the geometry of god

the geometry of god

a novel

Uzma Aslam Khan

First American edition published in 2009 by

Clockroot Books
An imprint of Interlink Publishing Group, Inc.
46 Crosby Street
Northampton, Massachusetts 01060
www.clockrootbooks.com

Library of Congress Cataloging-in-Publication Data
Khan, Uzma Aslam.
The geometry of God / by Uzma Aslam Khan. —1st American ed.
p. cm.
ISBN 978-1-56656-774-9 (pbk.)
1. Paleontologists—Fiction. 2. Mathematicians—Fiction. 3. Religion and science—
Pakistan—Fiction. 4. Pakistan—Fiction. I. Title.

PR9499.3.K429G46 2009
823'.92—dc22

2009010925

Printed and bound in the United States of America

Book design by Juliana Spear

Poems:
The couplet by Mir Taqi Mir appears on p. 140 of *Hidden in the Lute* by Ralph Russell
(New Delhi: Penguin Books India, 1995). Omar Khayyam *Ruba'iyat* stanza 37 is taken
from the translation by Peter Avery and John Heath-Stubbs (Middlesex: Penguin Books
Ltd., 1981).

Songs:
"Hound Dog": Words and Music by Jerry Leiber and Mike Stoller. © 1956 Elvis
Presley Music, Inc. and Lion Publishing Co., Inc. Copyright renewed, assigned to
Gladys Music and Universal Music Corp. All rights administered by Cherry Lane
Music Publishing Company, Inc.
"Losing My Religion": Words and Music by William Berry, Peter Buck, Michael Mills,
and Michael Stipe. © 1991 Night Garden Music. All rights administered by Warner-
Tamerlane Publishing Corp.
All rights reserved for both.

gateway the first: the world

I believe the soul is immortal but I cannot prove it.
—Ibn Rushd (Averroes)

All nature is perverse and will not do as I wish it.
—Charles Darwin

Amal

When I was eight, I developed the habit of looking down so Mehwish, my blind sister, wouldn't trip or fly down manholes or skid in filth, leaving me to swab her wounds or plunge in after. She was blinded on the same day I found the skull. Of course I didn't know it was a skull. I thought it was an ugly clump of rock. By the time I found out what it was, I had become my sister's eyes.

•

I'm walking with my grandfather in the Margalla Hills. Because it rained last night, the air is sweet and the ground moist, but Nana walks so lightly I know his slippers won't get dirty. They are soft, red leather slippers and the veins on his feet are large and fierce. I take his hand, rough and spotless like his feet. I take it because he never forces me to take it.

When we reach our pool I unlace my mud-spattered joggers, check for snakes, and settle on a lump of limestone that was once below a sea called Tethys. Nana sits beside me and I wait. From his pocket, he pulls out two small rocks. Brown and ugly. I was hoping for a baya nest, neatly stitched with a few dirty eggshells still inside.

"*Nazar se dekho.*" Nana's voice is firm. He's telling me to look closely, with the *inner* eye. "This animal was alive once. It swam in the Tethys."

I see no animal. Only the ugly rocks.

"See how the rock has split into two?" says Nana.

I stare at two people sitting under an acacia tree, away from the water's edge. Nana told me once that acacias help prevent soil erosion. They have small white flowers when they bloom. They couldn't have bloomed in the Tethys. You can tell by the way the man and woman under the tree are whispering that they aren't discussing soil erosion or ugly rocks.

"See how this part sticks out slightly, like the name on a rubber stamp? That is the fossil. A bone that has become stone."

I notice the color is different where he's pointing. But it's still an ugly rock. My father says Nana is very excitable. My mother says my father would only call *her* father excitable, not his own.

"The protruding half is called the positive." It's in his left hand. "The other half," he lifts his right, "the negative. Or—" he looks away, thinking. "When you press your pencil hard on paper, the front is furrowed. That's the negative. The bumpy back is the positive. Now imagine if your pencil nib got stuck between the pages of a book. That's what happened to this brachiopod, except the book pressed so hard it changed it. Isn't that amazing?"

I begin to see something.

If I stare in the mirror after a shower, waiting for the steam to cool, slowly, a wet head appears. I only know it's me because it has to be. Something like that is happening now. The longer I look at the rock, the more I can almost see *it*, except I don't know what *it* should be. It can't be me and I can't cheat by clearing a circle in the mirror.

I slide a thumb over rough sand. *It* is shaped like a triangle.

"You know, Amal, you are more like me than either of my children. Your mother and her brother are shadows! Dents! But you are a positive!"

Over the rock in my hand the mist keeps clearing. With my thumb I can trace inside the triangle *it*, counting seven, maybe eight arms. The top opens in a slit. I see it.

Nana asks, "Did you know I named you?"

I shake my head. I always thought my name was Aba's choice.

"Then you cannot know why." I shake my head again. I can tell he's going to give a speech. He begins, "Of the two kinds of intellects—"

"What's intellect?"

"Well, intelligence. *Aql.*" I nod. "*Aql nazari.* A talent for imagining. And *aql amali.* A talent for doing. A person with this talent can plant his ideas in the world. Your grandmother called it ambition, and she did not mean it kindly, though *she* was more ambitious in the kitchen than anyone I know."

I only remember a few things about my grandmother, who was a much better cook than my mother. People said she died young because Nana made her old. But she really died of a heart attack: she loved her own cooking too much.

"… I noticed that, like me, you had to touch everything, find out for yourself. I called you Amal. Practice." His moist lips peel back in a smile. "Mehwish is different, even though she's a baby. She is serene, not restless. She might change. Who knows? But I often look at you two and think: earthy Aristotle and dreamy Plato!"

I'm suddenly tired. I was enjoying the story of my name but then I got lost. I miss Aba, who gives me milk and asks me what I did at school. I wonder what he's doing now. He left Islamabad yesterday to inspect the site of a limestone quarry and took my mother and Mehwish with him. I'm staying in

Islamabad with Nana, even though Aba says if I spend too much time in Nana's company my hair will be white before I'm twenty and no one will marry me.

Nana looks again at the rock. "Some people do not like what is written here."

"Why?"

"Oh, because then you dig up letters that piece together a very different puzzle about how we got here!"

I think, What letters?

The couple beneath the acacia tree leaves and now there is silence.

Nana stretches his knees. He's going to give another speech. "People are always talking about a *real* Pakistan. The idea is ridiculous. It's the opposite of that rock in your hand. It's *not* real."

Another couple settles beneath the acacia tree. Aba says he knows what a man and woman are talking about by the way they hold their heads. When hers is lowered and his lifted, it's love. When his is lowered and hers lifted, it's in-laws. Hers is lowered.

Aba also says he knows Nana by the way he sits. When his long legs are bent, he might walk away and everyone can relax. When the legs are stretched, "he'll make us all tense." Aba only ever says this after Nana has walked away. In my family, talking about someone when they are present is not allowed. This is called respect.

The only time Aba broke this rule and showed his anger at Nana was when I was learning the Urdu alphabet. I learned the first letter *alif* is for Allah. Nana said *alif* is for *aql*. Aba shouted, "Allah comes before intelligence! You are teaching her to put herself before Him! She will first use *alif* for Allah then for *aql*!" Aba was so upset he forgot his own spellings. Nana always meant the joke to be on him: *aql* begins with the twenty-fourth letter of the alphabet, *ayin*.

Now Nana says, "Pray five times a day and be a *real* Pakistani! Speak Urdu and be a *real* Pakistani, or English and half as Pakistani! Well, here's my answer. Study whales and be Pakistani!"

He pulls something else out of his pocket. It's a picture of a very large dog. The very large dog has a very large head. He taps it vigorously with a finger. "Original Whale."

I blink.

"That is a whale."

I smile comfortingly and kiss his coarse cheek. "Nana, that's a *dog*."

"Amal, that is a *real* whale and we are *real* Pakistanis!"

•

The next day, I look again at the drawing Nana showed me, the one of the dog-whale, what he called Original Whale. I put a sheet of tracing paper on top, and, pressing carefully, I start to copy it.

I'm flicking my wrist for the tail when the doorbell rings. It's Nana's friend Junayd, who used to be a lawyer until he became an artist. In the room where we sit hangs a long panel with leafy shapes that look as if they want to crawl out. Junayd made it. As he sits on the sofa, I shade inside my lines on the carpet and listen.

"Welcome back!" says Nana. "Tell me all about your trip!"

Junayd has just come back from a place called Samarkand,

which I thought was a red drink with ice in it. Not the kind of drink Nana serves his friends. The kind Ama serves hers. But Samarkand is also a city and Junayd has photographs to prove it.

One photograph is of long narrow stairs leading deep underground to a place Nana calls an observatory. When I ask him what that is he says it's a place from which to see the stars.

Junayd adds, "This one was considered the last great achievement of a Muslim scientist."

Nana shakes his head. "It was constructed and used by Muslim scientists, but they were driven by an urge to learn about the world, not prove their faith."

Junayd says, "They did not feel the need to prove it. It was safe."

They speak their own language, while flipping through more photos.

Junayd continues, "Observatories like this were built to aid worship, through a science of fixed moments."

"I prefer a science of *fluid* moments. All religious moments are *un*fixed."

"And therefore man must fix them. The true believer is oriented in space and scheduled in time."

"I do not need to be pointed in the right direction. The world is my Ka'ba."

In my head, I repeat the last thing Nana said. *The World is my Ka'ba.*

I know the Ka'ba is the House of God in Mecca but I don't know what stars and fluid moments have to do with it. So I stop listening and go back to the tracing of the dog-whale. *The World is my Ka'ba.* I have it inside me and I keep quiet so it stays.

When I look up again, I notice Nana and Junayd are not talking any more but staring at each other, and their eyes smile.

Then Nana tears himself away to refill Junayd's glass. When he sits back down, he crosses his long legs and asks after Bilal, the man standing beside Junayd in many of the photos of Samarkand. "I heard he has become a Sufi?"

"Like you."

"Not like me." Nana looks at something far away. "A lapsed one, perhaps."

"Bilal says he's reverting to God's original idea of him. It's rubbish, of course. A man isn't capable of approaching intimacy with God, and besides, the Quran forbids it."

"What won't you say the Quran forbids? Union with the Beloved is hardly a sin."

Junayd smiles. "The Beloved."

Nana, smiling back, "How do *you* meet your obligations to this world, according to the wishes of *your* Beloved?"

Junayd raises his glass. "Not by worrying about it."

They giggle like children.

I forget what I wanted to ask.

Nana says, "Bilal seeks to submit to the way God first imagined him—"

"How can he presume to know God's imagination, or even call it that?"

"By self-destructing. That is the ultimate goal of his devotion: to revert to his original self. It's a belief in *pre-*existence. Or extinction. You could say the Sufi is the original evolutionist."

"If he *wills* his own destruction, then he thinks he can design himself. That is not submission to God. It's rivalry."

Nana has been silenced. I'm sure this has never happened before.

Finally, Nana says, "The disciple submits to his own personal perception of God. He does it out of love, not competition." Before Junayd can interrupt, he holds up a hand. "You need an analogy. Consider your own art. Don't you expect to preserve it, forever, the way it was first imagined?"

Junayd's eyes dart to the woodcut he made, hanging opposite us.

Nana nods. "That is the nature of all creation, to unite the real with the imagined. Or, if you prefer, to make the imagined real. Should any creative effort go into the world and exist independently of its maker, or, as Sufis believe, should the two never separate?"

"My art exists without me. I give it to you."

"Because you know I will not change it. If you feared I might, wouldn't you rather destroy it? Wouldn't it *live* better that way?"

Now Junayd is silent.

"I think you understand me now. But there is an exception, and this is science. A scientist's creativity must be proven, which means it must exist outside him. Outside me. It lives only when it mutates. If I keep my work to myself, so it yields to my will, it will not only die, it will destroy me."

Junayd shakes his head. "Your work on whales is not a creation but a discovery, though you know I believe it is neither."

"The Party of Creation and the Islamic Forum both believe I invented it."

"Then you should keep it to yourself."

Nana shakes his head. "That would destroy me."

•

It rains again after Junayd leaves. I climb into bed wondering, What does *original* mean? Original whale. Original idea. What does it mean? And why did Nana say, "That would destroy me." What would? I lie awake, hearing only the water fall.

•

In my pocket is my copy of the dog-whale. I decide to show it to Nana's neighbors, who look after me while Nana teaches at the university. "What is it?"

They answer in Urdu, and for the first time, I hear overlapping sounds in English.

The daughter who is my age: "*Geese.*" She does not mean two gooses but a shrew.

The brother from Aitchison College: "*Manduck.*" Not a man or duck, a frog.

The baby at her mother's breast: "*Titly.*" Not a boob, a butterfly.

The mother's nipples get bitten: "*Suer!*" Not a drain, a pig.

The father gets scared: "*Jinn!*" Not Nana's drink, a demon.

The gardener looks around: "*Robah.*" Not a thief, a fox.

The maid looks hungry: "*Gai.*" Not a man, a cow.

The cook rolls a pin: "*Bakri.*" Not a bread shop, a goat.

The driver starts the engine: "*Cargas.*" Not diesel, a vulture.

The big sister is tired of me: "*Humsai.*" Not a hum or sigh, a neighbor.

I decide to leave them alone.

At the gate, I pass the brother getting into the car. I can't help it. I say what it really is. He and the driver together snort: "*Joot!*" Not a plant, a lie.

•

I go with Nana and his friends to find more of this dog-whale, now shrew-frog-butterfly-pig-demon-fox-cow-goat-vulture-neighbor-lie. The men compliment me on being a clever eight-year-old and talk to me as if I'm eighteen, which is more seriously than anyone will talk to me when I *am* eighteen.

They give me the animal's Latin name, *Mesonychid*, and I see the Urdu–English ones to the door.

We leave as the sun peeps over the bald outline of the Margallas the way I once saw a butterfly tilt over the crown of Nana's head. First it crept. Then it spread its wings.

Inside his squash-nosed Toyota Corolla, Nana says, "Between the *Mesonychid* and the modern whale is a transitional mammal waiting to be found!"

Junayd ignores him, and helps me onto his lap. "Do you have a doll?" I shake my head. To him I'll always be three.

Nana laughs. He's in an excellent mood. The Toyota is as muddy as his slippers are clean. They flash orange as the sun warms his feet, one on the accelerator the other on his seat. I've never seen him drive with both.

Behind us sit Brian and Aziz Sahib. Aziz Sahib works at Nana's university, and Brian is visiting from somewhere with many vowels, an Indian name but not Indian–Indian. They say things like, "Eocene rocks in the eroding cliffs of the Himalayan edge" and the "ongoing uplift of the Potwar Plateau." Brian says hey a lot. "Hey, we got a great start! Hey, this lunar landscape's like the southwest!" Aziz Sahib always agrees with him, "*Bilkul* southwest," and Nana gets very excited about weathering alluvium.

The light is so bright I keep my eyes half-lidded, like a lazy lizard or a bride.

Nana tells me to locate myself. "Geography first exists in the mind. We're on the Potwar Plateau. Try to imagine standing on the right slope of a triangle. It sweeps south to Jhelum, close to your father's quarry, but we won't go that far. We'll cut a horizontal not far from here into the Salt Range, make a smaller triangle and walk slowly up the left slope, looking for fossils. Do you see it?"

Junayd answers for me with a groan. "It's too early for you, Zahoor. Barely seven o'clock!"

"What time do lawyers wake up these days?"

"I am an artist now."

"Then go back to sleep!"

Brian says, "Hey Amal, see those red and white bands? Salt from the Tethys. Before the subcontinent crashed into Asia rippling into these hills, it drifted in the sea for fif—"

"I know that."

Aziz Sahib tells me, "Politely politely!" and to Brian he says, "*Bilkul* continue."

Brian continues, "It was like a slow ship carrying monkeys, lemurs, and things with toed hooves. Things found nowhere else."

Nana adds, "The dog-whale had toed hooves. Do you have the picture?"

I have mine. I look at its feet. They are like a goat's, not a dog's. The cook next door was right. Though for my sake Nana calls it dog-whale, I think: goat-whale. After a while, I ask him, "Why didn't the animals stay in Africa?"

"Because no one had ever sailed across the Tethys before! It was a first-class adventure! And then the animals invented an even better one. They learned how to swim."

"Hey, like the dog that became the whale!" Brian adds.

"*Bilkul,*" echoes Aziz Sahib.

I think: It was a goat.

Nana smiles at me. "And that is the mystery that thrills us. Why did *some* animals stay on the boat, while others went back into the water?"

I say, "But goats can't swim."

"It was not a goat. It was becoming a whale."

Beside me, his eyes shut, Junayd yawns. "It was becoming Zahoor. The man who never says Zoh'r."

Aziz Sahib claps. Nana grins. "Bless the artist for his wit!"

Brian complains, "I don't get it."

Aziz Sahib explains, "Zahoor means becoming visible, like the day after noon, roughly the time for Zoh'r prayers. But our friend is not exactly a man of ritual…"

"But the day first becomes light at dawn."

"Zahoor does not mean first light. It is, how can I say? It is…"

Junayd says, "More than a beginning but not complete. Around midday."

"Well put," says Nana. "The artist has woken up."

Junayd yawns again. "*Zahoor* is the transitional mammal. I have found it. Let's go back."

Nana and Aziz Sahib laugh.

Brian asks, "Weren't we talking about continental drift?"

Nana: "Around midday."

The men laugh.

I've been turning a thought over in my head, looking at it

the way I looked at the dog-whale, trying to see what's wrong. It has to do with what Nana said earlier. I shut my eyes and ears and go back in time… There's the boat with the not-quite-goats jumping into the sea.

Who teaches them how to swim?

I can't swim but I've seen other children get in the shallow end of a swimming pool, always with an adult, who teaches them slowly. If I jumped in without any lessons, I'd drown. So would the not-quite-goats.

And something else. Nana said some animals go back into the water. Why *back*?

I finally ask, "Why did you say back into the water? Were they there before?"

"Yes, and that is a good question. We were all there before." Junayd snorts. Ignoring him, Nana continues, "The dog-whale was beginning to reverse its adaptation. It was developing underwater hearing. Its tail was growing. It was going to lose its fur, drop its legs. And it was happening very, very slowly."

I look at the goat-whale again. I try to drop legs and rub off fur. But it was drawn with pen, not pencil.

Junayd says, "Man was created on land."

Nana says, "If it's proof you need it can be found: *And We made out of water every living thing.*"

"*He it is Who has created you out of clay.* Man is *Ashraf-ul-Makhluqat*, God's Singular Creation. *No change wilt thou ever find in God's way.*"

From the back seat Aziz Sahib says something to Brian.

Brian mutters, "Uh huh."

Junayd grows loud. "These are *divine* laws. You cannot corrupt them!"

Nana is even louder. "If they are divine, how can man know them? Worse, enforce them. He will naturally bend them to his will the way *you* shape trees!"

"I do not *change* wood. I bring out what is already there!"

"Oh, *your* hand completes it? Such arrogance!"

"You accuse *me* of arrogance?"

I was dropping goats off a boat but now I look out the window, at a child running toward us from a field. He stops at the edge of the road and waves. I wave back.

I catch what Aziz Sahib is whispering to Brian. "The General's introducing Islamic laws that are going to change knowledge. In fact, reverse it—"

Nana snaps, "Irreversibly."

What does irreversibly mean?

Sweat from my hands blurs my drawing of the goat-whale.

•

We turn and the car's tires scratch the horizontal Nana described earlier.

The salt stripes of the Salt Range darken. Red salt would change everything I eat. If I sprinkled it on a boiled egg, I'd see the red kind better than the white kind and the egg wouldn't be too salty. Plus, I could annoy Ama by saying, My salt comes from the Tethys, what about yours? She'd tell me not to talk like that in front of Baby.

My mother had Mehwish after years of trying for a second child and now that she's pregnant with a third, all she ever says is Baby. Baby's milk. Baby's booties. Baby's sneeze, burp, fart. I'm glad I'm with Nana in the middle of these dark red hills.

It's quiet in the car. Nana and Junayd are no longer arguing. Maybe they've had a real fight, the kind Ama and Aba have.

I go back to throwing goats off a boat. They grow better tails and lose their legs.

After a while, Nana turns to me. "Do you have any more questions?"

I do but I don't know how to ask them. I shake my head.

He's disappointed. "Well," he looks at Junayd, "there must be proof of land-water mammals in these hills."

Brian folds a map. "After India collided with Asia, like a shipwreck—"

Aziz Sahib wakes up. "*Bilkul* shipwreck."

"—animals either stayed here, or tromped across Asia, or hey, kept going."

Nana pulls into a dirt lane and slows down. "But when man came it was to own the land." He sweeps a finger. "Everywhere you look, garrison towns. The crops are theirs. Buffaloes too. The rivers and the red earth. And of course, you. Our children."

Now it's Aziz Sahib who disagrees with him. "The Russians are coming. With the help of Brian's country, our army protects us."

Nana stops the car. "Their protection is what frightens me."

Aziz Sahib begins apologizing to Brian, who mumbles, "Too many sermons."

Noman

My father stands up, takes off his shoes, steps into the gateway of the Badshahi Masjid. I've already prayed. Now I have homework to do. Algebra.

I remember my teacher saying, "Did you know your Al Gorithms are named after the man who made them up, Al Khwarizmi? Or that civilization depends on the *sifr*, what you English-speakers call the cipher, what you *should* call the magic zero?"

No, I didn't know.

I sit in the park, watching Aba disappear inside the mosque. He's changed. We haven't gone out together for months, not to feed the pigeons in the courtyard of Wazir Khan Masjid, or lick our fingers at the fish shops in Mozang Chungi, or welcome the Sikh pilgrims who come from India every year to visit the gurdwara next to these gardens. We used to do these things.

In my copy book, I save the vision of someone long ago: 10, 100, 1000.

My heart isn't in it. I sip ice cream soda with a straw.

An odd thing happens.

The three pearly domes of the mosque start floating toward me. Three giant *sifrs* with the smaller *sifrs* of my sums swirling inside each like flies in a stomach. The giant ones burst, releasing the small. Tiny zeroes dance between the pages of my book, dive down the straw in the green soda bottle, one after another, till finally, they all burst.

A number is made up. It doesn't exist.

I look at the marble domes inside which Aba prays. Designed with numbers that burst, with made-up lines and made-up *sifrs*.

Inside me, a devil is unleashed. Like Al Khwarizmi, God needs empty space to create. Without it, He faces an impasse. His intersections get crammed, like the roads in Lahore.

He leaves.

By the time I've done the algebra and Aba slips through the gateway again—stoops, steps back into his shoes, walks toward me—I've finished my soda, and calculated that God has left this country. And this is why Aba's changed.

From now on, I pray for the return of the bloom of *sifr*. For the Unreal Zero.

Amal

We get out of the car.

The rocks are even more colorful when I step on them. Chocolate mudstone, limestone like mint powder, sandstone more pinks and browns than the paint-box grid of Ama's eye shadow. Nana says each shade helps trace the ebb and flow of the Tethys's slow retreat.

Junayd says, "She does not understand abstractions."

"Of course she does."

Brian takes my hand. "Let her feel concrete. Hey Amal, step here. Once this was an estuary. One foot over, oops, mid-ocean! And now, terrestrial rocks. That took millions of years to evolve."

I hop with him but don't see it. It's all completely dry now and in my imagination, there's no sea. Only a boat with goats dropping off. I leave Brian and lose myself in picking up rocks, turning them over, rubbing.

Nana follows me. "You have the scent!" He slips some of the rocks I hand him into a bag, always talking. "Crab claws… limpets…"

I hand him something small and sharp that even I can see is a bone.

He nods. "Good. Teeth are gold."

I'm beginning to see more shapes in the rocks around me.

"Ribs are handy too…"

I look up. The rocks at our feet look similar to the bigger slabs towering above. What else is up there? Bigger teeth? I start to climb.

"Careful," says Nana, canvas bag swinging, leather slippers finally collecting dust. The jagged cliffs are not like the soft moist

Margallas that grip my joggers and leave them muddy. This slope is as dry as Baby's talcum powder. There are no acacias, or other trees. The heat slams my head, tinting everything yellow.

Nana knows I'm getting tired and tries to give me a reason to stop climb-slipping. "You get more fossil deposits in the lower plains. Let's go back down."

I look down. Square farms float in the distance. Closer, tiny figures weave between our car and the Jeep that rode behind us with our tent and other gear. Behind them, trucks piled with fruit race by on the Grand Trunk Road that is suddenly remote.

Nana points out Brian on his knees at the bottom of another outcrop. Two men with shovels stand beside him.

"What's he doing?"

"Sniffing," Nana chuckles. "The best hills lie underground. The rest—the millet fields, the cliff you've scratched yourself against, the prickly grass that makes you itch, the rocks you've picked, the stinging ants and noisy squirrels—is as young and fleeting as the copper glow on your sunburned cheek. If you want to see more, dig. We shouldn't be climbing. We should be crawling."

I feel so tired I want to drop on a ledge and sleep. He could have explained it before. "But you said I have the scent!" My voice shakes.

"Amal," he holds me. "You're tired and hungry. I'm sorry. I wanted you to explore for yourself. And who knows, sometimes the riches are so visible we don't see them."

"I'm not hungry."

"We've been puttering in a dead sea for five hours."

"I'm not hungry." I've spent the whole day looking in the wrong place.

I don't argue when he picks me up and carries me back down.

•

Suleiman the cook has made the tastiest *aloo ki bhujia* ever to touch my tongue, but I'm still not hungry. I try to rest against a pink cliff but it's not a pillow, it doesn't bend with my back. And I can't straighten my knees. They're both cut and the hem of my dress sticks to a ring of blood. I feel worse thinking about the pain I'll feel when I pull the hem away.

Brian announces he's found something called the anticline and wants to return with a bigger team. Aziz Sahib's nose is in the site map I saw in the car. Junayd sips tea. Nana cleans my rocks with a toothbrush. He tricked me. I wish he'd put them away.

"Manatee molars!" says Nana.

It's just a brown clump.

"Hey," says Brian, "we'll add it to our collection!" He smiles at me. I see his teeth. There's a fly around my hem. "Doesn't look like teeth to me." He keeps smiling. "I'm going to get a closer look." He pockets my rock and points to the pit he was crawling around before. "Now let's smash the block and grab the matrix."

Somehow the men understand what this means and quickly finish their tea.

"Take your time," Nana says to me, walking toward the pit with the others.

I want to join them but the blood on my right knee has dried. The hem is part of it. I don't want to walk hunched like a monkey.

I shut my eyes, preparing to rip the hem off.

I could cut it off instead.

There's so much equipment around, there must be scissors somewhere.

To my left is the tent. Suleiman the cook comes out of it. I stand up. My legs are stiff and ache badly. Hop hop hop on my left foot toward him.

Suleiman says he packed scissors but doesn't remember where. "Wait here, bibi. I think they're in the bag next to all the rocks." He walks away.

I hop around the tent.

At the back, a man sits on his heels, his shalwar down, hands busy between his legs. It doesn't take me this long to do number one. Must be number two. I decide to leave, but turn around too quickly. The hem tears from my right knee. I squeal.

When he sees me the man stands up abruptly, clutching what I've never seen before. I don't have it in the same place. He grins. "Come here."

I run.

I pass Suleiman, zipping a bag after searching inside with both hands. "Sorry bibi, I thought I packed—"

I keep running, all the way to the pit.

Nana kneels at its edge, calling out eagerly to the men inside. A few feet away, Junayd also kneels, but in prayer.

I tell no one what I saw: a whale with fur and a growing tail.

•

It gets dark on the way back home.

As the sun dips behind the cliffs of an extinct sea, I realize I never saw that butterfly fold its wings and tiptoe back down Nana's head though it must have returned to wherever it came from.

There's a bandage around my knee. Junayd says I look tired. "The day was too long for a child. And digging in the dirt for magic rocks is no activity for girls. If your Nana forces you to do it again, at least bring a doll."

Nana turns to me. "Are you all right? You're very quiet."

Junayd pets the top of my head. "She's tired. Naturally."

Nana looks at me and I shut my eyes.

Brian and Aziz Sahib are discussing the rocks packed in the car's trunk. I helped make the casts. There are plaster smudges on my fingers that look like the white paint my teacher uses in school to cover up her mistakes. It will peel off.

I like the way the car sways on the GT Road.

Behind my eyes is a glass of red Samarkand Squash. I pour red salt into it. The salt collects at the bottom of the glass, where I never want to disturb it.

I half wake up. They talk of one of my rocks. The one Brian pocketed. Aziz Sahib had lightly tapped it with a hammer. Inside was a bit of skull. Oddly shaped. A bulb-like knot at one end.

Now Aziz Sahib says, "The braincase must have been tiny."

Brian says, "I'll take it back with me."

Nana again turns to me. "Brian's taking one of your rocks with him to America."

"Hey Amal, thanks."

The dog-whale dips into the salt pool behind my eyes as I finally fall asleep.

Noman

My youngest sister Sehr has three pet chicks dyed pink, turquoise, and orange. They skid across the floor while we sit at the table for lunch after Friday prayers.

Thrusting his legs under the table, Aba nearly crushes one—Sehr quickly dips to rescue it—and begins telling us about a very important meeting. "A bastard came uninvited! He will face the music!"

Sehr starts to hum a film song, gently releasing the turquoise chick. It cheeps loudly, hopping onto her feet, outraged at being back on the floor with his gaudy sisters.

Ama puts an extra chapaati on my older brother Adnan's plate. He's the good-looking one. While Aba talks, he sticks his lower lip out and nods sagely, though I know he isn't listening.

"General Zia was present. It was a pleasure to meet him! Great man! Great thinker!"

Aba's friends in the Jamaat-e-Pedaish, Party of Creation, want him to join their mission of introducing an educational system in keeping with the spirit of Islam. I wonder if this spirit has anything to do with the three zeroes that came floating my way earlier today, while I was trying to do al jabra.

I try to recapture the image of the man who filled me with a longing for a lunch out, just the two of us, while I watched him slip inside the mosque's gateway to pray. But he is not that man now—or else I'm not that boy. He says, "Everywhere you look, pornography, obscenity, women in sports and advertising, boys and girls together!" I feel no need to sit with him in a crowded café in Mozang Chungi with a slab of fried rahu fish on a red plastic plate and an oval of hot naan with the pattern of a grid pressed into the flour.

My other sister, Shaista—always the other sister—looks up from a plate piled high with chicken. Aba took her off her school's hockey team last year.

"What do you say?" He challenges her.

She eats.

"These are dangerous times." He burps.

Adnan nods with lower lip.

"The young Pakistani is a cultural freak! His religion is whimsy! We will save him from foreign influences—like science! Like films!"

I recall him slipping out of the gateway, bending, his toe catching in the heel of his shoe so he almost loses his balance. If I'd been with him, instead of in the park finishing my homework, he'd have grabbed onto me. And I feel no need.

Sehr pleads, "But Anjuman is Punjabi! And you *like* her films!"

"See what I mean?" Aba looks at Ama.

"If you argue with your father again," says my mother, "I'll hit you."

Sehr starts whimpering. Under the table, I find Pink and set her on Sehr's knee. I whisper, "He's seen her films more than all of us!" She strokes the chick and giggles. There was a time when Aba sat us on his lap and did just the same.

Now he announces he's accepted the party's offer to join its mission. Turquoise leaps onto his foot. *Cheep!* He kicks him off. "There are books circulating in this country today saying a newborn chick knows its mother by scent. Lies! Allah is the only cause. At every second, He intervenes."

Turquoise launches himself on Aba's heel. *Cheep!*

Amal

My life changes completely the next morning. The drive back to Islamabad from the dig was my last long rest. From now on, I have to stay awake.

Ama and Aba return from the resthouse. With only one Baby. The one inside Ama is gone. It left when she learned what happened to Mehwish.

"Infrared light," an ophthalmologist in Jhelum had explained, "can permanently damage the light-sensitive tissues of the inner eyeball. Mehwish was blinded by the sun."

While my father was at the quarry and my mother rested or vomited, the maid apparently took my sister out in the heat and left her alone while cavorting with local suitors.

Ama will never get pregnant again. The maid is sacked. Mehwish is moved to my room.

My world shrinks. I expand it any way I can. I look at Baby.

It's as if I'm looking at her for the first time. Her face is burned to the color of tea leaves. And her nocturnal habits are fascinating. She continues sleeping and waking the way she did before she went away and became blind. She still sees light. How?

No one else has noticed.

The more our house fills with relatives, the more Ama moans, "Shouldn't have trusted that *ayah*," or "they always *seem* reliable," or "God is punishing me."

Nana snaps. "Why is this poor child's deformity an excuse for *deiformity*? Who was that buffoon you took her to? The sun blinded her! Maybe she crawled into one of your husband's workshops and a piece of rock flew into her socket. Did the fool think of that?"

Aba sighs. "She was not blinded by man. She was blinded by God."

Nana glares at him. "Next you will say God was taking *your* sins out on her!"

Chote Phoopa scowls. "You know it's pointless looking for a cause."

Nana snaps, "This is worse than the boastings of super-powers! She should have more *tests*."

Even I don't relax till he leaves.

•

At home and at school, I begin looking for the mysterious thing called infrared light.

It'll come to me like a *sumbul* petal, twirling, falling lightly on my shoulder before exploding in a shock of scarlet. I'll look deep into the liquid guts of red and something urgent will be revealed. Then I'll understand what happened to Mehwish.

It doesn't happen. I look directly at the sun till my eyes grow teary and my head throbs, but no petals of light fall on me. I don't know what happened to Mehwish, alone on her back in the far corner of the lower right slope of the Salt Range. Did she meet her blindness with a gurgle or a scream? All I know is that the damage is—I learn the meaning of the word—*irreversible*.

I suppose, as I continued to watch her sleep, I made her my first experiment. Was this cruel and invasive, or the birth of a scientist? Was it my *aql amali*—my practical intelligence? I had to know how the blind see and if they have a sense of dawn and twilight, midday, night. I had to know this before I had to know why my mother's voice stopped ringing in the house, or even what tadpoles look for when they squirm.

So, first: I light a single candle. She doesn't wake up. I shine a torch in quick bursts on her face. Still she sleeps. Finally, I switch on all the lamps and even the tubelight, holding up a mirror to aim the reflection down her nose and across her shut eyes. Nothing, though the patterns on her skin dazzle and distract me.

It becomes clear: Mehwish won't wake up with artificial light but she'll wake up with the sun.

As I watch her anxiously every night, I begin to fear that *I'm* the one who's blind. I become an incurable insomniac. Mehwish sleeps steadily, while dark disks form under my eyes. I give up flashing mirrors and torches. I let her sleep. But now I watch her even when she's awake. I stroke her eyelids and look into her eyes.

They aren't like the eyes of shrews I'll dissect later at university. Theirs are partly scarred over. Theirs are almost *extra*. Mehwish's eyes are dead but not extra. They aren't scarred. And she cries with tears, just like other babies.

One day a fly lands on her left fat fist and I smack it. She cries. The fly gets away. I ask her why some flies know I'm going to smack them with a fly swat while others don't. "Is it the way I hold my hand, or is it a difference in the fly?"

She stops crying. "Fy!"

"I think you're right. I'm going to draw you."

"Fy!" She kicks happily while I draw.

I leave her and the drawing to ask Aba about her blindness. "Was it an accident?"

"Nothing is an accident. Everything is decided by God."

"But God made the eyes."

"Yes."

"Why did He decide what He made wasn't—?"

"You cannot question His will, Amal. You need to understand that."

I feel guilty going behind Aba's back, but a year after Mehwish's not-accident, when Nana is visiting and we're alone, I say, "God shouldn't have given her eyes if she wasn't going to need them."

"Exactly." He's reading a journal and doesn't look up.

"Did God make a mistake?"

"Maybe. Or started something He no longer wished to continue."

"If He knew it was going to get boring, why did He start?"

"Maybe He didn't know. Or did know but still wanted to try."

"Is that an accident?"

"Partly."

I think I have an answer now. "Mehwish is accidentally cleverer than me."

Nana looks up and laughs. "How do you know that?"

"Because she knows when the sun rises." I show him the drawing of Mehwish and the sun that I made last year:

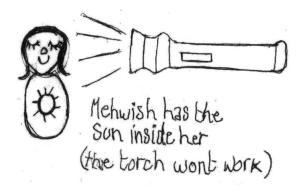

Mehwish has the
Sun inside her
(the torch wont work)

"Lovely! Show it to her. If you go over it again, pressing harder with your pencil this time, she will feel the marks and be able to see something."

"All right."

"Mehwish was born with a clock inside her, just like you and I. That has nothing to do with sight or intelligence. But your observation does. Why don't you bring her here?"

Mehwish lies quietly on my bed, chewing her fat hands. I know she recognizes me because she puts out a hand for me to chew. She never offers this to anyone else.

Nana sits her on his lap. She cuffs his journal with a wet fist. She can make more sounds now: "Na-na-na-na. Am-am-am-am."

We look at her eyes. I learn what's what. The brown muscle: iris. It opens and shuts the tiny hole in the center: pupil. From *pupilla*: little doll. I'm in it: a shrunken doll reflected in the center.

"Her eyes receive light but transmit no image," says Nana. Then his voice abruptly changes. "Listen, Amal. I've been meaning to have this talk and now you've given me a way."

He pauses. I look around. We both know we're checking that Aba isn't listening, though I don't know why.

"You probably know that your mother has always felt—" He looks at Mehwish and her soggy chin. "She's always felt, well, that I've been too strict with her." His small eyes are wet, and grayer than they used to be. "And she hasn't been well for a year now, ever since Mehwish's accident."

Anyone else and there'd be a full-stop sigh but Nana doesn't sigh.

"I haven't been much help but I hope she'll recover soon."

Does he mean my mother or Mehwish?

"Till then, you will have to be Mehwish's eyes. The little doll in her eyes is you, her guardian angel. So she won't have any more accidents."

When Ama and Aba talk about things like angels and devils he doesn't agree with them, so this part confuses me. But the rest has already been made clear to me by everyone else. "All right."

"You are a sensible girl. Much wiser than your years." He waits. I don't know what to say. He seems satisfied. He takes the journal from Mehwish and opens to a drawing of a funny-looking fish, damp with Mehwish's spit.

"What is it?" I ask.

He looks up again. "Do you remember going with Brian and Aziz Sahib to look for fossils last year?"

I nod. There's a movement behind my eyes. Fur, tail. Like an itch, it's gone.

"You found a scrap of skull up on the hill, though I said most fossils collect at the bottom, deep underground. It was a fluke, but such things happen."

I show him the scar on my right knee.

"Yes. Well, Brian took the rock to America, and now we know what it is. The ear of a primitive whale. We know because whales are the only mammals with a bone twisted in the shape of an *S*, called the sigmoid process, hidden in the middle ear. The dog-whale did not have it. But this one did. It is, possibly, proof of the evolution of whales. What we were looking for and would not have found, if not for you. It might have looked like this."

Long head. Sharp teeth. Fur. Paws. Thick tail.

"They've named it *Pakicetus*, though I think it should be *Amalicetus!*"

"Can I have it?"

Nana chuckles. "It has to stay in the lab. Brian is back and we have been looking for more pieces of the puzzle, hoping to find a complete skeleton."

"When are we going?"

He hesitates. Mehwish has fallen asleep against his chest. He smiles at her, then at me, and I know I have to keep my practical intelligence in the house.

•

Maybe because he feels bad I can't go with him, Nana gives me his old microscope. It's the first pretend eye I ever see through. I go outside and fish out half a dozen tadpoles from the pond under the rubber tree. I know what they really are from Nana's science books: sperm. I tell Ama this is what I'll look at in real life from now on.

Horrified, she whispers, "Sperm?" Then her head falls back on the sofa where she lives.

I introduce a grain of rice in the circle of wriggling sperm to see if they'll love it. They don't. They stop moving.

I look at my notes about my first experiment, in which I tried to wake Mehwish up with a candle, a torch, and brighter lights, till Nana explained the clock inside her: *Mehwish talks to the sun. She knows the different times of day. She has an observatory in her head as dark as the one in Samarkand and she is not much cleaner than a baby fly.* Behind the page I pinned the *Mehwish has the sun inside her* drawing, which I did trace over so she could rub her fingers over the lines and see them. I still consider this a successful experiment since I have watched Mehwish enough to prove it.

I have only a short note to make about the tadpoles, my second experiment: *Failed sex = death.*

With the microscope, I explore other things. Pond slime, sweat, and especially spit. I tell Mehwish, "Thuko in it." She understands me. She's not deaf. She spits and I catch her saliva on the rectangle of glass below the lens.

Another time I'm sliding her finger into the same slot in order to magnify a mosquito bite near her nail, when I hear a familiar voice outside our room. "Apa Farzana," I tell Mehwish.

Two years ago she would have said, "Goo!" Or, "Ap-ap-ap-ap." Now she says, "Fo weading!" and "Kiss myth!"

"*Kishmish.*"

"Kiss miss!"

Beside us is a small bowl of raisins. I put one on her tongue. She sucks it like a sweet.

Apa Farzana lives in Lahore, but whenever she comes to Islamabad she visits Ama. Together they read the Quran, which Ama keeps near her couch. If they call me, I start giving Mehwish a bath. They usually recite Surah Yasin. Apa Farzana says the name of this chapter comes from the mysterious letter-symbols, *ya sin*, and that the chapter is meant to help say goodbye to the dead. But there've been no deaths in my family since Ama lost her unborn child three years ago. And Mehwish is alive.

They recite together, then Apa Farzana translates and interprets. The only two people I know who understand Arabic and never ask for translation are Nana and Junayd.

Apa Farzana says, "*Glory to Allah, Who created in pairs all things that the earth produces, as well as their own kind and other things of which they have no knowledge.*"

I think aloud, "Pairs?"

Mehwish puts her hand over my face. "Pari!"

Apa Farzana starts explaining to Ama that *pairs* is a lovely reference to sex. "It was always written, hmm? What clever people say they have discovered today, it was always known about all things must having sex, things we cannot know and are not supposed to know, He does not want us to know, we must accept, as this verse proves, hmm?"

Ama repeats, "It is so true. We are not supposed to know."

I think of my tadpoles. They weren't in pairs but in mobs.

Apa Farzana explains, "There must be no having sex without opposites."

The tadpoles looked identical. What's the opposite of a tadpole?

She keeps explaining. "There can be no society without opposites. Now, that first daughter of yours, hmm? She is not opposite enough."

"She says I'm not opposite enough," I tell Mehwish, who releases the giggle she'd been holding like pee. "What's the opposite of a tadpole? What's the opposite of me?"

"I want barf!"

"Ba*th*."

"Wif shoap an sampoo."

Apa Farzana flips pages and arrives at Surah Tariq, Morning Star, which she says is like Surah Yasin, also a comfort to a person in dark despair. But I've heard Nana and Junayd read it differently, and for once they both agree: the star is a late-night visitor who knocks on a door. He doesn't comfort the house. He wakes it up.

But according to Apa Farzana, the visitor gives comfort by

discussing opposites. She reads the translation, "*Now let man but think from what he is created! He is created from spurting fluid proceeding from between the backbone and the ribs.*"

"It was always written, hmm? The backbone is the source of man's strength, his spurting sperm. Woman is the opposite. Her spine is created weak, for receiving and bending. It is written, and we must teach your daughter, hmm?"

Ama repeats, "It was always so." Then she calls out, "Amal! I know you hear me!"

I push Mehwish into the tub. Luckily, she loves baths more than anything else and doesn't start screaming. She knows temperature differences before I do, tells me her cold hand is colder when it hasn't been under the hot tap first, repeats the experiment with each foot. She also knows colors by scent.

"Want new sampoo not shame geen one."

"G*r*een."

She tilts her head and I wet each strand of her thick straight hair. Finer hair covers her spine, which isn't deep, like Ama's and mine. Her skin stays rough though I rub lotion on it daily. On the crown of her head I squirt a pool of new shampoo. "Turquoise."

She sniffs. "Too coy. Keen."

"Turk-oise. C*l*ean."

"Not geessy like geen one."

"G*r*easy. It has seaweed in it. Seaweed is like lettuce. When you eat lettuce even your shit smells c*l*ean."

She's delighted and says her first almost-perfect sentence, "My shit smell keen," quickly correcting herself, "clean!"

"Smell*s*. You're supposed to say number two."

"Clean!"

"All right." I soap her back, thinking about spurting fluid and spines. "Apa Farzana says *we* are the opposite of tadpoles."

She puts a damp finger to the wall and scratches the paint off. A flake catches in her nail. She pushes it into her flesh; a kind of nail-biting.

"Don't do that, you'll get hurt."

"Daw on my back."

Another almost-perfect sentence. I write words on her spine. She tries to call the letters out. She can call separate letters but she can't put them into words herself.

Sometimes I write the alphabet out for her on paper, pressing hard with my pencil so she can find the creases. Then I reverse the page and she feels the bumps. Other times, we use toothpicks and broken bits of plant-pots we've both cut our fingers on. She's learning these more quickly than I'll ever learn the dots in little squares, called Braille.

Now, in the bath, I scrawl on Mehwish's back: S-E-A.

It takes her three tries before she calls the letters out correctly, then I say the word. Next I write: W-H-A-L-E. She gets it in five. I draw a dog-whale and whale-whale. She likes it so much she begins to fall asleep. "This became that, because of evolution."

She turns around, smiling dreamily. "Big cof what?"

"Evolution. When this becomes that."

"Ewil ocean."

I never get shampoo or soap in her eyes, though I want to know if they'd burn like normal eyes. When I rinse her hair I hold my hand like the beak of a cap.

She surprises me by quickly turning and reaching under my shirt when both my arms are up. First she strokes my back the way I was stroking hers. Then she lingers on my new chest, always tender now and already too big. She rubs it with soap and my ears heat with shame. Mehwish grins. I slap her hand away, pulling my shirt down though she can't even see me.

She whimpers, squeezing all the shampoo into the bath.

"Stop it, Mehwish!" I snatch the bottle.

She scratches my face. I slap her again. She screams.

Ama opens the door. "What's this?" She grabs Mehwish's hand, with the paint flake dug so deep into the nail the skin has cut. A fine line of blood drips halfway down her finger.

"It's hardly anything," I say, rinsing the nail.

"You've become very cheeky, young lady. I was calling you. Apa Farzana was here."

It's Mehwish who saves me, with her first perfect sentence: "You stink orange!"

Ama's mouth hangs open. At last she says, "Pray your father's office moves to Lahore. Then we will all be closer to Apa Farzana." She leaves, shutting the door weakly.

In our bedroom I dress Mehwish while listening to old film songs, *Mehbooba Mehbooba* and the more recent, *Laila O Laila*.

She hums along, "Boob a boo ba." She fidgets so much I drop the comb twice before finally tying her hair. Delighted it's over, she begins to dance. She's never seen the films, yet she moves exactly as the actresses do.

I decide that, like the sun, she has it in her.

Noman

My first week at college I come home one day to find Aba looking very pleased. Since the beginning of the fifth year of the war in Afghanistan, his party's received another boost of American aid, and I presume this is why he beams.

"Noman!" He calls me with the shine in his voice I haven't heard in years. "You are so good at proving arithmetic equations and all, I want you to prove something else for me today." He grins. I sit beside him. "What kind of state did Jinnah want?"

I grow nervous. One of Jinnah's most famous speeches proves he wanted a secular state. But if I say this Aba will accuse me of accusing the founder of being an unbeliever, though several members of his Party of Creation have done just this, after opposing Jinnah for creating the state in the first place. I decide that all in all, this is a very tricky question if I think too much. I reply, "Islamic."

"Prove it." He hands me the famous speech, the one that proves the opposite.

> We are starting in the days when there is no discrimination, no distinction between one community and another, no discrimination between one caste or creed and another. We are starting with this fundamental principle that we are all citizens and equal citizens of one State.

Aba taps the page. "I want you to prove it from this."

I whisper, "How?" A pulsing thread of failure courses up my neck.

He pulls out a second page, a sort of consolation prize. "With this."

It is my belief that our salvation lies in following the golden rules of conduct set for us by our great law-giver, the Prophet of Islam. Let us lay the foundation of our democracy on the basis of truly Islamic ideals and principles.

Aba taps the first page again. "I want you to prove that this does not exist and this," he taps the second page, "does. That there is only one."

"But every one knows this one!" I look at the first.

He tears it up. "Which one?"

I stare dumbly at zero.

I read the second page again. *Truly Islamic ideals and principles...* "But it doesn't say these principles are *only* Islamic, it can be interpreted to mean—"

"Interpreted? There is only one reading." As he walks away, Aba adds, "One day I will need you to help me prove other important things. But first, you have to stop imagining the unimportant."

Amal

The year my mother finally gets her wish of moving to Lahore, Nana takes me for one last walk in the Margalla Hills. His soft leather chappals have become thin and worn and annoy his varicose veins.

"There are no such forests in Lahore," he begins.

It's cold for early November, as if the year has skipped this month. I bury my hands in my sweater sleeves as we walk to our pool.

Mehwish is at home with my mother and two of her cousins and two of their friends. I dub them TB: The Begumhood. Their conversation couldn't be more different from the ones Nana has with me and his friends. TB conversation flows:

"*Aur?*"

("Women are so sensitive.")

"*Aur?*"

("Women care too much.")

"*Aur?*"

("My daughter-in-law does not know suffering.")

"*Aur?*"

("My son has abandoned me!")

Poor Mehwish! I still don't know what my opposite is, but I know I want it to be the Book of Affliction.

I take a long drink of the cool forest air.

Nana continues, "There are lovely parks. A zoo I will take you to. Colleges that were once outstanding. But the new Lahore is filled with potholes, rickshaws, smog. Its heart cries Village, but its head indulges a foolish dream: Dubai. Lahore is a country child who once saw a skyscraper and longed to become it. So it chopped down the trees that already gave it height. It is giving up *lassi* for Pepsi as we speak."

Nana has been angering a lot of people at the university where he teaches. He points out what others overlook. While the Soviets bomb Afghanistan for the seventh year, Pakistan Television no longer broadcasts weather forecasts because predictions of rain have become witchery. Science and history books are being rewritten. Teaching evolution is banned. Nana says to learn is to search for what isn't written, or rewritten. He has become a dangerous man.

"Lahore has a past but no future. Heritage but no vision. All that old feudal money… The children sit and sit and inherit and inherit!"

The only other time I saw him this upset was when everyone said Mehwish was blinded by God.

"Lahore says it's the pulse of the nation, but its arteries are clogged!" He walks quickly, adding, "Many of the people who want me sacked are in Lahore."

I didn't know he could lose his job.

The pool is probably freezing so I keep my socks and shoes on. I perch on the same mound of limestone I've always sat on.

"You didn't check for snakes," Nana scolds gently, squeezing in beside me before announcing, "Lahore is property, meat, and late nights!"

Across from us a mother peels oranges while a father chases a boy around an acacia tree. The son models the rage of the decade: sweatbands. One around each wrist, a third at his forehead. He strikes an imaginary ball but doesn't know where to run. His parents cheer. Fists clench in glory. Everyone wants to be a star but no one has a court.

"What will you do if you lose your job?"

He doesn't hear me. "They call me western. As if scientific discoveries belong to the west! Are we to forget the calendar Omar Khayyam gave us? What about antiseptics? Who remembers Al Zahrawi? The war is giving this government a way to divide east from west, and all in the name of God!"

At home, Aba increasingly asks Ama what Nana is, *definitely*. "Is he even a believer?" Ama insists he is. She adds that with Apa Farzana's help, everyone's soul will be saved, including mine.

To me it's simple. Whatever he is, definitely, Nana will tell only when they stop asking.

That's why he talks to me. And that's why I can talk to him. "Apa Farzana says I'm not opposite enough."

He looks blank. "Who? Oh. *Her.*"

"She says I'm not opposite enough to a—tadpole. I mean, a man."

I expect him to chuckle but instead he looks away uncomfortably, turns back rapidly, glances around, looks at my knees. I know what it is. My breasts have started embarrassing men.

I also look away.

Finally, addressing my neck, he says, "Yes, well—I mean, no. Possibly."

We say nothing for a while.

The boy wipes imaginary sweat from his head with a wristband. His mother wraps her shawl around him. He slices it with an imaginary racket. His father eats a sandwich.

I'll miss these walks. And our house, which faces these hills. I can see their dark outline from the wide windows of my room at night. They are my Tariq, my late-night visitor, assuring me that if continents collide, I'll be able to rethink the contours of these hills before waking up the next day. *Geography first exists in the mind.* Without these hills, what marker will I have?

Nana still addresses my neck. "Yes, I have always felt you are too wise for your years. Good for Mehwish, but maybe not so good for you." He pauses, continues as if he did not hear this last sentence. "Now, what were we saying about opposites? Yes, people will even kill for divisions in the mind. Mixing is bad politics."

The war in Afghanistan is never introduced, yet we're always talking about it. Nana said to Aba once that because the conflict lives both inside and outside the mind, because there's no border there, it's more real than God. "And when it's over, it won't be over, not for Amal's generation, nor future ones, just as Partition is never over for my generation, and yours, and Amal's, and so on. Just as God is never over for a believer… So, is the closest analogy to God—*death?*" Aba stormed out of the room. No one talked after that, but no one was silent.

Now I kiss the thin skin of Nana's cheek and he finally looks at me. His lips spread in a sad smile.

The child in sweatbands shrieks as his father picks him up and his mother wipes dirt off his nose. They walk away, leaving a pile of orange peels. Troops of bluebottles begin their attack, homing in on blue-veined wings, antennae flaring, eyes cold. They've already ravaged *imli* wrappers, glass bottles, and packets of Peek Freans.

I hear voices from up the trail, where the white oaks that catch fire easily grow. From my street, I've watched thick smoke curl downhill before surrounding us—the fat and the skin and bones. It hangs for days, sometimes weeks, because someone left a cigarette burning. Apa Farzana would say God did it, because this land is His ashtray.

Nana stretches his legs. The first warning. "Listen to me, Amal." The second. I know that tone. "I told you to be Mehwish's eyes and you listened. Good girl. She is six years old now. A curious child like you were, and that will make your work harder in Lahore. Here you can pull her along while your head is up in this forest. It's hard to get lost here. And the manholes have covers, drains don't leak, drivers don't run red lights. But Lahore is different, and your mother still can't take care of Mehwish. You must keep doing it. You will have to stop looking up and all around, the way you do here. For Mehwish, you must develop the habit of looking down."

Leaves rustle. Deer, or maybe a paradise flycatcher.

"I know you'll miss these walks and talks." He keeps looking into my eyes now. "But they're inside you, and there is no need to be rid of them."

The sun bows to the trees. Inside my sweater sleeves, warm hands courier heat to my shoulders, while the rest grows stiff.

"And now," he smiles, "we should talk about your future. You want to be like me, don't you?"

"What will you do if they sack you?"

"What? *Oh.*" His smile vanishes. He calls it back quickly. "I'll leave the Punjab in a Jeep. Yes, why not? I'll park it on the Khunjerab Pass and walk into China." Looks at my knees again. "But we were discussing your future."

"It's Mehwish's bath time."

He nods vigorously.

As we descend the hill, I wonder if he'll wear slippers all the way to China.

•

In the Lahore house I hope for two things: a honeycomb window like the ones in Lahore Fort, and a pond. I get the second. I buy golden guppies from the plastic pouches sold everywhere on the roadside. Free them and watch. Many die of shock. Others grow.

The first time I bathe Mehwish in the new tub she complains the pressure in the taps is weak, but memorizes the order of the colors in a soap bubble.

She also memorizes the route to the Fort, and the order of all the British-built red-brick Gothic-style buildings on Mall Road—the GPO, High Court, Provincial Assembly, the museum, and the colleges. She knows as well as I do that the road leading to the layered heart of this city is Victorian. And on this Victorian street, Islamic laws are passed, while the Begumhood goes shopping.

The first difference I notice between my two homes: in Islamabad, roads have no history. Only mountains do. But here, in this city of parks, the trees are silenced. Brick and concrete speak. They ask: how secure is a forty-year-old state? If forty is barely mid-life to the royal elephants that once tromped through the gates of Lahore, soaped in gold and splashed in jewels, what is it to the republic that's left with the ghosts of their Sikh and Muslim riders? And the Hindu kings before them? And before *them*?

I remember the garrison towns of the Punjab plains, the fenced-off lands, the young soldiers, and I have my answer, as if Nana speaks through me now. To a republic, forty is infancy. And this is its horror, as it carves itself from ancient land, ancient water. (From where do we come, soil or sea? There are holy verses to prove both.)

Islamabad is the cosmetic capital of the infant; Lahore, the surgeon. From here the country's face is carved to remove our pagan features. But the surgeon is either clumsy or unconvinced. Scars linger. I've seen a shopkeeper stash rupees in a shrine near a broken gate, fingers accidentally grazing the small belly of the statue of a smiling god. He doesn't notice. Or women bathe their children on the balcony of an old haveli, nude deities scratched in the railing, entangled in love, coated in pigeon shit, witnessed only by the sun and by the living bathing children. Or an old painting of Kali on the wall of a college classroom. No one objects. No one will have to, till some mortal threatens them.

Seven years later, when Nana is arrested, I'll come to understand what he was trying to tell me on our last walk in the Margallas: in Lahore, I must search less for the designs of changing nature and more for the designs of unchanging men and women. I need a different way of seeing: nearsighted, sly.

But now my focus is only the designs of a rapidly changing Mehwish. This is my promise to Nana, who taught me to think like a rebel but act with obeisance. I watch Mehwish till I shrink to the point of a Moghul miniature hanging on a wall of the Lahore Museum. I am her pupilla.

•

People walk in front of her. They walk in front of me too, but I pay more attention to her, which means we both get bumped. Cars don't stop. Sidewalks drop abruptly. Manholes are left gaping. Thorny branches sprout in air. Beggars cling and make her flinch. She's quick to taste a difference between the air of a congested street and an emptier one, but won't admit to fear.

She loves to walk, almost as much as she loves me to spell out words and give her drawings to trace over.

One day, we leave for the park near our house. We're not supposed to go alone but Ama is with Apa Farzana. If I go without telling, she'll scold me. If I ask for permission, she'll not only refuse, she'll tell me to sit and listen.

We quietly slip out of the kitchen. I notice a change in the way Mehwish moves. It's slower, even *sexier*. What does a seven-year-old know about sexy? What do I know?

I've told a girl at my new school, Zara, what Apa Farzana says. "*Let man then observe out of what he has been created…*" In return, she's told me sex isn't only about tadpoles and their opposites. And shown me pictures of human genitalia, pointing with irritating authority, "Look at the sperm ducks."

Each time she says this, I remember the man behind the tent: Fur, tail. Instead of boasting that I've seen a real one, a real fertile furtail, I remember how he called me, and push the image away. Then I say, "It's written duc*ts*."

She flicks her hair. "The *t* is *silent*. This gland makes the sperm duck spermy." Her finger follows a green arrow. "It's all in here, the sperms whip around here."

"Then what?"

"They go in her." *Her* is so many tubes and arrows and circles she's a geography I can't imagine, she makes my head swim. Zara also looks woozy so we shut the book and burst into giggles. "We are made of spurting fluid!"

Then we have a *wuzoo* match, in which you press one nostril and spurt fluid out the other three times. Whoever blows hardest, wins.

Now I watch Mehwish and I know her mental picture of

her body is shifting. No one needs to show me this. She studies the length of her limbs, aligns her spine, arranges her mouth and chin. She combs her hair with fingers—the beginning of an old habit. Left hand lingers on neck, brushing shoulders gently. Whose hand does she make it? As always, she extends the right hand. This one belongs only to her.

I keep watching. Left hand falls to waist, strokes it with the same movements I use when I bathe her. "Do you want a bath?" I tease.

Irritated, Mehwish clicks her tongue. It's what she does when I tell her to stop retracing my drawings and drink her milk.

With a jolt I realize she's doing the same thing now. Revising my lines. Every cell on her skin that she strokes with one hand I've already touched many times, with both of mine. She wants to remove my imprints and stake out her own. She's looking for her original.

I understand other signs. Lately, when we come home from our separate schools, she insists on bathing herself. She locks the bathroom door. I don't hear water running. No steam when I go in later, or even a wet tile. I can guess now: she examines herself and doesn't want me watching. Maybe because the time she tried to see me naked, I slapped her. Who else's body can she see? Ama still lives on the couch, lulled and dulled by Apa Farzana. She never bathes Mehwish (she stopped bathing me when I was younger than Mehwish is now; by the time I remembered *her* fingerprints, I didn't have to erase them). I know this is one reason Mehwish will never ask to see Ama naked.

We walk, and my head throbs. I keep looking at Mehwish. Tall. Pretty. Blind.

I slap all hands away from her and grab her to me.

She pulls away.

"Mehwish, take my hand."

"No."

"You have to."

"No."

"*Please.*"

"No no *no.*"

"Are you in love with no?"

"N—" She grins. "Are the clouds tin-hazy, flat-gray, or round-curly?"

I give in, for now. "What do you think?"

"They taste dirty. Nana says I breathe the sky."

"We all do. Swallow it, heat it, send it back out. You're breathing the same sky as Jinnah and General Zia." I snatch her hand.

She snatches it back, making loud gulping sounds.

Those who see the earth as flat have never thought to consult the blind.

Her air is liquid. She can sink up to her waist in it. Her air is solid. She can cut herself against a sharp-edged cube. Her clouds are never still and never even, and she believes I can save her from a bad judgment. So she loves these walks, the way I used to love my walks with Nana. But this is a city and I have only two eyes. I keep one lowered. The other reads billboards, soars up minarets, drifts with kites. My two eyes don't connect. One always wants to pull free. Mehwish is becoming this eye, instead of submitting with the other.

We keep walking and she still won't surrender her hand.

The kite-flying festival of Basant is a week away. I feel no breeze, yet a kite jerks up into the sky, as if on elbows and knees. "I can't tell if it's being chased, or broken free."

"Where is it?"

I take her hand and point. The paper lashes between beams, like a girl between adult arms. On the road, traffic wheels by. It barely registers as I keep my hand on Mehwish's, following the kite as it soars smoothly now, nose in the air.

Then the movement below us stops abruptly, and it isn't right.

Before I've shifted my focus, before I can locate him, a motorcyclist jerks backwards and hits the road with hands to neck. I see this, though I'm somewhere in the long gap between him and the kite. The bike skids outside my widest focal range. A windshield explodes. Horns: never heard so many. Another bike spins on its side.

On the ground, a throat is slit by thin air. The first motorcyclist clutches his windpipe. Blood spurts like a rocket. It jets a scream. Loud. Ugly. *Infrared.* The second motorcyclist stands up. Brushes his jeans. Looks for his bike. Staggers. And I stagger with him: No Mehwish. I'm no longer pointing with her, at the kite.

"Mehwish!" I ran toward the collision and left her behind, my own throat sliced. "Mehwish!" *Even the air is not safe.*

I race back but I don't know where back is. I stop at a fruit stall. They haven't seen her. I ask at cloth shops, tire shops, a bakery. Nothing. Turn into another street. Reach a traffic light. Ask a pedestrian. Nothing. I start running again. I get lost.

I ask my way back to the park.

I find her in the park.

She stands beside a rosebush. She walked into it. Her right palm, the one that belongs to her, is scratched. Nothing else, except the sleeve is slightly torn at the cuff. She waits patiently. No tears. No perverts. No killer sky. And, to her mind, not even blood. Just a bush she tells me to smell. I squeeze her and she doesn't resist. I've been gone less than ten minutes.

On the way home, we pass by the accident. Both motor-cyclists are gone. On the road stretches a pool of blood glittering with glass. A car with a broken windshield sits abandoned. The first motorcycle lies smashed on its side. The second is gone. A crowd still lingers. One man coils the bloody weapon around his hand: kite string. Caked in fiberglass and released in the sky to slice away a life.

Mehwish points at the blood. "Tell what happened."

I don't reply.

"Tell what happened," she pulls my hand. "Cars were crashing. I heard it. You ran. Tell."

My first lie to her: "Nothing."

"Liar."

"At least it's the first time."

She smiles and the smile ripples outside my focal range. I admire her. I envy her. She wouldn't look so radiant if I hadn't made her darkness mine.

As Mehwish is again absorbed by the world inside her—feeding pictures behind her pupilla, where I can't get in—I remember Nana saying, when she was just a year old, that she lives in *aql nazari*, in her head, while I'm down-to-earth, literally. For her, I look down.

A warning in the sluggish wind stirring other kites, in the sky still bloody with a motorcyclist's neck: don't become Mother Martyr. Or the Book of Affliction. That is your opposite.

As she taps an inner source of fuel, gathers warmth from the flames lit at will, Mehwish's calm descends on me. Maybe, just maybe, a candle can light a candle.

I take her left hand, the way I tried to when we started on this walk.

Mehwish

Soon after Amal first lies to me she does some thing interesting. She keeps a roza. I also want to fast but Ama will not let me she says I am too young but Amal should she is fifteen. Amal never listens to Ama and Aba says it is Nana's fault her eticut is not high enough. So I am sir prized she listens to them now. I ask if it is "eticut" or "ex pearmint" and she gets angry. Then she tells me to call out the spellings and changes them to etiquette and experiment.

Nana is here and wants to visit the zoo. He is in a very happy mood I think big cause he is sacked. This is when you are made free. Amal is always busy I wish she would get sacked too. Nana has done many things since he got sacked. He went to China. He sat in a Jeep and went to the Hunza Valley and brought back ape rakats which were sweet. He also went to the Khoon Jirab Pass. Khoon is blood and jirab is socks but why call a pass Bloody Socks? I do not understand. Nana said he crossed Bloody Socks on foot and when I asked if his socks got bloody the room got quiet and then Amal said "He was wearing slippers not socks carry on" then Nana kept talking and no one understood.

In China the air is not tin it is thin. And cold.

In China there are guards that ask you questions like what is your per push and where is your pass port? Nana said to one "I have no per push but to be great full for this road into China and also to see some yaks on your side" and the guard got angry he said "Pass port?" So Nana showed him this is etiquette. I do not have a pass port I will have it only when I have etiquette.

In China there are Marco Polo sheeps.

These are different from the goat and sheeps near aboutrounds in Lahore before Bakra Eid they bleet then pee pull buy them quickly turning them into experiments. The ones in China are free big cause Marco Polo sacked them.

When the guard returned Nana's pass port and let him in he met a Chinese man about to cross into Pakistan who spoke English they said hello. They both liked long speeches. Nana says pee pull from old places always talk too much they carry all the words that came before and have to spit them out. Nana and the man said it is so amazing in only twenty years we have built the most difficult road in history on the tallest coldest mountins so many lives were lost who nose where it may lead and so on. Then the man said the making of the road reminded him that "a bird does not sing big cause it has an answer it sings big cause it has a song" and Nana started to cry.

When he tells this story later Amal hugs him he has a green smell like cold leaves and more later she says Nana was sacked from university for singing.

Goat can be one or many but only sheeps is many.

Fox can be one or many but only deers is many.

Wail can be one or many but only fishes is many.

Nana digs for wail in a few weeks. It is another thing he can do big cause he is sacked—

"We're leaving wear your shoes."

It is Amal inter uping me.

"Hurry up Nana is all ready in the car."

I sit on the bed she picks up a leg pushes a shoe on she was more gentle before. I was going to tell you other things Nana has done since getting sacked but first we are going to the zoo. Amal pushes me in the car.

•

It is so hot this July morning not a good day for the zoo I cannot believe how stupid they are. Before leaving Ama said Nana will make Amal who is fasting ill and me who is not fasting even more ill. But I was not going to stay home while they go out and any way it is not June the worst month when it does not rain it just blows dust on my face and in my eyes and the shampoo finishes quickly. The rains have come though it does not rain today the air is like Aba heavy and saggy and ready to fart. The zoo is smelly "steamy and tart" Amal calls it and when a breeze blows the tartness is mean in my nose. When it passes it is safe to breed again.

The lions are the high light which is when pee pull look most at one thing. When one starts to roar all of them answer and every thing goes quiet.

Amal holds me I am glad. But she says she is a "slave of the roar" and pulls me with her quickly pointing out the low lights: deers, bird, and bear.

Nana tries to stop us he says there is a new animal he must see we should hurry he promised Ama he would not keep us long in the heat. Amal ignores him she tells me my nose is still curled with tart smells or maybe loud lions. Then she describes the scene.

"We're at the pens."

"Are they in their cases?"

She clicks her toung she does not like me doing the same. "A pen is also a cage."

"I no."

"Then why—" She clicks her toung again. "One sher is curled alone in a pen—"

I inter up her. "A sher is a lion and a poem. Which one do you mean?"

Nana: "Oh, write it down quickly please! Release the caged poem from its pen!" I laugh but Amal clicks her toung again.

Amal: "Listen, Mehwish. Can you hear the mother lion growl in the pen? A cub is trying to play with her tail. Can you hear her get angry?"

Yes. "No."

"The cub is backing away in fright. *Aww.* He's looking with sweet yello eyes."

Nana: "Your ants throw per more flies ink."

Amal: "I can't help it. It's so cute."

Nana: "You're doing it again. Ants throw per more flies ink."

I hate it when they do this. "Who has ants that throw flies that throw ink?"

When they are finished laughing Nana says, "Repeat after me. An*th*."

"An*th*."

"Ro-po."

"Ro-po."

"More-fies."

"More-fies."

"Ing."

"Ing."

"Say it together: anth-ro-po-more-fies-ing."

"All right."

"Say it."

I get it the fourth time. "What does it mean?"

"Giving animals human character sticks. The cub's eyes are

not human eyes. It does not have human tots. Amal makes it sound as if she understands it."

"You sound like Junayd," says Amal her voice mean.

She has never shown Nana this Amal before though she loves me to see it. He is sir prized. "*Oh.*"

"Yes, as if I'm *for bidden* this aunty messy..."

He is silent. Is he looking at me her the cub or his slippers? Who am I looking at?

She does not stop. "It is you who taught me there are two ways of noing: intelligence and taste. Khayal and zauq. In the first, what is nown is seprit from what nose. In the second, it is the same. Without aunty messy, no taste!"

"Who is aunty messy?"

"*Inty*-messy. Mehwish, *please.*"

"Amal. *Please.* Junayd and I were talking about God—not cubs!"

"Junayd seprits himself from God. He believes God's eyes are not like human eyes. God does not have human tots. The problem is, his kind of belief seprits itself from *life.* It is not tasted. It is coded. *You* taste. And now you correct me!"

Nana mumbuls, "Oh deers."

I ask her, "What do you want to taste?"

"Shut up, Mehwish."

"Are you thirsty? If you break your roza you will go to hell."

"Shut up, Mehwish."

"Do not tell me to shut up."

Nana says, "Well, let's move on."

Amal says, "If a human character stick like courage can be dewine, why not the longing of a baby lion?"

"All right. Point taken. Onto monkeys."

"Do not tell me to shut up."

"*All right*, Mehwish. Sorry."

She pushes my right elbo forward. I tell her *I* am thirsty. "And I will not go to hell big cause I am not fasting."

She ignores me again. I want to go home.

The lists in my head are starting to swim. I do not speak about this list it is called Silent Let ers. There are no silent let ers in Urdu if you cannot hear them you are deaf. But English is sneaky. There are hidden let ers you have to dig up the way Nana digs wail. A wail has a hidden *S* in its ear which is how it can hear all let ers.

Amal teaches me to dig let ers. She says if you cannot hear the *t* in listen and the *o* in toung or young you have to store them like a mamry. *W* is specially sneaky some times a soft wail or wowel and some times a sharp *v*. It can also be a silent wrist or write two answers but I cannot remember other exam pulls. It has to be very quiet before I can dig them up.

Amal says I can spell some big words like intelligence and courage exact but not some small ones. I had lists for these also but they are also gone.

It is getting quiet they might come back. I can always hear the *qu* in quiet.

It is coming back. An idea is a tot that can be taught—

"Lee mars, Mehwish. Small, furry. And a red spider monkey from Central America." Amal is inter uping me more and more. "How they swing on their long tails! You would love a tail like that." She rubs my back. "Are you okay?"

"I am thirsty."

"We can leave soon."

But Nana starts again. "Maybe you are right. There is a

connection between how we relate to wild animals and to God. When we see the lion, what is ex perienced is not only fear or aww. It is the desire to konk er. The romance of taming the beast. If we could just open the lock, slide the chain, walk into the pen and smooth the snarling with our touch! It is the same as wanting to be chosen by God. To know Him, person ali. It is a sir ender but also a konk west."

"I remember a time when you believed only in the sir ender part."

"Yes, but that time…"

They keep talking and walking pulling me the let ers are pulling me. "Are we still on lions?"

"Mehwish." Nana stops walking. I think he had forgotten me.

Amal: "That noise is a chimp-an-zee. Say it."

It is very loud. "I am thirsty and I have a head aik."

Nana just kisses me and Amal pushes me on again.

Nana: "Mackawk. Langoor. Sucking on angoor. It is monkeys who *taste*."

Amal: "It is *you* who ants throw per more flies is."

Nana laughs we move faster. Then Amal stops suddenly and turns around I bump my nose in her big chest. She sucks in her breath as if *she* is hurt. "Oh!"

"*You* bumped me."

"No I mean oh!"

Nana: "Yes, this is it. The *new* animal."

"What is it?"

All Amal can say is oh.

Nana: "Latin name *Man der ill is finx der ill is man der…*"

He likes Latin names I do not they never stop I wait for Amal to give me ones that go away so I can store them.

But she will not till after we get home. This is what she will say:

"And then I was face to face with a buboon," and she will call the let ers out they are different from the Braille let ers no one calls out in school but Amal has always called hers and drawn them on paper or my back so I can call them on hers. She will also draw a lion but her drawings are not good. But I was telling you what she will say:

"It had swollen turkoise testy kuls an erect peenis it presented to the world with relish. Nana was also shocked. We looked away as if caught watching a dirty film."

"But what *was* it?"

"*Horrible.* The dewil's fruit."

"You mean a Latin word?"

"No I mean a big nose shiny blue a scar lit bump on the tip. Sharp teeth, red toung, eyes losty. A face like its bottom, with huge cheeks like testy kuls. Fur in every color of the rainbo, even on wrists and uncles. No one—*no one*—could imagine taming this thing. Its name was man drill—"

"Two words. Man drill."

"One word. Mandrill. Mehwish, stop splitting words."

"All right."

"Its name was mandrill both man and beast."

But now at the zoo Amal cannot speak.

"Yes," Nana says to some one. "Latin name *Man der ill is finx der ill is man der...* A lion's body and man's head. A monster. A riddle. Like *Amalicetus.* Wail or wolf? Monkey or myth? Why do we have to no?"

Amal squeezes me and now every one is silent. Even Nana.

Then he says, "You see some thing like this and have to ask why." He pawses. "Now I am having a real ijaz moment." He pawses again. "So, what is God? To define Him is to put Him in a pen and ants throw per more flies ink." He pawses again. "The Sufi way to God is the peri less but joy full flight of the alone. Now this poor monkey looks very alone. I hope he can learn to fly."

"I have two head aiks."

"Mehwish." Again he had forgotten me.

"It is very, very hot." Amal sounds like she has three head aiks.

"Do you want to no what I love most, a side from you two?"

We say yes.

"Very asian. What some call miss takes. Without miss takes there would only be one kind of rock, one kind of monkey, one kind of child. We would have no very asian or vim zee and die of bore dum."

He takes my left hand we start walking. I will not die of bore dum I will die of thirst. The lion roars again. It is too loud but I like this too loud it makes every thing else quiet.

Nana lets go of my hand to look for his car keys. "Pee pull have spells against this vim zee dewil! As they do against the wail we found. You will come to hear me speak, Mehwish? You will not find it hard?"

"No." I hear his keys the car door opens.

"I will also come." Amal pushes me in the back.

"I will be waiting." The engine roars differently from the lion. It does not bring quiet. "Let us hope mother wail is safe from dog ma!"

I go with Amal to hear Nana speak. There is a big crowd Amal says Nana is so stately he could be the UN Secret of State.

"What is that?"

"Doesn't matter. Women look at him."

"So? They look at me too."

"No they don"t."

"Yes they do."

"Not the way the glamris woman in the front seat keeps agling."

"What is agling?"

"*Og*ling. When you can't stop looking at some one in a losty way."

"She is ogling me too."

"No she isn't."

"Yes she is."

"I will take you home if you don't stop."

This is called a threat. It is mean. It has a silent *a*.

I wishper: "The mandrill was *og*ling you."

"That's right."

"It was horrible."

"And majikul."

"Is this woman horrible or majikul?"

"Please stop."

This is called a hidden threat. It has many silent leters.

Amal says I used to seprit some words that end in *er*.

This seat is not soft. Many pee pull think the same big cause they keep shifting chairs are moving it is noisy. A thing I do not no keeps going on and off loudly.

Amal feels bad she threatened me she tries to make me talk again without saying sorry. "That is a mike-ro-fone. Say it."

"No." She has started going to parties Ama does not no. She goes with her friend Zara Ama does not like her. Zara has a deep woice I like to hear her sing. "Did you inwite Zara?"

"Zara is only interested in parties."

"And boys."

She does not hear me she says, "Oh! I no that man. Brian. He was with us when I found the rock with the hidden *S*. And there's an other man with him. Cute."

"How can a rock be cute?"

"I meant the man silly okay be quiet Brian is about to speak."

The mike-fone or some thing makes that ugly sound again then the man starts to talk. "Hey it is wonder full to be here sharing our work I am sure you'd like to no how it all began the girl is here today! Hey Amal! Good to see you how you've grown!'

Amal shifts in her seat I no what she is doing she tells me I do it she is blushing. Pee pull turn in their seats there is more shifting and also there are laughs.

She wishpers, "Oof! I'm *fifteen*!"

Brian says, "But hey, let's get off the topic of seven or eight years and onto millyuns! Long before Amal was born some men found what turned out to be—"

I hear a but tin Amal says he is showing the dog-wail picture she has shown me except it was *her* drawing and I have said these are not good. This is called a slide show.

Brian talks again but I new it. He speaks Latin. "*Me so naked me so… un gu lati guni ungli…*"

I have learned to do some thing when Latin is on. I look for quiet. I tune out.

A dog can become a wail and a sound can become a word.

A dog can become many wails and a sound can become many words.

I tune back. Brian says, "So, hey, where is the truth if not in the feet? It is, ladies and gentlemen, in the teeth! In bumps points and cusps. The me so naked had the feet of a goat but teeth more like a wail's than any land mammal we no. Still some ex perts aren't conwinced. One pale into logic calls it ad hock."

I feel my teeth with my toung. I wishper, "What are cusps?"

"I don't no."

"What is ad hock?"

"I don't no."

"What is pale into logic?"

"Paly-un-to-lo-gy."

"What is it?"

" *Sh.* "

I do not no why I have to be quiet at least I am wishpering others are not listening to Brian at all they are talking loudly. "I hope Nana speaks soon."

" *Sh.* "

"Are you dying of bore dum?"

"Mehwish, he is nearly finished. Then the cute one will speak."

"How do I no he is cute? I want Nana to speak."

Amal puts her arm around me this is called desprit. *Ing* changes *ie* to *y*.

Her smell is like the smell of sin a men on my pillo case. When it is hot like now she is sin a men in hot ghee. She sweats more than me big cause of her big chest and thick curls. I feel sleepy. I like the dream I have later I will learn the word for it: sublime.

I lie in a bath full of salt. I feel clean it is better than when Amal scrubs me. This is an inside clean as if I am fasting. Some thing on four legs is beside me I can hear him drink the salt water feel the big toung taste the teeth but I am not scared. He is gentle. He is mine what I say he does. If I want seeweed shampoo I do not have to say it he makes bubbles in my hair I keep feeling clean inside. This new bath world has no color no green or turkoise there are no names. But there is a song that empties me. I do not want it to stop. I do not even want it to paws the way a melody pawses so you can store it away for always the way I store a new word. I do not want to store this song. I want to be in it.

When I wake up there is no song. I did not store it now it is lost. I can hear nothing big cause there is only shouting. I cannot help it I start to cry I miss my dream it is gone so quickly. There is no salt bath just chairs flying and Nana is angry I cannot hear what he says it is so loud and some one trips over me.

"*Excuse me*," says Amal angry.

Pee pull are booing Nana loudly.

Now pee pull are fighting for the mike-fone and one is Nana. It is not like him to fight he is always in charge. "What is happening?"

"Pee pull are angry," says Amal.

"I *no* that. *Why* are they angry?"

"Big cause Nana upset them."

"What did he say?"

"Oh, so many things, Mehwish. You were sleeping."

"Tell me why they are angry."

"Well, I don't no. He was talking about the mountins how

old they are and how there are more and more army fences around the area I found *Amalicetus* the men have to get per mits from this mince tree and that mince tree but they have no funds their labs and tools are so old it is why all our riches are taken a broad then some one got angry he said there is a war we should talk about important things not mountins what is rich about rocks can we feed mouths with them can we fight armies with them? Then every one started one man asked if Nana thinks we are disended from monkeys what about the special creation of man as the Quran says and Nana got angry and they called each other names till Aziz Sahib inter uped them and said there is bilkul no problem will every one please sit down there is proof of fossils in the Quran—"

"What name did Nana call him?"

"I'll tell you when we get home, Mehwish. Can you just sit qu—"

Some one is near us I can feel him. He is standing waching Amal wipe my face listening to her tell me to be quiet she does not sense him she does not turn round. It is not some one pushing or shouting just standing waching. *Og*ling. Like a sneaky silent English leter. "Tell him to go away."

"Who?" She turns round. The man walks away quickly.

"Who was that man?"

I can feel her shrug. "There's no man."

I will never no how she new his name.

Noman

I see the daggers of Amal's eyelashes and the peace disturbed in Mehwish's heart and know I'm in trouble. This bulbul loves too many roses.

How did I get here in the first place, in this stuffy room of a decrepit hotel on Davis Road, eavesdropping on a blind girl and blinking stupidly at her sister with the curly unkempt hair and full mouth half-bored, half-amused?

She turns around and glares and tells the younger one I'm no one.

Well, no man *is* an island.

I walk away.

gateway the second: the man

The utilitarian man is not capable of wonder.
—Muhammad Hussein Saffouri

Noman

Hours before I first see Mehwish and Amal, I'm on my way to Salman's house in Andarooni Shehr, the Inner City, what English speakers call the Old City.

It's a hot morning in August, already muggy and frenzied enough to lower my pulse and give me pleasure in trivia. I take my favorite route, eat a *mooli paratha*, examine ladies' underwear. In the Inner City, inner apartments flap outwardly: 42C. Yellow lace. Pink bows. Good pliability. My hairy fingers push cups in and out, in and out. Move on.

Nearing Salman's house.

Salman isn't just any Salman, he's Real Salman because he lives in Andarooni Shehr, where, according to him, all Real People live, and some Less Reals, like me, occasionally meet. Our families settled here after Partition but began moving to newer neighborhoods in the seventies, when the slums leaked into history. Through the eighties, the middle-class exodus continues. Only the poor and royals stay, the latter, like Salman, to embody all the clichés and cozy contradictions of a Lahori in love with his feudal blood. Oh, the glory that once was! Lost on lumpens like me! To the family's lands and peasants Salman's father piles a collage of businesses in some holier-than-thou planet like Dallas–Dubai or Jeddah–Jerusalem, sheikhing his moneymaker.

We always meet at his old haveli because he's an excellent host, lavishing us with whisky and pai and silk brocades on which to fall asleep. It's the kind of house that those who migrate to England or Canada love to return to for a jaunt around their roots. Salman's happy to oblige, parading his stash of Gucci and Johnnie Walker, Trotsky and Marx (he *is* a Marxist, he just grew up), sending them back scented with "authentic experience."

It's at his house that I'm going to get the phone call that'll change my life, and bind me to Amal and Mehwish. A part of me must know because as I enter Salman's skinny, gutter-sodden street (key authentic ingredient), my legs wobble. *Delay*, they seem to cry. *Go back.*

I spin around, exit lane, bump into favorite fugitive: Petrov. Note his blond bristle has flowered into beard overnight. Which white man once said the white man is more intelligent because he's less hairy? (Inventor of razor blade?) Should've met Petrov. This furry ape from the Caucasus towers a foot above me, swings a Kodak camera, wraps me in a suffocating hug, declares it too early for Salman, and of course I agree.

Petrov's life began when he defected from the Red Army and crossed the border from Afghanistan into Pakistan in twenty days. He looks Afghan. Or they look Russian. Or we look American. Every day he tells the same story. "The CIA dumps more dollars on the Islamic Jihad than it did the Contras. Bloody Mooj Jihadis have more Blowpipes and Stingers than prayer beads and Mr. Reagan compares them to his Founding Fathers! Do you know how many Reds are quitting?" Every day I reply, Nope, the papers don't say. He's still in touch with his Comrades—don't ask how.

We hop in a rickshaw, get on the Mall. His new love's reading. Discovered it here, of all places, the city with a lower per capita book consumption than Mars. We graze on rows of secondhand books on the pavement outside Anarkali. Personally, I'd rather graze on lacy C-cups. But when you're not from the Caucasus, you keep your mouth shut.

Petrov picks up a *Reader's Digest* for war talk. It's a back issue on booby traps (neither lacy nor pliable). A British reporter whose leg burst on a "horseshoe" reports, *Nothing is safe, even earth and wind explode. Nobody wants to walk or talk or even eat. Reds desert in hordes. Those left are disarmed before sleeping. Few get their guns back.*

Petrov tosses the digest back. He mutters that to fight or defect is the same when you're without cover. "There are more alliances between enemies than unity between invaders, or the invaded. The war will be over in a year, trust me."

"So, who's left in your unit?"

"Only the *hijras.*" Laughs. A thing about *goras*: they chew to the husk the one local word they learn—in Petrov's case, *hijra,* meaning eunuch—and expect us to cheer each time. A thing about *desis*: we do.

I also know this about Petrov. He was given asylum when his unit realized it wasn't the liberator or the conqueror but the slave. The Mooj were waiting for just this psychological victory: admit your country sold you and we, who were wronged, will set you, who wronged us, free. If you won't confess, we'll kill you.

He once told me, "That moment sums up everything this war taught me. I have no friends, no enemies. And freedom, like religion, breeds in a walled city deep in your head. When I own that city I will never have to admit defeat again." So he reads. Digests. Gateway to a walled city or slum? Fact is, in the time I've known him his English has become perfect so maybe there are winds in these ten-rupee tomes I should let inside my own head.

Speaking of which (that is, winds to let in *your* head), if you fail to believe a Communist turncoat can walk free on the streets of an American ally, you fail to understand the law of this Islamic

Republic: what shouldn't happen does. Which is why, according to Petrov, unlike his country, mine will never have a revolution. When small gains are negotiable, from families like Salman's or from God, but preferably from both, it's easy to lose sight of the big picture.

Let me illustrate. Right here in this Mughal capital Lahore—or Mahmud-pur, Lohar, *Laor*—on this dusty spot, I once found a pamphlet of the Vidya Bharati Trust, favorite son of the Hindu extremist Rashtriya Swayamsevak Sangh. Inside sprawled a map of Greater Hindustan, including Pakistan and Bangladesh, even Bhutan, Nepal, and Tibet. It said Adam was Hindu and so were his successors till one day a foreign race was born, created independently, by the devil. It comprised Muslims, Buddhists, and Christians. I flipped ahead: *That the Taj Mahal was built by Shah Jehan is a lie invented by Muslim-loving Hindus. Its real name is Tejomahala.*

I laughed out loud, thinking, Come on, yaar! We may not have done much lately but we did once love to death a woman who bore us a dozen kids. And build her the loveliest three domes in the world. Then I stopped laughing, stunned. We? Am I part of this We? And I thought, I want to be part of a We that envisions and erects the sexiest tomb on the planet. But after that, I am free.

I tossed the manifesto with the other books and the next week it was gone. And I have a feeling, and maybe by now you do too, that it wasn't confiscated. It was bought. A bitter fruit has value if forbidden. It can be bargained for. What shouldn't happen, does.

Afghan Muslims are refugees but a Red Enemy Blond Atheist, with a little help from Real Salman, is a guest.

Today, Petrov and I see only a halal display. Jules Verne on how to go around the world in eighty days (I tell Petrov to write the sequel. How to do it in twenty) mixed with Enid Blyton and Khalil Gibran. Then my eye falls on a paperback, which, if my life were a book, would be foreshadowing. *Selections from Charles Darwin.* Why does it glow in the dust? For me, only me? Something to do with Aba, but I can't decide what.

Since I now mention the man, I should take you on another mini-diversion. Bear with me.

Aba joined the Party of Creation soon after the day the three pearly domes of the Badshahi Mosque drifted toward me as three giant sifrs, showing me what's real and not. And showing me why Aba's changed. In the seven years since, I haven't been visited by the floating zeroes again. And Aba keeps trying to cast me into his Ideal Cabinet.

This morning, I heard him tell my brother Adnan about a sacked professor-scientist and Darvin-sisterfucker-believer: "The same who made rumpus at our first meeting! He will face the music!" (Sehr wasn't around to start humming.) My brother said the scientist must be harnessed, then drove away to harness a girl.

When Aba's in feverish suspense he says rumpus a lot. And harness. These are the things that cause rumpuses and must be harnessed: jinns, women, me, jinns, infidels, me, women, infidels like women, me, and Darwin.

And Darvin sisterfucker. Oh.

Who's this Darwin, anyway? There's a photo in the book and I swear he looks like Aba. Thick-shouldered, pot-bellied, long lush beard.

The bookseller wants fifty rupees. I give thirty, feel ripped off, scan the first few chapters, stop at a page that says Darwin's granny was his proofreader. He sailed around the world (not with Jules Verne, or Petrov and me) on a ship called *The Beagle*, kept a journal, and sent installments back home. Granny had nothing to say about his ideas but his spellings insulted her: "*It is lose not loose, highest not higest, cannibal not cannabal,*" I read out loud, tell the wind, "*do take note of the errors in your orthography lest the world ever get wind of them. I am under obligation to point these out. You see, I am still your Granny.*"

Petrov laughs, pays fifteen rupees for the digest, asks to borrow my book when I'm done. We head toward Real Salman's, passing the underwear *gali* I strolled through earlier.

I flip through pages as we walk. "*Evolution means to unroll a scroll.*" Petrov grunts, fidgeting with his camera. I glance down the page. "Apparently, a snake is on its way to being a fish, a fish to being—me. This man was a nut! I've definitely been ripped off!"

He takes my picture.

"How can I come from a fish when my mother's such a perfect woman?" I take his picture. "It says life's a dance between anatomy and behavior. Hello anatomy," I squeeze a mint-green 44C monstrosity, "I'm behavior."

We take more pictures. Then we dance like we're already drunk all the way to Real Salman's door.

•

Inside, we're immediately closed to the world and open to the haveli's own center: the courtyard.

The Inner City and the old houses in it are constructed like an onion, or a Russian doll, and this is why I keep coming back to Salman's mansion, keep listening to his boastful chatter, his insufferable hypocrisies. It's not just the whisky or the respite from the heat and fumes outside, though both help. What hooks me is the giddy logic of the design, the sense of falling into a smaller and smaller space, of stripping the doll to find the heart locked inside. Have never been able to decide if I love the journey or hate it.

Because the haveli rejects the natural skyline, as soon as I enter it, my eye floats down to the courtyard's red and black floor tiles. It feasts on the interlocked geometry of swirls and vines, looking for the void in between. The sifr. The zero from which God made the world.

There are days when (after smoking first-class hashish) I find inner peace simply by gazing at those tiles. Their repetition and symmetry, visual and audible, a prayer in perpetual recitation, a scroll unrolling, welcomes me. It brings heaven to earth.

On other days, the pattern offers no revelation. I gaze at the ceramic sky, with its floating red and black clouds, searching for a way to connect point, line, and space, to reach that elusive center. But the geometry doesn't bloom.

•

I hear voices from the first door on the left as I enter the courtyard. The group's already high: two journalists who frequent drug busts; a silent painter; a jobless musician; Salman the people's nawab; a German woman he's trying to impress.

Salman embraces Petrov and me. Introductions are made. I move straight to Ali, one of the reporters, to assist with tobacco threads. Salman says, "I was just explaining to Ann. This area used to have such taste but now it is a dump. What is the lesson there?"

Petrov grunts, lights up. He says you can't mix Blue with Red, all you get is Imperial Purple. But he knows he might not survive on our streets on good will and freakish nature alone. Help from above helps, and Salman's nothing if not above. So Petrov grunts and says nothing, though I'm sure "Ann" would be more interested in his nightly jaunts into Kandahar's poppy fields than Salman's purple lessons. But she's as gullible as *goris* get, and keeps listening to Salman.

"The problem is all about land ownership and law and order. Let me tell you. In the Mughal days this was a clean, splendid neighborhood. Then the Sikhs came. They looted homes and converted them to military barracks. The British reconverted them to splendid homes in a splendid colony, including the residence of that fellow-what's-his-name, Sir William. You know. It was called Bare Sahib ki Kothi. The First Punjab Volunteers of the British Army was formed right here."

Volunteers, my foot. Tell a man kill or be killed and call it a choice.

Ann's eyes sparkle. "Ja?"

Her racks: *splendid.*

"Now, a very interesting thing about this regiment. It played a key role in the 1857 uprising. Have some more tea?"

Nice. Glorify the Brits then say you fought them. Salman the prone warrior fills her cup with a silver samovar. First time I've seen him lift anything.

"And your family is part of uprising?" She blinks.

"Oh yes. There were many brave men on my father's side. Thanks to them—" he titters, he actually titters "—the British eventually began to leave. That was in the 1930s. Then families like mine settled here permanently. We kept the area so pretty for the next three decades you cannot imagine. We gave the people what they want: decent living. There was a good school just behind Sir William's house and we ran it. We housed them, fed them. You see, old families know. We look after our land, our people. We built the ties between them and their community. It is like the alleys in this old quarter, like the rooms to the courtyard. The people depended on *my* family for order. We were the center. Our schools, hospitals, madrasahs, shops, all were connected to serve a common social value. Now there is no center, no caring. It is each for himself." He shouts for the servant to bring more food. "The feudal structure, you know, it gets a bad name in the West. But if you look closely, it was a kind of socialism. And I am Marxist. Now anyone can buy plots and cut them up. Once an area like this had under a hundred residents. Now there are at least ten thousand and they are ignorant, uneducated people moving in even as we speak. It is a great loss."

Fresh plates of *dahi bare* and samosas arrive. Ali spoons the *dahi bare* for Ann (never seen him lift anything either, except a tennis racket), saying the "center" was plain monopoly. "You're a self-appointed ruler, afraid privatization will strip your power," he tells Salman.

Petrov winks at me. Ali's the only one of us who argues openly with Salman. To Salman's credit, he keeps inviting him back. The Salman that expects loyalty from "the people" also expects loyalty between friends.

Salman sits up. "Then why do they stay with us? Why do these poor men and women still come to our door when they need help? Why do they *trust* us?"

"Trust! They just have nowhere else to go! The same reason Arabs and Pathans and Kashmiris and Chechnyans are fighting in Afghanistan. They don't *trust* America or Pakistan or any other state. They need bread. And distraction. Killing, cooking."

"Ask them!" Salman insists. "Ask *any* of them. If not for us, all their children would be hanging around scratching lice and doing drugs!"

We all laugh, even the silent painter and jobless musician (also "helped" by Salman). All, except Ann and Salman. I hold up my wrinkled tube of burning evidence. Ann smiles. Clued in or still clueless? Who cares, I take the smile.

"I don't mean like *this*," Salman won't quit. "And you're wrong about the Mooj. They believe it's their sacred duty to fight." He steals a glance at Ann.

I say, "Their duty is not to God but to tribe." I steal a glance at Ann.

She's checking out Ali and who can blame her. He's built like a stallion and scratches a lean living chasing smugglers and thieves while I'm smaller than her and excel at mathematics.

Catching me ogling Ann, Salman smirks. "Dear Noman, you are oblivious to the realities of the common man!"

Ann asks Ali, "But *are* they doing it for God?"

Out in the courtyard, the phone rings.

Ali moves closer to Ann. "Some, yes. They do it for God. Their code of conduct."

Petrov shrugs. "Code of *hijras*."

The jobless musician compliments Petrov on his Urdu.

Ann beams at Ali; Salman frowns; Ali grins. Game point. Salman offers Ann more samosas. Ali offers Ann his half-bitten samosa. She bites Ali's. Game Ali.

The phone keeps ringing. "What are the sisterfucker servants for?" Salman hollers, illustrating his connection with the common man. The phone stops ringing.

The other journalist, Faisal the Vulgarian (can't say why, we're in ladies' company), more spin-bowler than tennis hunk, attempts a toss. Pipes up to say he's doing a piece on suicide bombers. "Did you know kamikaze means 'divine wind'?"

Ali shrugs. "Of course."

"Who was the first suicide bomber not hired by a state?" Faisal looks around, eyes Ann. Ali shrugs again. "Has to be a devotee of Ram."

"I'd guess Sikh," Salman plays along. Unusually sporting.

"No way." I stare at Salman, feeling my high plummet. "Must have been someone who didn't benefit from a Christian Wistian alliance with the Dream East India Company. And I'd guess Muslim."

The phone rings again.

Salman laughs. "That is interesting theory!" He shouts again, "Some bust tard get the phone na!" Some bust tard does.

"You're all wrong," Faisal smirks. "The first suicide bomber not employed by a government but fighting for independence was a Buddhist woman."

Salman laughs again. "Did it happen under a tree?"

I say, stupidly, "A peepul tree."

"Sahibji," a servant enters the room. "It's for you." He's talking to me.

"For Noman?" repeats Salman.

"I do get called, you know!" Why do I feel like shit? Is it just the hashish? Bloody Ali! I reach the telephone. "Hello?"

"It's your father."

"Aba!" My throat's prickly. Need scotch.

"Good news."

The worst kind.

He's been promoted to vice chairman of the Jamaat-e-Pedaish. His first task's to establish the Academy of Moral Policy, an institute to save the swiftly declining values of today. The first meeting is in one hour.

"I am appointing you personal secretary. It will harness your rumpuses, make you less of an issue. Your first job is to take today's minutes. Hurry!"

"I'll only take a few seconds."

Feel ill, curse this evil weed, shuffle back into the room.

"Who was it?" sneers the devil himself, Ann at his side.

•

In the car Aba hands me his papers and fumes about the same scientist he fumed about this morning. "He is having a meeting in the very same hotel! It is no coincidence. He has heard about the academy we are inshallah setting up and wants to make rumpus."

"What's *his* meeting about?"

"Darvin *bhainchod*! If you think we're descended from apes you're not my son!"

"I think no such thing!" I think I'm descended from hashish.

Did Darvin *bhainchod* say we're descended from apes? Can't remember. Think it was his granny. She changed cannabal to cannibal but how did she spell cannabas—or cannibas?

I look in the folder and find a newspaper clipping with no name or date. The author's name has been whited out. I start to read:

A Blueprint for Life

For a long time scientists suspected that whales descended from a terrestrial mammal, a Mesonychid, meaning "middle claw." It lived in the Middle Eocene, was approximately the size of a wolf...

There are two figures of strange beasts. They look all wrong—or is it my head? I slide the clipping away. We pull into the driveway of an old hotel.

•

Men congregate in Seminar Room 1. I recognize some faces from visits to our house over the years, others I meet for the first time: vice chancellor of the Islamic Forum (of the predestined acronym IF), religious scholars, clerics, delegates from the national space program, lawyers, JP chairman and party members, including tattered but resewn factions, and a handful of men who float around as "advisers." All unite to put Pakistan's youth on the True Path. I'm the youngest person here.

Aba opens my book and tells me to stop daydreaming and start copying. I fiddle with wires, blank tapes, my oily hair. Drink tepid water, turn up air conditioning. As Aba takes his seat between the JP chairman and IF vice chancellor on stage, my head starts to clear. Another 45 minutes, the audience finally settles, VC taps mike, begins opening address. I scribble in my copy book.

VC: "Bismillah-i-rehman-i-rahim. Asalaam alaikum distinguished scholars, worthy ministers, noble scientists *and advisers*, and a very hearty welcome to our foreign participants, in whose honor our meeting will be in English, Dr. Muhammad Lawrence—"

Tall physicist from Belgium intercedes. "Lawg*h*aw."

"Welcome! And Sheikh Abu bin Yaqub from Saudi Arabia, welcome! It is pleasure to inaugurate this, the fifth seminar on Islamization of Thought. To those present when General Zia ul Haq kindly delivered first address, hearty welcome back. New participants, welcome welcome. And now, a moment to remember our founder."

Prayers, followed by a summary of the first meeting.

"… As such, all efforts are ongoing. We have successfully banned obscenity and established shariat courts and an Islamic educational system and everything in between."

Sips water. Pauses. I check that the tape's running. It is.

"My focus is my passion is my knowledge. Teaching of any discipline, be it physics or biology or science, or history or the past, without reference to God and the Prophet, Peace Be Upon Him, leads us away. As such, we are taking measures (*checks notes*) for only men committed to restoring values that have been snatched from us like light (*searches for a metaphor*)—like darkness—can enter our educational systems. You are familiar with challenges. For example, humanities. In past, students dreamed up mindless fictions, and sciences crawled with foreign notions. I need not repeat. We discussed in detail in last meeting."

Sips water. Pauses.

"However, despite our best efforts, elements are working against us. They dispensate books that tempt children into believing they have own minds. Realizing urgency of matter, the President has given his generous support to set up of this institute of importance, the Academy for Moral Policy, headed by vice chairman, Mirza Inayat Anwar. (*Aba nods, pulls the microphone toward him, but the chairman snatches it. The vice chancellor quickly intercedes.*) And now I wish to invite the chairman to speak."

Chairman (*Rapid bismillah. No thanks to the VC, no greeting to the participants*): "There is pollution in our societies because of those who stray! (*Applause. I note the difference between an academic and a politician.*) Liars and cheats! Evil-wishers spreading falsehoods! Seeing in the Holy Quran and Sunnah what they please! Changing what is Eternal, Permanent, Im— (*searches*) Unchanging! Fixed as I am to this seat! They say it is gravity. We know it is Allah! (*Louder applause.*) But these elements against us (*sudden whisper*), whispering in newborn ears. Talking of senses, cause, effect. *(Shouts)* We will repair the damage with science that is pure!"

Continues for 27 more minutes. Room so loud I miss most of it.

Aba (*slower than the chairman*): "Bismillah-i-rehman-i-rahim. As the honorable chairman and vice chancellor describe, we are living in dangerous times. The reasons are many—from the Mongol invasion to the Crusades to Colonialism and Communism and so on—but these are the easy ones to identify, my friends. God give strength to those upon whom the burden of addressing *invisible* evil has fallen. (*Murmurs of consent.*) With His guidance, we are able to see where (*turns to me*) *invisible* cracks have risen. Our task is to repair their Eyes and our Road."

Heavy pause. Still hollows me with his eyes.

"The young Pakistani is a cultural freak. (*I sit up, remembering the last time he said this.*) His religion is whimsy. He has no concept of Al Sirat al Mustaqim, the straight path. (*Loud applause.*) He is a split. A small wind pulls him. People talk of brain drain when youth leave this country, what about the brain drain when they stay?

"Our immediate need, as you know, is to eliminate all gaps in spiritual education, especially in science. We are trying but have not had total success, as you heard. (*Fumbles.*) There are dangerous leaks, as you see, in this F. Sc. book (*holds it up*). What is this nonsense, 'earth sciences'? Do they not know the planet is a dead body? (*Loud consent.*) It is He who breathes life into it, and will stop breathing life into it, according to His will. Say: He is the only cause. (*Murmurs of consent.*) He who sets your house on fire. He who leaves your burns and your scars. *(Applause.)*

Aba clears his throat. He's the clearest speaker—why does this surprise me?

"Now, in this very hotel, soon, there will be an attempt to divert us in our struggle. If we cannot see evil under our nose, who are we to speak of Truth? (*Murmurs of confusion.*) I mean soon, in Seminar Room 2, I have heard through my sources, the former professor Zahoor ul Din, a man some of you know because he rudely interrupted our first meeting—"

A young JP member interrupts, requesting the mike. Murmurs of disapproval. I was wrong; he's the youngest person here.

Aba: "You see! The young these days have no manners and must be harnessed!"

Pipsqueak pleads: "Bismillah-i-rehman-i-rahim. My name is Muhammad Abdul and I am very grateful to be given this chance to speak and hope you will forgive my rude intrusion. (*Murmurs of boredom.*) I will not be taking too much of your time, I promise."

The vice chancellor mumbles: "Go on go on, quickly."

Pipsqueak: "Thank you, Hazoor. All my thanks. (*Clears throat.*) I agree with everything my eminent elders have said, wishing only to add that earth sciences, do not by definition imply, necessarily, heresy."

Sudden silence. Pipsqueak takes a deep breath, begins to look increasingly nervous as he continues.

"Whereas Islam does not, unlike Christianity, specify the age of the Earth, exactly, the Bible leading them to conclude it is six thousand years, but not in Islam. Islamic texts do not specify, exactly, the age of the Earth, necessarily. Howsoever, with the evidence of some astronomers (*silence ends as abruptly as it fell; loud murmurs of discontent*), we have necessarily calculated it to be approximately five thousand million years old exactly. (*Louder discontent; I feel a bit stoned again; Aba frowns, vhispers in the WC's ear.*) The Quran, in fact, praises the possession of this knowledge in two verses of Surah Al-Fatir (*recites in Arabic, then English*): "*In the mountains there are streaks of white and red of various shades, as well as others raven-black... Only such as are endowed with innate knowledge stand truly in awe of God: for they alone comprehend that verily, God is almighty, much-forgiving.*""

Murmurs of ameen followed by objections. Pipsqueak pauses, resumes.

"I wish to propose that this 'innate knowledge' is maybe, exactly, the earth sciences, helping us know these mountains of many shades, which are, in fact, the Salt Range of our beloved Punjab! (*Beams, no one beams back; status of my head is clear.*) In fact, the study of earth might be a (*licks lips, scratches beard with teeth*), a *divine* art."

Two men protest, "Haram!" Aba asks Pipsqueak to refrain from further offense. But he continues, though even less confidently.

"I want to propose only, as I was trying to say, those that possess the knowledge, necessarily, to study the earth's crust, exactly, which is not as new as some believe (*furious protests, Aba rises*), not either as old as others say. But returning to the text—"

Aba: "Young man, you are absolutely *not* in a position to lecture *us* on the Holy Word! (*Loud consent.*) I forbid you to continue. *Khamosh!*"

Pipsqueak, loudly: "It is *in* the Quran there have been, uh, other geological eras, and that after each, changes were made in the earth. I mean, according to His will!"

Chairman, rising; Aba, rising; myself, rising. Two men lift Pipsqueak by his collar. Aba escorts him out of the room. Aba returns.

Aba: "It is unfortunate this happened at our own very meeting. In our fight we will never be distracted by sudden rumpuses, but here is a lesson: beware how far the germ spreads." (*Somber nods.*)

Mujahid ul Sharif, JP member: "He was a mole planted by the secularists. I have had my doubts for a long time and regret not voicing them."

Aba: "You should not hesitate to come to me."

Mujahid ul Sharif: "That is my promise from now on."

Aba: "I apologize to our foreign guests, and beg them not to judge us by this one deviant. It will never happen again.

(*Applause.*) Now, I think, is a good time to break for tea. (*Loud consent.*) But only twenty minutes, please. (*Silence.*) After tea we will continue with the urgent matter of Zahoor ul Din and his wild fictions called 'transitional forms.' We will also welcome the honorable Sheikh Abu bin Yaqub, who will share his publication on djinn light, showing the correct use of the positive and negative ions of extraterrestrial djinns is to provide electricity, followed by Mohammad Lawrence of—"

Mohammad Lawrence: "La*gh*aw. Ph.D."

Aba: "Dr. Mohammad, uh, Ph.D. He has shown that evil forces cause the Earth to spin, but, as a nail holds down a tent, so Allah has made mountains to secure us in space. *(Men glance toward the door as tea aromas waft inside.)* And—"

Mohammad Lawrence: "What 'geologists' today call 'facts' were first proven in the Quran (*recites in English*): '*Have we not made the Earth a resting place for you and the mountains its pegs?*' We know not some concoction called Newton's Law."

Aba: "To name His laws after scientists is to deny that only He creates. (*Loud consent; clattering of plates outside.*) As I was saying—"

Mohammad Lawrence: "It is clearly written the mountain-pegs only—"

Aba (*hurries*): "Thank you, Ph.D. Sahib, we look forward to the rest. And we will welcome others, to mention a few, Dr. Khaled Mateen, Ph.D., who has shown the angle of God with carefully drawn graphs, and Dr. Ali Abadi, Ph.D., whose work on fish from river to sea and back shows that even in lower life, there is no instinct. Only revelation. In this most humble creature is a sign of the True Path." (*All men head for the door. Outside Seminar Room 1, tea is served.*)

•

I remain seated. Something vital oozes from my pores. Once Petrov said there are many ways to break a man's back. Louder than a stick is a speech.

Best way to save my back's by taking it for a long walk. A twenty-minute break means at least forty. I check that Aba's not looking. Escape.

Rolling words on my tongue feels good. Mountain pegs. Metaphor. Met a fir. A furor. A force. Met a force that fears metaphors. Puts a furrow on my face.

I gallop around the block with Aba's voice in my ear: *People talk of brain drain when youth leave this country. What about the brain drain when they stay?* I gallop around the block as Jamaat-e-Waste Product.

Posters of white beaches in windows of airline offices. If Aba paid me, I'd buy a ticket out now. Screw visa. I pass carpet shops, newspaper offices, an abandoned cinema house. Motorbikes blow black death up my nose. Rickshaws raid eardrums. Still, movement's good. Calming chemicals kicking in.

I pass a barber. A shave and massage would help, even here, at this jammed intersection. But he has a customer and I don't have time. Move on. Every inch of this road's taken—tea shops, paan shops, fruit stalls, and the men who strut up and down Lahore's pavements selling towels, hairpins, shoelaces. No corner free of fingerprints, no air pocket untasted. If the city was a virgin once, only God knows.

The talk at the tea stall is of sicknesses too expensive to treat, and of the war in Afghanistan. When will it end, and when will the General who grows fat on it leave? The money that godly America sends to fight its godless Roos rival—it was supposed to return us to our prosperous heritage, to an Islam that was rich and pure. It hasn't. So, where's the reward for hitching the Jihad wagon to the *Supra*power? Where's the golden past? A few eyes turn to me, and I think, this is the point at which the rich, the middle class, and the poor all meet: the present is dangerous, the past was glorious. It's our jammed intersection.

When you're not illuminated by history, you're encumbered by it.

If I think I know this when I return to the hotel, why don't I take my own warning?

•

After the break, when the participants are finally seated, the JP chairman taps the mike, about to speak again. Aba curls a finger, calling me.

I lean over his shoulder. He whispers, "It has gotten very late. That *bhainchod* Zahoor will have arrived in Seminar Room 2. His type is very punctual. I want you to leave the tape running and slip out *quietly* to the other room and slip back in *quietly* to tell me what that devil says."

I do as he says, except I almost trip off the stage. I drop the tape. The man sitting next to me asks loudly where I'm going. By the time I've mumbled an answer, everyone's glaring at me.

I tiptoe out, like a fish.

•

Inside Seminar Room 2, I spot the devil immediately. Tall and dignified, and at least ten years older than Aba, he paces before a screen where a white man projects slides of a thick-headed canine with short legs. Think it's from the clipping I tried reading in the car, a kind of cross between an Alsatian and a dachshund. (If I'd made it, I'd have crossed the opposite parts— kept the legs long and head delicate.) Zahoor paces back and forth, eager for the mike, just like the seated men in the other room. I don't know if he invented the ugly dog or not but I'm sure speeches were invented in Pakistan.

Men and women sit together, or stand comfortably at the back. No one notices me. I creep to an empty chair in front. Overall, there's a much smaller crowd than Aba feared, maybe forty, maximum. There are at least five times as many at his meeting.

The speaker ends his talk (Aba was right; they *are* punctual) and a younger *gora* stands up. "My colleague," he begins, indicating the last speaker, "shared the work begun by him and Mr. Aziz," he smiles at a round-faced man in the front row, "and Mr. Zoo Whore," he looks nervously at the one pacing. "You've heard how we began with this wolf-like *Mesonychid,*" he points to the first figure, "then found this freshwater *Pakicetus.*" The projector clicks. The screen displays a fish with sharp teeth on the dachshund's stubby legs. A film-starry woman in the front row nods vigorously, as if the speaker's flown in straight from Hollywood.

Next image: formless things in pale yellow piss. The American clears his throat. "In the shallow beds of the warm

Tethys lived things that defied classification. Mollusk or jellyfish, head or tail? Now here's the *inner*esting bit..." I scan the room. I'm not the only one falling asleep. Even Film Starry's yawning behind her bangles. Zoo Whore finally takes a seat beside two girls. The older one has curly unkempt hair and wears a half-bored, half-amused look. The younger rests her head on the older's shoulder, asleep.

The speaker skips on his toes. "What we do is look for murder weapons and fingerprints. Fossils are the fingerprints. We're the detectives. We're mad about burial grounds." The audience fidgets. "One of the most *inner*esting puzzles of science and a personal favorite of mine's why some land animals went back into the sea." The screen flicks rapidly. "Like these sea snakes, sea turdles, crocodiles, penguins, sea lions," he keeps on, the projector creaking, "and whales." Someone snores. "All sit between diverging branches of life. They're the mongrels of history. But this mutt," he clicks back to the fish with sharp teeth, "is a diamond key slipped into our fingers. It's the oldest whale ever known." A baby shrieks. "We're learning how it happened! It's the story of life, and we're... "

The star makes no attempt to conceal her yawn and more men leave the room. The speaker launches into an elaborate discussion of changes in anatomy and locomotion, and whether seals do the doggy paddle or torque like a platypus. When he announces, "The *Mesonychid* undoubtedly had a tail to keep it cool while it prowled the equator, while *Pakicetus*..." he has an audience of exactly twenty-one, including me.

Zahoor angrily stands up and takes the mike. "I told you these details won't *inner*est them, Henry." Henry reddens. "Please remain seated." Zahoor's long arms motion a downward sweep. "Please. I have something you will want to hear." Another couple sneaks away but others return to their chairs.

"Thank you." Zahoor bows to Film Starry, who sits up again, beaming. "Now. You have all heard of the French philosopher Pascal"—two others slip away—"I want to tell you what happened to him one night. It is a good story, you will enjoy it."

He paces, eyeing everyone, including me. "He was standing in a wheat field. The sky was clear. The stars, bright. It was a very fine night indeed. But then something changed. Pascal suddenly noticed a flea crawling up a wheat stalk. He had excellent eyesight this man, all philosophers do." The older girl giggles. He smiles at her. "You laugh but what did Pascal do? He cried." Now others laugh as well. "Why? Because when he looked up at the sky and saw the infinite world above, it felt *right*. But when he saw the tick in the wheat, he realized there was a *second* infinite, and this one worried him."

Zahoor stops pacing and looks around, making sure everyone's paying attention. Except for the young girl asleep on the other's shoulder, everyone is. "He saw that the tick was arranged like him. With a head, joints, veins, blood." He says the next sentence rapidly, like a riddle. "In the drops in the blood in the veins in the knuckles in the feet there was heat. What caused it?"

A man in the front row murmurs, "The Almighty." Others mutter and nod.

Zahoor smiles. "Pascal's mind blazed. He saw the heat churning, the blood burning, the fingers twitching, the wheat bending, the wind causing tiny flea wings to flutter, as the creature struggled for balance. He saw a chain of reactions with

no beginning and no end. He saw the universe inside himself."
He stops. Repeats, "He saw the universe inside himself. But not
the way he saw the outside universe. He would never *see* the one
inside. But he'd *recognized* it. So from now on, the only way to
see was by searching. And that is why he wept: his mind would
never rest again."

He stops. His skin's old but his stride, young. He wears red
leather slippers.

"Pascal should not have wept. He was given a gift, the most
precious gift there is, the gift of infinite curiosity. Many have
had it. Few have not been punished for it. We can recall the fate
of Ibn Sina and Al Kindi. Who cares about them today?

"The gift of infinite curiosity," he repeats. His voice is a low
rumble, a gentle thunder capable of extreme cruelty. I feel the
menace in him as much as in Aba, though his words have the
opposite effect on me. They revive; Aba's deflate. "My
granddaughter Amal has it too." He points to the curly-haired
girl. Startled, she blushes. "A lot happens beneath her feet." He
smiles broadly for the first time today. His skin sheds a thousand
layers. He glows. "She was only eight years old when she found
this," he picks up a bone, "a copy of the diamond key," he looks
at Henry, who doesn't acknowledge him. "Her sister Mehwish
also has the gift, even while she sleeps." Laughter.

Sensing his audience is relaxed, but still alert, Zahoor's
expression changes. It happens around the eyes. They grow icy.
"This gift is a great threat to some, inside and outside our
country." The air curdles instantly. I notice Mr. Aziz signaling
Zahoor to stop.

He ignores him. "It's a threat because they can't *control* it.
Now, I say to you: why are we losing the hunger to cultivate the

gift? These rocks," he lifts one off the table, "our soil," he stamps on the carpet, "building barracks on every field under every star is no way to protect them! They say it is not *safe* to pursue our work. If they leave, we will be safe!" Several people start booing. "We are suffocating between brass and beard, tank and creed!" Chairs fly back as a couple storms out. "And they are here today, in this building, spreading their campaign of fear, trying to put a spell on us!"

I freeze. Is he staring at me?

One man yells, "I have been listening patiently for one hour to this nonsense. Now will you please talk about Kashmir! That is why I came."

Another shakes his fist. "Without the army, the Roos would destroy Islam. So thank Allah and America for our tanks!"

A third declares, "I'm proud of my beard! Che Guevara had a beard! So did da Vinci!"

A fourth, "Why is a man like you wasting his talent on dogs or whales or what-have-you? Can you feed mouths with them?"

I start to lose track of who's saying what...

"It wasn't a dog."

"Then what was it?"

"Did you watch the rerun of *Ankahi* last night?"

"Think it was a mammal."

"Brought back such memories!"

"Shenaz Sheikh is *so* beautiful."

"A frog is a reptile."

"I hear her life is very tragic."

"Why a blueprint for life?"

"What about the special creation of man?"

"You know how men are."

"Where can I see the real *Pakicetus*? Is it in the London Zoo?"

"Every day every day."

"What's wrong with our zoo?"

Someone shouts above the rest, "My *arzoo* is to learn about scientific discoveries, not to be lectured on politics!"

As if waiting for this, Henry leaps up and takes the mike. "*Yes*. Why does politics have to come into everything in your country? This is science! This is science!"

The older *gora* wearily folds his arms. "Always prepare yourself for sermons. In fact," he shrugs, "hey, just prepare yourself."

Zahoor snatches the mike back. "It's all connected! It's how we live here—or try to!"

Mr. Aziz holds Mr. Zahoor back. "Calm yourself!"

"We didn't come to hear this." Two more men stand up. "It is shameful how you speak to our honored guests. We are grateful for their expertise." They shake hands with both *goras* and leave. The star goes with them, waving everyone goodbye.

Zahoor yells something after them, and then another man launches into another argument with him, while Aziz Sahib again holds him back. This time, they all curse each other freely.

Chairs tumble as the room empties. The projector's switched off. Charts are rolled. The two girls keep sitting. The younger (what was her name—Mehnaz?) has woken up. She looks around. I notice something's wrong with her but can't tell what. I move closer.

I begin to hear the rapid speech of the older girl, dressed in a loose shirt that doesn't conceal her voluptuousness. She looks about sixteen. She twirls her hair, unbothered by the chaos troubling her sister.

"Oh, so many things, Mehwish. You were sleeping."

"Tell me why they are angry." She—Mehwish—pulls away from her sister's arms and looks up, straight at me. I see what's wrong. She's blind.

As the older one speaks—"Well, I don't know. He was talking about the mountains an…"—I tell a tongue-tied me: now's the time. *Say hello, Noman.*

Instead, I keep staring at the girl (Amna?), as bluntly as Mehwish stares at me.

"—And Nana got angry, and they called each other names—"

I wish I was resting on the girl's shoulder.

Was it only this morning I was walking with Petrov, looking at silly books and frilly bras? Then that dope at Salman's, an afternoon with Aba and Co., and now this: the education of a blind child by a lovely girl who doesn't know my fatigue. The two have between them a heavenly intimacy. A bloom. I want to take off my shoes and step inside.

But I keep standing, listening.

Till I think I've finally found the courage to introduce myself. Yes, I have.

Yes.

"Tell him to go away." It's Mehwish.

"Who?" She turns around, with her grandfather's eyes: bold, cold, blazing. And with daggers for eyelashes, for snuffing a voice and slicing a bulbul's heart. Ashamed—of what?—I walk away quickly.

But not before I hear her call me no one.

•

And the day isn't even over yet.

I don't know what I was expecting back in Seminar Room 1, but it wasn't the words written in green marker across a white board. For a second, I think I'm still watching a slide show of a badly constructed dachshund. Finally, I make out: WHAT ONLY ALLAH SEES. Underneath, in smaller letters: The Path of a Humble Salmon.

The speaker's Ali Abadi, Ph.D., delivering the final words of his paper on revelation in freshwater fish. "So we see that a species does not, as Darwin claimed, *move*. It is simply fulfilling its purpose. There is no such thing as *patterns of growth...*"

I settle back down to find the man next to me fiddling with my cassettes. "Has everything recorded all right?" I whisper.

"Oh yes. Do not worry. It is all here."

Ali Abadi's final words have only just begun "... the malaise brought upon us by centuries of conquest, the Tartars from the east, Crusaders from the west, Communism, Colonialism, Oil Bonanza..."

Then the VC delivers final words. I neither record nor write. I wonder about the girl who ignored me. The challenge in her eyes, it's tweaked *my* eyes.

Miraculously, the VC's final words come to an end. The room fills with loud applause, which gradually subsides. Silence begins to fill the room instead, settling heavily around me. The men are waiting expectantly. For what?

I finally whisper to the man beside me, "What are they waiting for?"

He grins. "You are very modest."

Bewildered, I look up at Aba on the stage. He's gesturing toward my copy book. He wants to know what I learned about Zahoor. I've written nothing.

What will I report?

Now Aba's glaring at me. The whole room's glaring at me. My stomach hurts. The room starts to spin. (Where are mountain pegs when you need them? Aren't they meant to hold the Earth in place, for moments just like these?)

What will I report?

I begin to understand that there's a part of me I've never met before. The part of me who sees that Aba's giving me the power to say the words that he will speak. The part of me that stands up straighter, because of it. And my sudden influence rings as loudly in my head as the tension in the room. *I have the power to say the words Aba will speak.* This part of me I've never met before launches with shocking ease into a cold, lengthy calculation.

With what words should I speak for Aba? The truth is, hardly any one attended Zahoor's talk, and those who came, left divided. Zahoor is no threat. But as I look at Aba, I know he doesn't want to know he's safe. He wants me to prove he's not safe.

And Zahoor—what does he want? A little notoriety would help his popularity.

If Zahoor wants a public, Aba wants an enemy. I'll help neither by revealing that it's the secular faction of the disgusting fiction of *patterns of growth* that's in danger. I'll help both by exaggerating Zahoor's influence.

But if I exaggerate Zahoor's influence, what will these men do to him?

And another thing. In my bones, somehow I know, Zahoor

wants a public but not by being lied about. He wants it through his work in the mountains and his stories of philosophers, though I've seen how unsuccessful *that* is!

I grow confused. I lose the part of me I only just found. A few men start to cough and Aba taps his mike, still glowering at me.

As I prepare to meet his glare, I remember what he said earlier. *The young Pakistani is a cultural freak. His religion is whimsy. He is a split.* I understand that if I have any power at all, it's only the power of a child of the times. A child who blows with a small wind and bats for both sides. A Zia baby.

Aba's calling my name. Seconds pass. They feel like hours. I look at my skinny toes and long to do what's easy.

Maybe if I'd looked up a second time, I'd have seen that I shouldn't proceed the way I was about to. Maybe I'd have spoken the simple but shameful truth: Zahoor is no contest *and* I took no notes.

But I didn't want the shame. I wanted to feel as tall as I had only a few brief moments ago. Now I'm back to being no man!

"What do you have to report?" Aba demands. A few men mutter, "Hurry up," while Mohammad La*gh*aw, Ph.D., snipes, "How long must we wait for the youth of today?"

A hard weight slips into my belly. It isn't a creative bloom but a sharp resolve: *do it.* Exaggerate Zahoor and flatter Aba. Do both in one breath. Show them the cultural freak with no concept of the straight path.

I sift through the pages of my copy book as if I've written in them—holding the book to my nose so the inquisitive man beside me can't sneak a look—and begin:

"There were so many people they poured out into the corridor."

"I thought I heard them!" booms the JP chairman. "How many? Three hundred?"

"At least."

"That is twice as many as us!" calculates Ali Abidi, Ph.D.

"And?" Aba clenches a fist.

"Half of them were women. In jeans."

"Were they pret—" beams the man beside me, quickly biting back.

The vice chancellor stands up. "Hurry up and give the full report!"

"Read!" Aba pounds his fist.

Everyone's pleading with *me*! *Say he is against us! Say he has gathered an army! Say we are at risk! Say it! Say it!*

I flip a page and clear my throat. I read for fifteen minutes. I say it.

"At least four hundred people bowed in submission, while Mr. Zahoor smeared layers of falsehood over their innocent eyes. They looked upon him as a leader. Even," I look up, "a *messenger...*"

•

In the car, on our way home, Aba says I made him proud this evening. His once-whimsical son is finally growing up.

I'm assigned three tasks. The immediate one is to send warnings to Zahoor that if his army-building continues, he will face the music. The second is to publish a monthly periodical to be issued by the Academy of Moral Policy, called *Akhlaq*, in which I'm to prescribe ways to relieve young minds of *maghrib za'dagi*, westernization. And finally, I'm to accompany him to all future seminars as his personal secretary.

I remember realizing I now have one thing in common with Al Khwarizmi. The mathematician didn't write in his native Persian but in "foreign" Arabic. I won't write in my native Punjabi or "foreign" Urdu but in "foreign" English.

And I remember thinking of a time when sitting on Aba's shoulders meant looking farther.

And I remember reciting a saying of the Prophet Mohammad. *The scholar's ink is holier than the martyr's blood.* If I spill both, am I twice as holy or half as sinful? (I remember shuddering, why am I even *speculating*? Spill whose blood?)

And I remember feeling a sudden, surprising urge to know the man. The adoring grandfather of a curly-haired girl and her blind sister. The one who didn't flinch when others threw insults and chairs at him. Who didn't say what they wanted to hear. My opposite. I have an urge not to spy on him, nor warn him, nor even help him. But simply, to know him. Stand on *his* shoulders for a while.

And I remember turning in the car seat and looking at my father, who once laughed in merriment as he licked rahu fish off his fingers, and telling myself that the father–son equation is like the one of ink and blood.

Even Al Khwarizmi couldn't square it.

Amal

So this is how it is. Nana praises me to everyone. I'm the girl who found the fossil skull of the oldest whale. In its ear lay a bent tympanic bone. The hidden *S*. What Mehwish calls the silent-letter bone. Today, when we come home from the small riot at Nana's talk, she asks what happened to his. "Why couldn't he hear all the hidden threats and mean silent letters *before* they started booing him?"

And I reply, "We don't have the bone, Mehwish, only whales do. And anyway, Nana doesn't care about being booed." But she doesn't hear me, which is how it is with her now, most of the time.

Anyway, *I* sniffed it out, the bone, I mean. *I* brought it into the world. A blueprint for life, it has my thumb on it.

Nana's so eloquent about my "gift of infinite curiosity" but what did he ask me to do with it? Look after Baby! And I did. The girl who slipped the diamond key into his hands has become the girl that's talked about. She's the anecdote. She spices his speeches to give them a human touch. *Sweet.* She's the audience. Not the player. She's *she*.

Noman

Tonight my perch isn't Aba's shoulders but the roof of our house.

I should be drafting the first issue of *Akhlaq*, but maybe I can be forgiven this transgression. If not, Aba can come up to the terrace and give me a thwack. But this is my corner. He won't come.

Houses are stacked close in my neighborhood. When children chalk roofs in a hopscotch grid, they leap from one to the next, across chasms as dark and narrow as veins. I never fell, but other children did. Still do. When the wounds heal they leap again.

I spot a light a few houses away where my sister Shaista lives, under a roof of pigeon coops, under a sky of pigeon fugitives.

Our sky also fills with the floating flecks of community sentiments, rising and swirling like vapor, then re-inhaled. The planets in this galaxy have no copyright. By now everyone will know about my new job.

It's from up here that I first saw a thief, first heard a wife being beaten, a singer applauded, a minister elected, a maulvi promoted. Here I flew my first kite, saw an eagle crush a lapwing chick, heard a child being born. None of this has changed; its place in the Milky Way is fixed. Disputes are still resolved in the narrow arteries leading to each door below. When the men die, the sons that replace them aren't like me but like my brother, who'll never care how old the Earth is as long as God walks lightly today.

I like the roof best in winter, in the freezing air and romantic blanket of January mist. But this is a warm night in August. Too hazy for stargazing, too still for kites, but clear enough to scan the skyline for my neighbor, Unsa. Another thing you learn on roofs: it's where the pigeons that'll never fly are allowed out of the coop for a brief stretch. They appear around dusk. You can tell them apart by their location and their silhouettes. Unsa's small and moves quickly, like me.

The haze grows thick. No Unsa, nor anyone else. Must be late. I lie flat on the brick. It starts to drizzle.

When my sister Sehr shakes me awake later, it's stopped raining. My face and shirt are damp, my shoulders cramped, I can't stop shivering. "Hot colds are the worst," Sehr smirks. She's with her cat, Meow, who can say everything but her name.

I sit up. "What time is it?" My tongue, thick and rough in my mouth.

"I don't know. But Ama wants to know why you didn't eat dinner." She's sixteen and very plucky, but by some miracle, has escaped becoming an issue for Aba. Maybe because she's the youngest. Plus, her fussing over small pets adds to the innocent myth. Whenever Aba looks at her suspiciously, she pulls a furry chick or wide-eyed kitten out from under a sleeve and acts beseeching, as if she's also just popped out of an egg, into a world that must shelter her. So it does.

"Meow should go exploring rooftops and gutters. She's wasting her life as a cat. Stop the brain drain!"

"Aww," blinks Sehr, handing a freshly washed Meow to me. I lift her to my nose and inhale deeply. Fruity shampoo in a fireball. My shoulders begin to thaw.

Sehr snatches her back when I start to fall asleep again. "Ama's waiting!" Prances away in fake Puma joggers.

I'm sneezing and definitely running a temperature by the time I crawl downstairs.

"Have you eaten?" Ama calls from the kitchen. Her way of saying Come Here.

I change my shirt and dry my hair. Enter the kitchen.

She's worn the same fawn kameez for three days straight, without complaining. She says she's happy Aba's not like other politicians; he takes no bribes and leads a simple life. As his family, it's our obligation to live simply too. But I know she's smart enough to know his party's well-funded because of the war. And just once, I'd like to be able to give her something she never got. Or like her to say she wants it.

I blow my nose, watching her juggle tasks: reheating my food, making *koftas* and cutlets for a day when there are no more koftas and cutlets in the world, spooning away food she knows I won't want, wiping the counter. Sehr and I get our delicate frame from her, while my other siblings are stout, like Aba. (And Darwin.) My brother Adnan has his wide gut, and when he sits his shoulders slope and arms curve bonelessly. He's not good-looking anymore but hasn't noticed. After one child, Shaista's even heavier.

"Did you fall asleep up there?"

"Yes."

"Why are you so foolish?" By foolish she means *adorable*. She hands me a pile of *khat'te baingan* and *matar qeema* and I devour both, floating in a tang of tamarind and clove. She nods in a way that says, I have something to say when you're done, and rolls a wad of mashed potatoes to fry on Judgment Day. I think: these are the hands that created me. Wrinkled yet fine. They pat and squeeze assuredly, giving each cutlet equal care. Today I've been assigned tasks I need to do as smoothly. Why isn't *she* in my place?

I'm on my third chapaati when I notice the folder Aba handed me in the car lies on the table, open. So does my copy book. "Who did that?" I panic, leaving my chair and grabbing my papers.

"Sehr."

First, relief. It wasn't Aba. He doesn't know the book's mostly empty. Then I curse my sister. "Where is she?"

"Finish your food."

I try, but I've lost my appetite. I make her a glass of almond sherbat, not too sweet and with plenty of ice, the way she can't resist. She says nothing. My mother's a quiet woman who rests little and looks around a lot. Her way of coping with Aba and Adnan.

"Your father is sleeping." I wait. Here it comes. "He told me to tell you he wants you to start work on the magazine tonight."

"I know."

"What will you write?"

"I have to think about it."

"Your copy book is almost empty."

"So it was Sehr?"

She purses her oval mouth. *Don't argue with me.* "Your father's very upset. But he was pleased with your report. Where is it?"

Not wanting to lie to her, I settle on a scowl.

"Sehr found this book in your room with fuzool pictures in it." She opens a drawer that's supposed to have knives and forks inside and brings out *Selections from Darwin.*

I think quickly. After Aba called me at Real Salman's, I rushed home, stashed the book in a cupboard (with hashish!), and hopped in the car with Aba to the old hotel. "*Sehr* found it? Why are you checking up on me?"

"To make sure you do not slip away to be with your friends."

"I don't!"

She purses her mouth again, then puts the tray of cutlets in the fridge to set.

The ice in her drink melts completely before she describes one of the "*fuzool* pictures," and I understand *fuzool* means both *nonsense* and *fossil*. She gives a speech straight from Aba's mouth: "God is always testing us. Do we see what He reveals or what we think *fuzool* things reveal?"

"Do you want more ice?"

She waves a hand impatiently. "I am just repeating what your father said about that man who has upset him so much."

"What man?"

"The one you reported to your father." She stares at me, piercingly. "He was proud of you. You know he thinks you are weak. But he didn't today. Do not spoil it. Do not argue with him in that way you have. Do not ignore him."

"Do I need to tell you I did nothing but agree with him all day today?"

"That is what I wanted to hear." She smiles. I remember the way Zahoor's face changed this afternoon, when he looked at his granddaughters. That was nothing compared to the love my mother radiates now.

I add more ice in her glass and she finally accepts it, holding her back and chin straight, pausing patiently between sips. There's no trace of moisture on her mouth, nor does she look at me, nor exhale. She's unharried. Done, she sets the glass aside carefully, pushing it away from the counter's edge, near a colander of washed and drained spinach. She starts to pound the spinach with the dainty calm she employs on everything. I look for a wrinkle in her poise but don't find it. Not one of her children takes after her.

"Why don't you write the introduction?" she says. "Then you can sleep. You look tired."

"All right. But you have to help me."

She looks up.

"You seem to know more than I do about these fuzool things."

She giggles, dropping her guard for a second.

"You know if I don't do it by morning I'll be in serious trouble."

She tries not to smile, closing her fist around the pestle tightly. "Write about the meaning of the magazine's name, *Akhlaq*."

"Great idea!" I sit back down, find a blank page in my book (easy enough), find a pen. "What *does* it mean?"

She shakes her head. "Why are you so foolish? Can't you guess? It means *ethics*. It has the same root as *khalq*. Creation. Write that."

So we start this perfect introduction:

Virtuous behavior (*akhlaq*) cannot be separated from a proper understanding of the purpose of creation (*khalq*). It is an issue as much of morality as [took forever to find the word] cosmology. Scientific thinking blurs the relation between the two by insisting on a world of "facts." The purpose of our movement and of this magazine is to return us to the path of the humble salmon that follows divine laws not fickle experiments, and not transitional change (see appendix, *What Only Allah Sees*, by Ali Abidi, Ph.D).

"Now what?" I tap my pen.

"I'm thinking." She suddenly leaves the kitchen.

A minute later, Sehr bounds into the room, Meow at her feet.

"Why did you go through my things?" I snap, though I know it wasn't her.

"Ama did it." She helps herself to a paper cup of Igloo ice cream. Meow investigates my toes, hiccuping.

Ama returns. "Where did you put the clipping?" she asks Sehr.

"*You* had it."

"No, *you* had it."

"No, *you* went through the folder, *you* took out the papers, *you*—"

"That's enough!" Unlike everyone else, Ama's never found Sehr winning. Shaista, with a son at twenty, is *her* model of good ethics. "Find it!"

"Find what? What clipping?" I interrupt them.

"How can I find what I didn't lose?"

"The clipping about the dog."

"Oof!" Sehr leaves the room.

"What clipping?" I repeat.

"The one in the folder, about the fuzool dog or something. You will need it."

I'm trying to remember, when Sehr returns. "Lost. You look." She means me.

"He has work to do," Ama silences her again. "Look harder."

"Work!" She digs into the ice cream with a sliver of wood called spoon. I give it under ten seconds to snap. It always does. Then my sister can go "Oof!" while rummaging in the drawer with elaborate theatrics for an apparatus that'll serve her better.

"Yes," says Ama, "*work*. Put that away and either make the cheese for the spinach, or find the clipping."

Sehr returns the cup to the freezer, pours milk into a saucepan, puts it on the counter, pulls yogurt out of the fridge, finds a mulmul cloth—all while glowering at me.

"It was about an ugly dog and an ugly fish. Your father was very upset. Do not argue with him. How can I help you if you do?"

"I *don't* argue."

Ama fries the spinach, stirring with the long-handled wooden spoon that's become the sixth digit of her right hand. But I'm her focus now. "Good. I know you won't argue. You'll go along with him and soon you can have the job you want, a good job, just like your brother."

I finally understand that *this* is what she's been trying to say all night. The look in her eye: she's not talking about today. Not talking about the magazine, Sehr, or the food she cooks tonight so she can spend the morning with her grandson and still have a feast ready for tomorrow. She means: how can I *ever* help you, now that *he's* claimed you? She means: how long will these meetings and foreign wars and national feuds and family fragments and anti-this and pro-that continue before you, Noman, become a man? She means: what are you doing with your life? What's *he* doing with it?

She leaves the spoon and takes my face in her hands. They're warm and smell divine. She holds me, whispering, "God help him understand you are still a child. God give you health and prosperity. God release you from all you wish to be released from." I shut my eyes and hope she never releases me.

Sehr smirks. "A good job like bhaiya." Meow chirps for milk.

Ama finally pulls away, a bright smile on her face. "I remember where I put it!"

When she's gone, Sehr gets the ice cream out again and asks hopefully, "Are you in trouble?"

"You're getting fat."

She offers me a bite. I accept. The spoon snaps. We both start laughing.

"I said put that away," Ama re-enters the kitchen excitedly. "Found it!" She spreads a newspaper clipping with no name or date out on the counter. The author's name has been erased. I remember it.

A Blueprint for Life

For a long time scientists suspected that whales descended from a terrestrial mammal, a *Mesonychid*, meaning, "middle claw." It lived in the Middle Eocene, was approximately the size of a wolf, and in its habits demonstrated similarities to modern hyenas: carnivorous and hoofed, a running creature of sound endurance and limited speed (fig. 1).

Fig. 1: *MESONYCHID* ("middle claw"), *terrestrial prototype of modern whales. Reconstruction by the artist.*

But this ancestry was never proven. Then in 1980, in the Salt Range of the Punjab, a team of American and Pakistani paleontologists, among them a girl of eight years, found the link. The girl stumbled upon a piece of fossilized skull that revealed the secret hidden in the tympanic bone of the middle ear (next issue). Throughout this decade, scientists have unearthed more of the primitive cetacean. Though we still do not have a complete specimen (the nature of its limbs, for instance, is unknown), we know it lived fifty million years ago, had an amphibious lifestyle, and ranged in size from small dog to large wolf. It is the oldest whale ever found. We call it *Pakicetus* (fig. 2).

We are tracing the evolution of whales over a span of more than fifteen million years. One of the most comprehensive examples of macroevolution, it is a blueprint for the origin of all life. Life evolved much like the girl's chance discovery: in accidental stages. The random assemblage of fluke encounters between biology and geography might never have worked in our favor to create us, and it is not likely to work in our favor ever again. We are no more but no less than that.

Ama nods. "*Fuzool* things." She commands Sehr, "More yogurt."

Sehr points to the second drawing and giggles. "What is it?"

Ama clicks her tongue. "An ugly fish. And dogs are haram."

Sehr shakes her head. "A lovely fish. Fish are not haram." She fumbles in the drawer, finds a pen, sketches a silly bow on *Pakicetus*'s head. Just then, Meow leaps onto the counter, spills the milk, wriggles free from my grasp, and drips paw prints across the page. A startled Sehr jerks her pen, leaking blue ink on us all (the author did say *blueprint*).

This is what the creature becomes before I rescue it:

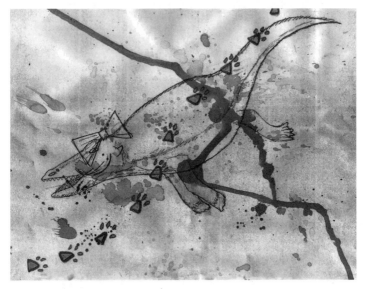

Fig. 2: *PAKICETUS* ("Pakistani whale"), *the oldest known primitive whale, found in the hills of the Punjab in Pakistan. Reconstruction by artist.*

•

President-General Zia dies in a plane crash. The country holds its breath.

When it cautiously exhales again, it's with the assurance that nothing will change as long as there's evil to fight, both at home and out in the big world. The war in Afghanistan ends exactly when Petrov said it would, the way he said it would, and the way all wars in Afghanistan have ever ended: without a political settlement. Since Communists aren't extinct yet, the

Party of Creation continues to thrive. The Academy of Moral Policy receives invitations to spread its mission in other lands. We accept.

The next two years fly. I accompany Aba to seminars around the world. I give free copies of *Akhlaq* to dentists' waiting rooms, peddle to pharmacies and supermarkets, drop the rest with *Reader's Digest* on the pavement outside Anarkali. None gets picked up as swiftly as the leaflet of the Vidya Bharati Trust. (And if you're wondering, the first issue Ama and even Sehr helped with was well-received, deservedly, if I say so myself.)

Aba's so busy touring the globe (and pulling me with him) that he forgets Zahoor for a while. I send the spry old man two warnings, as promised, but I don't have time to do what I've been wanting since the day I heard him speak: pay him a visit in his home in Islamabad. But I've found out where it is and know that day will come.

Meanwhile, I'm accepted at a school to teach math for eight thousand rupees a month. Could triple my income with private tuition but don't have time for either. I turn the offer down.

•

I fly with Aba to sleek hotels in cities with only conditioned air, where all the workers look like me. Everything's imported, the laborers and the food, wheels and tarmac. Even the bottle-opener a Bangladeshi bartender struggles with the night I tiptoe down to the bar, as Aba sleeps. I sip Mexican beer, open my copy book, draft an idea for a future issue of *Akhlaq: Scientists make tall claims about another geologic time but God made petroleum as petroleum, to trade land and people for technology and goods. According to His will.*

I ask the bartender how long he's been working at the hotel, but an elegant East Asian woman (Thai?) grabs his attention and he foolishly begins wiping all the glasses he'd stacked just moments ago. I stop jabbering and stick to scribbles: *There's no marriage between faith and reason. Only adultery.*

With few exceptions, meetings outside Lahore are similar to my first one in Lahore, with men uniting against a common enemy, and chatting amiably over tea. An exception happens in Rabat. Minds clash at a pitch that thrills me, as if I'm witness to an arranged adultery. As if I've brought Zahoor and Aba together.

Yousuf Saiid, Tunisia: "The debate between faith and reason is an ancient one. Have we learned nothing from men like Al-Razi and Ibn Sina? Their contribution to the civilizations of Fez and Baghdad, to the subsequent European Renaissance?"

Muhammad Wali, Indonesia: "Agreed. There must be a *synthesis* of thought. Without Aristotle, no Ibn Sina. Without Ibn Sina, no Galileo. Why would you draw a partition between them when they thrived without one? You cannot stop time from crumbling new layers over old, and blending them."

Muhammad Ibrahim, Egypt: "You are an idealist, my friend, and I envy you your fantasy. We are wasting time on philosophical debates. Our children see, with their own eyes, whose tanks and guns rule our neighborhoods. It is not Greek logic or Persian wisdom that will save us. What we need is security."

Yousuf Saiid: "But as an educator you have a duty to learn from the past and promote free inquiry in the present."

Muhammad Ibrahim: "As an educator I have a duty to keep alive a population to educate."

Muhammad Wali: "We are not talking about crude survival. We are talking about enriched living. You want technology. I want science."

Aba: "We *were* talking about Islam, and what is to be done about the secular elements infiltrating Muslim minds today. In this culture war, we need a defense."

Muhammad Lawrence, Belgium (*remember his mountain pegs?*): "I cannot imagine why the honorable Mr. Saiid says we should learn from Ibn Sina and other Mu'tazilites. I should remind you that they embraced free will."

(*Have to confess: till this moment, hadn't even heard of the Mu'tazilites.*)

Yousuf Saiid: "They argued that God gave them a will so they could use it! Would you give a child life only to deny him life? It is an outrage when foreign armies snatch our lives, our dignity, our capacity for thought. It is a sin when we do the same."

Aba (*red-cheeked*): "An outrageous sinful parallel!"

Muhammad Wali (*to Aba*): "You serve no one, least of all God, by denying a highly influential time of our past."

Aba: "It was a blemish, nothing else."

Muhammad Lawrence: "Agreed."

Yousuf Saiid (*to a handsome man who's not yet spoken*): "Will the honorable chancellor Kazeroun not acknowledge it was, if nothing else, a time when Sunnis and Shias worked together?"

Ashraf Kazeroun, Iran: "We are together now and I am in agreement with a Sunni." (*Points to my father, who nods his approval.*)

Aba: "Why did the Mu'tazilite influence not last? Because

the good majority understood the message of this small minority was heresy. Reason darkens the soul for a short time only. Sooner or later, people turn to light. Our goal today is the same as Al Ghazzali's a thousand years ago. To rid society of darkness." (*Murmurs of consent.*)

Yousuf Saiid: "It is a tragedy that you fail to learn from history. By rejecting rationality, the 'good majority' became an easy target for Mongols and Crusaders."

Muhammad Ibrahim: "The only defense is military. That is learning from history."

Sheikh Abu bin Yaqub, Saudi Arabia *(remember his djinn light?)*: "Technology and faith marry well. We need to *build* our countries. *Up.* We need to compete. We cannot compete on a camel any more than on skills in geometry or poetry. We need cars. We have no protection in tents. We need forts. We cannot guard them with a stick."

Aba and Muhammad Ibrahim (*simultaneously*): "Well said." *And so on.*

Afterwards, I leave our hotel and stretch my legs along Rabat's littered Rue Moulay Ismail, passing apartment blocks and musty cafés. A man stops me for "*dix* dirham," beer on his breath. I'm sure it's that nasty Flag stuff I had in my room last night when Aba was asleep. Sheikh Abu bin Yaqub offered it to me.

The street terminates at Boulevard Hassan II. I cross it, enter the Medina. All souks closed for a three-hour-long siesta. Oof! This is my only free time before we leave for Lahore tomorrow and my sisters will kill me if I arrive empty-handed. My mother won't, but it's her way of *not* showing disappointment that kills me.

I walk back to the boulevard, staring dumbly at the walls barricading the sleeping old quarter, feeling foolish for not knowing a damn thing about this place, not even owning a map. Felt shy at the reception. Would ask my way around Lahore or risk complete dislocation before peering like an idiot at a map—who carries *that*? Do we even make them? I stuff my hands in my pockets and look up.

I do remember this from a hotel brochure: the older wall was built by the Almohads, the dynasty that conquered Spain. The newer Andalusian Wall was built five hundred years later by Muslim refugees fleeing Spain during Ferdinand and Isabella's Catholic Holy War. The city that grew within both walls was all of Rabat till the French invaded, in 1912, and built the new quarter, the Ville Nouvelle, where our hotel is.

Yousuf Saiid's voice filters through the walls. *You fail to learn from history. By rejecting rationality the "good majority" became an easy target for the Crusaders…* In the hotel, he sounded convincing. But now I agree with Muhammad Ibrahim. You can be as learned as Aristotle or the Mu'tazilites, but in the face of bloodlust, what good is it?

My mood only lightens because of the women slinking along in short skirts and high heels. No Lahori larki shows so much skin, not even a Gulberg girl. Such voluptuousness! Such creamy skin! I follow one (ankles could be slimmer, but who cares, when a skirt's so tight) into a very chic café that serves a variety of patisseries (besides the women). She meets a man so I bolt. Almost get run over by a motorcyclist. The woman with him doesn't ride sidesaddle as in Pakistan, but with her legs open.

Re-enter Medina. Weave through, cross another boulevard, enter the Kasbah des Oudaias. Pretty garden inside. Café on the terrace. People in jeans and *djellabas* nibble *m'hencha* and tarts, calling out *Salut!* And *La bes!* Find a table. Stunning tiled floor: a blue so shimmering it purifies my blood. Over my right shoulder lies the river; over my left, the sea. My first view of the Atlantic. Brown river sludge pours into gray sea swells as I wait for mint tea. It arrives, pale amber in a gold-rimmed glass. I tilt it with thumb and middle finger, slurp sugar, inhale aroma. I watch two women in underwear and T-shirts towel themselves dry on the beach below, and feel blessed.

•

Before leaving the café, I approach a man I'd heard speaking English. From him I learn of an English bookshop near the train station. I walk there and find the book I'm looking for, *The Moment of Mu'tazilites*. It has them all: Ibn Ata, Ibn Sina, Al-Razi, Ibn Rushd—the whole sinning lot. I buy it.

The souks have finally opened by the time I return to the Medina a third time.

"*La bes,*" I smile at an old man selling leather goods.

"*Msa l'khir,*" he smiles back.

Red babouches for Sehr, yellow for Shaista, and, from another shop, a hand-mirror of inlaid cedar for my mother. Like her, it smells alive.

•

Usually there are no Yousuf Saiids or Muhammad Ibrahims to start a conflict in my soul, and no naked legs or seaside terraces to relieve it. By the end of the decade, the Party of Creation and its uniform speeches about division and freaks has bleached the color off every tile on earth, from Moroccan to Moghul.

One day I'm in my room in Lahore, trying to meet the deadline for this month's *Akhlaq*, but feeling vanquished. Why do I do it? Why don't I stop being Aba's peon and get my own job teaching al jabra, before I forget the magic in a *sifr*?

I scratch a line through dead notes.

Wish I were sitting at a seaside bar, chatting with a Bangladeshi bartender who was once Pakistani, and once Indian, but will never be Arab, not even if his children's children are born on Arab soil.

Is this why I keep working for Aba? For the travel?

Or to keep my promise to Ama? *He is your father. Just agree.* Doubt she's looked even once in the cedar mirror I got in Rabat. I wanted her to see herself as I do: always alert and always calm, never adorned and always beautiful, never bitter and always deserving. She put the mirror away, glass side down.

Or the same impulse that made me lie about Zahoor? Call it peer pressure, cowardice, or a hunger to please. Mixed in with a little bit of fear.

I'm not too proud to admit it. Aba's large and I'm small. When I was even smaller, he'd hit me with a ruler on my knuckles. Many fathers do worse—I've heard worse on the roof. But I remember the *whoosh* of that sting on my right hand when I used it poorly on school tests, or, once, on my left hand, when I used it too well, just as a video showing three buxom lesbians in a hot tub was hottest. That was soon after my epiphany at Badshahi Mosque, except that these three zeroes were different, in fact there were *six*, and I hoped, bittersweetly—as the sting from the ruler coursed up my spindly wrist, and the air rang with a shrill whistle a fraction of a second before the ruler struck again—that martial law meant the black market would be forever flooded with lesbian porn.

He used the ruler for many years and it worked better than a shoe or stick because, like me, it was a little thing. That my swollen knuckles were better soothed by my saliva and wimpy tears than Ama's ice cubes made me deeply ashamed. I know if I hear that plastic flick the air in a thin whistle again, I'll feel the same sore shame. Maybe this is why my right hand now serves him. My best glove is my copy book.

If I do it out of fear, loyalty to Ama, wanderlust, or innate weakness, it's all these things, but that's still not all. This is: he wasn't always like this.

He could always scare me and he never deserved his wife, *but*, he did love me, once. We had fourteen years of outings and conversation about everything from Lahore's crumbling gateways to the deep moat outside its city walls. He didn't only tell me what to think. He asked what I thought. Such as, Could restoration help the gateway of Dilli Gate? I compared the imitation to the original we found in books (books we don't try to find anymore) and decided it was a poor copy. I remember he thought this was worth hearing. Another time, while eating kachauri, he asked why there were five gates to the south, four to the north, three to the east, but only one to the west, Taksali Gate, now completely demolished and unrestorable. To prevent access to the coins once minted there? I licked the salt from my lips and said maybe, but two to the west plus three to the east would have made five—like the number of prayer times in a day—so I'd imagine a fifth. He laughed. Then we played more number games, guessing how many coins the taksal must have produced or *re*produced. And he taught me the two meanings of the phrase *taksali zubaan*. Chaste language and metaphoric language.

Then the war started. Almost overnight, metaphors were abolished. God was stamped out in endless repetition, on a mint of chastened tongues. Our outings stopped. He's never asked for my opinion since (and forgets that today his speeches are in my voice). Now he believes himself at risk of crumbling, like an old gateway of a torn city gate. Like the gateway, restoration is making him sickly.

Maybe I work for him in the hope of rediscovering his original. Because, like Lahore, I'm not illuminated by history. Only encumbered by it.

The Prophet said: *Every man has two Satans that beguile him.* If men like Yousuf Saiid and Zahoor are guilty of following the first, I'm guilty of following the second.

The first is free will, patterns of growth, transitional mammals and disgusting fictions like ugly dogs and ugly fish.

The second Satan is memory.

Amal

Mehwish and I are at Nana's house in Islamabad. If we don't return to Lahore soon, I'll be late for the New Year's party at Zara's house. Brian, Henry (if British, they'd be Mr. Sales and Mr. Walker), Aziz Sahib, and others from Nana's team lounge around the living room, discussing what they call "the two bookends of known primitive whales." The oldest, *Pakicetus*, and the youngest, *Basilosaurus*, recently found.

Mehwish asks me, "What are bookends?"

"Things that hold books up. So they don't fall off the shelf."

"Show."

I walk away from the group with Mehwish, to the wall where the shelves are, as Henry says, "Until we prove it, we're left to imagine the *inner*esting subtleties of adaptation…"

Nana declares, "A closed door is a challenge."

"What do they mean?" asks Mehwish.

"It means they've changed their minds about what *Pakicetus* looked like. It wasn't a swimmer. It wasn't fishy but doggy. Like the *Mesonychid*—remember, the dog-whale?" She nods. "They'll never know. That's what it means."

She starts nagging for bumpy drawings of "the new *Pakicetus*" and "the young other one."

"Do you want a drawing or a bookend?" I put a smooth stone weight in her hands. She rubs it, smiling brightly.

I look back at the men excitedly debating their discoveries. I still can't dig with them. They were more, hey, *inner*ested in me when I was eight than now I'm eighteen. But Nana says that's not it, nor is the reason to stay back only to look after Mehwish, who can walk, eat, dress, and even entertain herself better than most seeing adults. Now there are *security reasons*. I need permission from this and that ministry, and most of all, I need a man to guard me. The scientists don't want that burden. It takes away attention from their work.

It's the same at the university. Men don't want me in *their* lab.

I envy Mehwish for not knowing the spaces unavailable to her. She keeps smiling, turning a stone bookend over in her hand, feeling points and slopes.

I notice a piece of paper sticking out of a book placed horizontally, on top of others. Omar Khayyam's *Ruba'iyat*. I pull the loose page out. It's on the letterhead of the Academy of Moral Policy, and it reads:

Dear Sir,
Godlessness is a cancer whose favorite organ is the pen. It must be treated by every means available or it will spread. You are being watched. You have been warned…

I check the date. Two years old. Nana never mentioned it. Mehwish hands the stone back, and asks for a drawing.

"It's getting late, Mehwish. Tomorrow, promise." She frowns.

When we hug Nana goodbye, I think, *Be careful.* I push the thought away.

Noman

New Year's Eve. The roof. Another election. Another assignment: eliminate scientists from science books. Use verses from the Quran to prove their laws false. There have never been, and can never be, any discoveries because everything is Already Known.

I quickly run into a problem: I can calculate the side of a triangle faster than you can say *triangle*, but I'm not a historian of science. I don't know whom to delete. So I learn what to reject the same way I was exposed first to Zahoor, then the Mu'tazilites: through campaigning against it. But there remain embarrassing gaps in my knowledge, especially when it comes to the laws. I mean, is "perpetual motion" a law, an idea, or an event?

Second hurdle's even worse. I can't always find verses to fit and sometimes I find the opposite. Alone on the roof tonight, I worry. Am I misrepresenting God? I don't even want to *represent* Him. I don't even want to represent Aba. I don't even want to represent *me*!

I give myself an hour up here. If Unsa my neighbor shows up on her roof, I'll take this as a sign. Tonight's the night for holy rewriting. If she doesn't show, I should start the new year with a new job.

Two pigeon fugitives land on my sister Shaista's water tank. The winter mist creeps around them. I switch my gaze to the nearest roof, Unsa's, and keep it there.

After forty minutes, she shows.

She wants to run, I can tell this now, and whenever I see her. She pulls her shalwar up slim ankles then sets off in joggers, from one edge of her roof to the next, looking ahead. She's all slopes and arches: curved forehead; proud nose bent at the ridge; crescent mouth; chin and neck aligned in an angle so perfect Pythagoras would've cheered. I could recognize that profile anywhere, even in deeper darkness and thicker fog than the one swirling around her shapely legs, as if she creates it. (Seen the rest in my mind often enough to recognize it anywhere too.) While she jogs, I imagine lifting her up and releasing her, like a shooting star, or a dove. Then I scale the sky to find her.

I stand up so she sees me, close to our water tank so I can duck behind it if her brother appears. She doesn't look. She never does. But I'm content. One day I'll leap across to her roof. Now, I have another promise to keep.

Downstairs in my room, I start to write:

Pure Science

The Quran states: *Art thou not aware that it is God who has made subservient to you all that is on the earth, and the ships that sail through the sea at His behest.* (22:65)

If ships sink, it is by His law. If they float, it is by His law. Which we can't question or understand. Delete all references to Archimedes and his so-called principle.

It is He who holds the celestial bodies in their orbits, so that they may not fall upon the earth otherwise than by His leave. (22:65)

If an apple falls from a tree it is His will. If it stays it is His will. Which we can't question or understand. Delete all references to Newton and his so-called gravity.

And all the beauty of many hues which He has created for you on earth: in this, behold, there is a message for people who are willing to take it to heart. (16:13)

If color is perceived it is His will. If it is unseen it is His will. Which we can't question or understand. Delete all references to Newton and his so-called wavelengths.

Think of the Day when a violent convulsion will convulse the world to be followed by further convulsions. (79:6)

If energy is released it is His will. If it is stored it is His will. Which we can't question or understand. Delete all references to Einstein and his so-called relativity.

And God sends down water from the skies, giving life thereby to the earth after it had been lifeless: in this, behold, there is a message indeed for people who are willing to listen. (16:65)

Rain is His will. Drought is His will. Which we can't question or understand. Delete all references to Luke Howard and his so-called meteorology.

He creates whatever He wills: He bestows the gift of female offspring on whomever He wills, and the gift of male offspring on whomever He wills. (42:49)

Fertility is His will. Heredity is His will. Which we can't question or understand. Delete all references to Gregor Mendel and his so-called peas.

Have you ever considered that seed which you emit? Is it you who create it—or are We the source of its creation? (56:58)

Creation is His will. Destruction is His will. Which we can't question or understand. Delete all references to Charles Darwin and his so-called evolution.

•

The last time I saw Petrov, he was wearing a huge emerald on his pinkie. It was nearly three years ago, just before the Afghan War ended. He returned *Selections from Darwin* to me, grunting, "A scroll unrolling. Bloody *hijra* got it right!"

Faisal the Vulgarian and I walked home alone later. He asked, "Well?"

"Well what?"

"Notice the fat stone on his fat finger?"

"Of course."

"Where do you think it came from?"

I shrugged. "You're the reporter."

"Panjshir Valley." He nudged his chin as if northern Afghanistan loomed over my shoulder. "The rebels mine gems on a huge scale. Petrov sells them in Chitral, Peshawar, even here."

A thing about Faisal, apart from vulgarianisms: he whips dust for news. Conspiracies are made to leak from solid rock. And Petrov could be a solid rock. I remember the way he looked at me before we parted. As if *his* war would never end, or maybe his peace, proving he's a man with no friends and no enemies.

I asked, "What does he do with the money?"

"What do you *think*? Funding the Mooj, yaar. Next time you see a pretty girl with lapis around her neck, think: that's a bullet in a Red's neck." He smacked my back. "It's our duty as believers to decorate our sisters."

I was stunned by the news and confused by my reaction. "Petrov would help destroy his own army?"

"*His* army has destroyed *him*." He looked at me. "Why are you so shocked? It's better than killing *us*."

Now, nearly three years later, Mooj factions fight each other as ferociously as they did the infidels, while traffic in contraband still thrives. Petrov must have always known the best place to find the rarest gems: the refugee camps on the Afghan–Pakistan border. I can see him coolly bargaining over each stone while dodging projectiles. But I'm hurt that in all this time, he hasn't contacted me once. So I go to look for him in the park where we'd sometimes meet, on a hill frequented by hookers, journalists, and junkies.

Instead of Petrov, I find tennis-star Ali and Faisal the Vulgarian. Haven't seen them much either, since my travels with Aba keep me busy.

Since we're not in ladies' company, I can tell you how Faisal got the second part of his name: his endless fretting that the Almighty created his seed to serve humanity, while his addiction to blue movies forces him to waste it.

Now he's rolling a joint. I ask, "What are you reporting?" I know the answer: smuggling, corruption.

"Look who's here." He doesn't look. He asks me to get him tea.

"All right." I sit down. "What's the story? Narcotics?"

Ali paces as if a camera's on him, while a wife's in the next room giving birth. "Why are you here? Aren't you busy fixing the crisis in our minds?"

I look at Faisal. "You mean, crisis in our hands." Faisal scowls.

Ali laughs, then looks down the hill. "Elizabeth's crossing

the street. *Chup.*" He races to meet his current girlfriend, leaving me alone with Faisal.

"Seen Petrov?" I ask.

He shrugs. "Someone said he might be in Baltistan."

"Baltistan?"

"Warlords getting in the way of business, especially Hekmatyar's men. They rob the miners. But not in this country, not in Baltistan. It wouldn't surprise me if Petrov's set up shop on a glacier."

"What do you get in Baltistan?"

"Don't know. Heard of tamaline or beryl or something?"

"Don't know. How do you know all this?"

He smirks, knows he has me. "You've been gallivanting all over the world and have no idea what's going on here."

"Such as?"

He takes his time, gloating over his advantage. Let him. He never has any. Finally, "Such as Petrov and Salman are partners."

"*What?*"

He grins. "The last time I was at Salman's he offered Ann— you know, the German one—a six-carat rose beryl or what's-its-name. Ali nearly boxed him!"

"Did she accept?"

"Must have."

"Wow!"

He nods, still smirking.

"Let me guess, Salman uses the profits to feed the masses."

Faisal rolls his eyes, happy to complain about Salman, but Salman-bashing quickly loses its charm. We take his food and whisky, and in return, hate him. Pathetic! He's a better friend to Petrov than I could ever be. I cheer up by imagining myself in

Salman's place, kneeling before my neighbor Unsa with a six-carat rose beryl, confessing all the times I've watched her yearningly.

Such as: this spring, I saw Unsa running home through a dust storm, hugging a bunch of loquats to her breasts. Two rolled away and I longed to play hero and rescue them before they fell into a gutter, but her brother was on their roof, watching me watch her from mine, both half-blinded by the grit lashing around us. For her sake, I went inside.

And I'll confess that I've watched her from my roof as she eats strawberries outside my front door, taking ten little bites to consume just one, rubbing each on her lip, turning the fruit a fraction, doing it all again. The only reason I resist running downstairs is because she'll run away. So I watch her kiss five strawberries in fifteen minutes, and quietly moan. Does she look up? Of course not. Does she know I'm there? Of course. Why else does she eat at my door?

I'm still imagining kneeling before Unsa with a rose beryl that mutates into a strawberry that she kisses into my mouth, when Faisal rudely interrupts my sweet reverie. "What would your father say about it?"

"About what?"

Faisal shrugs with the defeat he must demonstrate every night, as he slides a tape into the VCR's cleft.

Then I get it. "He'd say God intercedes at every second, to punish those who do evil. So stay away from candles and stoves."

He nods. "Then it's not *only* my fault."

So we descend the hill and that's when I see her again. The voluptuous sister, less plump now and with even messier hair, nearly three years after I first saw her. Looks—eighteen? Nineteen? Sehr's age. But my sister's still a baby, and next to this girl, even Unsa would look like a child. Beside her, long-legged Zahoor, looking nothing like a man warned, strutting gravitas. That was never me and won't ever be. Next to him, Mehwish. Taller now, but just as thin. A mini replica of the old man, she walks upright, with calculated suspense. Doesn't carry a stick or lean on anyone, but keeps her right hand forward without falling behind in her step. Of the three, her face has changed the most. It's stretched. The cheekbones are even more prominent; skin darker; mouth focused. Not a bubbly child anymore, she's absorbed in becoming a woman, like her sister.

Why does this move me as much as it does? It's as if I've seen a niece grow up. After all, I turn twenty-five this year, and this girl, despite her best efforts, can't be more than twelve. The first time I saw them, it was Zahoor and the older girl that intrigued me. Now it's Mehwish. I recognize something in her, but can't say what. Something I've lost—or found? An inner knot, craving a dialogue. I want to say, a spiritual one.

I hold that picture. The curious trio. The curvy girl hastily untangling hair now at her waist; Mehwish determined not to need her; Zahoor determined to change us.

Their triangle needs a fourth point.

Amal

Look at Mehwish. Her inner eye grows while the outer one shrinks. She's like that curious whale, the narwhal, with one tooth four feet long, the other, barely an inch. The short tooth is her eyes. The long, her imagination. Where will it lead? She complains of being crammed into a classroom with too many children at school, with teachers who can't answer her questions. They don't care about her silent letters.

And look at Nana, still chasing a middle whale, but changed toward me. This is probably how it was with my mother and him. She grew up; he resented it. Except at public gatherings, where I'm still his pride. His prize.

This afternoon, he said, "Puzzles demand notice. For example, between the two bookends of the oldest whale, *Pakicetus,* and the youngest, *Basilosaurus,* there must be fossil evidence of whales that were beginning to swim. Things easily missed might be another diamond key, like the piece of skull *she*—I mean my granddaughter, over there—found, eleven years ago."

I didn't stand up and say, I was named Amal because I'm practical and I long to *act*. I didn't say, I want to find another diamond key, not *be* one. No, I sat. I smiled.

Noman

I'm traveling with Aba again, in Europe this time. I shut my eyes and listen to the Mediterranean as it slides between continents, linking fish and histories. *And He it is who out of this very water has created man.*

I open my eyes. *We made water out of every living thing.*

Lately, everywhere I turn, someone's pointing me to a passage in the Book. But not the ones I'm meant to hear. Not the ones that help rewrite other books. The passages I hear are the ones to ignore, like these references to water.

I could use them to prove we develop in stages, from, say, a loop of lizard in embryonic fluid. Instead of starting with an idea and searching for clues—and risk being led elsewhere—like Aba, I could start with the conclusion—the soapy membrane of a newborn child is a remnant of its reptilian origins—and point to the Quran.

I climb up to these ruins. Like a cock looking for a vantage point, every chance I get, I climb. The roof of my house; the terrace-café in Rabat; Simla Hill in Lahore (the city's only hump); these cliffs in Greece. I don't crow. I listen for shoulders to look out from. But all the necks peering around mine on this windswept rock belong to tourists, either shivery and searching, like me, or big and bombastic, like Aba.

It is God who has created all animals out of water.

I've become a man who can't even gaze at the stars and tune into cosmic radiation on the radio without searching for a verse to *prove* the crackling exists. Or one stating there's no point hiking up to this temple. It's Already Climbed.

•

Godlessness is a cancer whose favorite organ is the pen. It must be treated by every means available or it will spread. And while on the subject of treating cancer, delete all references to Marie Curie and her so-called radiation.

Lahore again. Lethargy. Headaches. *Please let me sleep.* Someone shuts the door.

•

Force myself to write: *Today our children are issues...*
What's it for?
When's it needed?
Can't remember. Curl back into bed.

•

Today our children are issues.
They have lost touch with real history; they believe Pakistan was created in 1947, when in fact Mohammad Bin Qasim discovered us in 712. Bin Qasim was only seventeen when he liberated this land from infidels, but what are young men doing today? The only words they spread are freaky.

Did I write that? I hear a faint whisper: *Consider the bee.*

•

"Enough!" Ama flies into my room. "Your father has been generous, but this time you must get up." She feeds me the same soup she plies her grandchildren with when they're ill. Then she puts my copy book on my pillow. "Your fever is gone. Try to sit up and finish his speech."

Someone—me?—has written:

The Blueprint for AFTERLIFE

Let us be like Al Ashari and Al Ghazzali, who saved the soul of Islam a thousand years ago...

I vaguely remember Aba has to present this speech soon, and I've been trying to complete it for days. My clothes stink. My face is oily. The stubble on my cheek itches. Slouched at my desk, I tap my pen. Ink in my face. *Think of something.* I look through all my notes of the past five years. My mind's *dead.* I step outside.

No Unsa at my front door. Only a few dozen honeybees swarming in the driveway, wiping their feet before their waxy temples. I marvel at their method: point, line, space. Here's the magic of abstract space blooming to perfect proportion! Al Khwarizmi bees. Honeycomb heaven. Again, I hear: *Consider the bee.*

Where did I read that?

Return to room, flip pages, find the verse: *Consider how thy sustainer has inspired the bee... then eat of all manner of fruit... (And lo!) there issues from within these (bees) a fluid of many hues.*

The translator chose "inspired" not "divinely revealed."

I visit Queen Bee. She's in the kitchen, making soup. "I'm glad you're here. Nadir has a cold. This will be ready soon, for you to take to him."

Nadir's my nephew, now three years old. I call the brat Nadir Shah, conqueror of India and Persia. "He sneezed *once.* In the eighteenth century. I'll have it."

"You're okay now." But she ladles some out for me.

While it cools, I find the honey jar and dip a finger inside. The honey tastes faintly acrid. A spot of peacock blue swells in a gold sea in the jar. As the ink tendrils separate, so the bitterness fades on my tongue, leaving a pleasant, grassy tingle. I dip a thumb, leaving a bigger stain, a heavier green.

"Use a spoon." Ama looks up from the pot, bubbling with pepper and chicken bones, and hands me a spoon.

I dip the spoon, lift green honey. A second line of amber pours back into the jar.

"Eat it. Don't play with it. You'll never grow up. Do you even know what year it is?"

There's less black in her hair each year, but otherwise, not much change. Still no wrinkles or fat or flurry. Even her hairstyle's static: center parting, thin and straight like gray bamboo shoots, combed across small ears, into a bun. Tiny gold hoops wiggle out of the sweep. Her grandmother's. Her one vanity. She turns the gas off and blows a prayer over the soup.

Then she tells me all that's happened in the weeks since I fell ill: the fraying of the alliance between the religious parties and the government; foreign funds and local popularity both dwindling, "even though the Shariat Bill was made law last year." Had no idea my mother was so informed. She keeps on, "Everyone is talking about it but you play with honey! This meeting in Lahore is very important to your father. He is always in a bad mood. Finish the speech, then take this to Shaista." She wraps the pot in a cloth.

I flit back to my room with a mild honey rush, amazed at what I find Already Written.

The Blueprint for AFTERLIFE

Let us be like Al Ashari and Al Ghazzali, who saved the soul
of Islam a thousand years ago from unbelievers like Al Farabi
and Ibn Sina. Let us remember that, as recently as the last
century, Islam's roots were rotting again. The infidels who
robbed our land taught us to think of a universe without
belief. And that time has returned. Again we must struggle
to save ourselves from becoming slaves of the senses.

Which leads to the question: what is science? For some it
is "blind nature." Proponents of this science are men like
Zahoor ul Din, who obscure the true message of Islam,
making it a puzzle full of hidden metaphors and poetry,
twisting it this way and that, and generating great support for
themselves. But they are themselves blind and the blind must
create what they cannot see. The seeing, who adhere to their
Shariat, are gifted with a "third" eye. We see Divine Proofs
Revealed. We have lifted the veil from our eyes. We need not
"interpret" or even "read." We see ALL, the visible and
invisible, angels and djinns.

Those not born with Vision will not cast shadow. They
will burn eternally, while we will be rewarded for adhering to
our Shariat and our destiny.

I know Aba will be very pleased, especially with the last line,
and the title, but I can't believe I wrote it. Did Ama?

I return to the kitchen to ask but she brushes me off, saying
she's getting late for Isha prayers.

Who taught me to believe Aba wrong and prove him right?
I've come full circle. Or crashed. I can argue anything. I have no
beliefs of my own. Light and darkness negate each other. The
ions of my mind are in deep freeze. Meet Noman, who is an
island. Not a synthesis, or even a cultural freak. But an absence.

I reread the middle paragraph, wincing at the reference to Zahoor. It shouldn't be there. I know this in my bones. I also know it's time to stop postponing the visit to him.

The scholar's ink is holier than the martyr's blood. We'll either save or destroy each other. I set off for Islamabad.

•

Zahoor lives alone in a single-story house in the Margalla foothills. When I ring the doorbell he answers it himself, looking distracted. "Yes?" Behind him flickers a gas heater in a small, crowded room. The guests dangle sweaters and glasses. They're either leaving or have just arrived.

"Uh. I'm a reporter." I smile.

"I'm not." He smiles back.

"Do you have a little—time?"

He steps back, points at his friends. "Do they look as if they'll give us time?"

A woman giggles. The older sister. Hair combed into a clip. Gray handloom cotton kameez with a bright purple dupatta. The colors suit her. Now that I can see her face completely, she seems friendlier, even younger, than earlier this year, when I glimpsed her near Simla Hill. Mehwish is nowhere in sight.

"Which paper are you from?" she calls out to me. *Hadn't thought of that.*

I'd made arrangements to stay in Islamabad with Faisal the Vulgarian's brother, saying I had to attend his wedding (ha, he's uglier than Faisal), got the green light from even Aba, packed a bag with a toothbrush, suit and tie, copy book, the article I assume Zahoor'd written, *A Blueprint for Life* (Meow's paw prints nicely preserved), and two forbidden books—*Selections from Darwin* and *The Moment of Mu'tazilites*. Hadn't thought of anything else. As if Zahoor would be alone, expecting me!

I gape at the doorbell.

"Oh, come in," says Zahoor. "It's cold. And you look relatively harmless." He shuts the door.

If late November evenings in Islamabad weren't cooler than in Lahore, he might not have invited me in. I step into his home, and the girl eyes me again. Her face hardens. Does she recognize me? She forces a smile and introduces herself as Amal.

"Noman." I smile again.

"Noman." She rolls the name on her tongue, slowly, probing coldly with her eyes. "Why do you seem so familiar?"

"A lot of short skinny men look like me."

"Or you look like them."

"What did you want to talk to about?" Zahoor settles on a weathered sofa.

Beside him sits a handsome middle-aged man, glass of whisky in his hand. He lifts the other to shake mine. "Junayd." I also shake hands with: the two white men I saw at the hotel, now seated with Amal on a second couch; two men slouched in chairs (one, also at the hotel); a seventh man on a floor cushion, stirring a teacup. I crouch on the cushion beside his. The group's just arrived and has no intentions of leaving.

Zahoor watches me, waiting for an answer. I'm the only one without something to drink. He doesn't offer and there seems to be no servant in the house. I stare at the faded red of the cushion cover beneath me. I fumble in my bag for the clipping.

"I—uh, I wanted to talk about this," I reach across the floor to show him, "ugly dog and—uh, lovely fish."

He waves me away. "I can see from here. What about it?"

"Well—uh, it's been a few years and I haven't read anything else."

"Why does a young reporter want to know about old sea-monsters? That is not usually the kind of thing to interest you boys."

"I'm not so young."

"From which epoch?"

The girl laughs; Zahoor's eyes twinkle. His humor's not mean but not kind either.

"If you have been following our discoveries you must know about the warnings this community of scientists," his chin sweeps the room, "has been receiving from certain primitive groups being returned to life with increasing power. And you would know that our work is severely hampered, not only for ideological reasons but for what is known as *security reasons*." He takes a long sip of a clear drink, watching my reaction from the top of his glass. "Though our digging and hammering continues, we are being more cautious. Our meetings have become even smaller and too exclusive for my taste." He puts the glass down on a table, loudly. I hadn't noticed the others were chatting among themselves till this moment, when they stop abruptly. "But you do not know, at least not all of it"—I flinch—"because you have not been keeping up, you are not interested in a time when the world belonged to whales. You are not even interested in your own time. Nor are you a reporter. So, what are you?"

Whoosh! A ruler whips the air in a shrill whistle before striking me.

Then, nothing. No crack. No burn. Only silence thicker than a winter fog, louder than a monsoon rain.

So, Zahoor and Aba aren't so different. Both give themselves the power to put youth on trial. A fury creeps up my neck, de-freezing me. I meet Zahoor's daunting gaze with ions fully charged. Yes, I'm in his house. Yes, I was wrong to expect his trust (of course I don't deserve it). Still, as I look in his small stony eyes, I see the expression on Aba's face the day I returned to his meeting after spying on Zahoor. "What do you have to report?" The room went silent, as this one does now. And a weight, harder than Zahoor's gaze but equally resolute, had slipped into my belly: *tell them what they want to hear.*

Except now, I'm not so sure what they want to hear.

I only know what I want to say: Do you know that in public I argue for Aba, while in private I argue for you? I've been batting for both sides. Now I want to bat for neither. I don't want to be in any game.

His friends start chatting again, as if used to his talent for intimidating strangers. Do I imagine it, or has the girl's face softened?

"Well," Zahoor repeats, "what *do* you do?"

"I match-fix." That gets everyone's complete attention. "Give me a sacred verse, and I can prove both divine will and biological evolution wrong and right. Or give me one of our founder's speeches, and I can prove he was a believer and a kafir."

Zahoor picks up his glass. Laughing.

Junayd leans forward, looking worried. "Who sent you? What do you want?"

"Are you a lawyer?" asks the man on the cushion.

"He'd make a terrible one," answers Junayd.

"What else do you have up your sleeve?" asks Zahoor. I pull my two forbidden books out of the bag and hand them over, like a confession. As Zahoor flips through the pages of both, including, I realize too late, my embarrassing musings in the margins (*If for Darwin God and Nature were equally dark, what did he think of extraterrestrial djinns?*), his mood brightens.

"Nana, this is no joke. I think he should leave," says Amal, stern again.

"Agreed," nod the two men in chairs.

"And when are you going to get a security guard?" Amal adds.

Zahoor smiles, flipping pages.

"Have you been sent by the Jamaat-e-Pedaish?" Junayd asks, pale with anxiety.

"Of course," says Zahoor. "He probably sent the warnings!"

"Yes. I gave the two warnings."

Zahoor laughs louder. He shuts both books and stands up.

"I hope you're throwing the wretched boy out!" says Junayd.

"No. I'm fixing the poor boy a drink!"

Amal

Since November, when Noman first rang Nana's doorbell, a lost bee in search of the sun, that small bundle of trepidation with the big nose and gap between his teeth has been visiting Nana every week. Nana always welcomes him, even though he's the one who sent the warnings. (I still remember the one I found: *Dear Sir, Godlessness is a cancer whose favorite organ is the pen…* I still remember how it frightened me.) I know that part of Noman's appeal is just this: he's an opportunity for Nana to spite his foes by welcoming one of their offspring.

Or is there more? Is he the grandson Nana never had? Or son (his *real* son barely speaks to him)—it's easy to forget Noman is six years older than me. He seems so young. I don't know how they've ended up being friends. I only know I don't like how Nana grilled Noman that first night, after getting him good and drunk. (He could barely hold his first drink, let alone the third.) I don't have a good feeling about that at all.

Now Nana's visiting us in Lahore. It's New Year's Eve, and for the third year straight, I'm late for the party at Zara's house. I can't decide what shoes to wear because Nana keeps demanding my attention, claiming I've been corrupted by the feudal culture of Lahore and have lost touch with the real things in life.

"Like dead whales?" Aba retorts indignantly, launching into a lecture of his own. Why won't girls wear traditional clothes to parties? Why can't he drop and pick me?

Ama nervously flits about. My appearance is her own. She spends less time on the couch. I find I don't need her to be anywhere else.

For the third year straight, I don't particularly want to go to Zara's. I've already drawn a mental map of the night's events. Swing from one drunk to the next. Spend under a minute on each. Complete no sentence. Smoke a lot. Laugh a lot. Spot VIPs at a glance. Swap phone numbers. Repeat. I'm going because it's better than staying. I'm going because it's better than hearing about it later. I'm going so I'll have something in common with my friends. Because I'm the only twenty-one-year-old in Lahore who cares about life fifty million years ago and fifty million years hence, and that gets lonely.

I leave Nana and duck into my room. I take off my tight gray pants and put on looser black ones, then return to the ones that fit me better. I also leave on the fluid maroon top that feels good on the skin. ("Like tissue paper that slides," Mehwish decided as I got dressed, rubbing me with those hands that make me naked.) I undo the second button. My breasts look huge. I wear two-inch heels.

I go back into the living room and wait for Zara's car.

Nana looks me over. "Landlords love fat."

"These shoes don't match," I mumble, fleeing to my room again.

When I brave them a third time, it's Aba's turn to pounce. "It's *winter*."

Nana: "The rich and powerful make their own weather."

Ama: "I have a sweater that will match."

Mehwish: "What did *Basilosaurus* eat?"

Nana: "Landlords."

Aba: "Give her socks as well."

Nana turns to me. "What tribe does this friend of yours belong to?"

Mehwish: "Islam united all tribes."

Nana: "Clever girl. You have illustrated the difference between fact and theory."

Aba: "Evolution is a theory. Fact: there are no divisions among Muslims."

Nana: "What a delicious fantasy! I'll give you another *fact*. Shariat never applies to those who enforce it. As long as she keeps their company, your daughter can go naked. She won't even catch a cold."

Aba: "There is really a lot of negativity in you."

There was a time when Aba didn't directly argue with Nana. This was called respect. Now they quarrel whenever they can. Ama lays a hand on Aba's arm and begins to say something but I remember my hair looks like shit and dash back into my room.

When I reappear Nana is even more fired up. He asks me, "Is invitation by caste only? Do you all stand around talking about each other's peasants and crops?"

Aba: "What on earth are you talking about?"

Mehwish: "What is the difference between tribe and caste?"

Nana chuckles. "You are almost as clever as your sister." He looks at me with those piercing eyes, insisting I pay him attention.

Mehwish: "I am more clever!"

I hear a horn. Zara's car. I say a silent prayer of thanks, and leave. Ama pushes a sweater into my arms.

I'm shivering inside the black Mercedes.

The driver is a thickset man with a coarse woollen jacket and a Frontier hat: flat top, ropy rim. I wrap Ama's gray sweater around me and sink into plush indigo seats. The car's also swathed in wool: the fog, very dense tonight. Headlights nudge fingers of mist that creep inside and brush my shoulders. I start to feel airborne. I exhale clouds. I lose track of the route.

Still convinced that a closed door is a challenge, Nana's still looking for a complete *Pakicetus* skeleton, and still looking for a middle whale, and I'm still not going with his team. But I can still learn their theories.

Theory: A middle whale had the feet of a water bird. If it swam, it moved like a penguin, weaving the spine up and down, aided by a long fluked tail.

Fact: I had a craving to draw for Mehwish the picture of a girl with a tail she doesn't need. I left it in her cupboard, to find one day.

Fact: In most families, women quarrel while men laugh at them. In mine, men quarrel while women wonder in silence.

Theory: I don't love Nana any less for aiming his ire at me or my friends.

Fact: I still wish he wouldn't.

Theory: Since closed doors exist, I'll learn to be a locksmith.

Theory: Adaptation, my middle name.

I roll down the window. The fog hides it, but I can smell the *ganda nala*, the filthiest part of the canal. We're approaching Mall Road. Zara's house is behind Aitchison College.

Zara, the girl who showed me sperm ducks. *Let man then observe out of what he has been created.* She still laughs about it— "Behold! Spurting fluid!"—adding that now I need to do more than simply observe. How we ended up being best friends is a mystery.

Well, so is Nana's friendship with Noman.

I go back to thinking about Noman. A thing I like: he's

good with Mehwish. He lets her examine his face, laughing good-naturedly at her announcement that God's hand slipped while making noses in Pakistan. But we were always a trio— me, Mehwish, Grandfather Clock—and now we're usually four. I don't know if I like the change. I know Mehwish doesn't. She says something about Noman doesn't feel right, but I'm sure she's just possessive.

I should warn her that if she doesn't learn the difference between love and possession, she'll start to think like Nana and Aba (the only time they agree) that because the war in Afghanistan spoiled our countryside by peppering it with bandits and guns, city women should stay home. If Mehwish doesn't understand this, she'll not only start believing *I'm* better off at home, but also that the world is closed to *her*. Her imagination will wither. Her long narwhal tooth snap. It'll hurt her worse than it hurts me to know that the hills where I once found an ear, have since grown deaf to me—and to her.

What can I give to a blind girl in a troubled land as long as her safety is my obsession, and even I need permission to live?

As the car pulls into Zara's driveway, I worry: *Will she turn the heater off before going to sleep? Will Aba check that the gas lever is up?*

If Nana asked me to do it again, to develop the habit of looking down so Mehwish never flies down manholes or skids in mud or gets lost the way I nearly lost her once, I would. She's the tail I need.

•

I take off Ama's ugly sweater and throw it on a chair.

Over three hundred bodies are packed inside a house at least as old as 1922, the date scratched on the square spoons that were wrapped in cloth and tucked under a tile of the veranda. Everything else in the rambling structure was looted during the Partition riots. Zara's sister found the spoons years after their grandfather moved his family to Pakistan from India. They came by air. They were able to save their own belongings. The highest-ranking antiques are Zara's grandmother's *paan dans* (treasured more than her grandchildren) and the sun-bleached carpets she's able to hear the servants step on.

Tonight the carpets have been removed. So have the *paan dans*. The servants have multiplied. The floors throb with dancers. The smoke's blinding. I can't locate the laughter. I have a Mehwish moment of sensory surplus. The furniture in every room has been moved to make space for guests. If she were here, I'd take her to the kitchen, the only space left untouched. But she isn't. I force myself to go where she wouldn't. The dance floor, pulsing with lights that would prick her perceptive skin.

I look around for Zara. She's not dancing. Must be on the terrace. Near the staircase, I hear the gravelly voice that Mehwish loves. (She also loves Zara's bones. She needles her chin and elbows, knees and heels, finding her to be "like many spoons.") It's the voice of someone who somehow outgrew the need to flaunt her family's power and her own sexual savvy, to become a person with everything except anything to prove. Unlike her equally well-connected friends. They flash; she flows.

She's perched on the bottom stair, barefooted, icy beer warmed by hands in fingerless wool gloves. A slinky dark cat with white front paws and legs in brown satin. She points a foot at me, "Amal! Meet Kamal!" and does something provocative with a spiky shoulder. Yes, I've noticed him. No, she shouldn't put me on the spot. I want to tell her the braces make her mouth look especially big today but she'd only laugh.

"Hi." I kiss her cheek. "Bitch," I whisper in her ear. "Hi," I say to Kamal.

"Sit sit," Zara sings. As soon as I do, she'll whisk away on a pretend errand. "Can I get you something?" A thin coffee-colored pullover with delicate bronze sequins clings to feline waist and hangs below the knees, matching her complexion, as if all five feet eight inches have been rolled in gold dust. I surrender a smile. "Sans alcohol?" French was a former fad that clings as stubbornly as her clothes. I nod. She leaves.

Kamal has been staring at me. I mean, at my breasts. His name means perfection, proving that the first checkpost up the steep slope called Parenthood is naming your child his opposite. I smell his cologne, his gel, his smirk. I walk away.

In the kitchen, Zara's of course forgotten my drink and is chatting up another debonair dunce. I pull her aside.

She feigns horror. "But you *must* say hello to Riz!"

I pull more sharply, nudging her into a corner. "You have to stop doing this."

"Whatever it is, I'd never."

"Where do you get them from?"

"The sweaters? This one's from Milan. Rip not."

"You know what I mean."

"Oh, pour yourself a drink. Come on, you'll have a whale of a time."

"Corny, Zara."

"What did you learn today? Are we extinct?"

"It's not about death. It's about *life*. But forget it, you won't understand."

"You're obsessed with the past."

"I'm obsessed with the present. And the future."

"You have a morbid fascination with rocks."

"I have a healthy fascination with life."

"*This* is life," she swings her arms, indicating the crowd around us.

"*This* will disappear."

She slides a finger down my sleeve. "Good texture but maroon's not your color."

"Shut up, Zara."

"Come to my room, I have something for you."

"Keep it."

"The shoes are definitely extinct."

"Zara."

"You need to meet men, not dinosaurs."

"And you're going to arrange that?"

"If you want."

"If *I* want!"

"Riz's checking you out."

"*Fine.*"

He's pouring another drink, announcing, "Opposition to the army is elitist. Who else can protect us?" Zara's sister Tina and her friends NinaDina all nod emphatically. When he asks me to dance, I nod emphatically.

They're playing Elvis. The last hour of 1992 and they're playing Elvis. *I'm* obsessed with the past!

His gut bulges. Hips sag. Feet hop. Head keeps vigorous time with the beat while midriff spills: polar extremities compensating for the center's sluggishness. He whispers in my ear, "I study law."

"The way you dance," I say, "is the opposite of the way the Earth spins."

He frowns, repeats, "I study law."

Clearly, not the law of gravity. "Can the army protect us from Elvis?"

Blank stare. Lips amphibian. "These shoes are from Milan."

"Did you get Zara's sweater or did she get your shoes?"

"Our fathers got them. They went together."

"Nice!"

"Naturally. Armani."

> *When they said you was high classed*
> *Well that was just a lie*

"Law and order," he yells above the music. "That's the challenge. Before the bloody mess in Karachi corrupts Lahore." Drumroll. Throws his head back.

The song changes. His feet tread more slowly. His stomach globe begins to rotate. A reedy voice Mehwish would call yellow light summons:

> *That's me in the spotlight, losing my religion...*

"Losing my religion." Riz looks at me. "Is it the latest?"

"Naturally. Armani."

Once, Mehwish and I were driving by the cantonment area while the army practiced for a parade. The bagpipes were so loud she got cranky. The only way to calm her was to park the car, peer inside the barracks wall, and describe it all: the bellows and bellowing cheeks, flapping arms, kilts, bare hairy legs. She marched around the house mimicking them for days, begging Aba to wear a skirt (he refused). If she were here now I'd tell her Riz puffs and parades exactly like a Scottish-Punjabi soldier-piper.

Trying to keep an eye on you
Like a hurt lost and blinded fool, fool...

Midnight. Riz leans into my nose. I give him a friendly wave. Other couples either embrace or find ways not to. Applause. I'm about to sit down when the song changes again. Behind Riz, a woman with a bob haircut steps aside for her partner, who's balanced on his toes, knees flexed. Slowly, he winds upright. My eye falls to his hips. They have that tight yet liquid quality you see in Russian gymnasts on television. A long minute. Eyes shut. Face serene. Multiple scissory legs.

When the music stops, I head back for the kitchen, noting the Rhythm retreats to a chair at the edge of the dance floor, his partner beside him. They don't speak.

I can't find Zara and Riz's following me, maw moving. I catch a fragment, "Have you...?" swing around too fast, bump into his grin. "Books are so expensive."

"Toilet emergency." I push by him.

I cross the floor to look again: moustache, drooping eyes, wet fringe. If I hadn't seen him dance, would I look now? Moustaches are crumb collectors and hair-in-the-eyes, fussy. Then someone approaches him and he looks up. Eyes come alive.

"I see," a familiar voice at the back of my neck. "You like to be the one who chases. How come I never knew that?"

"You're not as clever as you think." Behind me, Zara snickers. I add, "A closed door is a challenge."

"Bravo. You've homed in on the loudest bang."

He's still speaking animatedly to the man who approached him. We watch. Teeth prominent. Very white when he laughs. Brushing the tip of a quite delicate nose (no proboscis mischief from the Maker here), his mane is suddenly winning. "Gay?"

"Don't think so. Just with the wrong woman." She pulls my hand. "Wait."

"For what?" She bats her eyelids.

"Those braces make your mouth look especially big today."

On cue, she breaks into laughter. "Most girls seem to need an Omar in their lives."

"Omar?" I quickly go down a mental list of women-with-Omars. Disasters, all.

The DJ plays Fine Young Cannibals (rainbow light to Mehwish) and Omar stands up. This time, his partner keeps sitting.

"He's dancing for you," Zara nods. "Sexual selection and all that."

I laugh. "You're a naturalist in chic skin."

She caresses my arm with a glove. "Sheep skin."

I pinch her wrist. "Cheap skin."

"Men and women need a way to find each other, right? No display, no pay."

"What?"

"*Play*. No display, no *play*. Whales sing, peacocks strut, flowers bloom. What do you do?"

I tsk.

"I'm serious. You can't dress, you can't cook, you can't even—"

"I'm the *female*, remember?"

"Act now or Riz later." He spots us from the kitchen. "Riz *soon*," she hisses. But he gets tangled in the lights and we lose sight of each other. Zara resumes, "What's the point of your *healthy fascination with life*, if you can't apply it?"

"I *am* applying it. Now shut up!"

Omar bows and slowly spins. We aren't his only audience. A large circle has been cleared for him, and the room—normally crammed with Gandhara Buddha statues—explodes with applause as the tempo of his twirling builds. I watch, but more with admiration than attraction. A closed door isn't a challenge if everyone pushes in.

So when it's over and he sits down and devotees surround him and he loses the smile to preen his feathers, I consult my watch: one-thirty in the morning. I was supposed to be home an hour ago. The whole house will be waiting up for me. Except Mehwish, asleep after stumbling into pajamas—after she or Aba switched off the gas. Definitely.

"I should go," I turn to Zara, but she's gone.

I spot her beside Omar. The man he was talking to earlier gives her the attention she demands. The first part of her scheme. The second: Omar's looking at me. He's standing up. He's moving in my direction, alone.

He grazes my shoulder, says, "Sorry," considers, asks, "Where's the staircase to the terrace?" Adds, "I need some fresh air. Do you?"

I don't reply.

"Do you have a sweater?"

"No."

He crosses back to his chair, collects a heavy shawl (gray like the sweater I don't have), returns, smiling toothily.

•

The route home is barricaded by fog, pillars of white mist that magically melt for us.

At four in the morning he drops me at my gate. It's bolted from inside. I leap across, carefully clutching his shawl around me so it doesn't tear.

I have left the sweater behind.

Mehwish

"Explain myself?" shouts Amal. "Has Ama ever explained herself? Has Nana? Why should I? What is there to 'explain'?"

Putting a word in in verted commas gives it a secret "meaning." For instance Amal has not been allowed out at night for a month big cause of her late night "experiments." What are these "experiments"? She should not have to explain.

"Jail Road. Left onto Gulberg, bastard!" I hear the horn. Between cursing motor cyclists, flashing brights and being over taken from the left, she calls out the names of roads so I know where I am. I hear the horn again.

"Driving gets you worked up."

"At home my toung is a rinkled worm. Driving washes the salt off."

So does screaming at me but I do not say it.

Sprinkling salt on slugs that ate our zinnias used to be one of her "experiments." I would touch their soft dried up bodies in the flower beds their meat smelled white when it decayed. Only some had eaten the zinnias but all were punished. Ox gin broke them down. This is good for future zinnias.

Ox gin = Decay

When we die the same will happen to us. We will feed flowers. And smell white.

"The marigolds are in bloom, Mehwish. They are a beautiful lemon."

I will tell you about my Periodic Table of Stinks and Sounds later but beautiful lemon means a yello smell. That is not a clever code big cause a lemon really is yello I am told and a marigold is gold or it would be marired or mariblue. I was saying that putting a word in in verted commas gives it a hidden "meaning." For instance Amal's late night "experiments." What are they? Aba calls them "dangerous" Ama calls them "shame full" and Nana calls them "tribal." If you listen care fully to pee pull you see they all say or do what they do not want to have to explain so Amal has a point.

"More ugly bill boards! Should we go round and round the Liberty round about?"

"Please no." I do not know why she thinks this is "fun." I cannot see how much we are turning I over do it in my mind it makes me want to womit.

"You're growing very quiet. Was I like that at thirteen? I can't remember."

"I am almost fourteen."

I remember her at almost fourteen she did not wash me as much I stopped touching her big boobs and hairy thighs that were smooth under neath. It was also when she told me about gravityG. There are nine planets flying around the sun and a man called New Tin put a difficult idea into a simple sentence about pull. I am light so my gravityG pull is tiny. Amal would stand on the floor or bed or roof and drop things and time their fall. I liked guessing what she dropped by the sound when it landed. I used to be in her experiments and in verted commas were not necessary.

"What are you thinking? Is it your period? Have they finally arrived?"

"I do not want to have to explain."

She laughs. 'That's my sister!'

I listen care fully to pee pull. Nana says some children do not know about New Tin and the planets as if big cause we cannot hear them they do not exist. He likes that I slow down to listen but Amal says I have the extra time big cause she does things for me. She says this more these days I do not like it. Soon she will sound like Miss Fauzia at school who says God has punished us with things we cannot do by our selves like eat or read but I do. Miss Fauzia asks what will you do when you grow up? and answers herself Pray.

"Bastard's going to cut in. Right is your doctor's, left is Tahira Syed's—"

"I know where we are." I also know she does not drive as fast as she wants when I am with her.

"*Fine.* I was just trying to help."

"With what?"

"*Fine.*"

We start moving again. She always jerks into second gear then blames it for being "sticky." Third gear is like gliding on to a floor after nearly tripping on a rug. Fourth is the same floor polished like a hotel's. A hotel is given stars maybe by the army.

"I'm going to pull into Barkat Market to buy some mithai for the school team. And tube roses for Miss. Do you want to come inside?"

"We are not there yet."

"*When* we are there do you want to have a look?"

"Ask me when we are there."

She mutters *oof* under her breath if a bastard is cutting in she does not say or blow the horn.

I was going to say the round about we passed is called Tahira Syed's Hand big cause it has a tall shape that looks like the hand of the singer when she sings I am told. The straight hand goes side ways to hold a note. The note comes from a thing called a vocal chord. The vocal chords of her mother who was a singer first are always loose and long and deep and I love her song about being young. She sang it when she was old. She sang what she felt this is what made her famous. And she went blind.

Amal says my spellings are improving my sounds are clearer my vocal chord is not dried up like a slug with salt on it. I used to say wocal and wisual. There are still *v* words I cannot hear. I used to hear about round now I hear round about. But Amal says I still separate words that are one. It is sometimes not some times mistakes not miss takes. There will always be too many silent letters I can only think of some the *h* in whale or which and after *g* for exam pull weigh not only way.

Amal takes a deep breath. I am sorry she thinks I am difficult. "Okay, we're here. Do you believe me now?"

"I never did not believe you." She sucks in her breath. "I can hear you."

"I'll be as quick as I can. Do you want to smell the flowers?"

I like to do that. "I will wait in the car."

"See you soon."

"You too."

I like that Amal uses normal expressions with me like see you or have a look or dekho. It is quiet when she is gone even though it is noisy.

We do not do much writing in school and there is no Braille book shop but Amal makes me try at home I will explain how in a minute. I have difficulty with commas Amal says they are a "blind spot." Uptrophies are crowded I am is better than I'm. Para graph breaks do not speak or stop speaking. Except whenever Amal leaves there is a big one.

I get out of the car. I am not sure where in the market she has parked I cannot guess where the flowers should be. The air is full of adult petrol. Adult petrol is when cheap things are added to petrol to cheat young pee pull into buying at normal price. Nana says young pee pull get stupider every day and maybe he is right big cause the air is very dirty. This is called pull ocean which is different from pull nation which is what bees do not slugs.

There is a lot of traffic. Motor bikes shake trucks groan. I stand still. Doors slam pee pull get in and out of cars some with soft engines some loud. Children try to sell them flowers. Not the kind I like but single paper roses in plastick rap. I hope they do not uproach me but they do. One touches me she says Lelo tries to push a rose into my hand. Others pull my dress and laugh. Amal has told me they are Afghani children not gone home. Though the war is over a "civil" one has started so they stay. They are screaming something probably blind in their toung. I climb back inside the car. They tap my windo I roll it up all the way or they will drop a flower into the space and tell me to pay.

Sometimes you can sit still and not know where you are more than when you are moving.

The tapping continues. I blow the horn. First shortly then long. The children move to her door so I know she is coming.

She throws my hand off the horn. "What's the matter with you?" She is very loud.

"You said you would be quick."

"It hasn't even been ten minutes. It takes time to rap the sweets and flowers."

"What if our team loses?"

"Don't change the subject." She grabs my hand the same one and squeezes it with commas. "Do not, ever, throw tan, trums, like that, again, in public, under, stand?"

She makes more noise than a tree full of owl lits. "Ouch!"

"Stop pretending, promise me you will not, do that, again."

I think her door is still open sounds are coming to me very loudly now but the children seem to have gone. This is like eating choc bar when I have a sore throat part of me is glad the other part hurts.

"Promise, me."

"Ouch! I am not pretending."

"Mehwish."

She loosens her grip I quickly pull my hand away. I notice the milky wanilla smell of tube roses like the nuts in a melting choc bar. Her door shuts she starts the car. I hear her arrange the gifts in the back seat then she re verses suddenly and we are off.

I was saying I do not like Amal inter uping me she used to give me more time she used to understand that if I am quiet it does not mean I am empty in the head she should not jump into my thoughts in a loud way. It just means I am turning the dial of my radio maybe a voice tells me this is Radio Pakistan and a song comes maybe I like it or maybe it is a salty vocal chord. When I am listening hard it hurts a lot to be inter uped. She does not understand any more. She keeps talking all the way to school where there is to be a match of blind cricket but I tune out.

gateway the third: the word

عجب نہی کے پریشاں ہے گفتگو میری
فروغ صبح پریشاں نہی تو کچھ بھی نہی

علامہ اقبال 'تصوف'

No wonder that my talk is scattered
It is but the scattering of the rising dawn
—Allama Iqbal, "Mysticism"

Mehwish

The first pee pull to play blind cricket lived in a city far away called Mel Burn which is also a type of cigrit something Amal's friends like a lot. It smells worse than adult petrol and is another way of tricking young pee pull so her friends are stupid except Zara who loves me. Her vocal chords are relaxed. There are seven continants Mel Burn has its own. Nana says if the sub continant had kept floating instead of bumping into Asia we would have more space to get on with our selves.

"There's Miss Fauzia," says Amal inter uping me.

We have entered the school grounds I cannot locate any one thing just a lot of cheering wishles bells and always traffic. Amal's right free hand has my left. She does not seem angry now so I say "I want to give the flowers to Miss Amna not Miss Fauzia."

"Why?"

"I do not want to have to explain."

"Please, Mehwish. Please tell me."

"I like Miss Amna she told me Australia is a continant I do not have to put what she says in in verted commas."

"Okay," she wishpers walking more slowly.

"It is Miss Amna who wants us to play but Miss Fauzia—"

"Oh!" She drops the box of mithai gravityG pulls it with a thump. "You're early!"

"I just got here," says a voice I do not know.

"Let's go sit there," says Amal.

"That your sister?"

"Yes. Mehwish, I don't see Miss Amna. Let's just give these to Miss Fauzia."

"*No.*"

Again she squeezes my hand roughly hisses in my ear. "Don't, be diff, cult!"

I stare in the angry way she says makes me look like an owl lit. If she can sound like ten I can look like one. "You told me to explain I did I will not ever tell you again!"

"Shit! Mehwish, I'm *so* tired!"

"Who told you to get flowers? I did not."

"Just do this for me, please? I want to sit and we can't have this on our lap the whole time."

"*No.*"

"I'll carry them," says the voice I do not know laughing.

I do not like pee pull laughing at me thinking I am deaf. "*No.*"

"Oof! She's a firecracker!"

I start walking. I can hear the cricket ball now so straight means field and left means seating. Amal grabs my elbo pulls me straight. She wishpers something to her friend I try to tune out but cannot help it I ask "Is he an experiment in in verted commas?"

First there is silence then he laughs so much he coughs. Before I know it he is tapping the top of my head like a holy man except his voice is not old and says, "I like your sister."

"Are you talking to her or me?" I speak to him directly fed up.

"I was talking to her about you but now I'm talking to you about her."

"One leg up, Mehwish. Stairs."

We sit in the third ro I feel confused. They know each other but I have been put in the middle. Nobody answered my question I have the feeling this *is* an experiment. Amal is dropping books and pulling my hair out to put under a micro scope except this time no one is telling me. But I like the way he said that sentence to me it was in a normal voice not sugary or salty so I ask him if he knows anything about blind cricket.

"This is my first match. Why aren't you playing?"

"There are many degrees of blindness and only two girls on our team are completely blind like me. One is bowling the other fielding I am not good at them."

"What about batting?"

"I do batting in my head."

"Wow!"

"The first pee pull to play blind cricket lived in Mel Burn in 1922."

"Wow!"

"The same year as Zara's spoons. They are square."

I hear a russling I think it is Chili Chips. "Want some?"

I lift my fingers he finds them puts them in the packet. Usually pee pull put things in my hand instead of letting me find them. His fingers are cold. "What is your name?"

"Omar. Want some?" He repeats but this time to Amal who reaches across me and moves the flowers they are wet my lap feels cold. I put them in her lap. She makes that windy sound he laughs again. "I can take them." He taps the top of my head again.

"She should hold them," says Amal. "As punishment."

"I have done nothing rong!" I am very angry now and speak loudly which is not normal.

"Be quiet, Mehwish. There's Nadia, let me to take you to her."

I sit with Nadia in class and do not have to keep sitting with her. "I was talking to Omar."

"We were chatting," Omar agrees.

Amal mutters Omar does not hear but I am good at hearing. "Some ghondaywoo."

I have heard this word before Zara uses it it is French. A language is like a person or a whale it comes from something else it is mixed not pure but not mixed like adult petrol in a harm full way more like double roti which has lots of things mixed in it like flower and sugar and is not harm full but should be called quarter roti big cause you have to have four to be full. Nana says my school is not like Amal's which is private and "tribal" but a gowment school where we do not learn English or Urdu it is a sim tim of the times. He says I am lucky to be learning both languages well at home thanks to Amal do I thank her?

This time the cheering inter ups me. Omar says, "Did you see that?" Amal giggles. He says quickly, "I'm sorry, I meant—"

"It is okay," I say. "I did not see. What did you see?"

"Well, that girl just hit a chaka. Wow!"

"The outside ball is rubber but there is a metal one inside. Can you hear it?"

"No, but that girl did. Wow!" Everyone is clapping wishling too.

"It must be Urooj the cap tin."

"It is," says Amal who usually describes everything to me but not today.

"Urooj is also thirteen. Miss Fauzia thinks we should stop playing at thirteen."

"Why?" asks Amal.

"Big cause she is Miss Fauzia," I say loudly.

"Wow!" says Omar. "Another six runs!"

I am getting used to his wows. "Urooj has seventy percent vision in her left eye. Wow!"

"Mehwish!" says Amal.

Omar is cough-laughing again. "You're really sharp, more than these chips!"

"Be nice about Urooj."

"I am nice about Urooj. I think we will win big cause of her then you can give everyone the mithai. She is five feet five inches and her brother is six feet three inches he was not in the car when she had her accident she told me. She has a scar on her neck—"

"All right, Mehwish," inter ups Amal.

"—and scars on both her knees she could grow another two inches like her sister who was in the car and died."

There is silence now. Then I hear Amal put the flowers on the floor before the stair bends and the second ro starts. There is not much space so my toes are touching the buds. They are small some are still damp. Omar leans across me I think to offer her more chips I want some I reach into the packet and feel his hand in Amal's. I do not know what ghondaywoo means in French but in English I think it is something like round about big cause I am in the middle and Amal and Omar are going around me. I remember gravityG. Heavy objects have strong pull. Omar is fat. "How much do you weigh?"

"What?"

"God, Mehwish," Amal hisses.

"I—I was just wondering if you are heavy."

I hope he laughs but this time he does not. After a long time he says, "I'm five feet eight inches and quite thin. I've never weighed myself. Once a doctor did, I think I was about sixty kilos. For a man that's not heavy."

I raise my hand and find his face. I feel his sir prize. His cheek is not soft and not hard. It is like one of Zara's leather jackets. I move a finger up in the other way hair grows the under

166   the geometry of god

neath hair wants to come out. He has scars and bumps on the cheek bone his eye brows are long and rinkled. He has shut his eyes. He is consintrating like I do I like that. His hair is silky and long it falls in his eyes. He does not have a funny nose like Noman. He has a must stash prickly and long and moving big cause he is starting to smile.

"Now you know," he says. Amal pulls my hand away as if it is blowing a horn. "I think you've won."

Everyone is cheering high heels gall up down stairs Amal tells me to give Urooj the cap tin mithai and starts on flowers for Miss Fauzia again I give them to Omar "You take them" he says "Good thinking" I say "See you" and we leave.

The Periodic Table of Stinks Shades and Sounds

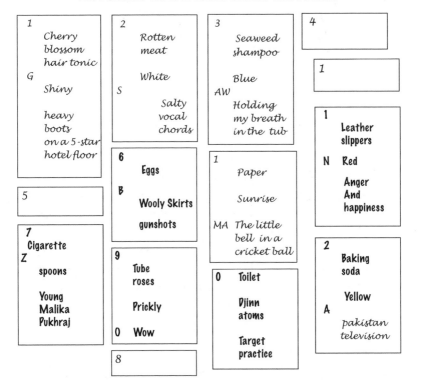

I was saying.

I keep a table of things it began when Amal was teaching me to make Braille with matches stones and broken pots if I got cut she would clean me with Det all which smells like a corner and burns.

The big letter is for the name. The small words are what I smell touch and hear if you say the big letter name. There are empty boxes of all sizes big cause the table is never complete and each box is in pencil in case you have to rub it out quickly to make a change. Sometimes a feeling is repeated for different things and boxes are not really needed. But the periodic table was made by someone who wanted to explain. He wanted tidy ness so if I use it I should also be tidy even if in my head I am not.

G = Generals
S = Slugs
AW = Amalicetus Whale
B = Bagpipes
N = Nana
A = Aba
MA = Miss Amna
Z = Zara
O = Omar

First Amal helped with the table but she stopped at Pakistan Television for Aba. Miss Amna finished his box she helps when Miss Fauzia is not looking. We keep adding and taking away. Today we added Omar. To fit him Miss Amna made the bagpipe box smaller though Amal had already drawn it and she moved Zara to the left also making her again. Miss Amna did not want to make Miss Fauzia's box till I promised it would be our secret.

First it was also number one then Miss Amna told me the Braille story which I will repeat a little now and more later.

In the 1700s which is before I was born a French man Valentin on a ghondaywoo saw clowns pretending to be blind though they *were* blind reading books up side down wearing ugly glasses pretending to be deaf going ee aw like don keys the crowd cheered. This made Valentin sad. So he built a school for the blind clowns. His first student was a beggar who could see a coin by rubbing it. He was twelve years old he was younger than me. He learned to read with coins then wood blocks the way Amal taught me with matches and stones. His fingers could feel letters at the back of a page so can mine. When Amal and Miss Amna write or draw I read the creases Amal calls negatives then I flip the paper and read the bumps called positives. It is the way Amal reads rocks.

Miss Amna and I were playing this word game one day then I started drawing her feeling front and back making sure she was neat. I heard Miss Fauzia's foot steps like target shooting and her toilet smell before I could hide it she stole the page and told Miss Amna off. She slapped my hand and said drawing and writing for fun is not allowed the Prophet said those who are punished most by God are the makers of figures. Later Miss Amna said the sayings of the Prophet were spoken "out of con text" which pee pull do when they want to make their own unimportant idea sound important. They make a place for it. A pretend box.

Miss Amna said we should do our learning secretly which makes it better. And she said if someone does not like how well I read and draw it does not mean they are important or even Miss Fauzia. They are just someone and if I give them a number or a name I give them a "con text." In my periodic table I made Miss Fauzia zero.

I have made many boxes for Amal but she keeps hopping out. I leave them empty in case she feels like staying. I put zero someone in a box big cause I do not want her bumping into Amal.

I have not yet made a box for Noman but *Amalicetus* at the top has moved a little to the left to make a small space for him. He is always at Nana's house in Islamabad. They are always *khus puss khus puss* discussing discussing. Noman's father does not like Nana. He says all the boxes are all ready made they can never move they are not in pencil. He is in the gowment. Junayd thinks Nana should be care full but he does not even keep a guard. Amal says all the guards are for her.

•

Corrections: moustache not must stash. People not pee pull. Religious not real ijaz. Lust and lusty not lost and losty. Zara told me that. Also adulterated not adult or adultery.

•

Corrections: Amal hit me the day I touched Omar at the cricket match. She hit me when we got home. She said I was doing more than seeing his face. What did she mean? Then she said sorry and cried. She said things I do not under stand for instance Omar was so relaxed how come he is not that way with her? Everybody *trusts* me big cause I am a child I am blind I can do anything it is always in oh cent but everybody thinks she is too grown up they do not *trust* her most of all she does not trust *them* and does Omar really love her? She cried so much and kissed me so wetly I had to put a pillo on my head.

•

I like waking up with the sun when the mozzan who calls the prayer is the one who sings. He is like Omar with a wide tooth brush moustache thin nose and a packet of Chili Chips. But if it is the man who is angry to wake up for God then I wish I had put a pillo on my head.

Today is the Omar type. I lie in bed and listen. His vocal chords are long and relaxed. When he says *Allah o Akbar* it is the *ah* which makes me glad. He holds it for four seconds each second climbs higher in the sky like a kite enjoying the breeze no other kite can come near and cut it. Then he says *bar*. This is a cut. It means stop playing and climbing and flying. *Bar* is Miss Fauzia. Four more beats everything is silent. Then she is zero the kite is free. It starts to fly again.

The mozzan ends on a note that stays for a long time longer than four beats.

Once Amal told me what this silent note has. It has "longing" which means to keep looking for what you know you will never find. Like Pascal in Nana's story. Pascal cried when he saw the tick big cause it was small like him. The note *ah* is the tick and I am in it. So is Miss Amna Amal Nana and Aba. But the silent end note is the tick falling. Not just falling. It is the tick lost. It has gotten mixed up with big things in a big field it does not have enough gravityG pull it is alone.

The silent note has still not left. I want to chase it away with another song maybe Hari Prasad on the flute or the tape Nana loves of Pathanay Khan who is a Sufi with more silent longing than a millyun mozzans. I specially like *Ghoom Charkhara Ghoom.* Spin spinning wheel spin. When he says it I have to twirl. I know where the tape is but I do not play it not big cause of the music but big cause of how I feel when the music stops.

•

Miss Fauzia says to real eyes my drawings and questions serve no purpose. To understand "purpose" I have to hear the difference between "calling" and "singing." She says the mozzan calls not sings. He is to be obeyed not enjoyed. There is no use imagining who he is or what he eats big cause he exists to serve Truth. That is why I exist also. Instead I get "pleasures of the senses" which is very rong it stops me from feeling the pain of the world. The mozzan does not exist except to call the doctor does not exist except to cure the teacher does not exist except to correct all of us must be the Voice of Rem dee. Do I get this channel on Radio Pakistan? No. I get it from saying sorry my charts and figures are no rem dee they are use less and use less is ewil.

•

Today I have woken up in time for sehri I can hear Ama in the kitchen. I cannot hear Nana he is visiting for Eid which is either tomorrow or the next day no one knows.

Amal is asleep. I want to touch the skin under her eyes it used to be puffy from watching me too much but she will wake up and get angry. She tapped on my window in the middle of the night. If I do not hear her tapping and open the door she will get into trouble the way I would have if she had not saved me from manholes and thorns for so long. When I opened the door she said "If you say a word or make any shor I'll kill you!"

I said "I have to make sure no one hears *your* shor" but she did not get it. I meant *sure* in English meaning positive and *shor* in Urdu meaning noise. She used to think over lapping sounds were funny but not now she is too busy tapping on windows and running.

Window rainbow and yellow end in *w* even though toe ago and buffalo do not. Amal and Miss Amna think knowing this is use full.

When Amal is not tapping on my window she is working in a lab with boys cleaning rocks they find though she found the best one when she was smaller than me on the same day I became blind. I do not remember that day she does. I have heard her tell Zara "I am stuck looking around for Mehwish!"

Her breath is on my neck. In, one two. Out, one two three. I leave the room on tip toe.

I can make my own way around the house without making shor. I would be better at coming home late at night and tapping on my own window only I would hear it.

Ama is arranging the table if she sees me she will tell me to wake up Amal. I slip outside. I draw with dew on the car. It tastes dirty but is my first taste of the day. *Ah.* I like the smell of wet grass and I know the song of a bulbul is a soap bubble. A tailorbird never sits on the same leaf for more than a second. It will always tell you when it lands but not when it leaves big cause it will be back soon. It is calling and singing both. A sunbird can squeak but usually only shakes like a moth. Amal says its wings are rainbow. Some birds rarely talk for instance hoopoes. When the grass is freshly cut they walk in it.

Inside Aba is at the table. I smooth his hair with my dewy hands he squeezes me like a pillow. "You smell so fresh!"

"I want to keep a roza."

"Maybe next year. You are still too young to fast." He gives me a big kiss. A spoon taps the shell of an egg.

"When Amal was my age you said she should fast she did not want to."

"*You* are my baby. *She* was always grown up. All that time spent with your Na—"

"Where is your sister?" Ama puts a glass in my hand. "Finish your milk then go wake her up."

"Where is Nana?" I have learned this trick from Ama. If you do not want to answer a question ask another one.

"What have we done rong?" says Ama. "Apa Farzana was right all those years ago. We have been too lean ant with Amal. She is as free as a boy." Ama eats quarter roti with fruit jam.

I drink my milk slowly. "Bulbul is one word not two."

"It is your father's in flew ants." Aba mixes sugar in his tea. Sometimes there is halwa puri not today. "Do you know what he's done now? I have it direct from a parent at the school he is lucky hired him. Do you want to butter my toast?"

"Yes." I like to slide the small knife over the top of the smooth butter block. His tea must be too milky big cause I can hear Ama fix the color.

"He's going around teaching 'Look around you are really monkeys.' One little boy began to cry. Then your father said to visit the zoo and bow in wonder. One little girl said she visited the Lahore Zoo and bowed in dizzy ness it was so smelly. Your father praised her for having a reaction and told the boy he was a silly thing who made all the children scared and a few went Oy bandar! His parents are out raged rightly so. Thank you Mehwish that is enough. They are saying he is a Hindu who were ships the monkey god. Others are once again suspecting he is a her tick. Rightly so."

"He is not a her tick. He is my father."

"I have found out other things. To an older class he gave a speech. You know which one, we have all heard it. We accept a thorty blindly and what not look at how the Party of Creation rewrites our creation one minute Jinnah is a kafir the next a save year. So what does he do?" Now he is eating pawridge. I think the subject of Nana has confused him he normally eats the pawridge hot before the egg and toast. Now it is cold. "He gives them a multi pull choice test and in it is a trick question." Cold pawridge flies out of his mouth onto my cheek. Ama has stopped chewing. "What is this question? I will tell you. It is so shocking I cannot forget. It is: If God is perfect why did He make us? The choices are a. There is no God b. He is also flawed c. We are also perfect."

"Maybe we can talk about this later."

"Why? Mehwish is a sense able girl, am I right?" I think he is looking at me so I nod. "I am a librail man who does not need to go around giving speeches about how librail I am. I just am! I do not marry my daughter off! Let her study use less things if she wants! I do not force her to fast. Let her sleep if she wants! She thinks like Dubai Airport she is Duty Free? Let her sleep all day!"

"Mehwish, go and wake her up."

"She does not know how lucky she is to have *me*!"

"I have not finished my milk."

"Not *him*! *He* failed everyone. He said those who ticked a and b were doing what they always do. Guessing. And those who ticked c were thinking but not enough! Now you tell me. If the man is so keen to have young sters express them selves why punish them when they do? He has *one* correct answer and that is his. Let me tell you though I am sure you can guess."

"*I* can guess."

"Poor baby." Aba squeezes me. "You are upset."

"But I *can* guess."

"Hurry up and finish your milk and wake up Amal."

"The correct answer big cause it is his is that they should have ob jacket to the question! That would have proved they had minds! Instead, they went home and told their parents. Well, I have said it before. He is a her tick."

"Is a her tick different from a his tick?"

"Haven't you finished your milk yet?"

"Was Pascal's tick a he or she?"

"Where do my children learn these things? Who is this Pascal?"

"What is taking you so long?"

"Do you like this kind of buffalo milk?"

"There is only one kind of buffalo."

"I like the other kind."

"She must have met this Pascal boy at Zara's house."

"This kind of milk is too thick for a tick."

"Your father should be care full. Hasn't he heard of section seven eight nine?"

"What is section seven eight nine?" I hear something. Maybe a lizard on the carpet. Or a moth in the corner.

"He has *never* said anything for it to up lie. He is just play full."

"Play full? Wife, what is rong with *you*? I do not think much of Apa Farzana but maybe you need more of her! Next you will say there should be no shor yet!"

"This is really not the time."

"Did you mean sure or shor? We are all ready making shor!"

"Poor baby." Aba kisses me again. "Are we too loud? These are very adult things. But a Muslim state needs Muslim laws. *Shariat.* One word." He spells it and puts down his spoon. "I should brush my teeth before the siren goes off."

The front door opens I hear Nana's slippers. "Lovely morning for a walk."

Somehow I feel guilty. I think Aba and Ama do too they do not speak or move.

Nana comes closer. "I went to Jamia Hajveri. Haven't for a while. Well, maulvis can hate Sufis but their shrines give people jobs. Hello, Mehwish. You're up early."

I run to him rap my arms around long legs in a thin pajama which smells of leather and leaves. "Sufi is with capital *s* and I know how to spell shrine and shariat!"

He laughs dragging me to the table. Ama offers him tea.

"Later. I don't want to sit here drinking it when your fast begins." He relaxes into his seat. I squeeze in beside him. He asks Aba, "How's business?" They sometimes start politely.

"Good. Good. We have located another sight. More lime stone."

"There is no short age of wealth in our mountins."

"No. None at all."

Everyone waits I know what for. Nana to say the army steals the land Aba to say it protects it. Amal would say both Nana and Aba can dig the land for different things but not her she is a security issue. She is angry with both but most of all she is angry with me.

I notice I have finished my milk and hope Ama does not notice.

Aba asks Nana, "And how is—school?"

"Good. Good. I have located another sight. More young minds."

I start to giggle.

"There is no short age of wealth in our youth."

"No. None at all."

They are silent and I am giggling.

Nana says, "I had an interesting talk with a young boy yesterday. Noman. His father is a JP minceter. He pointed out that Zia band the teaching of evolution but allowed the digging of fossils to continue"—he stretches his legs I fall off his chair he pulls me back—"as if the two are some how un related. People are so touchy about the first and so in different to the second. The abstract is more real than the conk reet. Isn't that interesting? Is it big cause our religion is so abstract? Any way, with religious parties now in civilian gowments, their in flew ants has spread. They not only hate ideas but rocks—the same rocks they see no problem buying and selling."

Ama begins to clear the table. I slide my empty glass under it.

"You always speak as if you are above us!" Aba's voice shakes. "We chairish our religion, which says nothing about *extinction*. Only Judgment Day. The next life is what this one is for!"

"And buying and selling."

"That is a day to day matter! The best way to protect our faith is to keep it separate from day to day matters."

"Then why do we need religious laws?" I sit up. The moth in the corner. It was Nana. "If heaven is not on earth, then keep them separate."

"You—you have dillbritly trapped me!" Aba stands up. "You are very clever with words. I am just a simple man. Now, if you will excuse me, the siren is about to go off."

"It went off ten minutes ago."

•

Amal finally wakes up and leaves for college with Aba. Usually he also drops me to school on his way to office but today Ama lets me stay home to play with Nana. I am hoping now that Aba is gone he will be more happy than angry. I show him my periodic table. He grunts in a happy way I think big cause he is number one. Aba is number two.

"Why red?"

"Your slippers are red."

"Did Amal tell you that?"

"Maybe."

"She used to like how clean they stayed even when we walked in mud. She hasn't noticed they are brown now." I wait for him to finish. "Why isn't Amal here?"

"I put her in number five—"

"No, I mean where is she?"

"She just left for college."

"She did not say good bye."

"You were in the bath room and Aba was waiting in the car."

He grunts not in a happy way but I think he is finished.

"I am making a box for Noman what color—"

"*How* is she?"

He always inter ups.

I want to say angry but it would make Amal angry. I also want to say sleepy but then I would have to explain she was with Omar and that would make her more angry. Zara would want to say she is Inlove. I say nothing.

Nana waves the page. "All right. Why isn't she *here.*"

"I put her in number five and made it number one like yours then I put her in number four and also eight and even—

"I am about to say box number nine with Omar but I know she will be angry so I just look down.

"Yes?"

"She is in all the boxes."

"I see. And your mother, where is she?"

I do not know how to answer that question also.

Nana is quiet also. "I see. Who is zero?"

"Someone."

"Someone like djinn atoms?" He chuckles. "You heard Noman and me discuss that?" I nod. "You hear everything." Should I tell him I heard him come in earlier when Aba was talking? No I hold back with respect. He wishpers, "They are after me."

I do not understand. Who is after him? I want his happiness only. I touch the page hoping he will say something about the other boxes. But what if he asks who Omar is? I take it back quickly.

He always brings something to show me he used to do the same with Amal. Before she found the whale ear with the hidden *S* he showed her a rock she read it with her hand. By now she must be in her lab reading other rocks. She has told me how. She compairs one bone with an other from a different time. This is called co relation. Amal says co relation is only possible big cause people do not only see with their eyes ears and hands but also with their memories.

I under stand why she is angry with Nana and others for getting in the way of her reading. I under stand she thinks they make her "blind." It is why I am angry with Miss Fauzia. But Amal does not think I can under stand big cause I *am* blind. I have not told her about Miss Fauzia who got angry when I told the class about the hidden *S* she said it was a lie and only one type of story is not a lie called all gory dewine story telling. All gory dewine story telling is when real animals like birds not imagine airy like whales speak use fully in the Voice of Rem Dee. When Miss Fauzia re sights the Quran she speaks in the Voice but no one under stands.

There is one Braille Quran in class we do not read Arabic we touch it only.

Nana puts a coin in my hand. It is small I can feel a tiny star and cress ant with my thumb nail when I scratch. "It is the flag."

"How much?"

"Smaller than two rupees." I keep scratching.

He is sitting in the rocking chair made like a baskit with holes that leave star marks on skin. I squash beside him the chair squeaks we rock. "A clue. It is less than a rupee."

Then I know. "Twenty-five paisas."

"Clever girl. Twenty-five paisas wouldn't get you roti today though it was minty just five years ago."

He rocks I scratch. When Amal first told me a coin is minty I thought it was a sweet and put it in my mouth. She slapped my head so I spit it out quickly. She said mint has many meanings. For instance Nana is a mint of use full ideas. But he is not a sweet.

I ask, "Is it Eid tomorrow?"

"We sell brit Eid when the mullahs say so. Their Moon Sighting Commit Tea goes off in a plane in search of the crip tick sat light."

He explains what crip tick and sat light mean and spells *committee*. Each committee has its own plane in its own sky with its own stars that hang with gravityG pull and each committee wants to see the real new moon first.

"It is a comic race."

"What is a comic race?"

"*Cosmic.*" He spells it, laughing. "They play their own blind cricket and we are the last man in!" His breath smells a little like Det all but I will leave it as leather in my table. "Pakistan will be split on Eid. Some will eat tomorrow others will be made to wait, hungry for a better real newer moon." He rocks harder.

I have lost his happiness. I was hoping he would help with the box for Noman. And also that we could listen to songs that make us happy.

Nana scratches the coin with me. "This, Mehwish, is all the moon we can have."

I know why he is upset. Amal did not say goodbye.

We have lunch alone big cause Ama is fasting.

He is happier after wards chats to me as if I am Amal or Noman. Did I know Aristotle was rong about the eye? He thought it creates light like a torch but one thows and years later Ibn Haitham said the opposite. The eye reflects light it does not create it. Ibn Haitham did many experiments for instance he made a hole and lit many lamps and noticed all the lights go through the hole in a straight line. They did not mix. Later people used the experiment to make a pin hole camera.

"The eye is also a pin hole camera."

"Is mine?"

"Not exactly. But the eye is not the *only* pin hole camera."

"My nose?"

He laughs. "Your nose, ears. And *inner* eye. Memory. What do you think, does the mind create light or reflect it?"

"Ask Iqbal Bano."

He laughs again. "You are a funny girl. You get that from me!"

We are listening to Iqbal Bano sing ghazals and Nana is humming along. He stops and asks me which I like best a qasida, ghazal, or qita.

This is a trick question the only one I know is a ghazal. "Ghazal."

"Ah, beautiful but me link holy!"

"What is me link holy?"

"*Melancholy.*" He spells it. "Cup lits for the love sick. What do they say to *you?*"

"I want to make a box for Noman."

"Do we create love or reflect it? Does it all ready exist? Is it dewine?"

"I want to make a box for Noman."

"Which one?"

"Next to number four Miss Amna made the lines straight. I cannot by my—"

"No no, which ghazal do you like?"

"The one we are hearing."

He chuckles. "Give me a cup lit or two. Your own. It does not have to be about love. It can be about anything, even a sher, as long as it is not in a pen!"

I was thinking of boxes but this inter uption stops me thinking completely.

He waits. "It does not have to be *me link holy* and we can change other laws. But your cup lits should rime. This law has a fine if broken!"

"I cannot do it."

"Come on, Mehwish. Your Nana needs three cup lits."

"Can you make your own?"

"All right. I will give you three cup lits and one box!" He clears his throat.

A golden sunset on the River Nile
Ibn Haitham reflects on the eye
"I see the moon not with a sun
No fire no heat I speak no lie
But with a nudge a nose a coin
And most of all a play full child!"

"That did not rime!"

He laughs. "It was all rong. You do it."

I clear my throat and think. Nothing happens.

"Do not think so hard. What is on your mind?"

"My table."

"You are stuck on your table."

"Before lunch you were stuck also. On moons and mullahs."

He is quiet.

I start to feel for rimes on my toung out loud Nana does not inter up. "*His hair is always greesy.* Greesy. What rimes with it?"

"Easy rimes with greesy, but poorly."

"Messy? It does not rime."

"It will do. You are right. Noman should sham poo more."

"And he talks all the time. About the Mutzil lights. Spell."

"M-u-t-a-z-i-l-i-t-e-s. From Mutazili. To dis agree."

"Who were they?"

"Well, that's a long story. We might get stuck!"

"Tell me in a ghazal."

"It was *your* turn."

"I promise I will give you one also."

He clears his throat.

They're called Mutazili who dis sent or leave or split
They lived a thows and years ago and now they are extinct
The first was Ibn Atta a man who cried free will
He said a man has reason a voice a rime a wit
His words lit a candle and others dipped their wick
Ibn Rushd Ibn Sina Al Kindi all men of free spirit
But with Al Ashari and Hanbal the flame was extin guished
Now we have all become slaves of dead lit rilists!

I repeat the last line to see if it adds up. "*Now we have all become slaves of dead lit rilists!* It is okay even with the *s* it rimes. Spell the last word."

"L-i-t-e-r-a-l-i-s-t-s."

"What does it mean?"

"You *know.* In your heart you have felt the fear they put there every day. In schools, at home, in laws that try to make you use less."

"Miss Fauzia."

"There you are."

"She is zero."

"Good point."

"No I mean she is the zero someone in my table."

"I see." He waits. "Now what about your ghazal?"

"I have a bad ghazal about Noman."

"Wonder full."

I clear my throat.

His hair is always greesy
His teeth have a gap
His toung is always messy
I think he should nap
He will fit into a small box

I stop. "I have for gotten the last line."

He gives me a big kiss. "When you have five perfect lines you do not need a sixth. New law!"

"I want to finish it." I clear my throat. I think I remember.

He will fit into a small box
If he wears no shoes or socks

Nana claps. "Excellent!"

But it is not the last line I wanted and I do not like this one. "You end it."

"It is yours, Mehwish. And it is perfect."

"Please."

He waits. "All right." He clears his throat.

He will fit into a small box
Bend knees free of or the dox

I go over both last lines in my head but cannot decide which is better I do not even understand his. But I understand we are both rong.

His toung is always messy
I think he should nap
He will fit into a small box
If feet are on his lap

"Oh, that is the best!"

"Will you make the box? You have to use a ruler and press hard with pencil."

"I think you should do it. So what if the lines are not straight?"

"You promised."

"All right. You have such a *sis tim*."

I hear his pencil scratch the side of the ruler. I do not say it is not my sis tim but the man who made the table first in my head nothing is neat I hear different alphabets one English one Urdu plus the Braille one Miss Amna is teaching me. Amal says we any way listen with at least two sets of ears big cause we are always under sir whale ants What Others Say is everything girls specially are born with crooked necks it is partly fear partly sir wival big cause we depend on others for everything even roti.

"It is small." Nana inter ups me. "As you wanted."

"What color are his socks?"

"I have never noticed."

I ask him more questions I am sir prized how little he knows. Noman and Nana talk so much they do not even notice each other. But in the end we make this box:

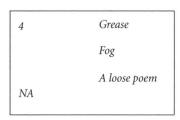

4	Grease
	Fog
	A loose poem
NA	

Since Nana is all ready N he is NA for Noman Anwar his full name. He smells greesy and is the color of fog big cause it was foggy the night he first came to Nana's house I was not there. He sounds like a loose poem big cause he and Nana always *khus puss khus puss* discussing discussing.

•

After two more days it is Eid in Peshawar after three in Lahore. Nana says the Pakistan Sighting Comedy divided the moon and fed it to the poor instead of meat or roti. For that they must pray to God and goras. Aba cannot wait for Nana to go back.

We make many poems before he leaves and I learn the structure of a love poem Nana explains it with *Tum ai ho na shub intizar guzri he.* The first two lines of this poem end in *guzri he* this is the tag. But in the next cup lits only the second lines end in *guzri he.* You can play with the form only if you stay inside it. In a way it is like my table. I can put anything in the boxes but they have to stay in the lines and they have to have a number even if it is zero.

Until now we were stepping outside the box the lines were loose. But now Nana wants to follow the laws he wants a legal ghazal. While we think of one Nana says, "Everyone under-stands love through the images of love like the bulbul and the rose or the hunted bird or eye lashes like daggers or we have made up our own. But a ghazal in English is illegal!"

I repeat what Amal once told me. "A language is like a whale it comes from something else. Urdu from Persian, Hindi and Arabic."

"That is very clever, Mehwish. All form is fluid, poetry, moons and whales. I myself prefer an Urdu verse to an English one but would rather hear a lively one in English than a stupid one in both. Like you I also get tired of *me link holy* and bulbuls and roses, though it depends on who says them and how. Speaking of which, Mehwish, does Amal have a bulbul?"

I am sitting on his lap in the rocking chair and nearly fall off. He says it so suddenly I am "caught off guard" which Amal says does not happen if you listen with two sets of ears. But I was only listening with one set and now I do not know what to do.

Nana caught me so I did not really fall but he is no longer rocking he is waiting. "I see. Is he a nightingale or a crow?"

I still do not know what to say.

"I see. Are you all right?"

"I do not want to have to explain." I am very proud of my next sentence: "When I have to explain I feel like a hunted bird."

"Wah!" Nana is also proud. He forgets Amal and keeps repeating, "Wah!"

But then I know we both start thinking of her again.

After a long time he says, "Will you allow me one almost legal ghazal full of *melancholy*?"

"Yes."

He clears his throat.

The world belongs to who ever takes it; it will change
The trunk of a road, the fluke of a toad, the seat of a court;
    it will change

A slip pery wish a flying fish a man der ill us finx
Croc dile teeth man tea feet grand child speak; it will change

The slant of a hill the depth of a sea the eye of a bee, life is flux
A boy with no socks in a little girl's box; it will change

When girls dig hidden whales they pre wail,
When adults get in their way they fail; it will change

A bone not revealed but created
A book not preserved but con fiscated; it will change

A prayer unheard is not without creed
A land unfree is destined to bleed; it will change

A heart birdined is still die lated, it receives it bends
It remembers to lend it makes light and gives heat; it will
    change

Like a pin hole it sees dim inshes deceives in creases con seeves
Grows rusty and creeks, irroads with the wind or like Tethys
    reseeds; it will change

But there's an other wise a way the heart waits dif eyes time
    and stays true

Quite simple it is, wise and won deris, in loving You there is only one rule; it will not change.

"That was a cup and a half lit!" I kiss Nana's cheek.

"Well it was only half legal! I am no good at last lines!"

"Who did you mean by You? Me or Amal?"

"Who is her bulbul?"

"When I have to explain I feel like—"

"I know. Do not spoil a good line by over chewing it. Now, this Omar in your table, at least tell me if he sings like a nightingale or croaks like a wet crow?"

I forgot his name was below the periodic table where I explain the boxes. I pretend to be in oh cent. "I like his voice."

"Just what I was afraid of."

"But Amal smells like sin a men not a rose. *He* does. A tube rose."

"Yes, I see that in the box. He is both the bulbul and the rose. Dizz aster."

•

It is late at night Amal is not home. I know she is with Omar looking at the sky. What is up there? To me it is not Pascal's tick that is scary a tick or musk eat toe or fly you can touch it is the stars and moon that are scary they have no smell no sound not even longing. They are not funny or melancholy or legal or illegal. What are they?

Amal

Tiger lilies in spring bloom on the Mall. Noman telephones in a panic. He'll only talk in person. We agree to meet after lab, where I assist students of comparative anatomy.

I walk to the room that exhales formaldehyde, wondering what to make of him. He swings between insufferable neurosis and delightful warmth. He always wears the same ratty trousers. His hair smells stale. He shares with Nana a knowledge of philosophy and a dislike of ideology ("one develops, the other dictates"). Though their growing attachment still makes Mehwish jealous, she's smitten by the gap between his two front incisors when he smiles for her, which is often. She touches it; his tongue meets her finger. They laugh like children—though he's twice her age!—and then I feel outside *their* growing attachment.

I still try to keep her in a visual pouch. But *Mehwish Marsupium* needs more room to hop around by herself, pretending to blow bagpipes, singing, "*We have all become slaves of dead literalists!*" Apparently a line from a poem she and Nana invented last year, when Nana spent Eid with us in Lahore. (Aba glowered; Mehwish saw it.) The two have many codes now, the way Nana and I used to, they way he and Noman are developing. We're beginning to feel like four shifting chambers of the same heart.

Nana's supposed to visit again this year but there's some delay. I'm not sure what.

●

After lab, I wait for Noman in the cafeteria but he doesn't show. Remembering how frightened he sounded when he called, I feel uneasy. I don't call him.

Mehwish

This year Nana does not visit us for Eid. I am hearing things
about him. Yesterday Amal said "His toung is under arrest it
has a collective copyright and copyrong and his mind is not
working legally it will have to have a hearing." I did not
understand.

Noman does not visit Nana any more.

Next month, I will be fifteen.

•

Ama and Amal are at Nana's hearing on my birthday. Before
leaving Amal said Nana's accusers had dug up a hidden *S* in a
rock that did not exist. From the Trial Court in Pindi it will be
carried to the Pindi Bench of the Lahore High Court on the
Mall.

While Aba and I eat cake I tell him I know the order of all
the brick buildings on the Mall they were built by the British
some of them wore skirts. "The High Court is next to the GPO
which echoes loudly it is also a good place for hearing."

Aba grunts. "Do you want more cake?"

"No thank you. Amal says the Mall is Go tick-Victorian
and the pipers who march around the Go tick-Islamic heart of
Lahore today in the same old red skirts look—"

"Do you want more cake?"

"I said no thank you."

After cake he watches Pakistan Television.

I ask "What happens in a hearing? After you find the
letter?"

"Letter? There are no letters there are witnesses in a box a judge on a bench and an accused all alone in a chair."

"A folding chair?"

"Mehwish, you are too young for this. Go to sleep."

"But it is not night."

"It will be if you try to sleep." He carries me into Amal's and my room.

"Will you help me make a table of boxes, benches, and chairs?"

I hear the door shut.

Noman

Fixed a time to meet Amal but let it slide. I wanted to tell her: The charge against Zahoor is made because of me. I always knew it would happen. I was pushing toward this day. Now that it's here, I try to pull away. I did the pushing toward badly and do the pulling away even worse. I couldn't tell her what I know: when JP members run out of things to complain about, they look at back issues of *Akhlaq*.

In April, during the long days of Ramzan, the Jamaat-e-Pedaish runs out of things to complain about. The Communists are dead. The JP's kitty's drying. International experts decide Pakistan can have its experiment with democracy. They rewrite the religious parties that rewrite them thus:

> Islamic laws bad.
> Nuclear democracies good.
> Nuclear democracy in Pakistan bad.
> Female Secretary-General in the UN bad.
> Female President in the US bad.
> Female Prime Minister in Pakistan good.
> First female head of a Muslim State, elected twice. Very very good!

April is bad. April is cursed. April sends the Prime Minister to the White House to "save" Pakistan's "foreign image" thus: "I am against Islamic laws and Islamic laws are against me. I love you. Can I have my fighter planes? Please get rid of my rivals. I did pay for them—I mean the F-16s. I love you." For a second, Pakistan flickers back to life.

Aba checks his calendar. No invitations to conferences on the stationary world on the horizon. He travels less and so do I.

Bad. At meetings in Lahore, the Party of Creation decides how to reignite interest in Islam in increasingly freaky masses.

Someone suggests taking Jinnah's speeches to the lab again. The one that proves he wanted a secular state and was an unbeliever. Or the one that proves he wanted Sharia and was a believer. This is quickly vetoed. "We have already done that! Think of something original!"

Someone else suggests I do several short features in *Akhlaq* on ____ *and Islam*, liberally filling in the blanks, beginning with Women and Islam. This is easy.

I pluck and prune syntax and gist. A woman's weak judgment forbids her from holding authority. It's already written. Regarding adultery, I ignore, *"Leave them…"* And see, *"Flog each…"*

And so on. But then at one meeting, while I'm mentally rehearsing other options, Aba asks, "What about that man Zahoor?"

All the blood rushes to my ears.

He continues, "You have said nothing since you—" he hesitates. I think he means the speech I wrote for him, Blueprint for Afterlife, but he doesn't want to say I wrote it. I still can't believe I did write it. "—since you sent him the warnings."

There are murmurs of recognition. Fleeting impressions of a man against whom I collected evidence. Whom I revised and abstracted. And they forgot. Until now, as we face International Rebuff. Periphery breeds a Second Satan. They start remembering a man against us. A man gathering an army. A man putting our life and afterlife at risk.

I blurt, "That was a long time ago… " and stop. In the year-and-a-half since I've known them, Zahoor and his granddaughters have become my family. We're a triangle with four points. Even a sifr. A magic bloom. How can I turn attention away from them? From *us*? "I can do a short feature on bees and Islam?" No one hears me.

One man scowls. "I remember him well. He spreads lies against us." Murmurs of consent. Louder consent. And then a wave's unleashed:

"He is a threat. Future, present, and past." Applause.

"You said they think of him as a *messenger*." Pounding fists.

"I say we at last press charges against him. According to your proofs." My face burns. Shoulders, icy. Shiver and sweat.

"You said he defiled our Prophet."

"You said he burned pages of the Holy Quran."

"You said he is an Ahmadi."

"Who calls himself a Muslim. You said."

"He is, you said, a kafir."

"To many gods said you he prays."

"To animals he said you pray."

"No awe, you said, of the divine, he said."

"Our Great Leader he said you."

"Outraged a said tenet with life, he."

"You said with fine or death or both to court."

"Ordinance section amendment as above federal shariat section as above Ameen, you said."

The chairman rises. "I say He says. Agreed!"

Mehwish

A hot night in June the cooler is on. Each year I like to smell the new grass mats and listen to the water drip from the pipe. I like the fan it drowns out everything the news Aba watches about the President stepping on the Prime Minister and the Chief of Army Staff stepping on them all and Ama asking Apa Farzana how to put Amal on the True Path. I am glad the cooler fan blows all the noise out with the heat.

I lie awake with the small coin Nana left before going back to Islamabad last year at Eid. I have still not seen him since. He is in police protection which Amal says is an oxen moron. Other oxen morons are secure cell and awarded imprisonment for instance for one hundred years. It is good Nana has not been awarded yet.

I scratch the dot moon and star on the coin. If Nana were here we would think in cup lits not fully legal he would tell me if the moon this month is plump or crip tick and tell me to draw boxes and figures so what if they are not straight they are not use less.

Four lines come to me I suppose more qita than ghazal or maybe knee the.

> *I have never seen the moon*
> *I do not care who does*
> *If I cannot touch its lines*
> *Then it is not but was*

I put the coin away and go to Amal's cub bird and find two things. One is a drawing. I think she made it for me big cause it is scratched deep into the page so I can feel it. But she must have forgotten it is at the back under her old torn panties she uses them for waxing her thighs. I feel the drawing.

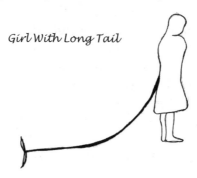

Girl With Long Tail

Who is the girl and why does she have a tail maybe it is Amal her self?

The second thing I find is a soft ball. I hide it and wait when my fingers open the moon will rise. I make this drawing and leave it on her pillow:

I am a new moon

•

Corrections: I do not know where Noman is he is not in his box. Nana is a lion in a pen. Miss Fauzia is too loud for zero. My periodic table is not true any more.

Corrections: I hear commas more now and I know it is interrupt not inter up, thousand inverted commas surrender neither devils nor cigarettes.

I organize my thoughts, the way I do shampoos and soaps along the edge of the bath tub. The lines of my drawings are more even I can link them, without pins or chips. But there is a lot of noise in my house, Ama and Aba always talking about Nana and section eight seven nine which used to be nine seven eight and school is also not quiet except when Miss Amna and I read, by linking dots.

I was telling you about the Braille story which is also made of dots.

In the 1800s still before I was born, a child called Louis Braille became blind in an accident like I did. His country fought many wars against Russians who later fought Afghans who are still fighting each other and Louis Braille's home was full of people escaping wars, one was a man who made a code for reading messages in the dark.

The secret writing was made of dots, it gave Louis Braille an idea for a new alphabet in Valentin's school. The new alphabet was straight and made with holes so b and d became:

Louis Braille kept improving the alphabet playing making mistakes the way God played with a man der ill us finx. But lots of seeing people did not like that reading made the blind who loved Louis, see. That is why I am telling you this story. I am "co relating."

In the 1900s I was born. If zero someone catches me reading or drawing or humming she does not only say stop and hit me she keeps pulling my ears my hair and shouts, in a very loud voice.

I need a pillow on my head.

One day I brought a pillow she took it and no one not even Amal noticed we had one pillow less in the house. I drew a bird flying fast:

I made a whale with toes a cress ant ear with a hidden dot star S I called it Nana's Hearing:

It could talk.

I asked "How long were you lost before Amal found you?" and soon I was asking if there were sunbirds on long leaves millions of years ago and do you know a lot of people are wondering today if you could swim or not? and again I was stupid. I did not smell, the toilet smell.

"What are you doing?" She pulled my ear.

"Nothing."

"What are you doing?"

"Nothing."

"Then what is this?"

"Nothing."

Did I not understand the purpose of stories drawings poems science history songs everything, is to spread the message not What Is Your Age Scientific Name Diet! She kept on I could not tune out "Who do you think you are why do you think you're different why can't you be like others sit quietly pray someone marries you use less?" I asked if I was awarded imprisonment for one hundred years but I do not want to repeat the horrible things she said about Nana.

Then she and Miss Amna had a fight the other girls cried my ear rang Miss Amna, kissed me.

Later she said "Miss Fauzia needs to save young girls but you will not let her save you." I did not understand. "Miss Fauzia is too bitter for art." I still did not understand except that it was the first time she said anything bad about Miss Fauzia. When she said "Do not worry" I think, she was also crying.

•

Today Miss Fauzia has not come to school she is sick Miss Amna is like before. Her vocal chords are relaxed commas. She asks the class what we remember about Louis Braille and his "in sight" which is when you see inside. Then I have an "in sight." I say "Miss Fauzia wants to join the Moon Sighting Committee so she can fly over Amal and Omar and report them to their mothers." The class goes silent. I know I am going to make someone angry.

At break time Miss Amna is the first to be angry.

"Why did you have to say that thing about the Moon Sighting Committee now the children will tell their parents and Miss Fauzia will be very angry." I do not know how to answer this question or if it is a question. "And what is this business with Amal and Omar? Is this the Omar I put in your table?"

So I tell her. "Yes. That year after the match I was looking for you and you were not there Miss Fauzia called Ama to say she had seen Amal with a boy. Ama and Amal any way did not like each other now it is worse. Amal and Omar still meet but in secret."

Miss Amna sighs. "Their *love* is the moon. Well, you have fed it to the whole school now your mother will get more than one phone call."

My stomach hurts it is worse than a tick getting lost in a wheat field. I hold it with both arms.

"Forget it. There is never any use in crying over spilled milk."

"I have never spilled milk."

"You just did."

"I have never spilled milk."

"It's just a way of talking."

"I have never spilled milk."

"Mehwish. *Forget it.*"

The pain does not go away. I say what I have been wanting to say for a long time but have not big cause of Miss Fauzia. "Amal says when people force you to admit they have all ready decided you are guilty."

"Yes. It's like that."

"She says she does not have to admit her love for Omar big cause it is not rong." She strokes my hair. "But she does not say what Nana has to admit."

"Because," she keeps petting, "I'm sure it's not true."

I drew a bird flying fast for Nana. When he has to explain he feels like a hunted bird. I drew the hunted bird flying away quickly.

I keep squeezing my stomach. I have questions in my head like Amal in traffic lines are crooked cars are over taking left and right. It is as noisy as the silence when she leaves me in a place I do not know.

"Let's read. You like that, don't you?"

I try to feel less upset about what I said by mistake and Miss Amna saying I would get Amal into trouble and Nana all ready in trouble. I agree to do some reading.

She gives me a book I have not read before I get stuck on many words Braille is more difficult for me than the raised curly letters of a seeing person big cause I learned those first Amal taught me. Now I feel two raised dots which is *b* or *c* and three for *l* and three again but in a different order maybe *o* and then four I think make *g*.

"Clog creates all boys—"

Miss Amna starts to giggle she should not I get confused with all the missing dots.

"Which word is rong?"

"Clog."

I rub the page again. "Clod?"

"One letter you are miss reading one you are imagining."

I rub again. "Clue?"

She gives me the word. "God."

I still only feel the two upper dots though I want to believe her. "Then *C* is for God."

"Read it properly, Mehwish." She tries to stop laughing.

Now I like her laughing so I say it again. "*C* is for God."

"All right, but you will read it properly for Miss Fauzia."

"All right, but you also want Miss Fauzia to go off in a plane with the Moon Sighting Committee and never come back."

She laughs very hard now sniffing tears which happens sometimes when you hear something very funny it is not crying though if someone did not hear the joke they might think so.

"Don't you?" I repeat.

"Oh, Mehwish." She sniffs. "Promise me you will never say that to Miss Fauzia."

"All right but you have to tell me I am right."

"I do not!"

"Then I do not have to promise!"

She finally wishpers, "You are right but you can't tell anyone. So now you have to make me *two* promises. One, you will never miss read *God* in front of Miss Fauzia. Two, you will never reveal that my deepest wish is to see her off on a one-way plane."

I make her two promises.

•

I have made a drawing that talks to me. I have named it Clog.

"When is Nana coming back?"

It answers but I do not understand.

"Where is Noman?"

It answers but I do not understand.

"Will Miss Amna be sacked?"

It answers but I do not understand.

"Does a dog always become a whale?"

It answers but I do not understand it does not speak English, Urdu or Braille.

Should I tell Amal the drawing talks to me? I cannot decide. She is home early from college in a good mood after a long time. The milk I never spilled has not spilled I try to forget it like Miss Amna said.

We are making a zoo in the lawn the way we used to soil shapes that collapse and never live exactly the same way again. She used to like the half water half land things the best was a crocodile. She smashed clay pots we pushed the pieces all the way down the tail all the way down the lawn. It was our pride, a dragon we tamed.

I think what we are making today is supposed to be a foot.

From the kitchen I smell butter and choclit. She has made brownies with wall nuts for Zara who will be here any minute so she will be late. I like Zara. I will like today.

It is November the weather is just right. Ama is inside with Apa Farzana. I say, "Ama does not like Zara."

"No. She doesn't like her parties till dawn in rivers of alcohol. And of course, she doesn't like that Zara talks in millions. What are we making?"

I thought she knew. "A tail." I help her carry loose dirt from the pile near the pond where we used to have tad poles and fish. We leave the foot and start a tail. She cuts the tip of the tail it has two points one half I pull out like a wing or Omar's moustache. I am satisfied with my half of the split tail and the mud on my fingers.

"Red smudges all over your face." She brushes something racing up my dress maybe a prickly caterpillar.

She is not angry with me. She is—what is the word? I do not know, I cannot find it. But I mean she is easy with me today the way she used to be without thinking she has to play with me but only because not big cause she enjoys it.

I still do not tell her about Clog. But I am going to ask if a dog always becomes a whale when suddenly she says, "Do you remember when Nana took us to the zoo and showed us a mander ill us finx?"

"Yes. It was the year you kept rozas and began to not want to explain."

She is silent but not in an angry way. "I was about your age. I asked Nana if everything is or isn't like something else then what is or isn't God like. He told me of two ways to know Him. Khayal and zauq. Do you know what they mean?"

I have heard the words but I do not know what they mean. "Yes." She does not believe me.

"Khayal means a thought, or an image. But where does it come from? What's the seat of intelligence? And how can the same intelligence that calls Him by many names force a man to admit what he didn't do? Or force a woman?"

I hear her play with mud maybe she is back on the foot. I want her to keep talking so I ask, "How many names?"

"Many names and many meta firs for instance jugular vein." She spells it. "You don't really *see* the vein but you can say God is like a built in pulse, reminder or warning. Whatever your khayal is." She puts my finger to the side of my neck I feel a throb. "Bet you don't understand a word I've said!"

"I understand some words."

She laughs. "What about zauq."

"Which one is better?"

"Don't answer my question with a question!" I did not know she knew my trick. "Okay, I'll tell you. Zauq is taste. Joy. When your mind is empty you surrender completely you become the jugular vein."

"Which one is better?" I ask again.

"Zauq. It is even lovelier than khayal because—" She wishpers so softly even my ears miss it.

"Because what?"

"It's physical. Not abstract. To understand, first you need a mortal."

"I do not understand."

"No, of course not. Any way—"

'Is it an image of God?'

"What?"

"You said khayal can be an image."

"You can have an idea khayal of Him such as 'God is great' but not a picture khayal."

"But Ama wears a tavis around her neck."

"Those are His words. Not picture."

"How does she know? They're written in Arabic."

"You either believe it or you don't. Any way, we were making a zoo."

We hear a horn. Amal brushes her hands clean and stands up.

I wish Zara was more late because Amal has not talked so much to me in so long. I tell her I am glad she gave the flowers to Omar not Miss Fauzia she says that was a long time ago. Then she says, "Ama does not like Zara but Ama is clever. She knows Zara's is the kind of family you might need one day. With Zara's father now a core come under and Nana the topic of every drawing room and Aba's business not as good as he admits and me behaving like a boy and you asking questions, not sitting on Apa Farzana's lap, that one day has come. So, despite their promise kiss ways, she doesn't stop me from meeting them."

"Where is Nana?"

"The court proceedings will soon be quashed."

I do not understand and she has not answered me at all.

Amal

I brush my hands on my jeans and realize the report's still in my pocket. I'll show it to Zara while Mehwish waits by the mud zoo.

> *Zahoorul Din verses The State* 1995 Pcolg 78987 (Criminal Misc. Application No. 50-Q)
>
> The accused, Zahoorul Din, aged 70 at the time of the occurrence of the offense, April 1994, of moving about merrily in school saying all things are accidents calling himself a prophet and gathering a huge army. The principle was called and to avoid further shame the school was closed for the day. Other evidence has come to light. It is known that he wrote the names of all four caliphs on the souls of all his feet and a student has come about he is indeed eye witness to the feat there was a name on each written in blue ink…

I remember that day in April last year. It was just after Noman called in a panic. We arranged a time to meet but he never showed up, or called. Still hasn't.

I spent the day of Nana's "offense" in the lab, preparing rocks the men brought back from a dig. In my mind, I saw inside the skull of *Pakicetus*, this time with adult eyes, all the way to the sigmoid process in the middle ear, what Mehwish still calls the hidden *S*. (*S* for what? She says Sleep. I say Sin.) Then I looked at the rocks around me and thought, No skeleton is ever complete or completable.

But I always have to try. So I kept chipping at quartz, coral, clay. A fossil bone is rare and I usually only find traces. A bird crest. A reptile claw. But that day in April, I got lucky. I scratched off dirt and bleach to find ribs and ankles. A crocodile's? I lost myself in the delicate insistence of scraping and brushing, dogged by one worry: Suppose I reassemble the bones wrong and the copy in no way resembles the original? Am I revealing or creating? Thousands of people, maybe millions, will carry an image in their heads of a prototype that never was. And *I'll* be responsible for this terrible corruption!

Though I can't dig in the army fields, in my lab-kitchen, I'm given the power to cook, lay the table, serve the banquet. But with ingredients missing, rocks poorly dated, fossils hastily cast and left to crumble on the floor. The wrong acid's in the wrong bottle. Key bones dissolve. Because I have to present something, I do. It's like being told to play a raag with broken strings.

There might be a recitation but no revelation.

I slid a kneecap in a femur. It fit poorly. I was looking for a trace image in a blind girl's visual cortex, rubbing creases and dots and shaping a different language. In the lab, I'm more like Mehwish than she can know.

I came home unsatisfied with the way I reassembled the leg.

To confess my complicity in forging antiquity, I phoned Nana. "My crocodiles are counterfeits." He laughed, wheezing in a way I wished I couldn't hear. "Are you sick?"

He cleared his throat. "All first models are necessarily lost. It's the people who deny this who make trouble—" He coughed again.

"What's wrong?"

Ama snatched the phone. "Aba, you need rest." I heard protests but she hung up. Then she told me what had happened. "The student witness was clearly bribed but your Nana still needs to deny the nonsense charges. Calling himself a prophet, of all things! Walking on the names of caliphs! But you know him. He says because he's innocent, he has nothing to deny or defend." Then, weeping, she pleaded, "Can Zara's father help?"

When I called him from university the next day, his voice was clear, and he sounded angrier than last night. "They grill me to ignite the very physics of my faith! My faith is what they bury when they force me to expose it!"

I knew as a child that Nana would only say what he is when others stopped asking. They never did. His accusers have created a prototype and now it exists. Nana is no more than a counterfeit crocodile.

As Zara gets out of the car, I show her the report, which concludes:

> The accused was arrested on 5th May 1994 and held under police protection. He filed an application under section 15-P locg for quashment of proceedings. On 1st February 1995 the Trial Court held that the evidence of the crime left no room for further examination the appeal was dismissed and the accused sentenced to life imprisonment. The case was transferred to the Pindi Bench of the Lahore High Court and awaits court proceedings till 1st Dec 1995.

December 1st is less than a month away. Zara pulls two pink braids, looking ridiculous. I want to tell her he's in solitary confinement for his protection. (The other prisoners have been told he's a thief, but of course they know.) His cell stinks. No toilet. A guard takes him to a pit four times a day. No fan. No window. This bothers him most. No light. "*How will I read?*" They even took his slippers.

He doesn't know his lawyer's strategy: plead senility.

He doesn't know mine: use Zara.

Her father's a corps commander. Ama knows this is the favor I have to ask. It's why she says nothing on days when I slip into Zara's car to be with Omar.

But when Zara finally looks up from the report and starts to giggle, "*On his feet?* You didn't tell me!" I understand why she's taking so long to read it. She's stoned out of her mind.

Mehwish

I usually put what Zara says in inverted commas.

She is wearing baggy denim over alls *swish* as she stretches on my bed lights a cigarette and tells Amal, "You haven't given me the week's Omarnama."

I would also like to hear news about Omar, not just for the week for at least two years. But I know Amal makes a sign "not in front of Mehwish" because Zara puts an arm around me and says, "It's just Mehwish."

"You don't know what goes on in her head."

Zara laughs. "I can find out." Her hair is in two braids she says are party pink.

I say, "You are the one who talks in millions."

She laughs harder and Amal goes, "*See.*"

Zara covers my ears but not well a cigarette is in one hand. "You were saying."

"Mehwish. Not one word."

I nod, smiling as well as I can.

Amal talks. "I'm tired of the *scene*. His friends—your friends. Thrill-seekers who drive-by gossip. They boast how much *pai* they eat, how many four-wheel drives they own, how many girls they de flower. Strut to Hira Mandi to collect gold, not spend it."

I know Hira Mandi is near the Badshahi Mosque and it has only red lights.

Zara says, "While their girlfriends clutch them for protection from *those* women."

"What a dumb expression, de flower!" says Amal. "What did you carry between your legs, lily or pitoonia?"

"Dog flower."

A pillow lands on us Amal has thrown it they giggle as if they are my age not twenty-four. Maybe the cigarette has fallen and we will catch fire.

Zara says, "Ignore them, silly. They're just DIs."

"DIs?"

"Desi In vertebrates. All worm, no spine. In their dreams, a girl's a breeze. A dick a kite. Where can he fly?"

"Omar's the kind of man Nana once warned me against. Meat and late nights rolled into one. Speaking of Nana, Mehwish—"

"But what meat!"

Another pillow lands on us they giggle and fight I almost fall off the bed.

"Mehwish," Amal says again. "Why don't you go play zoo?"

"I do not want to."

"Let her stay." Zara puts an arm around me. "Let's dress you up!"

"She doesn't want to. Speaking of Nana—"

"So, where are you with Omar? Still stirring the halwa?"

Amal wishpers, "This is impossible," and stands up. "Time for a sweetener." She leaves the room.

"What's wrong with her?" Zara asks me. "Is it Omar?"

"No. It's Nana."

"Where did she go?"

"She made you brownies."

"Oh yum. Where's your mother?"

"In her room with Apa Farzana. Are you modling?"

"Yes, baby. I'm on this week's cover." She takes a magazine out of her purse I feel it, it is shiny. "You're thin and leggy like me. You could also do it. Not like your sister with those boobs that drive men crazy!"

She blows smoke on my face I hear a scratching she is putting the cigarette out. It is her job to stand in front of a lens while the lens looks for the best in her. If she is on the cover it means the lens found the best.

"Do you want to come to the studio some day?" A long finger rubs my neck. Zara likes to give massages and rubs and is better at it than Amal when she would bathe me.

"Yes."

"Are you a woman now?"

"I have not started my period yet."

"Lucky. But late."

Ama also worries she says at sixteen I should have my period Amal started at twelve and Ama at nine. "What is a dog flower?"

She laughs loudly her laugh is deep and rolling it does not hurt my ears.

"Is it more dog or more flower? The dog whale was more whale."

"It is a flower and you have it too!"

"I do not think so. We do not have dog flowers in our garden we have lilies I like."

She keeps laughing. "I like lilies too."

"Amal says you are promise kiss."

"I'm what?"

"Promise kiss."

"What's that?"

"I thought you would know."

"Does it mean when I give a kiss I keep my promise?"

The door opens I smell warm brownies and coffee steam.

"We can ask Amal."

"She knows I do just the opposite!"

Amal hands me a plate. "Ask me what?"

I touch a brownie dotted with nuts oozing with choclit. I forget what I wanted to ask Amal and she does not ask again everyone wants to eat. I stop minding when Zara says things I do not understand.

"Is it loaded?"

"Of course not."

"Your mother's busy with Apa Farzana. Invite Omar over."

"Can I have more?" Amal puts a second brownie in my hand.

Zara is giggling she has not stopped laughing today. "I did dove at a raven London."

"Zara, shut up," says Amal.

"We'll have one like it with music that puts you in hard trance." She gets up. I hear her flip the stereo on a terrible beat hits me like stones.

"You can dance to that?" asks Amal.

"Clubbing with Zara. You me Sanjit Omar and disco biscuits."

She raises the volume and I cannot enjoy the brownie any more.

"Are you crazy?" Amal laughs lowering the volume. "Who's Sanjit?"

"The one I love. His mother can't stand me."

"Whose mother can?"

"How to impress your Ama, your Apa Farzana? So many begums, so little time! Want to know my latest craze? Uncut men."

"Zara, shut up!"

"Do you mean his hair?" They do not hear me.

Zara says, "Do you remember that thing about a male dear? Before his horns are full blown, a young dear is very shy."

I decide Zara likes shy men with long hair.

"How old is this Sanjit of yours? Ten?"

"The young ant ler has a protective skin like the four skin. When the skin pulls back, he's as beautiful as—"

I touch Amal's knee. "Where are the brownies?" She does not hear me.

"As beautiful as what?" asks Amal.

"It's like this," says Zara, and shows Amal something but I cannot see.

"Where are the brownies?"

"Oh Mehwish!" Amal puts one in my hand again instead of helping me find it.

"Come here, Mehwish. I want a promise kiss!"

Amal changes the tape and Zara sings along about a mission airy man. I like Zara's voice and the singer's voice is also not salty but today the noise in my head is getting louder.

Zara and Amal fight over volume.

Now the music is lower but the throbbing in my head takes more space suddenly I do not want to be here with them. They are hopping on my bed shouting:

"Believe!"

"Beli*eve!*"

"*Believe!*"

"*Belieeeve!*"

I do not think Amal and Zara notice that I am gone.

"Finally you are here," says Ama. "What is your sister doing with Zara?"

Instead of asking another question I answer, "Jumping and shouting."

"About what?"

"Parties. With ravens and doves."

"At a party? Next it will be snakes and cheetahs. All they think about is parties!"

"They are slaves of the senses," says Apa Farzana. "There is still hope for this one. Come here, beti," she pulls me. I kiss her damp cheek. She always sweats even when it is not hot and her sweat is sweet. Her voice shakes it is high sounding, like a small child's. Amal calls it sugary and says even salty is better. To Amal Apa Farzana is zero someone.

When I became blind Ama's face went loose her eyes drooped. She says Apa Farzana got her mussles back. But she still says "all my fault" someone did not want her to have the child she was pregnant with so I became the target. Apa Farzana has helped many women find forgiveness through Quran and Sunnah and being care full of the evil eye which looked at me and took my good eyes.

But Ama still feels guilty because of me. When Apa Farzana turns a page and starts to read, "Alif Lam Mim…" she is really explaining Ama's shame to me.

"There are many sex but be wear of false sex interpreting Islam according to their will, hmm? On the final day it is against them God will unleash his most severe penince." She re sights and trance lates: "*And every time their skins are burnt off, we shall rip lace them with new skins, so that they may taste suffering in full.*"

She has an other book I hear the pages turn. "The miracle as explained here is that no matter how deep the burns of hell fire, the sinner finds no relief her nerves will not be damaged, there is no loss of pain, her skin is put back immediately, hmm?"

Ama says, "So that they may taste suffering in full."

"You are forgiven. That is also a miracle. But it is because you feel pain. Hmm?" She puts a hand on my back I jump her cold fingers burn. "What do you think, Mehwish? Is it not a miracle?" She pinches my cheek shakes my head side to side.

I wonder if I should tell them Zara was also talking about skins. Four skins. Instead I ask, "What is the other book?"

"It is not polite to ask Apa Farzana questions."

"It is all right, hmm? This is a pam flit the Jamaat issues every month for us."

I have another question in my stomach it rises and sinks.

Apa Farzana re sights from the beginning in her child's sugary but old person's shaking voice but she has missed something. My question comes up again. Letters start to swim in my mind there is a huge tub it is very dark instead of soaps or boxes there are just these letters she has not spoken. They are made of dots and they are made of bumps. Then I know the question. "How come you did not begin Alif Lam Mim?"

"Mehwish! That is *two* questions you are disturbing Apa Farzana it is unacceptable do not interrupt her say sorry."

"Sorry."

This time Apa Farzana does not say it is all right and her voice is not sugary or shaking. "It is just like that. Sometimes it is just like that. You must be care full with her. She is at the cups of woman hood. It is not good. She should be watched. Or she will go the way of your other daughter and your father. Now, it is time for my next up ointment."

When she leaves Ama slaps my cheek for making Apa Farzana angry.

•

Amal is not slipping out tonight. Our room still smells of smoke. "Did Zara find ravens and doves?"

"What?"

"She said she would have ravens and doves at her next party."

"Oh God, Mehwish."

"Do shy men have four skins? Apa Farzana says only false sex do."

"Please stop."

"Why do some surahs begin Alif Lam Mim or Ha Mim while others do not?"

"What?"

"Why do some surahs begin with letters but others begin with words?"

Amal sits up in bed in a temper I can tell the springs shake she says, "Shit!"

I know she will start complaining about wanting her own room in a bigger house we cannot have. So I ask, "Do you want a house as big as Zara's?"

"*What?* A house? What do you keep talking about, Mehwish? Why don't you let me sleep? God!" She has become angry like before not like when we were making the zoo she punches her pillow and probably puts it on her head.

I start to cry.

It feels good and bad at the same time I cannot stop.

Amal touches me. I kick her. It feels good and bad. I do it again.

She holds my legs down. "Stop it!"

I am stronger than I know. I can shake her off.

She tightens her grip. Now I am stuck.

I sit up and slap her.

"SHIT! What's gotten into you? STOP IT."

"STOP IT YOURSELF."

"SHUT UP."

"I HATE YOU."

"BITCH!"

"BITCH YOURSELF!"

She slaps me. "BLOODY MEHWISH."

"BLOODY AMAL." I slap her back but she dojies me. I have never been so angry. "YOU KNOW I CANNOT SEE YOU CAN HIT ME I CANNOT HIT YOU BACK WHAT EVERY ONE DOES YOU MISS FAUZIA AMA I HATE YOU ALL I HATE YOU I HATE YOU BLOODY AMAL!"

She is crying. "I have tried. I have *tried*!"

"YOU ARE ALL THE SAME."

The front door opens. It is Aba's voice but I cannot hear the words.

•

In the morning Amal says she does not want to live in our house any more. I thought she would say sorry to me like she has before when I have been upset. But I have never been this upset neither has she and she has never cried in front of me *because* of me before. I feel guilty and I do not. She should say sorry.

"Don't be ridiculous," says Aba, eating breakfast. "You two should say sorry and forget about last night. You are both *animals*. I do not know why women say they are soft and loving and what not and go marching and what not about piece and justice and how gentle the female race is if you ask me they are more than any man should have to handle! And I have to handle *three!*"

"I am not a woman yet," I say.

"You *are*," says Ama. "And a cheeky one. Do not forget what Apa Farzana said."

"Another woman!" says Aba. "Now what nonsense is she putting in your head?" He is eating porridge hot today.

"I can go live with Nana," says Amal.

Aba drops his spoon.

"Your Nana has more than enough to cope with right now," says Ama.

"I want to know what is happening to him," I say.

"Drink your milk," says Ama.

"He'd love me to stay," says Amal. "We have a special understanding."

"So do *we*," I say.

"Pha!" says Amal.

"We *do*."

"You don't. If you don't want me living with Nana I'll live at the college hostel."

Aba slurps his tea. "Don't be ridiculous. You do not know what kind of boys and girls live in hostels! You come from a good home you should be grate full and stop this grumbling. Have you ever heard *me* complain?"

"We *do*." I repeat. "We have a very special understanding!"

"You do *not*. Or you would know where he is!"

"We *do*. I *do* know."

"Stop it, both of you!"

"You understand nothing! You know nothing, you speak rubbish and you never let me sleep! I'm going to live with Nana."

"If you live with Nana in Islamabad how will you keep seeing Omar in Lahore? And go thrill-seeking in Hira Mandi?"

She gasps.

This does not feel good. Only bad.

"What?" Aba's chair creeks. "*What?* Is this the fellow at the cricket match?"

"Yes," says Ama her voice shaking like Apa Farzana's.

"Yes? *You* know but I do not? What else do you know? What else, Mehwish?"

"She has seen him often since the cricket match. She knocks on my window at night. She goes out with his friends who eat a lot of *pai* and own a lot of cars and fly a lot of kites and the girls are a breeze. She is tired of the scene."

His chair falls as he stands up. I put the milk back on the table. It spills.

Aba is walking toward Amal. The words did not come out of me.

"We told you to stop seeing him. I don't understand!"

I am sorry, I say to Amal. Except that I do not hear it.

Ama blows her nose. "There have been more calls. Everyone knows!"

"*Pretender.*" It is Amal and she is not crying her voice is not loud or salty or sugary. It is a thorn. A branch of red thorns. "*You* know. You know, and you have known, and you have said nothing and you meant to keep saying nothing as long as Aba never found out. Now *he* knows, you act *wronged*. You act *wronged*."

Ama sobs. "Listen to her! We should never let her out of sight! And her language, did you hear them last night? What is she teaching Mehwish!"

I am sorry, I say again.

There is noise in my head Aba shaking Amal she telling him to stop he hitting her they do not stop for a long time Ama cries but not Amal. I made her cry the night before but Aba and Ama cannot make Amal cry.

•

She is in bed beside me but a part of her has left.

Aba did not even give her the chance to do what she hates most: explain her self.

When the moon goes down she says, "It's not my seeing Omar that troubles Ama it's being found out. There's no such thing as a proxy mother, Mehwish, remember that. Ama doesn't work for Aba or God or Apa Farzana. She works for her self."

Does this mean she is not angry with me only Ama?

Before the sun rises she says, "At least you didn't repeat the bit about de flowering and four skins. Why not?"

It is not a question but an accusation. *A pulse, reminder or warning. Whatever your khayal is.*

I fall asleep with a finger at my neck.

•

The second time Amal leaves will be to marry but it will not count because she will have all ready left me.

The first time Miss Amna leaves will be for ever but not because of me. She says it is to get married but the girls agree with me. She has been sacked for teaching use less things. I remember when Nana got sacked he went to the Khoon Jirab Pass. I hope Miss Amna will do the same and take me with her.

She does neither but our last day is still a good one.

She sits with me at break. I chew a cold omlit with tomato and pepper but no onions I do not like them cooked they become slimy. I try to imagine eating alone from tomorrow. I cannot. She is in my periodic table and the place is fixed. I will never wipe the box or even move it. When I tell her she says it is the best thing anyone has ever said.

"Thank you, Mehwish." She kisses me and I feel sad. I stop eating omlit.

We sit quietly till I tell her what happened last night. "I had pain under my belly button and in my legs also between my legs where Zara has a dog flower I felt sticky."

"A dog flower? Sticky? You must have started your period. Did you show Amal?"

I shake my head. I have not told her she was right about the milk spilling.

"What about your mother?"

I shake my head again. "Amal has told me where the pads are so I put one in my panty like she said in case that was it."

"What if it wasn't? Stand up."

When I stand up she checks that the back of my kameez is not stained. It is not.

"You have worn the pad correctly. Or not started. You should show someone."

"No."

"Was there a smell?"

Yes but I do not know how to describe it. Then I remember something. "Once I found a hair pin left on the wet sink. Amal said it was covered in rust. I tasted it. That is how it smelled."

"Oh." She kisses me again and stops insisting.

I could ask her the question that made Apa Farzana angry and that Amal also did not answer though I do not think she even heard it. I could ask Miss Amna why some chapters in the Quran begin with letters like Alif Lam Mim while others do not. What do they mean? But I like the quiet around us so I do not ask the question. Maybe some letters do not have to mean anything except make a pleasing sound under the quiet. I clear my throat and hum a tune.

Miss Amna smiles at me. "Winter comes so quickly in Lahore there is no warning one day you need no sweater the next you have caught a cold! Aren't you chilly?"

"Ama has given me a sweater but I know my arm pits will smell worse than Det all if I wear it." She laughs. Her laugh is a big cricket ball bell. "Do you want my omlit?"

"No thank you, Mehwish."

I decide to tell Miss Amna. "Clog talks to me."

"Clog?"

"I asked about skins burning again and again like Apa Farzana said about Nana."

Miss Amna strokes my hair. "I'm sorry to leave you at a time like this."

I have still not seen Nana but everyone talks about him in a roundabout way. He is "repeatedly taken to court" I do not know where or when and if Amal and Ama visit him they do not take me.

The bell rings. Normally Miss Amna is afraid to return to class late but not now.

She keeps stroking my hair so it never tangles again. "Mehwish, who is Clog?"

"I made him."

"Mehwish, I think I know who Clog is. Please listen. He is not yours to play with."

"But I am his to play with."

"That is very different."

"It is just Clog."

She hesitates. "All right. If you're sure."

I am happy she stops insisting. I need to think about all the things we have not discussed for instance single letters like rhythms.

"What are you doing?" She touches my finger which I did not realize was on the side of my neck.

"Seeing something."

"Remember your promise to me. You are to keep Clog hidden from Miss Fauzia."

"All right." I am sir prized when she removes my finger it is an interruption she knows I do not like that.

She keeps holding my hand. The bell rings again. "I have to leave now, Mehwish. But before I do, tell me, what's this about a dog flower?"

"Before Zara was de flowered she carried a dog flower between her legs."

Miss Amna gasps and starts laughing like a bell. It is very different from the bell calling me back to class. It is as if I have just hit six runs and everyone is cheering.

•

Clog talked to me more after Nana left Noman left Miss Amna left and a part of Amal left. I did not understand till tonight. Now I begin to understand.

Clog lifts his head takes a drink.

Here is the seat of intelligence
Bring a cushion for your thoughts
Sip a sin shoe us wine
Tell me what is your taste?

His words are as clear as a dream I had once asleep on Amal's shoulder. I was inside a song. When it stopped I felt empty. The same happens now.

"Clog?"

There is no reply.

I say the word again and again hoping it creates him. "Gloc?"

Nothing.

•

Clog lifts his head takes a drink looks around. He likes being newly born. He likes the taste of salt. It does not make his toung shrivel like a bitter vocal chord. He bends, sips again, looks up again. He notices me. His toung is sweet.

"I made you."

"And I: You."

"Between us there are no inter me dearies."

"No. Between us there is only sheer good."

•

I am again alone in the house with Aba. Amal and Ama are at Nana's second or third hearing no one knows maybe the Moon Sighting Committee. Aba shouts at Amal a lot now he says her friends are rubbish and does she think a university degree gives her the right to question him and what not. Amal says his word is stat tick. Stat tick makes the crackle on my radio when I turn the dial for a song.

Aba is watching Pakistan Television loudly he will lose his hearing. He is hoping the Prime Minister will not be stat tick. He is hoping she will be sacked.

If the President tells her to "get out" then she and Miss Amna and Nana can all meet in the Khoon Jirab Pass. Nana will arrive on foot in slippers Miss Amna on a bus at sun rise and the Prime Minister in her jet in a sugary dupatta. Aba says she used to be attractive but is getting fat. He likes the President in sherwani who Amal says Nana calls use less or *bekari* and Amal calls Not At All Attractive.

•

Clog lifts his head takes a drink looks around takes a step makes a frown.

I mean no variation in very asian
No particular party cooler
Nor can analogy make Plato
play toe or have an allergy

I say, "Do not make fun of my old spellings your lines are illegal I can rime better than you!"

"It is Clog verses the State!"

"You are a her tick!"

"I would rather be a his tick!"

I hear stat tick. "Do not go! I am sorry!"

•

Nana is home in Islamabad I went to see him. I have not seen him for two years not since we made half legal ghazals I have so much to tell him but I have to wait.

He is in a "dead lock" which is when you are neither sentenced nor freed. He says Power knows the best way to break is through monotony wear and tear.

The student who accused him falsely is the son of a wealthy feudal and core come under by working together with the Party of Creation they have become Power Plus. But Uncle Junayd who once gave up law for art has now given up art for law to help Nana. He knows many good lawyers who know politicians with stars and there have been protests for Nana so this gives our side a plus.

Nana and Amal are back to *khus puss khus puss* discussing discussing.

He has kept a security guard because Ama and Amal insist but he is always letting the guard go so he is not really under protection and like Amal he gets angry when you talk to him about "security issues."

•

Corrections: Heresy and heretic not her see and her tick whisper not wishper commander not come under.

Corrections: Noman is back! He is here at Nana's also after two years he smells different. I want to ask where he went but he talks a lot he says, "The blasphemy law was penned by two British men one I think was Sir Peacock, soon after the War of Independence. Pakistan made it a weapon of..."

I try to listen politely but Clog is also here. He says,

Learn to tell between
Hearsay and heresy

I whisper, "You are not supposed to be here get out!"

"Who are you talking to?"

It is Noman. I smell him again and know what is different. He has shampooed. When I touch his hair it is silky. I shut out Clog and Noman begins to joke with me saying he is an old man he is thirty-one. He asks how old I am now I say I will be seventeen this summer. I touch his mouth and feel the gap between his teeth but something else is different I have to remove my hand quickly. I never did that before.

I have to think about it. Amal hit me once for touching Omar she said I was doing more than seeing his face. She was wrong. But if she said the same now about Noman? I do not think he felt any change. I move away.

Noman likes Amal but Omar is still her only bulbul I know it is the same though she does not knock on my window or let me near when Zara visits.

Clog will not leave Nana's house. He used to only visit at school but I pretended deaf or Miss Fauzia would grow mean. That was my promise to Miss Amna I have kept it with a promise kiss. He clears his throat.

To understand the aww of law
Pick a lock or pen and draw
Trace a dot and let it sprawl
Feel from where it had to crawl

It was in eighteen sixty
The Empire was not thrifty
Muslims and Hindus lost
Freedom at highest cost

Sir Peacock fanned his tail
Wrote the penal code like Braille
Full of holes and gaps it was
Though it claimed to be for us

So the blasphemy law was penned
Sections seven eight nine and ten
For the Christian Crown to punish
Damage to temples and masjids

While it secretly felt glee
Lack of harmony brings ease
To the handling of rupees
Makes them sterling quickly please!

So today we have a mode
To find a verse create a code

Duller than death or the lock up
This gnawing sentence without full stop

And I hope you enjoyed the tale
Of when Sir Peacock fans his tail
There is still a lot to tell…

"I did not enjoy it at all!"

"Mehwish! Why are you shouting?"

"I am tired of you always discussing discussing!"

"Poor child, come here." Nana pulls me to him says "this is too much for you" and would I prefer to stay home next time? That was Amal's idea but I wanted to come.

"I do not want to stay home while you are taken from court to court!"

"Shh…"

I finally fall asleep listening to section seven eight nine ten eleven…

•

It is Noman not Amal who shakes me awake later. "Chicken soup. With peas and carrots. Amal says you like peas and carrots they are sweet not sugary."

He gives me the spoon I give it back. I have always fed myself but today I do not feel like it.

"My mother thinks it cures everything even hic cups!" I hear him blow so the soup does not burn my toung then I open my lips. The peas are still round. I eat in silence just him cooling the broth, me sipping. He talks about his sisters.

Shaista has three children. Sehr has married an engine ear in Canada and taken her cat with her.

"Meow is older than you."

"Where were you?"

"When?"

"When you were not here."

"I—I was doing penince."

"Did you know there is a silent *g* in gnawing?"

"I have felt it."

The next time I wake up I am back in Lahore.

•

The new teacher is Miss Hina she is afraid of Miss Fauzia. She wears flowery perfume her skin is soft she must be very pretty. She wants to "help poor people."

She leaves in one week.

•

Clog lifts his head takes a drink looks around takes a step makes a frown licks his teeth finds a crown neath his toung on the seat with two feet on her lap sits Miss Ad Hoc.

I tell him, "I want to hear about Miss Ad Hoc not Sir Peacock or death or the lock up."

I hear a flutter like a tailorbird taking off.

"Come back!"

•

After three more teachers Miss Raheela arrives. She is very tall with short hair and a forin degree. A forin degree does not come quickly from Lahore it comes slowly from a broad. Miss Raheela has come to Lahore to live with her new husband and new in laws. Miss Fauzia does not like her she says, "A forin degree does not make you clever nor your high airs!"

"But *all* schools must have a bookshop!"

She should not argue back but I like her for trying. This is my last year at school but it would be nice to have a bookshop in the last months.

•

Nana is still between penalty and dismiss.

Clog always follows me to his house with Sir Peacock and his tail and the gnawing sentence without full stop. Finally one day the weather is cooler it has rained the leaves are washed when I for bid law talk he agrees.

"A fine notion what is your motion? A silent wrist a Latin twist? A scientist—"

"Latin names long sentences and winding speeches are all devil's fruit! I want an early ghazal. When words were simple!"

"You want the melody of birds! The executioner is lofty words!"

"Oh hurry up!"

I am secretly hoping someone will explain why I no longer meet Noman by finding the gap between his teeth touching his lips letting my fingers sweep the rest of his face.

He clears his throat.

An early ghazal would be
Before the fifteenth century
When the form was loose and free
Not pure and proper like me

An early ghazal without girls in painted nails
Flicking lashes in a trail sending poets scented mail
Ringing bangles like a spell no true man can curtail
His love deep as a well for an object who will fail

If she speaks for herself.

She is only spoken of
Her voice fills us with mistrust
What does Laila know of love?
Or Shireen know of lust?

Let Farhad spin the tale
Of a passion
That inflames and ignites
With each dharkan
When ladies speak of flesh
What low fashion!
But Mujnoon is requested
To please cash in
On desire without restoration.

In this early ghazal find a hemi stitch
Tie a knot in it keep the petals rich

Catch the seeds in fists plant them in a ditch
Feel his mouth on tits lie back don't flinch

"I want to go home!"

"We just got here, Mehwish." It is Amal, angry.

"I want to go home."

"I told you not to come. Why don't you listen to me? I told you to stay in Lahore. We'll leave tomorrow, as planned."

"I want to go home *now*."

"I can take her back." It is Noman.

"*No.*"

"I think you and Mehwish should both leave today." It is Nana talking to Amal sounding tired.

"But I want to stay with you. She should not have come."

"But she *is* here and I am asking you to please go back with her."

"What's the matter, Mehwish?" Noman is moving close to me. "Do you want soup?"

"*No.*"

All three of us take the next bus back I stay quiet.

I do not to go to Nana's for a while.

•

In August Nana is taken away. No one will tell me where or why. Not even Clog.

•

In November three things happen. The President tells the Prime

Minister "Get out!" A small shed at school becomes a bookshop. Aba agrees to let Amal marry Omar.

It is Ama who asks him to let them marry. She says Amal has been "good" this year and Omar's family is also "good." They come to meet us. They say "Aur?" we say "Aur?" they say "Aur?"

Amal is twenty-five. Aur? Ama did not think she would ever marry let alone at a normal age to some one so good looking. Aur? Omar is allowed to visit our house "openly" and there is a small engagement. Aur? They keep discussing when to have the wedding. Amal wants to work and save and wait. Ama wants it as soon as possible so the good looking boy does not get away.

It is over three years since I met Omar at the cricket match he seems more stiff he sits in the drawing room without saying wow or aur. I do not talk to him it is not polite when adults are discussing important things for instance "Who all should be on the guest list not forgetting anyone?" I know Omar would be more interested in the new bookshop at school. He would laugh that all the books are for seeing people! The bookshop was built because Miss Raheela pulled a string. I wish I could show the string the books with no dots or bumps though it does not make much difference to me since I leave next month.

Nana did not attend the engagement he is still away. But we talked on the phone.

"Is this *the* Omar bulbul?"

"Yes. But I cannot hear his voice anymore he does not speak."

"Let's hope he sings."

I do not think he has told Ama or Aba that he already knew.

"Where are you?"

"Somewhere safe, Mehwish. You know how everyone is about security."

"Are there Marco Polo sheeps?"

"I will find out." He blows me a kiss.

I did not touch Omar's face I kissed him quickly on the cheek he patted my head like a holy man. I do not touch men's faces anymore except Aba's.

•

There is an old baba who sits in a chair in the bookshop I like to visit him at lunch he has nothing to do except stare at the books that no one buys or reads in case they are stolen. He is not blind he is illiterate.

One day I say, "We would be better off if you were blind and I could see." I do not mean to insult him I hope he will not be.

He is not. He laughs. "Well we are both blind!"

We play a game he pulls books from the shelves and describes their color paper size and I guess the inside. The first is thin with a hard cover. "It is all about a hidden *S*."

"What is that?"

"Look inside are there whales?"

"There is nothing but a lot of small writing." He puts it back and pulls out another.

"Look inside are there moons and aeroplanes?"

"No. There is no moon and no aeroplane."

"Then it is not about Eid."

He tells me to eat my lunch before the bell rings so I unpack my tiffin.

I chew one shami kebab he chews the other. I say, "My sister can read rocks."

"What a silly girl! Doesn't she have anything else to do?"

"She is going to be married soon."

"Mahshallah."

"Do you know where the rocks come from?"

"Only Allah knows."

"Amal says the rocks come from a time after Africa kicked."

"Acha?"

"Yes. The kicked off part was like a comma floating up to be an apostrophe."

He stops listening I walk back to class. The way is easy left at the bookshop exit straight for eleven steps at the banyan tree go around to the hallway, my class is the second door on the left. I know Clog will visit me tonight with a better way to tell Baba about Africa kicking.

•

I was right he is here but his mood is serious his voice is old.

Before it came under attack
Apostrophe, 'tween front and back

The stench of fish slime cartilage
A backdrop is the frontal stage

The backbone is a fine design
But does it put you in the front?

The yellow yolk is even better

Feed up front and guard your back

A pigment spot its only sense
A push that cleaves from back to back

In all transitions keep close contact
Shut all back doors fly open fronts

My pigment spot tells me whenever someone is in the room. Clog stays. I fall asleep with a feeling Amal described to me when the charge against Nana was first made. A feeling of doom.

•

The next day at lunch it is my turn to play the guessing game.

I hide a book behind my back. Baba guesses the color and cover design. Blue floral, plain green, small figures on a red carpet. He always says he has guessed correctly but I cannot know. Though I am tall there are books I cannot reach so I stand on his chair.

I feel a draft from up here and something prickly on my skin maybe light. "I did not know the bookshop had a window."

"Behind the bookshelf is a door not window."

"Is it open?"

"Yes."

A cool breeze blows between the shelves as I find a book on the top shelf. I tell him, "I did not know this shop has two doors."

"It was a storage shed and the back door was the front door."

I pick up the heavy book on the top shelf. Baba says to put

it back unless I am clean. It must be the Quran. I am not supposed to touch the Quran if I am "bleeding" which by now both Amal and Ama have told me I do. Today is the third day of doing "bleeding." I put the book back and since our game is over, I jump off the chair.

"Milk toffee?" He hands me one.

I like milk toffee it has a special texture almost sandy. "Thank you."

"I will get more from the canteen. And some lunch for myself."

While I wait for him to come back I eat my own lunch a boiled egg and chaat. The egg is just right not drippy or dry. It has been cut in two so I can eat it from the inside out if I want, by licking the yolk.

The yellow yolk is even better
Feed up front and guard your back

"Clog?"

He does not answer but he is here.

I keep eating.

When I was standing on the chair I wanted to ask Baba something but I did not. Now I think about it. If he cannot read how did he know what the book was? What if it was another big book with a hard cover and big curly raised writing not in Braille?

I stand back up on the chair and touch the book again though it is wrong. I open it. I rub it like a drawing. There are no lines bumps or dots so I leave the book get off the chair and finish half the egg. I start eating chaat. It is also good full of hot peppers and small raw onions, not cooked and slimy. I wonder where Baba is. Maybe he has gone to the small barbecue restaurant outside the school. There is one near our house also. I like to hear the small orange sparks that Amal says blow out from under the grill like stars while a planet grows into a chicken tikka, breast piece.

I do not get cramps on my third day. Only the first. When Amal confirmed I did "bleeding" I told her it was white.

"Why?"

"Because it is not real and meat smells white when it decays."

"But it isn't meat it's blood, which is red. And it's happening. It's real."

"The papers on Nana are called white paper they exist but they are not true." I kept trying to explain but she did not understand. I meant that just because something is done to you it does not make it real. Maybe it is not this way for Amal but I feel my period is being done to me and this me is not me.

The door shuts. I expect to smell chicken tikka but instead I smell fish.

The stench of fish slime cartilage
A backdrop is the frontal stage

"Baba?"

A soft laugh answers, "Baba is gone. I am—his son."

He comes closer the fish stink grows. "What are you eating?"

"Nothing. Why?"

I decide not to tell him. "The bell will ring soon." I close my tiffin box.

"Wait! What's the hurry?' He pulls up a chair, rubs my back. "I see you often in this shop no one else ever comes to. Why don't you sit with the other girls?"

I move away in my seat. Even worse than his smell is his voice.

I think about his question. Before the shop existed, I spent the break with Nadia and Urooj, walking to the pitch where younger girls play cricket and made up games like throwing a ball instead of rolling it. The shop is what Amal would call an "alternate space." Long ago she told me her alternate space with Omar was Jinnah Park.

The man moves closer, he strokes my head, his face leans into mine, he touches it with his other hand.

"If you are Baba's son how come you never visited before?" I stand up to leave.

He pushes me back down, holds my hand, pushes it over his face. It is a horrible face, greasy in a different way from Noman's used to be, this one is slimy onions.

"I do not *want* to touch you."

"You will never get a second chance. Have you *seen* yourself?" He laughs.

He moves my hand, down his onion neck, buttons are open, hairy. "Stop it!" I pull.

My wrist twists his voice changes. "What part don't you like? This? Or *this?*"

I stand up he pushes, tiffin box opens, food rolls. I feel the floor for my food. Again, wrist twist.

"Don't be afraid. Nothing you can do. The door is, shut." One hand still on mine, other, around neck. "Keep your hand here." It is not, my hand it does not, exist he has many hands, in many places. Small boobs, too big. "Relax! Enjoy your only chance!"

I pull.

"Okay, *be* like that!" Hand around neck, tightens another pulls, I know what. Amal always tied my shalwar in a double knot. I always do the same. He pulls the knots.

The bell rings. He stops, laughing forces me up. "Open it!"

In all transitions keep close contact
Shut all back doors fly open fronts

He growls. "Open it!"

"It is all ready open!"

"*I said open it!*" He leaves mine opens his, with my hands.

I start to cry, say the only thing. "The *door*. It is all ready open!"

He stops. "Liar! I locked it!"

"The other one!"

"What other one?" Rubs panting bites neck. Pushes me choke into wall.

A backward lunge across a front

A push that cleaves
A push that cleaves

"The door behind the bookshelf is open some one is coming I hear him!"

He hits me. "Lying bitch! No one comes here only Baba who is busy doing something for Miss maybe *this*." My right hand on a stick. Unties my first knot. I scream. "Shut up! What is that?" He is hitting two napkins hidden in panty hidden in shalwar. "A cock? Are you a boy? Or are you filthy? I am going to find out!" Pulls second knot, it gets tighter, curses, rips. A hole in the front of my shalwar.

"Go and look I swear by the Quran on the highest shelf the door is open and someone is coming!"

He stops. "Bitch, if you are lying, see what I do to you!"

He sees it on the highest shelf he begins to move away.

I breathe three steps, walk so quietly to front door really the back.

"You were right about the door—"

Reach the wall. Feel for the door.

"—but no one is coming." He shuts the door.

Knob. Key. Turn it left. Nothing.

"You lied about that."

Turn it right. Nothing.

"Oy!"

Leave key, turn knob. The door was not locked.

"Miss!" I shout more loudly than Amal ever could.

Where are the voices coming from I am running too fast I bang into a wall.

"What happened?" Miss Raheela reaches me I am bleeding white above one eye.

•

Amal touches my stitches softly. There are three.

"Does it hurt a lot?"

I say nothing. My eye cannot open fully. She lies with me the way she used to, my back to her big chest. She breathes on my face she has raised her head to look at me.

When she thinks I am sleeping she looks at all of me.

•

Amal keeps asking did you fall or was it something else...? It is many days since she began sleeping next to me again.

•

Nadia attends the graduation party I do not. Later she tells me Miss Raheela arranged for music paper whistles fancy hats and some girls were even dancing. She says, "You should have seen zero someone's face it was all gory." And she says next year the shop will have fewer books and more "supplies" like tape and paper Miss Raheela says so. "If we were starting now instead of leaving you could draw all you want!"

Ama and Aba do not force me to attend the party.

No one mentions the "son" no one knows what happened in the bookshop probably not even Baba alone in the shop, dusting his blue green books.

•

Nana is still Waiting but he attends Amal and Omar's wedding in November next year there is a lot of security everyone is tense.

He sits on my right side Noman sits on my left. They watch the bride and groom on stage. It reminds me of when Amal and I sat together while Nana was on stage there was a slide show I fell asleep that is when I first heard Clog. When I woke up people were angry with Nana while a man was ogling.

This year Amal told me who the man was. Noman. I have not met him like I used to I have not touched his face.

Clog lifts his head takes a drink looks around takes a step makes a frown licks his teeth finds a crown neath his toung on the seat with two feet on her lap sits Miss Ad Hoc.

To her side she can see a boy with shampoo seaweed tween his nose and his mouth lies a dent so sweet if she draws her thumb down there's a gap she will meet.

I will meet the gap between the teeth of the boy with shampoo seaweed.

But I will wait for the right note.

Nana puts an arm around me. "I do not know why your mother finds Omar good looking. And you were wrong about his voice, Mehwish. He is not a bulbul but a crow!"

Noman whispers in my ear, "If she wanted a crow she would have picked me."

Nana hears him. "Oh?" He is so surprised as if he has just seen Noman for the first time. His arm around *me* grows tighter. I rest my head on his shoulder. He will always smell of leaves.

Noman

One rose plucked. Two, actually. After a long engagement, my neighbor Unsa finally did marry, leaving me to tumble like a loquat from her bosom, straight down a gutter.

And now Amal.

I look at her, this crisp November in 1997. On stage, next to her groom. She's always been in love with Omar more deeply than I was ever in love with Unsa, whom I know I did love. Hope he deserves it. Silver threads dance across her blue top under the bright lights: the moon breaking in a pool of water. It becomes her, but anything would. Even a potato sack. In his white *sherwani*, Omar is surf to her deep sea.

From time to time she looks at us admiring her: me, Mehwish, Zahoor.

Why did I just say to Mehwish, "If Amal wanted a crow she'd have picked me"? To make her jealous? To make her lean closer to me?

She's grown very silent this year but we don't know why. She hasn't been going for walks. She doesn't swell—in figure or complexion—like a girl entering womanhood. Like Amal always has. Yet, to me, she's beautiful. Her face is delicate. Her skin, thin, translucent. It's a beauty I don't want to consume, like strawberries. It's a beauty I want to receive, like light. I must receive it while waiting for her to resolve the conversation I believe she's been having with herself for too long. When it happens, she'll be lovelier than either Amal or Unsa. And I'll still be able to feed her chicken soup.

But why does she turn away from me? Is it me, or worry for Zahoor? Missing her sister already? I want to ask but don't know how. I'm nearly thirty-two. She's eighteen.

Am I a dirty old man? Is Zahoor right to pull her away from me?

Tonight she sleeps on his shoulder but I wish it was mine.

I will always regret that wish.

Because she wakes up, mumbles something to Zahoor, and reaches for me sitting to her left, exactly two beats after I've scrunched forward with elbows on my knees, to try to make out what Amal's mouthing in some frantic sign language, from up on stage. Mehwish's right hand extends, feeling for me the way she used to when still a child, before Zahoor's arrest, before she started avoiding me. Her hand finds my face. She slides a small finger in the gap between my teeth. Hearing the noise behind me, I briefly turn my back to her.

Did she sense the killer—the way she once sensed me? Or was she ending this year's silence? Had she resolved that conversation playing out like a radio in her head? Was it—just an innocent stretch?

Mehwish, why did you have to wake up and look for me?

Amal

People are avoiding Nana. Even his son, Munir Mamu, recently arrived for my wedding, walks around him, ashamed. *He's not polluted!* I want to shout but brides don't do that. Poor Omar's sick of hearing about Nana's trial. Junayd's trying to tell me something. Where's Zara? Picking up someone, at *my* wedding? Who's that behind Nana, Mehwish, and Noman? *What?* I shrug at Junayd, Noman flicks a palm up. *What?* Cameraman says smile. So much security, Nana doesn't look well, all of us an oxen moron called Secure Cell. Try not to give photographer hennaed finger. *Do your best.* Munir Mamu again. Thriving abroad. He can't stand that his own father's at the front of the culture war in the Motherland he can't stand to live in. *Smile.* Motherland should be unchanging, idealized not loved, arms open, legs open, traditional finery fading familiar, dusty antique, abused authentic, screaming to be fucked. (All Zara's fault I've started swearing. *Where is she?*) Zara, finally, congratulating me on my groom. "In full breeding plumage," she winks, floating off. Mehwish is lovely on Nana's shoulder, sleeping the way she always slept on mine. Why sleeping? I could never sleep at her wedding! Munir Mamu stands behind Nana, casually fanning a first-class ticket back to land of booze and pork, saying something deliberately annoying. I know the anger crawling up Nana's neck.

Oof, all my wedding pictures will be shit.

What? (What's happening over there?)

Then I see it: *infrared.*

gateway the fourth: the love

We think of what we are, what we have become with our souls
and words, but we don't think much about what we gave
up along the way.

—Carl Zimmer, *At the Water's Edge*

Amal

November 1997. I'm in the hospital and I don't want to be here.
There were five shots. I'm in the hospital. It's my wedding night. I
don't want to be here.

•

I replay all the days that might explain something. When
Noman first came to Nana's house, when he first came to my
lab, when he called in a panic then blew me off. When Mehwish
betrayed me. And Omar proposed. Do I remember more, or
just differently, to suit my desperate needs?

Whatever the answer, it doesn't explain a thing.

•

"Oh, come in," Nana had said that November in 1992, when
Noman first showed up shivering outside his door, claiming to
be a reporter. It was the month before I met Omar. "It's cold
and you look relatively harmless."

Have never known Nana to be more mistaken.

He said his name was Noman and that he was doing a story
on fossil whales. "Noman," I said. "Why do you seem so familiar?"

He mumbled that a lot of skinny people looked like him,
and before he could get too comfortable, Nana began mentally
carving him, slowly, slowly, like an experimental rat.

"Sea-monsters? That is not usually the kind of thing to
interest you boys. You are no reporter. What do you do?"

"I match-fix. I work for the Party of Creation."

Junayd told Nana to throw Noman out.

But Nana was delighted to welcome an offspring of the *other* side. "I'm going to fix the poor boy a drink!"

As Noman relaxed, Nana probed. "So, aside from getting you to send me the two warnings, what else do they plan to do?"

Noman volunteered an answer easily. "Nothing. You're not enough of a threat."

He didn't say: *though I've already made you one.*

He put down his drink and Nana refilled it. After the second gin his temperature changed again. From shivery pup to fake reporter to guilty stooge. "I bat for both sides! I edit the Word of God and the Word of Science!" He made himself a third drink.

Junayd motioned to Nana to get Noman to stop. "The boy can't hold his liquor one bit. He's a complete mess and I don't trust him!"

Nana kept sitting. "I need him to relax. Trust has nothing to do with it."

But Nana couldn't get him to say more. Noman was too drunk. He should have told Noman to go, or let him be. Interrogating him was cruel.

I was about to ask Nana to stop when his next attack made me hesitate.

"I've been wondering where I've seen you before. I have an excellent memory, you know. Of what use is a bone unearthed if you can't hold it against another? Well, you resemble someone I saw at one of my early talks. There was a modest riot that day. Few people came, fewer stayed, and when I searched the room, you were lurking around my granddaughters. It was you, wasn't it? Are you fond of hovering around young girls?"

Noman looked as if he'd found an icy comet in his mouth. *Swallow or spit.* He shook his head. "It must have been someone like me."

Nana wouldn't release him from his gaze.

"Okay, it *was* me!"

I stared, remembered. "That was you."

"You called me no one."

"That was you."

He blurted, "I'm riled by guilt! I'm a sheepish, self-effacing thief! I've snatched a first-class ticket to purgatory! Thank you, anguish! Thank you! Thank you!"

Nana, more satisfied, replaced Noman's empty glass with fresh water.

I wanted everybody to leave. "It's getting late."

"Yes," agreed Bilal Uncle, balder than when I first saw him in a photograph of Samarkand. He stood up. Aziz Sahib, Henry, and Brian did the same.

Henry added, "A man I admire once said that if you want to understand what ordinary folks do, a thoughtful deviant teaches more than ten thousand solid citizens."

"*Bilkul bilkul,*" echoed Aziz Sahib.

"Is that what we are?" laughed Nana. "Thoughtful deviants?"

While they talked, I glanced at Noman. Across his face appeared the silliest smile, as if he'd just beheld a houri. Then he passed out.

Six months later, he shows up at my lab, looking at me with the same silly smile. I feel uncomfortable remembering the way Nana had grilled him that first night in November.

Noman

I lie in the hospital with a bullet in my back. Amal comes to give me blood. She starts talking about the first time I visited Zahoor, and four months later, when I came to her lab. She thinks I can't hear her say, "How did you and I get here, Noman? We are nothing but clay to dig up, assemble, reassemble." I want to say, "I don't know about you and clay, *I* have nothing but time to calculate my mistakes."

All I can do is wheeze.

•

All right so that night at Zahoor's house, after the third drink, I grew silly. I don't remember what I said, something about guilt and anguish, gratitude and sin. There was also a confession. And someone quoted something to someone, maybe me. What I do remember is sipping water, cold and lovely. Deep in my bosom, serenity cut across fear. I'm not a cultural freak! I'm a thoughtful deviant! Throw anything at me, even angels, and I won't stray from the straight path!

I looked at Amal. So poised. I mean, so *so* poised. Why are some people a wreck while others float high above the weather? Amal's magic sifr, her holy bloom, was so vast I vanted to veep.

I dropped unconscious on the tattered floor cushion where I sat.

I return to his house often after that. Sometimes, Amal and Mehwish are there, though not as often as I'd like. By next spring, when I learn Unsa's getting married, the only person whose company I crave in my miserable state is the girl with the magic sifr. Not at Zahoor's house, but alone.

I go to Amal's lab. Not as a suitor, but still, a man can't help thinking it's a shithole for love. Long filthy tables with sharp tools that would stun even a roadside dentist. Tubs and trays, hammers, brooms. A ball of fur. It moves. The stench of acid. Cracked microscope. Torn shelves, dusty bottles, fermenting fluid, a squashed goat head, leering.

Of human life, the lab's empty. I know through Zahoor that Amal was recently hired as a lab assistant. I also know this was fiercely contested, the Department Head arguing that men and women both pray and work separately. It's the Natural Chain of Being. (So, Aba's party and Amal's campus create each other.)

Then a new Head arrived, all for equality. "If we can have a woman Prime Minister, we can have a woman senior lab assistant! We gave the PM a chance and we will even give a second! Many western countries do neither!"

The debate fueled, till eventually, the new hierarchy won. She was hired.

(And in October, the former Prime Minister will return.)

On the floor is a stack of books. I choose the one about dinosaurs. According to the author, dinosaurs were wiped out by a natural disaster, but not the one we'd thought. Death didn't fly in from outer space. It was tucked innocently in an earthly flower. The lizards developed an appetite for its poisonous seeds.

"They were drug addicts!" I laugh out loud, missing Petrov. Millions of years before his nightly jaunts into the poppy fields of Kandahar, giant lizards were doing the same. I stamp my foot and holler, "No wonder Communists are also extinct!"

When I look up a group of men and women is staring at me. Among them, Amal.

It's been a couple of months since I saw her, and she looks different. Slimmer, though still shapely. That's not the main difference. The difference is in her face. The half-bored, half-amused look's gone. Something else there now, more serious, but also more beautiful. I want to understand where it came from.

The second thing I notice is the man beside her. I've seen him before. Wide hips, light beard, light skin. Where? He hovers around her possessively as she focuses on her students, who go about their bizarre business of pouring liquids and scraping shapeless things. Then she comes toward me, feeble bodyguard in tow.

"Noman! What are you doing here?"

"W-well." I look down, at the book in my hand. A smile around her eyes says she heard me about the dinosaurs. I'm an idiot. I shouldn't be here. She smells lovely.

"If you are not a new student," says Hips, "it would be quite better to leave."

Ignoring him, I ask her, "What's that?" I mean the object in her hand. She studies it with an expression that again hooks me: serenity, curiosity and—? What lingers around a corner of her thinly parted mouth and in her dark pensive eyes, like a physical thread?

"*That*," interrupts Hips in a Huff, "is maybe exactly a skull found near here, slightly."

I stare at him. Yes, it's the JP member Aba verbally castrated at that first seminar. The one who said geology was a divine art. Abdul. He's found a second calling. Amal.

Also ignoring him, she addresses me. "When I finish, we can have tea at the canteen."

We do. Our conversation's comfortable and light. Her grandfather and sister—at this time—are safe. She has nothing to protect. Her caution vanishes. She talks happily about the afternoon class, then changes the topic abruptly to tell me about Omar. A kind of sexual repellant she sprays while maintaining sisterly ease. I identify that third ingredient lurking around her mouth, like a palpable ribbon: love. It must have sprung up recently, because I know it wasn't there when we last met. It's made her face softer. Wiped the knowingness away.

I tell her about Unsa. I frisk her for sympathy and she offers it, generously, while I mope. Next I tell her how I know Abdul.

"You JP wallahs get around! I've told him about Omar but he still hovers. So, Nana enjoys your company." Again, subject changes abruptly. "I know he was a bit—examining. At first. But, he likes you. He evokes strong feelings. People either adore him or fear him. What is it with you?"

"The first." That is not exactly a lie, or I wouldn't keep going back.

"He has a big heart that wants most of all to love and be loved."

Does she somehow sense that I've already hurt him? That no matter how much I seek his friendship now—and hers, and Mehwish's—I can never make up for the day I turned him into a foe?

I keep visiting Zahoor till his arrest a year later. When I leave—our foursome, and my home—it's Mehwish I miss the most.

•

Did I imagine it, or did the bullet that entered me pass through her first?

A nurse arrives to replace my drip...Oh, blissful sleep.

Amal

Spring '94. Tiger lilies in bloom on the Mall, all the way down to Charing Cross, not quite all the way to the High Court. Noman telephones in a panic. He'll only talk in person. We agree to meet after lab, where I assist students of comparative anatomy. It's exactly a year since he first came to the lab to see me alone.

I walk to the room that exhales formaldehyde wondering what to make of him, his friendship with Nana, and even with Mehwish.

How to trace the anatomy of our growth? Preserve the geometry that binds us? Slow down the sequence of changes in the time we've been given? Since Nana is our parent entity, our Pangaea, I choose his way. I devote myself to the *jan* of *janwar*. The anima of animals.

The students arrive but the teacher's late. Often he never shows, then they relax. I'm just a few years older. Like Mehwish, they see me as the dependable older sister.

On the center table, I've put two trays. One with a frayed chicken. The other, a lewd-looking shrew. They're doused in chemical and kept on ice but the stench of rotting meat dominates. On these days I eat an extra toast for breakfast and skip lunch.

To understand extinct vertebrates, we begin backwards. We examine the living. "Internal supporting structure" is a phrase I use frequently. So is "correlation": know the gaps, how they fit. (Hoist up on parallel bars with Omar's multiple scissory legs. Keep swinging.) Birds and mammals always slow us mental gymnasts down.

I could pick something other than a shrew—goat, sheep—and sometimes I do, but I like hearing the women laugh when I call us shrews taming shrews, and even enjoy the smirking men. (They're in almost equal number now but by the time they graduate, the ratio will drop—no, crash. Nature is something she needs to stand for but not share in.)

The chicken's already skinned. Dermis and epidermis snipped and slid under the microscope (the way I once slid Mehwish's finger). A week on fat. "The next time you're in the kitchen, think: chromatophore, not garam masala!" A lot of what we do is learn names. A lot of what we do is what Nana always told me to do: pay attention. Nothing's taken for granted. Not a sweep of spine, nor the lock of each component bone, nor the interlocked barbules of a single flight feather. Not—today's lesson—a ratty knot of skull.

From the tiny nasal apertures behind the bird beak, we move to the mammal. Two students flip the shrew on its back. Mouth hangs open, gums black, molars exposed like an alphabet. The textbook (a pirated old British handbook) says to avoid contact with chemical preservatives by wearing gloves and eyewear. We have the gloves but our eyes are exposed. We throw windows open. Flies amass; wasps bump heads. Temperature twenty-seven degrees (in a month, it'll hit forty). No air conditioning.

Nose to rump, fifteen centimeters. Tail another ten. Weight, before dissection, two hundred grams. Age: at least three years old. Close to end of life. Male.

The instructor (still not here) made an incision from chin to groin with scissors so blunt the edges are jagged and won't fold back as they should. Each time we "reopen" the shrew, a blood vessel bursts and tissue crumbles off. Now I trim the tattered ends of the neck with sharper scissors, just below the transverse jugular vein. A student hoses the blood away. The drain clogs. Muscle drapes the sink.

After enough time wasted on reskinning, I scratch a line in marker to divide the skull into facial and cranial. Then a circle for the brain, and for the middle and inner ears. Each time I see a mammal skull, I look for the ears. In these smallest of bones are the subtlest changes of weightiest significance in the largest, most elusive mammal of all, whales. I point out that the shrew has also evolved the ability to echolocate, not underwater but underground. Then the tiny eyes, not blind but not keen either; whiskers; deadly teeth.

I ask, "This isn't a technical question. Just think out loud. What surprises you most about this form?"

A woman with a long braid, Bushra, replies, "How its fur gets everywhere. In the scissors, the sink, even my clothes."

A smaller voice pipes, "How it's not so different from the chicken."

A third, louder, "It's *completely* different."

I ask, "Size? Does that surprise you?"

"Yes," answers Bushra. "Creeping in ficus it seems longer. Because of the tail. And snout."

I nod. "You think this is a small mammal with a sizeable span but remove the flesh and it shrinks."

Salim, slim-faced, yawns. "The old 'dimension is just perception' argument."

I try to explain that our practicals (I am, after all, *amal*) are a way to be oriented to a different balance: the width of a nose hole, the cleft between eyes. These millimeters build a warren behind my eyes, just as Mehwish's sleeping habits once did. The need to scratch the surface, to quantify with a thumb, to nourish a sensory chart, to *taste*, becomes a primal pursuit, like Mehwish's craving for depth and contour. I satisfy my three-dimensional curiosity in the lab the way Omar and Noman satisfy Mehwish's fingers.

I can always tell the students who have the craving to *sense* not simply *control* from those who don't. Except for Bushra, there are none in this group.

When we've examined the exterior of the shrew's head, a student—as if reading my mind—suggests we cut it open.

"That's the instructor's job."

"He's not here. And you can do it."

Another student, Arif, adds, "By the time he shows up, the rat will be dead." Laughter.

The next time we meet the stench will be unbearable. And I *can* do it. Probably better—though I've never tried.

Bushra adds, "If it gets messy, Arif can catch another one."

I take the shrew's chin in my hand. Close lower jaw. Open it. Swivel torn neck. Pull tail. Feel the point of a claw. My eye rests, as always, on the pinna. The external ear. I pull back the skin. It's thin. The face has little fur. I draw another circle. With a razor blade, I start to shave off skin. Soon I'm in the sheen of the inner left cheek. I cut through the olfactory tract. On my gloves, red and white mess. "Optic nerve." I point, feeling a little sick. I wasn't ready for this. But I've begun, I continue.

Bushra pokes something soft and pulpy. Others do the same. "We're in the brain."

Salim cuts the optic nerve.

"Leave some attached to the brain," I warn.

But he lifts it out, clumsily. Brain spills on the table, shivering like a birth. Salim scoops it as it slides, while others squeal. "Dimension is only perception, but look how little this rat *is*!"

I start cleaning up before it's time to leave.

•

In the cafeteria, I wait for Noman. I carry a bottle of rose attar in my bag and pour some on my neck. We haven't reached the point in our friendship when I can forget how awful I smell, though he never bothers about *his* scent.

I needn't have bothered either; he doesn't show. I look for him at the cafeteria all week. Nothing. Remembering how frightened he sounded when he called, I feel uneasy. I don't call him.

Glued to the wristband of my watch is a speck of intimal rodent vein.

Noman

I'm at Real Salman's. Fixed a time to meet Amal but couldn't face her. Called Zahoor. Hung up when I heard his voice.

This is the plan: find a student with a grudge. Zahoor's past record makes this easy. It's not his popularity with God that's on trial.

This is my relief: the charge won't be made by me. Aba said, "Better you stay out of this."

Ha. If I hadn't lied about him all those years ago, this wouldn't have happened.

At Real Salman's, Faisal the Vulgarian plies us with pot.

"What's this?" I ask, coughing.

"Rat poison." Ali spits. He has a new squeeze, Baltic Hilda.

"Ant powder." Faisal exhales across Hilda's cheek on Ali's shoulder.

Ali misses the Afghan stuff. "The Roos were great. These *bhainchod* Taliban only get high on *tihara* and *ta'zeer*, purity and punishment," he tells Hilda, "not dope. I'm too young to miss the old days!"

Salman tells Hilda where it all began to go wrong, "for my people."

Faisal tells her the Americans shouldn't have deserted the Afghans. "You can't just leave them with the weapons and the mess once they win for you. Now look what's happening there. They were nothing but a hit and run."

"A long hit," says Hilda, inhaling.

"Eleven years," agrees Salman, leering.

"We want to be friends with the Taliban *and* Americans," says Ali. "We don't hit and run. We *stick*!" He squeezes Hilda's hand.

Faisal: "We F-16 it. Pay first, beg later!"

I listen dumbly to their ramblings, writing tomorrow in my head. Zahoor will be arrested without a warrant. The Rawalpindi Police will detain him for weeks. I'll visit the jail but won't go in. Stand outside in the heat with a few dozen men who won't know what happened, exactly, except that they want blood, their honor's on trial, and its thirty-five degrees celsius. Balls will be scratched and thirst will conquer pride. Once they know he'll be convicted, they'll leave. A secure cell in Adyala Jail. Appeal. While the case is transferred to the High Court, I'll stand outside the jail. Forty degrees.

An odd thing happens.

I've been staring at the red and black tiles of Salman's courtyard, my eye shrinking to smaller and smaller spaces, looking for a void, a view, a flight, a light. A portal. A zone of transition. Like the vaulted honeycomb arches leading to the inner chambers of a mosque. Dizzying shapes—hexagon-diamond-triangle-circle—simple in repetition, complex in repetition. All that I feel for Zahoor, his granddaughters, even Aba, transforms into a simple resolve. No more batting for both sides. *Get your own apartment, get your own job. Leave. Ama will manage. She always has, better than you.*

I keep staring at the tiles. And then I start to hear them.

Many times at his house, Zahoor showed me different examples of this simple/complex visual recital, both on floors and ceilings, including a picture of the finest one: the cupolas of the Great Mosque in Cordoba. I remember his words exactly. "These logical yet random forms—from square to dome to octagon—are gateways to deeper worlds. They are an exact intimation, causing you to leave your skin in a leap both mystical and sensual. You praise each movement. You search for alternatives. An arch is open melody. The world is your Ka'ba. At one time, *faith* meant devotion to multiple pleasures—mathematics, poetry, music, anatomy, calligraphy. Knowledge was holistic. It had to be *tasted*. The mosque in Cordoba reflects that vision. It could not be built today. Tell me, how can an eye so penetrating have grown so dim—all across the globe?"

Now the texture of the design of Salman's courtyard grows so audible, I start to float. I squeeze through its interlocking bars as if through my own skeleton. Dangling in a corner of the dark ceiling, I watch the others. Circle them. Circle again. Circle a third time.

Blow.

I'm gone.

Amal

Last night Ama told me what happened to Nana. This morning I walk to the lab, still hearing his voice, "My faith is what you bury when you force me to expose it."

When I was eight he gifted me a dangerous ambition: to understand where we live. I'm still her, the girl who gazed at a brown clump in her hands, waiting for the mist to clear, the image to surface. Hoping to strike the right rhythm so the eight-year-old can devote herself to the creatures that speak to her from antiquity.

But sometimes the rhythm is broken, and today is that kind of day.

I wipe the tears I shed for Nana, and enter the lab.

•

Inside are Abdul, a few unobtrusive others, and Fawad and Ibrar. *My* accusers!

Like many members of the many student offshoots of the Party of Creation, baby-faced Fawad has a Master's in Victorian literature. (The road to the heart of Lahore is Victorian.) He says he's descended from the Prophet Mohammad *and* Rudyard Kipling.

Ibrar: co-party member, enormous, loves leather.

They both left the Military Academy to pursue Victorians and skulls (and Victorian skulls), and to hunt wild boar. They relish the taste of what they kill.

In the lab, they exhange accounts of hunting races, and of their own race: God created man as stratified layers of rock, whites (like them) at the top, on a planet that's static and forever. And roughly a million years old.

After Kipling, their hero is the Saudi astronaut who became the first and only Muslim to land in space. Ibrar believes he'll be the second—provided the spacecraft carries boar.

They upset Abdul a lot. They enjoy this. When I arrive at my worktable this morning, Abdul's arguing, "Your belief in a chosen race is, exactly, westryn and unIslamic!"

Fawad lights a cigarette. A beaker of highly combustible fluid rests inches from it. He exhales. "It is written: *To all are assigned ranks.*"

Abdul leaps off his stool. "*To all are assigned ranks according to deeds.* See! See! This is how your type exactly bends and twists to suit your purposes, calling it Islam!"

"Go to hell, with the rest of *your* type," growls Ibrar. "Your *nichi zaat!*"

"The things you say!" Abdul squeaks. "There is no caste in Islam. No high or low, you fools! Not even maybe!"

I try to ignore this family I've been thrown in with as accidentally as a real one.

My focus is the knee of a possibly counterfeit crocodile. I hear Nana's voice from yesterday, *All first models are necessarily lost...* I shut my eyes and try to make the puzzle fit by finding a *khayal* image. I see a pool in the Margalla Hills, and a tracing of a very large dog with a very large head.

I open my eyes.

The limestone on the table in front of me I've already washed, but I move to the sink to wash each piece again. I don't want anyone seeing my face. I dribble cold water over my wrist (on the band of my watch, shrew blood still sticks), splash it on my face.

The story of water is written in stone.

While Ibrar keeps arguing with Abdul, Fawad's eyes strip

me. I tell myself, *He's the opposite of that rock in your hand. He's not real. Like plastic, he won't mix well with time.* But the way he grins and licks his teeth—it *is* real. He's broken my rhythm, gotten to me, gotten *into* me. A mound of gold flashes white on his pinkie.

Abdul moves to obstruct Fawad's view of me. Abdul wants to marry me.

Behind them all, I become *she.*

Fawad says to Abdul, "If she admires the natural world, she should know her natural place is at home."

She: Silence. Abdul: Silence.

Ibrar adds, "Our concepts are too advanced for the weaker s—" He swallows "sex."

Silence.

Fawad smirks. "You can tell she does not have our detachment or discipline. She looks at dead things with *feeling!*"

"She does not have a scientist's eye."

They see how well the shrew lies carved and mounted, in the adjoining lab, where her students (not Fawad's—she was chosen over him) have finished analyzing its frame. They also know that she's the girl who found a diamond key when she was only eight. They've only ever found chips of Paleozoic crab.

Then why won't she argue back?

She knows their aim is to wear her down, distract her, make her quit. She fears if her voice is heard it'll prove their success. But she tells herself this isn't why she's silent. This is: if they aren't her equal, why should her reaction be? She can be a funny corner of history. A *better* funny corner. A deviant. A woman scientist. Ahead of her time.

But in her heart she knows her silence is less than equal.

She doesn't want to be a corner of history, funny or not. It doesn't make her better than those who put her there. She's *aql amali*. Practical intelligence. She's carried her potential long enough. The gestation has become a burden. She needs to push her talent outside herself, into the world. This need to bridge her isolation, this hunger for acceptance, community—she isn't able to name it exactly—it washes over her in waves of increasing force. Each time a wave recedes, she tries to brace herself against the next ache. And fails.

Her grandfather once confessed to a similar yearning. A way to light a candle, and be lit by more. What good is a candle vacuum-sealed? *That would destroy me.*

Look at him now.

Noman

The day I'm going to tell my mother I've decided to leave, I wake up when her day begins, before Fajr prayers. She goes to sleep late and rises when it's still night. She mothers the sun.

She always does her ablution in the bathroom I share with Sehr, because Aba takes theirs. It's her habit to leave the door open so the splashing wakes us up. It seldom does. Today I sit up. I want to memorize all her rituals, holier to me than to Him.

The way she rolls each sleeve. Such bony elbows. Such slender arms. Wipes chin. Wets lashes. Gargles. Spits. Scours nostrils. A dainty woman who blows her nose with gusto. Smears water behind each ear. Spits. Purifies fingernails. Lifts right foot. Rubs between toes. Down. Lifts left. Raises each so high. A heron in a previous life.

I recite, "*Ma khalqum wa la bashkum ila kanafsin.*" He created you and recreated you in no other way but as a single cell.

Some say "resurrected" not "recreated," and call it true. Some say the verse proves evolution wrong, some right. Some prefer "single individual" (Adam) to "single cell" (Hawwa). If she came first, by what name, Hawwa or Eve?

Some say there's no evidence of Hawwa springing from Adam any more than Adam springing from Eve.

Some say. Let them. I am no longer part of the sum.

I want my knees to be so supple at sixty.

Left foot leaves sink. Spits. She's done. Bathroom flooded. I always thought Sehr made the mess.

"*We made from water every living thing.*"

"What are you muttering?" Sehr wakes up, scowls.

I lean across a small table with red Moroccan babouches underneath, and gently pinch her cheek. "Go back to sleep."

"Are you being sensitive?" She yawns.

"I don't know how."

"True." Content, she falls asleep.

I slink back under the sheet. Ama's movements will change if she knows they're being admired.

She lays the prayer mat on our rug. Her *salat* is silent. No bones creak and words are spoken in her heart. She bends, kneels, gets back up neatly, quickly. A single movement, as fluid as rolling and unrolling her hair. An exact recipe.

But at the end, she changes it. Knees curled, feet sliding, she lingers. A conference with God, in her way. About what— me? Today, I'm content to not know.

When she has an answer—or is satisfied without one—Ama folds the mat. Back in this world, she scolds Sehr. "Wake up and help with breakfast." Sehr moans. Ama leaves our room.

Outside her kitchen-womb. *He creates you in your mothers' wombs, one act of creation after another, in threefold depths of darkness.* I watch her boil water, heat milk, roll parathas, arrange a tray with a butter dish, sugar pot, and wool tea cozy as old as her marriage. Parathas flipped. Tea leaves heaped generously, like her blessings.

As if their separate spheres are synchronized, the moment she lifts the tray, Aba—who prays and dresses loudly—snaps his briefcase shut in their bedroom. Ready to eat.

His first appointment today: a private meeting with the JP chairman. I'm not needed there, but I have another assignment. I delay it.

His cherry-blossomed shoes approach. I scurry up to the terrace.

"Were you on the terrace?" Ama, putting away breakfast plates.

"Yes. The sky's a pink grapefruit."

She looks at me quizzically, stuffing paratha into my mouth. Unsa wasn't on her terrace. Unlike Sehr, she must be helping her mother clear the table she helped arrange. Her last weeks at home. Only brides leave home, to enter the territory of in-laws. Good men keep fattening in the womb.

I lick buttery sugar off my lips. "It's a good time to start my own job."

"What do you mean start your own job?"

I take a deep breath: Filter Worry, Exhale Slowly. "I applied to a school and got the job. I'm going to tell children about Al Khwarizmi and the magic of zero. They'll love it."

She stares at me.

"A number's made up, have you ever thought about it? Do you believe that praying alone brings twenty-seven times less reward than praying in congregation? Why would God be a boring accountant, like bhayia?" I try to laugh, but choke instead.

"You should eat something." She turns her back to me.

I stare at the slope of her shoulders as she lights the stove. Today, I can't face rejection. I want to tell my own mother how I see the world and what I need from it. I want to tell her this with the faith that she'll listen.

I try to share my vision at Badshahi Mosque. "The three sifrs said, Build something, no man. We weren't imagined for you to keep score of the blessings received *after* life. We were imagined for you to live well now, in this one!" I laugh again.

My stomach hurts. "Everything changed. Are you listening? It finally makes sense, how"—follow her to the fridge—"I mean, what was I saying? To try to live"—follow her to the sink— "which is, by not staying with him. Maybe not even with *you*."

The counter, the kitchen table. She keeps turning away.

My voice grows louder. "Are you listening?"

"You promised you wouldn't argue with him."

"I'm not going to argue. I don't care what *he* thinks. I care what *you* think."

"You have to care what *he* thinks."

"You said to go along with him till *I* get the job *I* want. I have done that."

"You have to continue till *he* lets you go."

"I do not."

"Do it for my sake."

"That is coercion. Not peace."

"I do not understand the difference! Neither will he!"

Her hand trembles. I take it. Despite their use, her fingers are so soft. Her mouth trembles. I whisper, "Don't say what you should. Say what you feel." She tries to pull away. I finally understand that I'm making her show me her weakness— something she's learned to conceal from us all. She and Aba are synchronized, even if they aren't in love. Happiness? Who am I to say she doesn't have it, when *she* is part of *him* and part of *us*? If it's taken me this long to find the strength (or weakness) to defy him, it'll take her even longer.

And what then? What good will pulling away do then, when she's found such dignity in her place here? God give a rebel half as much grace. If I had to say who has more, my mother or Zahoor, I couldn't.

She looks at me and she knows: I've made up my mind.

I answer the questions she won't ask. "The apartment's rented, starting today. I borrowed money from Salman. He was thrilled. 'I always help my people.'" I squeeze her hand, hoping for a smile. She guards it.

"Only brides leave home."

"I know." I kiss her hand and return to my room, to pack.

•

Upper portion. Studio apartment. Faces the park. Good condition.

Every one lies, so why not landlords? Except for the upper-portion bit, nothing else in the ad is true. My apartment's smaller than a studio, faces a corner, windows are broken, taps leak, the boiler needs replacing, all the bulbs are dead. But it's mine. And it's cheap. By next month, I'll have my debt paid to Real Salman.

It came with a two-burner stove and a rickety table and chair. Everything else—the mattress on the floor, secondhand fridge, pots and plates from Ichra Bazaar, batik bedcover—mine. I make a good bride, shopping *is* fun, but no facial, no thank you.

Everything's good, except for one thing: the space I've risked so much to make is filled with the people I miss. As much as Ama and Sehr, it holds Amal and Mehwish.

I haven't seen them since the charge against Zahoor was made this spring. On weekends, I lurk outside his jail in Rawalpindi, not daring to go in. During the hearing at the police court next week, I'll wait outside.

Amal

Rawalpindi has two notabilities. It was the largest military outpost in nineteenth-century British India, when Sir Macauley wrote and Sir Peacock revised the Blasphemy Law. (The Pakistan Penal Code again amended it; lost the original.)

Its second claim to fame: where Pakistan's first Prime Minister was assassinated.

Ama and I head for the police court, escorted by a guard. It won't be a hearing but a silencing.

Mehwish is in Lahore with Aba. Ama asks how much she knows "in the weeks since five men filed an FIR against Nana." She gets stuck on little details, such as, *five* men filed the FIR, not two or three. That's how big their vendetta is, she keeps saying.

"I don't think she knows much." I don't tell her Mehwish recites "oxen morons" like secure cell and prison award while falling asleep. Or that she asks me to never copywrong, only copyright.

Ama keeps fretting. "I think she was awake the night I told you about the five men." She takes my hand. She's started doing this now.

"I don't think so."

The guard marches energetically. Too many high kicks at Wagah Border.

She pinches my hand. "Does she know he was in police lockup with *drug addicts?* You know she hears everything."

"Why don't you ask *her*? Why don't you *tell* her?"

"Did you *see* them? They had marks everywhere. Why do they *do* that? Why would any normal person want to stick needles—there?"

"Maybe they're not normal."

"I have heard the magistrate is a nice man."

"Why don't you make friends with his wife?"

"But your father doesn't think so. Your father says a magistrate is a minor official and minor officials are very insecure."

There's a mob outside. A few hold placards for Nana. No More False Arrests. Amend The Sham Law. Faith Is Private, Proof Is Public: Where Is It? They seem to know who we are and two start clapping. Others chant, "Heretic pig!" One spits on Ama. A small figure darts by us. Noman? Couldn't be. Haven't seen him once since Nana's arrest. I turn around but whoever he was, he's gone.

The lawyer says to wait outside. "As I tried explaining over the phone, Mrs. Ansari, this is where personal vendettas are spiced with questions like land mines. They have no evidence so they will try to get it from him. If he's not a heretic, then why does he argue against legislating faith? Who is he trying to protect? Others like him? Who is he really? And so on. We need your father to say he is a believer and I think he has finally agreed."

Ama starts to cry. "He will never agree. He is *stubborn*."

"Then he must be stubborn about wanting to *live*! I'm telling you all this because you should be prepared. Once he, well, *confesses* his faith, the prosecution will be ready. They will have other evidence waiting. It could be anything, and it could be very upsetting to you. Maybe you should—" He looks at Junayd, then at me. "No magistrate is likely to release him. Their authority is limited and they fear for their own safety."

Though Nana insists he doesn't need defending, he's lucky to have this lawyer. I say, "I'll wait here with Ama." Junayd gives me a sad smile. I reach over, kiss his cheek.

The lawyer concludes, "We will appeal. Do not worry." They go inside.

I wait outside with Ama as she weeps, thinking of the spring Mehwish became blind and I developed the habit of looking down, though I didn't know any of this—not Mehwish's accident, not Nana's trial—when he and I arrived at our favorite pool in the Margalla Hills of Islamabad.

He showed me a drawing: a very large dog with a very large head. Tapped it vigorously. "That is a whale."

I smiled comfortingly and kissed his coarse cheek. "Nana, that's a *dog*."

"Amal, that is a *real* whale and we are *real* Pakistanis!"

•

The magistrate takes fourteen days to decide. While he "examines the evidence"—and the evidence, as the lawyer warned, has an added layer: a student saw Nana walk into class with the names of the four caliphs on each foot (he has only *two* feet, and his soles are always tucked in leather slippers)— while the magistrate examines Nana's imaginary feet, I skin mammals. And chip and clean and reconstruct petrified bones.

Noman

Zahoor's lawyer appeals. The case is transferred to the Pindi Bench of the Lahore High Court. Protests for his release. And for his death. I watch Amal and her mother go in and out of court. When Amal was plump and radiant she was like her mother is now, while she herself grows thin. Mehwish is never with them.

I return to my apartment craving the company of the family I had for so short a time.

At school, I burden youth with trigonometric equations. "Draw the Canal perpendicular to Ferozepur Road. Now calculate the length of Jail Road. Is it a right triangle? No? Make it so. How? Build a bridge parallel to Jail Road. Figure out the cost." While they complain, I read a book Zahoor once lent me, about Ibn Haitham's pinhole experiments. *He shined light through a tiny, tiny sifr.* It's a private school, so none of the changes the Academy of Moral Policy still makes to textbooks apply. (We measure triangles without saying God Willing.) I once created the antidote to the pollution in our society. Now I create the pollution. Cause and effect, I tell them, only appear as two divergent roads. Link them.

Figure out the cost.

Amal

Sheer physical fatigue causes Nana to behave well in the courtroom, even when he and his lawyer are booed. In between the hearings and silencings, he's put in solitary confinement, for his security. Ama usually comes with me, crying no less.

This morning, as I left for university, she pinched my hand and said again, "Zara's father. A corps commander?"

Now at lunchtime, I collect my books and leave the lab. I usually have lunch at the canteen, but today's a good day to nibble *shami kebabs* alone under a tree and come up with a way to apply Ama's repeated hints. If I ask for a powerful military man's help in saving Nana, he can't know. To help him, I must betray him...

As I walk toward a banyan tree, Abdul intercepts me, in his sincere but grating way. "Miss Amal, if you have time, can we talk? I have good news, maybe."

I hesitate. I want to avoid him, but I also want to be nice. (At home I'm told my etiquette isn't high enough, but why then do I get trapped by niceties?) "I have time," I tell Abdul. "Do you want to eat outside?"

"Outside where?" He looks around nervously, as if we're about to be ambushed.

"On the grass. *Outside.*"

He dusts his trousers. "The canteen, I think, is quite better?" He points to a paved section where a few tables and chairs are arranged and a few couples sit. Wagah Border for the sexes. Where I had tea with Noman once. Still no word from him.

We head for an empty table littered with cold chicken and splashes of Coke. I pile the garbage to one side, wipe the table with waxy paper, and wait while he shuffles sheepishly forward in line. I wait a long time. No breeze, not even a nudge. I smell armpits. I stare at men's behinds. Abdul's flare like a woman's. He walks with his hips.

I daydream about Omar. Omar walks with his legs, one foot before the other, hands in pockets. Alert, graceful. Silent, suspenseful. Like a panther with hunger and loads of time. Together, we've circumnavigated many of Lahore's parks (I like the contours beginning to shape my calves). His hips are lean and shoulders spherical. A man as beautifully proportioned from the waist up as waist down.

"Miss Amal, I'm sorry that took so long?" Abdul sits down tentatively. When he's nervous, I am Miss and all declarations become questions.

He sets down four kebab rolls and two Coke cans. I didn't tell him what I wanted, he didn't ask. The stench of stale ghee erases the memory of Omar like pesticide in a tangle of leafy undergrowth. "You're very polite, the way you kept waiting in line."

Another timid look, then he exhales air through his nose while inhaling half a roll into his mouth. It doesn't seem possible, even as he does it. He repeats the move; the rest slides down his gullet. "Aren't you hungry?" he picks his teeth, unwrapping a second roll.

"No. You can have mine." Nasal cavity clears; second tube disappears; third's unwrapped. "What did you want to talk about?"

His nod says he'll explain. He cracks the soda and drinks. Coke drool on the bristles of his chin, like a second stubble. "Two things. One happy one difficult?"

I hope neither involves me. But I've thought about it, realistically. Who in his right mind would want to marry a shrew-skinner and whale-worshipper?

"First difficult." He burps. "It is always difficult to begin? But I have wanted for a long time to tell you that I do not agree at all with Fawad and Ibrar."

I smile, surprised and relieved. "That's obvious. I mean, the way you argue back."

"What they say is not Islam. I have wanted to say, exactly, about real Islam."

My smile disappears.

"You have noticed the campus militants? But the clever thing about Fawad and Ibrar is that they come from big big families. Power, maybe, how can I say…?" He shifts his weight on those wide hips.

I consult my watch: almost two o'clock. Sedimentology at two-thirty. (*Will you marry me? I sex sediment.*) Then I meet Omar. Ama watches from a window when he drops me home later. Our silence knows I'm safe if this is before Aba returns from office.

"Power watches its back with religion," Abdul declares. I note it's not a question. "Islam embraces all." He looks up shyly. "It embraces women."

"I have a class." I swing purse strap around shoulder, collect books.

"Please, please, five more minutes, thank you?"

Still clutching bag and books, I sit.

"Long before Christian kings were divorcing wives and Hindus were burning widows, Islam was caring for you tenderly. The Quran says a wife is as tilth to a farmer."

I think I'm being cultivated. Tenderly.

Only one minute has passed.

"I want only to know you? You are a decent woman. You keep your gaze low and work hard. I have noticed. You should not feel harassed by men like Fawad and Ibrar."

I finally blurt, "I feel harassed by this subject!"

He doesn't hear me. "The glory of Islam is that it codified laws to guide women. Men like Fawad and Ibrar do not know, they are not Muslim."

"I'm not bothered about Fawad and Ibrar (why can't I lie?), but—"

"Miss Amal, please let me finish?"

"—but as with them, so with you. I'm a woman first and that won't change."

He blinks. "But you are a woman?"

"Maybe, exactly?"

He doesn't crack a smile. I still don't leave. Because a thought nags: he's not malicious. Be nice. My mother, whom I thought too frail to bring me up, apparently did, enough to keep me sitting. Shit, I'm thoroughly bred.

"Women have all the rights. In return for their purity? And what I want to say," he bites his lip, "I want to say you should be careful? And I want only to protect you."

I stand up and start to walk away.

From behind me, I hear, "I have good news! I heard the director say he wants you to start going into the field with us!"

I turn around. "What?"

"Exactly. He is happy with you and has told the others he wants your help."

"What did they say?"

"They are not happy. And that is why I am here." He smiles smugly. "I will protect you."

•

The director has allowed me Outdoors but Aba and Ama still refuse. Underneath my fury is a growing seed of rebellion. No, not a seed. A bloody field. I'll cultivate it. Tenderly.

That night, I slip outside, warning Mehwish to let me in later. Her turn to pay attention!

•

Against the brotherhood of boar-hunters like Ibrar and Fawad, against their verbal and physical pinches, women form their own tribe, with its own rules.

The first rule: don't talk to men.

Other rules: what your family does, how your siblings marry, who proposes to you, who doesn't—the business is Ours. Likewise, your work is Ours. It has no copyright. You don't do it; we do.

And finally: we are *mujboor*. Helpless.

To woman: microcosm. To man: macrocosm.

If I know my work is higher than our petty prejudices, why do I let myself get tangled up in microscopic meannesses?

"You are leading him on," Erum whispers, meaning Abdul.

"And Omar," says Shehla. Must have seen me at the canteen with him.

"And the other. The little one with bad teeth." Must mean Noman, though we haven't met in nearly two years.

"Too good to sit with us at lunch?"

"She attracts attention alone. In a crowd, no one would notice her, no matter how much she shows."

The women cram together in a tight little square, their righteousness frozen hard, and I don't know what's worse: the gloating of female chastity or the bloating of male conceit.

•

I stand alone outside Nana's cell, a guard behind me. "How's Mehwish?"

"She doesn't know where you are."

Nana squints at the filthy walls. "I think I've overstayed my welcome."

He's developed a urinary infection. He's at risk of cardiac arrest. The lawyer wants him put under house arrest, if refused parole. As the months drag, I wonder what's worse: a second summer barely survived, still with no fan or even a window. Or a second winter without heat. The first left behind a cough. The second could kill him.

"And Noman?"

I shake my head. "Still no news." It pains me that he still asks after him.

On the high ceiling is a bulb switched off at 7 PM. He's always done his best reading at night. "I can't read." He folds his glasses and pushes them through the bars.

I push his hand away, something I've never done before. "You have to keep them. Sunlight would only make this room hotter." *And without sunlight, in the cold Potwar Plateau darkness creeping toward him?*

"*Room?*" He drops them on the floor, folds his arms, walks away. Mutters, "This is what it's like for Mehwish all the time."

I try to say something but can't. They have even taken his slippers.

His lawyer will plead failing health. If that doesn't work, failed health. Senility.

My plea, forming resolutely as I watch him wither: Zara. Ama was right.

•

A rumor: Zara's father was involved in the mysterious death of the last Chief of Army Staff. After he became a corps commander, Zara distributed sweets. People publicly congratulated her family and privately called them corrupt, the same way they publicly sun themselves in Zara's glamour and privately call her a slut. I don't know the truth about her father, but I do know Zara proudly echoes him: "Our people can't handle democracy. They need the military to oversee politics." (And the maulvis to oversee legislation? She'd have no opinion—she'd never need to have one.) She always concludes, "Together we will build a real Pakistan."

The last one was fake.

While the brownies cool and we wait for Zara, I agree to play with Mehwish. It'll help me come up with the right way to seek Zara's help.

But Mehwish is very chatty and won't let me think. "Ama does not like Zara."

"No. What are we making?"

And somehow we get on the subject of understanding God through *khayal* and *zauq*. "Do you know what the words mean?" She nods but of course she doesn't know. "*Khayal* is an idea, or an image. But not a picture image."

"What about the *taviz* Ama wears around her neck?"

"It's not an image of Him. It's His words."

"How does Ama know? They're written in Arabic."

"You either believe it or you don't."

"But you can't see it?"

"Well you can but you can't *read* it."

"Then you can't *see* it."

"All right." I put her finger to her jugular vein. I tell her about *zauq*. "The only way to taste divine sensuality is through love of a mortal."

"I'm glad you gave Omar the flowers."

How does she know I meant him? "That was a long time ago, Mehwish." I'm glad when Zara arrives because our mud sculptures are dull and she starts asking about Nana.

•

Mehwish finally leaves us alone, after hearing too much about Omar, and Zara's latest craze, uncircumcised men. We're listening to the Eurythmics. When Zara's dope-induced hunger finally begins to fade, I stop the tape. She says she met her boyfriend Sanjit through her guru in Delhi, who she believes is spritually linked with the family in whose house she lives, the one who left the spoons. "We're all connected through the One Great Cosmic Dance." Puff puff. Her cigarettes smell like frog farts. Today her stubborn jocularity frustrates. Nana's alone in his cell. People are fighting for his life. Zara doesn't even read the paper.

How do I present him to a family like hers? How do I beg for their help?

If I don't ask I'm guilty of abandoning him. If I do I'm guilty of betraying him.

The wall behind her is dotted in mirrors—a humble substitute for the honeycomb windows I wanted when we first moved to Lahore. The glass reflects us in picoseconds.

"What's the matter with you?" She takes out green nail polish from a purse also haphazardly stocked with silver and brass shades. "It's subliminal, don't you think?"

"What is?"

"Rock picking."

"Zara. Not today."

She flicks a hand, dries nails, pulls a pink braid while cackling wickedly. Her mouth's smeared in chocolate. "Seriously, think about it. The colliding of the peninsula. The cause of the thrust. Going into the field. An out-and-out lily hunt. Consider yourself lucky your parents won't let you go. *Very dangerous.*"

Ignoring her, I open the window Mehwish opens for me at night. She couldn't if I'd gotten my honeycomb pattern instead.

"Does Omar know about Abdul's generous protectiveness? Good looking?"

"Find out yourself."

"Ooh, a duel would be delicious!" She comes up behind me, folds long arms around my waist. "Just teasing. Come on. Chirp for Zara."

"Nana's in solitary confinement. He's very sick."

At last I find the words to affect her.

•

That night Mehwish asks annoying questions, then starts crying. Enough crying for one day! Even Zara left in tears once I told her Nana's started *shuffling*. "He was always more light on his feet than even you!" (I wasn't lying.) I try to comfort Mehwish but she kicks me. I hold her down but she slaps me. I hit back, hard, harder than after the blind cricket match, because of the way she touched Omar.

It was a mistake, but I didn't expect her to turn so vicious.

The next morning the dining room echoes and echoes and echoes:

"If you go to Islamabad to live with Nana how will you keep seeing Omar in Lahore?"

Before I'm sure I've heard right, Mehwish adds, "And go thrill-seeking in Hira Mandi?"

And before I register *that*, Ama's whimpering, "They are still seeing each other, everyone knows!"

Her hypocrisy rips through me, like a bullet.

Noman

Zahoor's temporarily released, though still not acquitted. He comes home to Islamabad. After almost two years, I visit him again. He now lives behind a taller gate, barbed wire and two armed guards. He says he's still in prison, but adds, "At least I have sunlight." We both know this is the absolute minimum security, but I don't dare say it.

I watch him closely, glad that we're alone. He coughs a lot. Looks gray. Goes often to the bathroom (tries not to shuffle). Says little. Icy with everyone now, or just me?

Another change: an extra heater.

I've rehearsed what I want to say. I'll admit the lies I spoke about him. I'll show him *The Blueprint for Afterlife*. A fiction for your fiction, I'll say, about that dachshund-Alsatian thing! It was well-received, and then forgotten… Till now, this mid-decade slump. These years of International Rebuff. What's a man to do, I'll ask, when he's no longer invited to five-star hotels around the world? When today the world bites, where yesterday it kissed? ("We helped you build a laboratory of faith, now fry in it!")

And I'll answer, I'll tell you what the man does: he digs in the dirt of archives, as you, Zahoor, dig in the dirt of dead seas.

I could recite this speech backwards.

But Zahoor has a nasty habit: he makes it impossible to recite. His silence is a judge. *Look deeper. You are just a little tick.*

Damn him! "I'm sorry!"

He's wiping his reading glasses. "Now what have you done?"

I start babbling. I think I tell him Aba's party hired the student who accused him of blasphemy. I think I say, "I wish they'd targeted someone else."

He squints at me. A thick goo collects around the corner of each eye.

"... I couldn't say all this before (*babble*) I promise I didn't know how much it would matter one day. I should have told you earlier. I—I'm sorry. I was (*babble babble*) scared."

He says nothing.

The second time in his life he's been reduced to silence. Only now do I feel the cruelty of what I've done. Just as my work for Aba was never meant to help anyone but me, ditto for this confession.

I repeat, "I'm sorry."

"You look older than I do. Come back when you feel young."

So at last he tells me to leave, as he should have done the night he first let me in.

Amal

Nana's been granted conditional release. The condition is that he act senile.

There are two types of people. Those who come out of prison refired. Those who come out of prison cold. Nana surprises us. He comes out cold. It's as if he knows only a military man could have helped him. We've been selfish. More valuable to him than his life—or ours, or *mine*—is his pride. I understand now that pride is his seat of *zauq*. He wrestles with himself to preserve his taste.

Support helps. He gets it both in Pakistan and internationally, mostly from strangers. Articles appear in newspapers. Letters arrive. A fan in Sweden wants to write a book on him. But many of his own friends and family are ashamed. They walk around him as if he carries a germ. His son, who lives in Paris, writes a letter of such disdain ("How could you humiliate me? We need you to represent us, to show the world the pure face of our motherland, not make us look bad. How am I to live here with your dishonor? It has spoiled my image…") that Nana actually weeps.

I take Mehwish to visit him, and we become a triangle again. Two guards stand watch outside, plus a police van shows up at odd hours so no one can keep track of its schedule. Nana says all this security only attracts more attention to him. No one listens.

•

A few weeks after his release, I spend a weekend alone with Nana. I don't take Mehwish. Ama calls twice a day, both to make sure we're safe, and to make sure I'm not with Omar. If Nana gets suspicious, he doesn't show it. Maybe he decides one person on trial is enough.

While the police van waits at the head of the trail, the two guards follow us up the Margalla Hills. Nana is seventy-two years old and, for the first time in his life, unequally mobile in mind and step. He doesn't exactly shuffle, but he pauses between steps. If he forgets—or resists—he hacks. Under his jacket, he wears an extra sweater. And socks. The prison guards never returned his slippers. His new ones were several times more expensive and are already torn.

But this morning: snow on the high peaks encircling us. I inhale sharply. Clean air. It tastes sweet. Our footsteps crunch frost. We'll reach the pool by a different trail. The old one is too crowded now. My eye, now used to billboards and supermarkets, flat plains and diesel smoke, has to readjust to mountains as stark and regal as the tall man beside me. I'm revived with such vigor, I hurt.

I last walked these slopes ten years ago, just before moving to Lahore. He said, "*Many of the people who want me sacked are in Lahore.*"

He said sacked, not dead.

Earlier today, before setting out, he told me he had something to say about who was behind his arrest. Now he says it again.

I'm only half listening. I want to leave his trial behind us as we climb. Cars trudge up to Daman-e-koh, the viewpoint looming ahead like a giant heel. When did that happen—was it always there?

"Pay attention."

I smile. "You can stop saying that to me now."

"I will, when you start listening." He tells me Noman visited him, repeats everything Noman said, and ends abruptly with: "Do you blame him?"

I can't speak.

Empty cartons of Milk Pak by my feet. A sanitary napkin with a brown smudge.

I stamp a foot foolishly. "You trusted him! You treated him like a son!"

Nana coughs impatiently. "Do you blame him? Think before you answer." He walks ahead.

The security guards look baffled. "Follow him," I say to the one who'd never even loaded a gun before he started shielding Nana. When Nana showed him how, smiling, the guard had said, "First class." Later, I found him asleep, gun at his feet. Now he thanks me for telling him where to go, and races on.

I follow. "So that's why he disappeared? Did you throw him out?"

"Answer my question, Amal."

"I can't. *You* have spent time in jail. *You* are sick. *You* are being watched. *You* hate protection even more than I do. *You* have lost your job. *Jobs*. *You*—"

"I will ask you a fourth and final time and I hope you will keep in mind everything I have ever said. *Do you blame him?*"

Before I know it, I've said no.

He looks down, at his new slippers. Grimaces. "I was half hoping you'd say yes. But you *have* been paying attention."

I start to cry.

"Now you'll have to bring him back."

He wipes my face as we start to walk again.

The pool is smaller than I remember. The acacia trees that protect it, shorter. I take his hand. It hasn't shrunk at all as I've grown.

Noman

Evenings and weekends I'm usually at Salman's, or he and the others visit me. We smoke. Listen to music. Play rummy. Drive around. But this Saturday afternoon in February, I put the stove burner on and slide under a blanket. Don't feel like moving. On the bed, beside me, like the stain of a last night with a jilted lover, *Akhlaq*. The stain's from the summer I left home. After all this time, I still sleep with it: my last issue of the magazine, in which I publicize my reasons for resigning. The printer printed it, as he always does, without reading a single page. Once you decide not to censor yourself, you find all the policemen are asleep. Till someone like me grossly exaggerates your strength.

Then you're revised. Translated. Sentenced. The Word you become is not You.

I wonder if Zahoor knows how he changed me.

This was my front-page editor's note:

Al Qalam

The title, as all good readers true readers know, is of the sixty-eighth surah, The Pen. It begins: Consider the pen, and all that they write therewith... It says that God alone is aware of who strays from "truth." Good readers, true readers, is the scholar's ink holier than the martyr's blood? Aren't both only spilled for this life—for you and me and nothing higher? Your righteousness about the next is noise and clothing. I use this pen to go naked today.

My clearest memory of Aba. In the ruins of Taksali Gate, he said to always speak with a shiny minted tongue, and always think with a shiny minted mind. But a tongue is to use, not hammer into shape like a coin. And a mind must breathe or it sours. It becomes a cultural freak. I use this pen to be less freaky today.

Good readers true readers, members of the Party of Creation, scholars of the Academy of Moral Policy, if the second Satan is memory, you create the third: distortion of memory. You are the Past Patrol and Present Police. You pervert Him the way you do all our laws and bills and histories and sciences and Life Itself. I use this pen to cease editing today.

I filled the pages with this and that: a poem by Mir Taqi Mir—*To save their souls they kill themselves with care/ A Paradise like that can go to Hell!*—you could get away with that, two hundred years ago; a sketch of a crocodile-rat called, *My Landlord*; a photograph of my barber; another of Petrov wearing a 44C bra; a third of Unsa's favorite fruits. And on the cover: the Hot Roofs of my old neighborhood, titled, *Where is she? I have her loquats.*

I'm flipping through the pages on this cold Saturday afternoon, when I hear a knock. The JP? Here, at last, is reckoning! I've been exaggerated! I'm seconds away from hanging!

A second knock. A hangman with a soft fist.

From inside, I shout, "Who is it?"

"Amal."

"Amal!" I fling the door open.

She doesn't come in, though how can she, I'm standing in the doorway. Seconds slide. We stare at each other, dumbly. Haven't seen her in two years. She looks—sad.

"Come in."

In the time it takes her to cross the threshold, take in the sparse furniture—stove, table, mattress—notice the space is small but scrubbed, strut to the window, and finally swing around, a hand has wiped her face. She's collected herself.

"How did you find me?"

"Abdul. Remember him?" I nod. "He knows your house. Your mother told him."

"He's not waiting downstairs, is he?"

"No. But I can't stay. My mother—" she hesitates. "So," she flaps her arms, "I like it. You're no sloppy bachelor. It's tidy. Even—*sweet.*"

"You're the first person to say that."

"You've left the party?"

"I was never really invited."

She smiles. I make us tea. We sit on the mattress and slyly look at each other. Sadness behind her smile. At last, "Nana sent me."

I drink my tea. Too hot. Burn my tongue.

"Why didn't you say everything—that first night? If not to him—to me? Later?"

"I don't know. It wouldn't have helped."

"It would have."

"I don't know."

"Did you feel interrogated?"

"Maybe."

"Do you feel it now?"

"Maybe."

"Did you hear what I said? Nana sent me."

"I'm *sorry.* Give him this." I hand her a copy of my last *Akhlaq,* many months old, many months too late. "I don't expect forgiveness, but maybe his opinion of me will change, a little."

"Give it yourself. And don't tell me what to do. And don't presume to know his opinions." She stands up. "He wants me to forgive you but I'm not sure I can."

"I'm sorry. I didn't know. I didn't."

"I thought we were friends! Coward!" She breathes heavily, turning red.

"I am." I mean a coward and a friend. Strangely, I'm comforted by her anger. Anything but her chilly composure. "More tea?"

"I said I can't stay."

"Five minutes?"

She sits down. She flips through the magazine, skips the editor's note—I think, *please read it, it's good!*—reads Mir's couplet out loud, mumbles, "He had the best worst etiquette," laughs at, *Where is she? I have her loquats.*

"Is *she* Unsa?"

"Yes. She'll be married by now." I pour her a second cup, trying to smile.

"This living alone. Opening or penance?"

"Both."

"What do your parents say?"

"My mother's trying. She brought me lunch the other day. Good sign. My father's furious. I've broken up the family. Brought dishonor. But at least he's in Bahrain these days, then on to the United States. Foreign invitations after ages. They keep him busy."

"Sounds like Munir Mamu." She begins to relax, reclining slightly.

"Who?"

"Nana's only son. All three generations—Nana's, his son's, ours—face each other with fangs. I hope Mehwish's is different."

"How is she?"

She hesitates. "Talkative."

I wait but she doesn't say more. "And Omar?"

"Still smells of tuberoses."

I didn't know he ever smelled of tuberoses, but I'm glad she's talking, even if this is the closest I've ever been to a woman without touching her. And I know I'm not going to.

When I'm good and worked up, she suddenly tells me of her fight with Mehwish. "The cost of my progress with Omar." She pushes the magazine away. "Traitors, all of you." She shuts her eyes. "I used to watch Mehwish sleep. She sleeps beautifully. Is that possible? As if for those hours, she overcomes something."

"Her second Satan. Memory."

"That's it."

Within minutes, it's Amal who's fallen asleep. My turn to watch.

I smell the pinhole gap between her voluptuous lips: tea leaves. Underneath, another scent. Honey? Cinnamon? A thick green sweater hangs in folds, hiding her breasts. She rests on her side. The angle flaunts the fullness of her hips. The shalwar of her top left leg clings; I see her thigh. I want to take off her shoes, roll down her socks, press her feet. But I leave her exactly as she is. I get the feeling she hasn't slept like this in a very long time. I can't remember even being awake like this.

Amal

The flying foxes are in Jinnah Bagh's northwest corner, beyond the library, in the branches of enormous banyan trees. Omar and I have made it our alternate space.

Today I'm skipping sedimentology to be with him. He looks at me, a smile in his moustache. "Will never understand this love you have of strange animals."

"Are only dogs and cats normal?"

"I used to have a rabbit."

"Was it normal?"

"It never bit me." He gives me a sidelong glance. "Unlike you."

Behind his light-hearted exterior is my first image of him, sitting by himself after his trancelike dance, an aura of caginess cautioning his girlfriend at the time to sit apart.

We find a bench under thickly colonized branches. A bat flaps, sending a ripple of sleepy wing-adjustments around it. I know why I bring Omar here. He's grown less like a panther with hunger and time, and more like the bats. Free in flight, twitchy in rest.

As the fidgeting continues, the tree with upside-down roots turns into a house of irritable upside-down residents. They yawn, gazing about their gravity-free world with large limpid eyes. A few fly off to hunt. Others find a better angle for stillness and disguise. They become pods. Lanterns. "Look." I point to one licking fur the color of Lahore's soil. "They groom like *normal* animals. And they echolocate, like whales."

"I've heard of whales," he laughs. "Come on, yaar, tell me what's new. The last time I saw you, you were running away from a party."

"It was boring. I've already told you that." We talked the next day. I told him I go only to be with him, risking echolocation at home. Ama's loosened the leash a little since Mehwish squealed, but if I'm caught again, Aba will grab it. I'll probably be married off to a computer dud in Texas or Singapore.

Omar sits with arms on the back of the bench, legs open. "The music was great."

"No it wasn't. You know I don't like U2."

His knees flap, sleepily, peevishly. He pouts. "What *do* you like?"

I look at upside-down roots and aerial swingings. A world against gravity. Frustratingly, my eyes tear.

He plays with my hair. "No problem, yaar," and louder, "how's your nana?"

He always asks after him, and that means a lot. "The security bothers him. His cough bothers him. Brian's work continues but Nana's housebound. That bothers him. But he's a little less aloof. And Noman is back." I don't tell him his reasons for disappearing.

Pout extends. "I never liked the sound of that Noman character."

I look away, smiling. All girls flirt with Omar but no other man should like me. I haven't told him about Abdul. Maybe Zara's right, I should, just to experiment! But I know the result: he'll forget it bothers him by partying more.

A skink brushes his foot, flaming orange tail glistening wet in the sun. He won't care but I say, "That was a lizard on its way to becoming a snake."

"You need books to tell you? In Punjabi that's a *samp di masi*."

I laugh. "A snake's mother's sister! Exactly. Related but different."

"The oddball's on the mother's side."

"*Of course.*"

"Learn Punjabi, drop your Urdu–English, you might learn something." His father's car bumper sticker reads: *Pakistani by birth. Punjabi by the Grace of Allah.*

"All right, Smug Sahib, what can *you* tell me about *chamgadar?*"

"*Chamgidar* in Punjabi." Pulling moustache hairs into his mouth, he folds his wings. "All I know is my mother'd say not to go into strange houses or the *chamgidars* would get me. But it didn't matter because they were always flying into our old house, when we lived on Nisbet Road. When I wanted to be a dancer." It's the first time he's sharing this. "I even took *kathak* lessons. But at thirteen, it stopped. Aba wanted me to know I'd one day work for him, in his leather factory. We both have the wrong passion. Girls dance and boys do business, if not science."

"Girls don't dance much either, not professionally."

"At least those who do aren't called lesbos."

"No. They're called whores."

"Maybe Mehwish would understand. It's like that Miss Fauzia and cricket."

I consider telling him that both Abdul and Noman badly want me.

"Anyway, I didn't like the *kathak* stories. How many times can you play a girl getting decked up, especially when you aren't even a girl?" He pretends to apply mascara and rouge. "It takes practice, being coy."

"Let's see."

"Not here."

The sky darkens. Trees recede in purple light, swallowing their restless tenants.

"I have a friend nearby." He stands up. "He will—he will leave us alone."

When it comes to being alone with him—completely alone, not in a car, or at a party—we've always parted here. I'd thought, feared, I'd make sure we always would.

I was wrong.

Noman

Spring 1996. The year before Amal's wedding, and the shooting.

This time when I return to Zahoor's house, I don't feel interrogated. I'm not the one he accuses, though his withering physique, the stifling security, and the restrictions on his work—American and French scientists get permits to dig up our fields, but not him—remind us daily: he can fight but not win.

Maybe he believes the fight can be won by my generation—or Mehwish's. Maybe that's why he chooses to forgive. Maybe it's not a choice. He *has* to. Hope is his religion.

Mehwish's happiness the day she finds me at Zahoor's again puts a silly smile on my face. From then on, Lahore's where we live our separate limited lives, while Zahoor's fortified house in the foothills of Islamabad where the four of us reunite becomes an opening. A magic bloom.

One day she shyly calls us *shir-o-shakar*, milksugar, adding, "I don't like milk, so *shir* you can keep." She speaks in her own rhythms and doesn't need an audience. The exception's when I tell her I turned thirty-one last year, and she wants to have a party. I say we'll have one when she turns seventeen in the summer but she wants one now.

So Amal bakes a cake, Junayd plays the harmonium, Mehwish sings, "*Happy gap teeth to you!*"

When Junayd tries to sing Ghalib—"Your favorite apostate," he tells Zahoor—Mehwish insists on making her own poem up, and she wants us to hear it.

It has nothing to do with my birthday but it gets our attention:

I like sugar without shir
Not a sheer that is steep
Like the steps of a balcony
I cannot see or sheer see through
Like Amal's shirts can be

She smiles, waiting for acknowledgement. Zahoor clears his throat. Amal looks worried. Every one claps. Zahoor says, "Come to me, Mehwish." He starts coughing, so she does as he says and sits beside him, not in his lap as she used to. She's too tall now and he's too weak.

Junayd fiddles with the harmonium keys and hums.

When he pauses, Mehwish says, "A god who is sheer good rehearses and hums."

Around the room, eyes meet. How much does she know? Zahoor's trial's never mentioned in front of her. She doesn't know he was in jail. But there are slips. We say the words heresy and apostasy. (It's hard to be in Zahoor's hollow silence; he's a man who has to speak.) So, why do we protect her from something no one's guilty of? We say all this while Junayd stretches his voice, gradually rolling into a rich raag.

Mehwish smiles as if she's composing rhymes in her head. Amal and I eat more cake.

•

All spring, Zahoor's house fills with visitors. I often catch Mehwish talking to herself and usually can't make out anything. Once I hear, "Clog. What kind of name is that? Flat!"

When I interrupt her she touches my face in that slow, intent way she has, poking her little finger in the gap between my teeth. Then she announces, "Of all God's names, Fareeb is the most magnificent."

"You mean *Fareed*. Without comparison."

"No. *Fareeb*."

"But that means fraud. Cheat."

"Oh!" Her voice is surprised. Her expression isn't. "In Braille the difference between *b* and *d* is just one dot!" She pinches my cheek, as if *I'm* the child. So I pat her head. Abruptly, she skips away. "I am all gory. I am a fish in a dish of a sensuous wine!" She leaves a space ringing with joyous murmurings. I stand still, absorbing it. The way she said it, it sounded *sin*suous.

Later, I find Amal outside, talking to one of Zahoor's guards about the weather. I ask, "Have you noticed Mehwish lately? Do you understand what she says?"

She shakes her head. "No. She's tasting."

Amal

"Marry me," says Omar.

He's the coast I want to collide against. I open for him like a sail. But do I want to be a boat called *wife*? Our rhythm swells. I suck his breath.

He repeats, "Marry me."

Muddy nipples on a shallow marine shelf. Kisses, my deposit. They taste of him. More than anywhere else, his teats hold his warm scent of sweet basil best. He wriggles, pushing my mouth closer to his. "*Here's* your narcotic." We are iron matter, swirling in a dynamo.

(Maybe Zara's right: geology is sex.)

When he pulls out he's still hard granite, and covered in me. On the inside of my thigh, he peels away like fish scales.

•

Something's happened to us since Nana's conditional release. Noman manages by himself in his flat, without complaining, even with dignity. Mehwish's betrayal is a minor Himalayan uplift. Our hearts rust, unity corroded. The rift keeps her to herself, but I think she prefers this. And I've gotten bolder—both in love and at work. It takes an old man on trial for youth to find itself, as if this was also part of the condition for Nana's release.

In the lab one day, Ibrar hovers around me while I remove the latest set of rocks brought back from a dig. I lean across the table. He peers down my neck. Then he pushes a slab off the table, Fawad laughing, Abdul bristling. I pick it up. A corner crumbles between my fingers. The rest, I start to clean. A rib?

A manatee's? An oddly calming chemical begins to course through me. What triggers it? Something I ate last night? Whatever it is, I'm suddenly able to ignore them. Instead of Fawad snickering, I see a pig-hippopotamus feeding on seagrass. I scratch the nub of bone, thick and tubular, and sketch the rest in my mind. I think, So what if their theology is as mixed up as this backbone? As the spine takes shapes, Fawad recedes. Eventually, all of him vanishes to the place that he had, till now, succeeded in putting *her*. I don't become she.

I become a separate ear, cushioned in oil, isolated yet better able to listen. Singularly in tune with an antique rib smaller than my thumb.

While Nana waits for the final verdict, I summon a center from which to chart the distant past of a land as much his legacy as that of his accusers. And as much mine as Fawad's, or Ibrar's. I overcome that unnameable hunger—a longing to be understood, or more, believed. I lose myself in my work, deaf to those that watch.

•

I sustain the calmness for months, even the day I get to the lab to find the solution I'd made to seal the slice of backbone in a transparent, protective coating, dribbled all over my worktable. *Don't react.* I clean up the mess and look for glue and Sufi detergent to make more solution. Can't find them. *Look later.* I focus on the bones I dislodged from the rock matrix, all shaped like arches and blades. Three I coated with the mixture. One's now missing.

They snicker. I keep calm. I look everywhere: the floor,

littered with old casts. Shelves, drawers, even the windowsill. I move to their table. They both sprawl across it.

They've done nothing since returning from the dig except talk—about last weekend's boar hunt, about tonight's feast, about their villages and peasants. They're supposed to make a copy of each fossil I prepare, and then catalogue it.

Erum and Shehla are supposed to help prepare the rocks. They avoid the lab when the men are in it, which is most of the time.

Abdul is supposed to scan the rocks with the electron microscope we don't have. He does Fawad and Ibrar's work instead, filling a mold with plaster of Paris, while they opine: the plaster is too thick, too thin, or too little. Abdul scratches his chin, streaking his beard white. (Mehwish streaking her smooth cheek with soil sculptures.) Leaving the cakey copy to dry (it's identical to the fragile original), he moves to Ibrar and Fawad's table, where I still linger.

"Do you want something?" Fawad asks.

"She is looking for the bone," answers Abdul.

Ibrar says, "What bone?"

Fawad says, "What she?" They both look at me. "There's no one else here."

"The bone you were supposed to maybe make a mold of, I think, like that." He points to his model.

Fawad sneers. "Are *you* tellling us what to do? Why don't you *eat* it?"

Abdul turns red. *I will protect you*, he promised. Now he can't even look at me. I tell him, loudly, "I'm not looking for a bone. I'm busy."

Fawad mutters, "I have a bone." Ibrar hoots.

Keep calm. I finally find what I need to make a fresh seal, return to my table, tell myself: *You need glue and Sufi Soap to make macrocosm!* Force myself to laugh. When I leave the lab later, I slip the remaining bones into my bag so they won't disappear as well.

On my way out, I meet Shehla and Erum. "What did we do today?"

I tell them how far I've gotten.

Shehla starts groping in my bag. I reach inside, hand her my book. She takes it with no thanks. I snatch it back and leave.

•

It's Noman I talk to. In his apartment, I tell him about my peers. "Their insults eat creativity. They're vultures, salivating at the temple of doubt." Omar would fidget. Omar would take off my shirt. Noman listens—in his way.

"*You* let their silly comments get to you?"

"*You* know what peer pressure is."

That silences him.

He stretches on the bed and smokes, not for the flavor but the rings. He says, more tenderly, "I understand. They have to smear their fingerprints over you."

"They make me feel like a lab rat."

"A rat for afterlife," a smoke ring wobbles at my heel, like an anklet, "in a laboratory of faith. But you're doing the right thing by talking to me."

I whisper, "You're easy to talk to." And this is true. His malleability's his weakness, but it's also his charm. He knows it. He knows that, like Nana, no one believes him capable of doing harm. His smile's too beguiling, his body too slight. Maybe if I weren't in love with Omar, I'd kiss him now. Instead, I look up the knees of his pants to his face, and the angle enlarges his nose. I ask, "Remember when Mehwish said God's hand slipped when making noses in South Asia?"

He flicks ash in my hair and I thank him for listening.

•

It's Noman, not Omar, I can talk to but it's Omar, not Noman, I want. I'm reckless about meeting both. But I maintain Ama's second silence, and I say nothing about Omar to Mehwish.

We go often to his friend's house in the Inner City. The house is always empty. A few broken tiles cling to a pillar dividing the kitchen from the living room, the oldest part of the house, where I like to lie in the tight curves of Omar's arms. (The rest is reconstructed more clumsily than the molds poor Abdul makes in the lab.) If Lahore won't preserve its beauty, we have our own way of trying, in our own modest space.

Love makes me lazy, as if I always have a full stomach. Our foreplay—or *bo's-o-kanar*, as Omar lovingly calls it, shedding his manly Punjabi pride to ladylike Urdu—is lavish and fat. Pretending to be at our own private court, we massage each other like Mughals. (The King's Hammam, now in ruins, is just around the corner.) The oil has a rich, woody scent. I take my time around his neck, watching those clitoral nipples stiffen. Even stroking the soles of his feet won't get such joyous results. He giggles and protests and feeds me falsa berries, strawberries, lychees.

I learn to taste. Item by item, the way I watched Mehwish's baby spit flower under a lens. (If the wonder of our childhood has helped make me a more attentive lover, Mehwish will love well. I learn to taste and so will she.) So, one day, drizzling oil down the thin line of thick hair that runs through his navel, and drooling lychee juice over his thighs, I have an urgent need to know which he noticed first, his chest hair or pubic hair.

I'm about to ask, when I realize something. I look up. "My religious vocabulary's Urdu–Arabic, social vocabulary Urdu–English, but sexual vocabulary only English, while yours—"

"*Ouch.* Do it again." I stop. In a flash, he rolls me onto my back. "Stop thinking."

Between laughing and hurting, I struggle to remember what I *was* thinking, "You've only looked at yourself—"

"I prefer to only look at you," he mumbles.

"I mean, you've only looked at both of us, sexually, in Urdu or Punjabi. Isn't it?"

He sighs. "Maybe English is like your endless questions. It helps you hide your *jinsi bhook.* Do you even know what that is?" He pulls off his white cotton briefs, the only kind of underwear he thinks he's allowed. It's as staple as rice.

"Of course I know. Sexual appetite. If you wear a different color next time, I'll have more."

He bites my nipples and I squeal. "No, I mean, do you *know* what that is?" He slides a hand into my shalwar, slides it higher, lower. The tip of his penis oozes lubriciously as he tells me to name myself in *my* tongue.

I can't. My mother tongue is as chaste as my mother.

He nods. "Urdu isn't as proper as you Urdu wallahs think. You leave out all the good words, forgetting the language comes from those who loved to love. There's a specific word for *female sexual desire*. Did you know that?"

"What is it?"

"Find out. You won't, because inside, you're still a *munh band kali*. No, excuse me, I mean a *virgin*."

"I know what it means." Absurdly, I remember what kind of closed bud Zara calls a virgin: a dogflower bud. I start to laugh.

"Why are you laughing?" he sulks.

I try to suppress my laughter behind lips I hold shut, like a bud.

He opens my mouth and starts naming me.

The words are hotter than the oil down my back, sweeter than the saliva on his tongue. They belong to me. They loosen me. *Geography first exists in the mind.* My names give me shape. ("What's this? *This*? Do you finally understand *jinsi bhook*?")

He starts to kiss my kus and I don't care how I should call it.

Noman

Abruptly, it stops. Mehwish won't poke between my teeth. She won't read my face. I try to sit beside her at Zahoor's but she moves away. I ask Amal if I've upset her but she shrugs, wanting to talk about Omar. He's asked her to marry him. She doesn't want to but she loves him, madly, he *is* the one, she's just afraid of being *wife*. Et cetera.

I don't give up. One evening, after a light rain, Amal and I lie in the damp grass while Mehwish sits apart in a chair. I try again, "What's the matter with her?"

Amal turns her head and looks inside the living room. Zahoor's coughing violently, Junayd beside him. He covers Zahoor's knees with a blanket. Brings cough syrup. Wipes Zahoor's forehead with a hanky drawn from his shirt pocket.

Amal smiles. "I'm glad I turned my head."

"He never married—Junayd?"

Amal looks at me and we both fall silent.

Mehwish's head is lowered but I feel her awareness of me grow.

After a long silence, Amal says, "In an environment where you can't light a candle with a candle, you risk being burned by your own flame."

Zahoor lies back and Junayd tips a teaspoon between his lips.

Mehwish stands up. On her way into the house, she passes us, murmuring, "Hanky panky swimming in a tanky. Kun fe kaf noon, kith ne half moon."

"What on earth…?" I turn to Amal.

Amal gazes dreamily at the sky. "What do you think, should I marry him?"

"If it'll help you listen, yes."

Amal

"Marry me," Omar repeats. "We'll live on our own."

That's one of my conditions. Omar's feudal-industrialist family lives together, but we have to live separately. I don't underestimate the problems this will cause between us and them. Or how sweet the reward: no in-laws listening to our passion or our fights, our peace or alienation. I don't know if their intrusion will be real or imagined but I know I don't want to be consumed by the need to find out. And if it *is* real, I don't want to "suffer," like Erum or Shehla, Ama or Apa Farzana.

If you want to tell a different story, live a different life.

"I'm going to do a little preliminary research."

He throws an arm around me. "Stay."

"I can't." I trace the bulge of his jugular vein, his *shah rag*, the shah of veins. Kiss it. Between my fingers, he starts to pulse. I show him a breast and he salivates. Happiness is being in the right skin.

We roll names across each other. He says, "These are too good for tits or chest or *choochi* or *chathi*. I pronounce you: Milk Pak."

I remind him where my hand is.

"Okay okay," he pleads. "I pronounce you: Malika Boobs."

"Then bow."

He bows. "And this," he holds me holding him, "is more than cock or *lund*. It's the biggest. *Lora*."

Happily for him, I can't correlate. But I still tease, "That's a girl's name."

"Not in our country, you angrez!"

•

When I finally tiptoe outside, I find a rickshaw easily. As the hefty driver weaves the rickshaw between two police cars and all three of us race to run the red light, I remember asking once, about a sketch I drew, What is it? To me it was a dog-whale, but not to Nana's neighbors.

I decide to start my experiment right now. I don't have a picture of a person-wife, so first I tell him to imagine it.

"I don't have a wife, baji."

"*Imagine* you do."

He looks at me quizzically in the rear-view mirror. We hit a ditch and I nearly fly out, almost don't become a wife.

I repeat, "Just shut your eyes—uh, no don't do that, keep your eyes on the street but imagine, you know, a wife. What is it?"

"I would have to ask my mother."

"What do *you* think?"

"*She* would know."

"What kind of wife do *you* want?"

He shakes his head, grins.

"This investigation is a failure."

He laughs. *Can't wait to tell my friends about this nut I picked up today...*

"Okay, one more time. Do you know any wives?"

He looks worried.

"What is your brother's wife like?"

"Bhabi? She is a very good woman."

"Yes?"

"She helps my mother. And she doesn't complain."

"And she looks good?"

"Oh yes. I mean, of course. Bhabi."

"How many children?"

"Three, mahshallah."

"Boys?"

"Inshallah."

I pay him and wave goodbye.

•

For the next several days, I continue with my investigation. This is what I find:

She must be *surily*. Not gruff, melodious.

She must have *silica*. Not a mineral, tact.

She must have *naiky*. Not nudity, purity.

She mustn't have *jurm*. Not disease, wrong.

She mustn't have *man*. Not a lover, arrogance.

She mustn't make *churcha*. Not a place of worship, a commotion.

She mustn't be *zehny*. Not silly, intelligent.

She must give *awlad*. Not one wondrous lad, several.

She must love *taskeen*. Doing chores and giving comfort.

But I'm losing the picture, more blurry than the dog-whale. The last speaker is a saleswoman at a lingerie shop. I cut her off. "Don't say what she should *do*. What *is* she?"

"*Shahdarah.*"

"A gateway? But a gateway to what? What is she *already*? From inside?"

An orange-haired woman looks me up and down, from my

muddy toes to my messy hair. "Already she is a *qatamah*!" Not a mother cat, a whore. "Already she has no *hookum*!" The orange-haired customer leaves with her bag of panties.

"Already she has no authority?" I ask the saleswoman, who simply shrugs.

I go to a men's store to buy Omar something more interesting than his staple-as-rice underwear. I leave with our panties, now as a hooker with a little *hookum*!

Noman

Mehwish stops coming to Zahoor's. Rejection, how you stab me!

And just as suddenly, Zahoor's acquitted. It's over: the judge decides there was no evidence. Case dismissed. Within days, one of his guards goes missing. Within hours, the other's found dead.

Zahoor finds him, "curled like a cashew," both eyes open, gun in his crotch. Probably poisoned, but his family won't allow an autopsy. In the muzzle of the unloaded gun, a single ominous line scratched in blue ink on a scrap of paper: *Jaise ap ko pata hai.* As you know.

"He was sweet and could barely load a gun," Amal tells me. "No blood. No broken bones. Not even a bruise."

So the wronged are remembering Zahoor, again. Who knows how it began this time. A column printed somewhere, maybe in *Akhlaq*, maybe by the new editor, if such a person exists. All I can do is speculate. I'm out of the loop now, and this is almost harder. I'm not the agent. I'm just another powerless witness of a trajectory now moving by itself.

Amal

Two days after Nana's security guard is murdered, the guard of the judge who freed him is also killed. This time, the skull is smashed and the note rests across his eyes: *Jaise ap ne dekha hai.* As you've seen.

The judge leaves the country. We start telling Nana to do the same.

I can't sleep. I watch Mehwish again while she sleeps. I barely see Omar. I worry that our sublime months of *bo's-o-kanar* are over. And at university, I lose the ability to float above the gossip and intimidation.

Within a week, Nana's lawyer's guard is also dead. In the same handwriting in the same blue ink, a roll of paper dug into his ear: *Jaise ap ne suna hai.* As you've heard.

The lawyer leaves the country. Junayd moves Nana to a secret place. A hidden *S.* (*S* for sanctuary.) Even I don't know where it is and could never climb the right hill to find it.

What we do is build a sound barrier around Nana, so he can't be seen or heard or even heard *of.* He becomes *al ghayb.* The absent. We're to stop even imagining him.

•

I return to my afternoons with Omar and the sound barrier of our hidden sanctuary. But now it feels less as if we're moving toward each other, more as if we're running away from everyone else. Do we need this, or a different nest? Not his friend's poorly reconstructed hideout in the Inner City, but a home built together, with windows to throw open to a world that welcomes us? Without that, will our refuge grow stale and our love self-destruct?

Omar means too much to me to risk that happening.

I lie beside him while he sleeps, my mind spinning. Today he asked me again for an answer. Today I think I'm coming close. I've done research on "wife" and gotten no answers. But I've found my own: she can't be quantified. Mehwish understands me better than I understand myself. She never framed me in a table of stinks and sounds...

I wonder what "husband" is to Omar. He sleeps as serenely as Mehwish, as if his memory has flown, leaving an early morning glow to this late afternoon.

At last his eyes open, the corners wrinkling in a smile as he looks up at me. I want him to always wake up next to me with that smile. As he tries to wipe the sleep off his eyes, I pull the hand away, finger by finger, and the wrinkles around his eyes expand. "Will you be a pompous pontificating married man with speeches and what not?"

He groans. But miraculously, the smile doesn't leave him.

"As a person-husband, what's the first thing you'll always be?"

"Oof!" He covers his face.

"I see. The first thing you'll always be is oof!" Again I pull his fingers off his eyes.

"God forbid, the last thing I'll always be is oof!"

"Ask me the first thing I'll always be, as a person-wife."

"Oofless?" He kisses me, finger by finger.

•

I get home late. The television's on, and it's loud: Aba. Ama meets me at the door. "He hasn't noticed," she says, as if I've asked. She's so panicked she pants.

The assurance of my day with Omar fades behind her need to "save" me.

She pulls my elbow. "Marry him. If he's asked you, you're a fool to say no."

I said *yes* today. Now, as I look at her, as I feel her paranoia slide into me like a poison, I almost change my mind. But then I would be a fool.

Noman

Quiet since the death of the three guards this summer. News about Zahoor still vague. If the family's in touch with him and Junayd, I don't blame them for keeping it secret. When Amal gets engaged, only close relatives are invited.

•

I walk around the city, take a rickshaw to Bhati Gate, consider drifting to Salman's for whisky, keep walking, all the way to Mehwish's school. Haven't seen her since before Zahoor left, when she stopped touching me, then stopped visiting him. I wasn't with her when she turned seventeen. Yet, Mehwish is so *known* to me. The scent of her many shampoos—seaweed for blue, wood for purple. Her little finger between my teeth. Her intimate chatter. The sweet low ring of her voice. I don't exactly think of her as blind. Exactly. But now at lunchtime, as I look inside the school gate, I feel disoriented. The girls walk slowly and stare blankly, or nibble sandwiches without seeing chicken bits or tomato rings slide from between the bread, and onto the ground. Mehwish would have sensed it. Or maybe not. Maybe sometimes I only assume she knows so much.

I think that's her, walking toward a small shed with her right hand extended. After a while, I see an old baba come out of the shed. And then the guard at the gate asks me gruffly what I want and I move on.

Am I a dirty old man? Honestly, for Mehwish I don't let myself feel anything lower than my heart. For Unsa, yes. And briefly, I'll admit, for Amal. Mehwish is different. With her, I'm not a bundle of trepidation, as Amal cruelly described me once. Mehwish makes me the way I want to be. Mehwish is my peace. Living alone's giving me the discipline to wait for her to grow up. Or just wait.

A rickshaw stops. I could visit my mother. She's very lonely now that Sehr's married and moved to Canada. She even misses Meow, Sehr's cat. The last time I saw her, she sat with me on the terrace, something we've never done before. Her hands weren't making or putting away food. They were free and I stared at them till I heard the front door open: Aba, home early, to suck the color from my blood. I took myself off his roof, and fled.

The rickshaw driver impatiently pulls away.

I walk by the Canal, sometimes green and fetid, sometimes brown and oily. Today the water's high, earth red and flowing. Wonder how Mehwish sees its moods.

It starts to drizzle. A late November drizzle, before the fog rolls in. A billboard announcing *God is Great* hangs like a menacing shield, waiting to crash into a car, or tumble down the bridge, for stray cats to fuck under.

The rain grows loud. I get the smell of Lahore I usually only get in summer, when it's so hot people water their driveways. They turn on the hose to crack the whip on heat. And then that smell: of watered roads, of the earth opening its maw, of tension released. Vapors slide over my tongue and deep into my lungs. It's the smell of the fertile tunnels of Lahore's past. It's the smell of a woman.

I lie flat on my stomach. Stick my face in the wet earth of this city.

•

It rains into December and I walk. Catch a cold. Grow skinnier.

One evening, Amal's waiting for me outside my door. "Finally! I was about to leave! Just wanted to say we've agreed on a date next November. Plenty of time to convince me not to do it."

"You're already engaged." I smile, hold the door open for her.

She opens my empty fridge and puts chicken ginger inside. "I made it."

"Thank you." I take off my shirt, wear a dry one. Boil water. With my back to her, I try to ask after Mehwish as casually as I can. But Amal's a shrewd devil and takes this opportunity to say what I know she's been dying to say for a while.

"Noman. *You* are thirty-one. Almost thirty-two. *She* is seventeen."

"Oh, I know! I have not—" Shit, shouldn't have paused. "I mean, I haven't—" Deep breath. "I don't think of her, you know."

"Noman, you've never told me who you sleep with, but I know you never found the guts to tell Unsa you wished it was her."

Even for her, too bloody much. "This is none of your business."

"Are we friends?"

"Good question."

"Thank you."

We try to stare each other down. Stupidest thing I've ever done.

Finally, she says in haste, in a surprising quiver, "I know I hate it when others are protective or interfering but she's my baby sister. She still is. And something's—happened. I can sense it. She won't tell me. She's just so—*quiet.* It's not *her.*" She breathes deeply. "I *raised* her."

She picks up her purse and runs away before I can ask, What do you mean something's happened?

Amal

I found Mehwish crying in our room, her shalwar torn. Ama brought her home early from school. "Her teachers said she fell. She was playing."

"Playing what?" I asked Ama.

"I don't know, Amal. What do girls play these days? We used to play pithoo and hopscotch. The cut above her eye is deep but not infected. They cleaned it well."

Mehwish had three stitches and a bruise above the eye. She let me touch a corner of the bruise very softly. "Does it hurt a lot?" She didn't reply. "Is that why you're still crying?" She wouldn't say. I held her as she lay in bed, my chest to her back, arms around her waist, craning my neck to look in her face. It was unreadable.

When she fell asleep, I don't know why, but I checked her shalwar, which she'd taken off and thrown in a pile of dirty clothes. A small tear along the cloth's right thigh. Another at the knee. A little blood at the knee. Nowhere else. I wondered if she still tied the cord in a double knot, then wondered why I thought that. Heart pounding, I looked in the dirty clothes for underwear. Found two, both unstained. Her self-grooming's meticulous. Even with her period, her clothes stay clean. She can smell the tiniest leak. I returned to the bed and lifted her nightie slowly. Two pads bulged in her panty. Except at the knee, I saw no bruises or cuts, definitely none near the scent of her discharge. But a pair of fists knocked at my temples: *Who or what has scared her? All those years spent looking down for her weren't enough. Her safety will always be my tail.*

I gently covered her again. I thought, no, I *knew*. Today she learned it's not only my tail, but hers.

I shut my eyes and tried to remember her new moon.

•

Tonight I lie with her again. She's not asleep. Behind the air conditioner, a lizard laughs. We'd lie like this as children each spring. As the weather warmed and the reptiles crept awake, I'd think, She'll never see the silver of a snail's walk but she'll always hear the lizards first. Now it's December and getting cold. The gecko clucks goodbye.

"Remember the one you found, in the sofa?" I remind her of the day she was searching for a squeegee ball—the one she turned into a moon—digging under cushions, probing between the backrest and the seat. She came away with a dead lizard. I, who've skinned cock and shrew, would have screamed.

She only frowned, asking, "What is it?" The pressed bones were tightly locked, like a sheaf of dried tobacco. "Light and papery," she rubbed. "Oh!" The skeleton snapped. "What *is* it?"

I found an analogy she found an allergy: lizards are like cockroaches. They fall on you. They're dirty. They creep.

"But this one isn't moving."

"It's dead. Its skin's been picked. That's the skeleton."

When she finally understood, she dropped it and screamed.

Now she says nothing but I know she's listening. "You were only afraid when I told you what it was. Now you've learned to know by yourself." I stroke her hair. "It's good to listen to that." I keep stroking. "Did you only fall?" The fourth time I'm asking. Still nothing. "All right." She doesn't attend her graduation party.

•

Finally, in March, the geckos return, dust storms rage, Nana calls often, the scar above her eye fades, a tiny one at her knee remains. Her silence begins to thaw.

"I won't tell if you tap at my window," she says.

"It's all right. Since we're getting married, seeing Omar isn't so secret."

"Is it still a little secret?"

"Some things, yes."

"What things?"

I hesitate. "Some day, you'll know. You will love well." She tilts her head, hiding a smile. "Did you hear me?" She nods shyly, moving to the cassette player. Should I try to ask about the fall again? No. She'll speak when *she* wants. Give her time. Time is hers.

We listen to Hari Prasad on the flute. She moves around the room, swaying, humming.

I watch, remembering her dance like the film stars she'd never seen, and never will see. I miss that her real ijaz moments have become only religious, that Khoon Jirab Pass is not Bloody Socks but just the Khunjerab Pass, that we only go around roundabouts not aboutrounds to get petrol that's not adult but only adulterated though person ali, it should be. Is this why Noman has fallen in love with her? In making you miss her, she brings you closer to yourself. Better than even Nana, Mehwish understands why Pascal cried when he saw the little tick. In the drops in the blood in the veins in the knuckles in the feet there was heat *there was Mehwish*.

Noman

The invitation to Amal's wedding is a simple card, rough in texture, muddy brown with blue trim. It smells of Lahore's mud. Of a woman. "For heaven and earth. And for the creatures who decided to return to the sea. For *Amalicetus*." She laughs.

"Congratulations." I hug her, comforted by her voluptuousness, but not aroused.

She kisses my cheek. "I'm sorry. For the last time I was here. You know, when I told you to stay away from Mehwish. I had no right."

But when I try to ask after Mehwish, she's still guarded. Still protecting her.

So I say, "And Zahoor, will he attend?"

"I can't get married without him."

We spend the rest of the day discussing the islands she and Omar will visit on their honeymoon. I don't see her again till the wedding.

Amal

We hear of a two-bedroom apartment in A Block ("A block of what?" says Mehwish). Good location for a rent we can afford, though just barely. The floor's littered with dead and dying cockroaches; the drains limned with mold; the Azan blaring from the mosque down the street rattles the windows. "We'll take it."

Omar didn't tell his family we weren't going to live with them till after the engagement. Then the wedding was almost called off (Ama of course said to stop making a fuss about living arrangements), and Omar almost sacked from his father's factory. Eventually, his father kept him, but the price is being constantly reminded of the favor, though he earns almost as little as I earn at the lab. He's looking for another job.

We'll move into the apartment in December, the month after our wedding, once we've returned from the Maldive Islands. Zara's wedding gift to us. I've never seen a living whale and am hoping to spot winter migrants. Neither Omar nor I can swim. But we can buy swimsuits, for splashing in the shallows and peeling off at night. Mine's parrot green and makes me feel more like a ten-year-old than when I was a ten-year-old. His, scarlet.

When we're alone, he tries it on. It hugs his hips and warms his skin. He glows.

"Primordial return."

"What's that?"

"God's original idea of you."

Dark hairs line the lewd red triangle as he stands, hands on hips, grinning.

Noman

On stage, next to her groom, Amal adjusts the neck of her aquamarine top. Satisfied that both ends are even, she looks up at us: Mehwish in the middle, Zahoor and I her two bookends.

Zahoor looks like the lone old wolf he's had to become. He's lean, he's haggard, his eyes are starved. He's quiet. But he can still insult others just by turning his neck. Still incite admiration with a nod. And he still softens for Amal, and especially Mehwish, asleep on his shoulder. With me, he's changed yet again. Instincts are now his sharpest teeth. They tell him I've fallen in love with the girl between us. His arm around her's a challenge: *I forgave you but did I say you were good enough?*

Except for the time I think I spotted her at school, this is the first I've seen of Mehwish since last summer, when she stopped coming to Zahoor's. Last year she looked younger than sixteen. Now she looks older than eighteen.

She doesn't show any sign of having missed me. I keep looking. It's not there.

More people arrive. Between the angry and the adoring, there are those who give Zahoor cold, calculated indifference. Security's tight. Armed guards at every door. Invitations closely checked. But from the look on Amal's face, not closely enough. Because she insisted on Zahoor's attendance, only relatives and close friends (not their relatives and their close friends) have been invited. I'd guess three hundred people. These days, if you don't have three thousand, you're nobody.

There goes Amal's hot friend, Zara, in fitting bronze-toned tunic, orange dupatta blazing behind her like a scent. Golden eyeshadow. Stars in her hair.

Junayd hovers, smoothly blending in the crowd while keeping an eye on Zahoor. I'll never have any one that devoted to me. At least ten years younger and always reverent, tonight Junayd assumes an authority over Zahoor that's almost fatherly. No, daughterly. No, wifely. He tells him where to sit and what to eat. And when Zahoor's son, arrived from France (where he lives in shame of Zahoor), stands behind us and announces, "It's our *values* that mark us. They're the materials God designed us with, to be his singular creation, as the Quran says," Junayd shakes his head at Zahoor, pleading, *Ignore him.*

About food and seating Zahoor will grudgingly agree. Not this. He turns around (Mehwish shifting in her sleep). "What does it say about singular idiots? With what materials are they designed?"

Good for him. He and Junayd will quarrel about it later but they always make up.

Funny what you're thinking when the world explodes. This was my thought: Zahoor won't be in his house in Islamabad when he and Junayd quarrel about it later and laugh and drink and forget. He doesn't live there anymore. He lives in some secret place, isolated but safe.

What was the chronology of events? What caused me to turn? Did I *know* the bullet was making the commotion, *see* it, or *hear* it? Who screamed first—Junayd? Whose blood's still on my shirt?

Why had Mehwish reached out to me, just before?

I feel a stab in my back and a cold finger—no ionized djinn this, but a soft soft angel—and wetness in my eyes and just like that, there's an explosion. Followed by a second. Amal runs down the stage, Omar pulls her to him, her sea-blue top ruined, her wedding dress for life, covered in what I know by now, as I lie here in Emergency—the drip, drip drip, in the intima of my veins. Amal gave me the word when she gave Mehwish and me blood. *Intima.* The innermost wall of a vein. We three talked from vein to vein, without once touching. *Intima.* An exact intimation. An opening: from gateway to gateway, square to circle to triangle. What was I saying? This will be the wedding dress Amal will look back to, covered in what I know by now is my blood and Mehwish's and Zahoor's and Junayd's and most of all, Zahoor's specially created son.

Amal

Mehwish shifts. *What's going on?* I mouth to Noman. Nana tosses his head, says something to his son. The photographer aims a video camera away from me, the geometry of arms and shoes, glasses and chairs, more photogenic than just another bride. Someone shoves Junayd. Mehwish wakes up. Leans forward, hand outstretched, toward Noman. His hand lifts, I think, to take hers. Then he turns.

The movement stops abruptly, and it isn't right. *This has happened before. When?*

Everything that happens next happens before I can tear my eye away from the chaos of men standing behind Nana, Mehwish, and Noman. In that long excruciating gap between all the pushing and shoving and Noman jerking backwards, I see it: infrared. A splash of heat outside my focal length. A tumult of blinding color. A hurtling explosion that would spark a beginning if it weren't created to end.

Kite string? No, a silent bullet. No, two. The second, I hear. I run. Omar holds me back. Screams. Never heard so many. Zara sprayed in blood, the drops oddly dazzling on her rust-gold silk. She springs forward, pushing me into Omar. "Don't let her see."

A third shot. "Mehwish!" *Even the air is not safe.* "Mehwish!"

Nana falls onto the floor, where Junayd lies open, an enormous pomegranate wet for the gouging. They both keen.

Mehwish is screaming, I'm screaming, Aba's screaming. "Ambulance!" Blood oozes between our fingers. "Ambulance!"

Noman and Munir Mamu—the only ones not screaming.

gateway the fifth: the afterlife

When we were children we went to the Master for a time
For a time we were beguiled with our own mastery;
Hear the end of the matter, what befell us:
We came like water and we went like wind.

—Omar Khayyam, *Ruba'iyat*

Amal

I'm in the hospital. I don't want to be here. I'm in the hospital.
I can't escape.

Mehwish still unconscious. A doctor infected her wound. A
second doctor recleaned it. He doesn't think she'll die. Noman
might. He wakes up, clear-headed, tries to talk. Still, he might
die. Nana also might. Junayd, definitely. Munir Mamu, already.
Omar's gray shawl around me, the one that smells of us. Omar
alive, definitely. I don't stop shivering. Around my head, true
and false bullets.

On my wedding night I learn that there are true and false
bullets. A true bullet spins just so, it doesn't wobble, it releases
full energy inside the target. A false bullet passes through the
target. It doesn't mushroom or explode. It performs badly, like
the bullet that hit Target Mehwish. Actually, she wasn't the
target. Nana was. It was false. The second doctor doesn't think
she'll die.

After my wedding night I learn that the type of bullet's
crucial, so's the type of gun—the police say it was a pistol—but
most crucial of all, is the distance a gun's fired from. No one had
a measuring tape. Wherever it came from, the bullet that hit
Mehwish ricocheted like a bird in an eclipse, darting from surface
to surface, knocking into the ceiling and at least one wall. By the
time it entered her it had lost enough velocity to cause only soft-
tissue damage. And the angle of entry was also false.

She leaned forward to touch Noman. If she hadn't, she
wouldn't have been hit at all. But if she'd looked for him with
her nose not arm, the bullet might have torn her esophagus. Or

jugular vein. Instead, she stretched her right arm, the one that's only hers, and the bullet slid through it almost clean. It behaved badly and miraculously.

Almost clean. The first doctor tied the tattered corners of the exit wound shut like a child learning daisy stitch with a dirty needle and a hair. Tissue swelled with pus, "like a caterpillar trying to get out," she cried. The second doctor, Dr. Bashar (Dr. Human—good to know), shot her with antibiotics and reopened her the way I once reopened a shrew. He sewed her back evenly and sterilely.

My blue-green wedding *jora* (for Mehwish's favorite color, seaweed shampoo), soiled in everyone's blood, is at the cleaner's.

Today Mehwish wakes up and moans. "The caterpillar got out."

"Her fever has broken." Dr. Bashar puts the thermometer away. "Had the bullet flown a little higher, little upperarm bone pieces called humerus bone pieces would have shot through her with maximum energy. You should give buckets of thanks."

"Where's Noman?" Mehwish whimpers.

"In another room. Also being dressed." Not true. Noman might die.

"And Nana?"

"With him." Bigger lie. The bullet that struck Nana performed well. The one that hit Junayd, even better. I start to cry.

"Then why are you crying?"

"Same reason as you, Mehwish."

Dr. Bashar says I'm in shock and should go home. He changes Mehwish's dressing, shaking his head with approval. "She is going to be fine." Mehwish scowls at him, trying to look like an outraged owlet, looking instead like a petrified kitten. He bandages her and keeps chatting. "I have never heard of a wedding like yours."

He's young and should be forgiven.

Before Mehwish drifts asleep again, she asks, "What happened?"

"It's a miracle your bone wasn't hit," I tell her again. This is no lie. (The doctor smiles at her. *She can't see you.*) "The bullet pinched the only fleshy part of your arm, the part of me you say sags." And—I leave this part out—entered Noman. In him it released its potential.

If he hadn't turned away from Mehwish, it might have pierced his heart. Instead, twisted away from her, his upper back absorbed the shock. Small bone fragments have broken off and punctured a lung, filling it with fluid.

When Mehwish is asleep, I join Ama outside Nana's room (the way we once waited outside the courtroom). I also want to join Noman. I also want to join Omar, waiting outside Junayd's room. Munir Mamu's dead. Burial tomorrow.

•

Noman is temporarily off the respirator. He opens his eyes and wheezes. "What …?"

I don't know what he's asking so I say, "You need oxygen and plasma."

"What …?"

"Plasma."

"Sehr …?"

"Flying in from Canada today."

"Like cheese." He smiles.

His sister Shaista asks me to leave. I know she wouldn't mind saying a thing or two about my wedding.

I stand up, but Noman whispers, "Mehwish."

I tell him only her arm was hit. Then I realize probably no one's explained what happened to *him*. So I say, "The same bullet hit you high on your back, but never exited." I try to smile. "It's now somewhere near your—"

Shaista begins to cry. Her brother steps forward, asks me to leave, adds, "You are a very cold unfeeling woman." Her mother holds both palms out, praying.

I *feel* cold (I *un*feel cold), as if I'm the one who's lost blood. Like an accountant, I *list* Noman's pain. (Like a scientist is said to be.) It helps to call out the events of my wedding the way I once called out letters for Mehwish. But it isn't helping anyone else.

I pass Noman's father in the corridor. Though I've seen so much blood, I wouldn't mind seeing his.

•

If knowledge helps: The false bullet sits in muscle near Noman's spinal column, near his aorta. To remove it is to cut dangerously close to the artery. The doctors decide to leave the bullet as a permanent guest. They hope it'll never turn in its sleep. They hope that over time, it'll petrify in its new home.

To prevent worry from fusing with the dreaded lead poison to create a worse poison, for now, no one tells Noman. And I don't tell Mehwish.

•

By January, the hospital releases Noman. Not Nana and Junayd.

How to begin describing their wounds? *List their pain, item by item.* I tell myself I'm good at that. But I can't do it. I only get this far: they were each struck by a soft-nosed bullet, both from a local rifle fired by the same security guard. I learn this because the guard next to him, who carried an American assault rifle, had never cleaned it. If it came with an instruction manual, how was he supposed to read it? When he pulled the trigger, the bullet slipped and blew off half his face. With the half left, he tells us that all five shots—the one that backfired; the two that hit Nana and Junayd; the one that hit first Mehwish then Noman; and the one that killed Munir Mamu—were fired by three guards hired to kill Nana. We asked what Nana had done. He didn't really know. We asked who hired him. He didn't really know. The other two guards got away. He confirms that the one who shot Mehwish and Noman carried a pistol, though which kind, he didn't really know.

When the half-faced man's rifle was opened, the barrel was a mine of limestone deposits. I can recall such details.

•

A gusty April morning, five months after my wedding and a week after Junayd dies. All the biggest events in my life happen either in November or April. April: Mehwish is blinded; Nana's arrested; Junayd dies. November: Noman arrives at Nana's door; Mehwish betrays me; I get married.

April: my first dig. Now that I'm Omar's, not my parents',

they can't stop me. And now that Omar's mine, he doesn't try to stop me.

I'm standing on a steep outcrop overlooking the Valley of Dhun, one of the highest points in the Salt Range. The Jhelum River flickers ahead, sliding into the horizon like a fish. Around me, a mat of soft green plain. Behind me, Abdul and other colleagues kneel at the edge of a pit, picking stones.

If I fall off this rock—or jump—the river will snare me with a quick flick of its silver tail. If I leave behind no trace, I'll exist as God first conceived me. As abstraction. I'd pre-exist, if He exists. But I'm a creature of this world and can't renounce it. I need to scratch fingerprints, and leave my own. Sometimes I collect records of ancient life because I'm unafraid of my own mortality. Sometimes, because I'm afraid.

Before my first ride to these hills, when I was just eight, Nana and Junayd talked. What they said resonates louder now, in this valley, than in Nana's house. *Why create?* To unite with God? Rival, or reject Him? Junayd praised an orthodox God whom no one could presume to know. When Nana jokingly asked, "How do you meet your obligations to this world, according to the wishes of your Beloved?" Junayd didn't truly answer him then. He answered at my wedding. With his answer must have come shock, that his stern, formal deity would reward his humility with the most gruesome end.

He threw himself in front of Nana to take the second bullet.

In the end, it isn't theological debate or scientific inquiry or artistic devotion that proves you, but a sudden act of courage. Junayd couldn't have pre-empted it. He didn't do it to be remembered or immortalized. He just jumped. His impulsiveness, his selflessness, is the closest I've come to witnessing the divine.

The bullet billowed inside him like an A-bomb. The water in his body rose like a tsunami. Smashed him. Flooded him. Swept him into its maw, like this pebble I chuck into the river below. Enough description for me.

I don't want to know how many bones were broken, how many veins burst, how many organs crushed, how many inches of flesh were lacerated when the bullet finally exited. I don't want to know whose idea it was to leave the soft nose poking out of the bullet jacket so it kept expanding. I don't want to know that it was a *true* bullet, while the one that struck Mehwish and Noman was false. I don't want to know if she leaned in front of Noman for the same reason Junayd threw himself in front of Nana. I don't want to know why he didn't die immediately instead of suffering for so long. I don't want to know *that* miracle. I don't want to know. I just want Junayd alive again.

I never thanked him. He defended, nursed, and saved Nana. He sat me on his lap on my first ride to these hills and asked me if I had a doll.

I've waited so long to dig alongside my colleagues, as an equal, I can't let them see me now! Better to leap off this cliff than give them the satisfaction of seeing me cry—like a *girl*!

I keep my back to them.

What I have to create: a dike against decay. This is the burden of the witness and I'll carry it with pride.

I pull my eye away from the silvery light of the piscine river below, and walk toward the pit. Inside is a segment of thigh about five inches long and two in diameter. We place it on a plinth of dirt. Abdul and I start preparing the cast, dipping burlap strips in a tub of plaster of Paris, winding the wet cloth first around the pedestal, then around the thigh itself, slowly, as if shielding a sprain. I can feel the bruises as I wrap.

•

Now that Nana's lost Junayd, I know I'll soon lose him.

The bullet broke inside him. I can say that now, nearly a year later. I can name his pain. Two surgeries, each to pick out two bullet scraps. The second surgery caused an infection. There's a splinter of metal still embedded in him, but the doctor says Nana's too weak for a third attempt. "A younger target would have had better immunity."

I should have been the younger target.

Aba sells Nana's house in Islamabad and Nana moves in with his only surviving child, my mother. Mehwish recites poems to help him sleep.

•

When I remember that I'm married, my marriage is a relief. Our little home in A Block is covered in ivy and has a large bamboo tree with delicate shoots that hang over the balcony where Omar and I have breakfast every morning. He likes to begin his day on a hot stomach: toast; melting butter; strong steaming tea. I like to begin mine cold: fresh lemonade; almonds; dried dates. Followed by a pill. We never did have our honeymoon, but Omar warns me not to lose more weight or my swimsuit will droop unbecomingly when we finally get to a beach. Zara promises to buy us the honeymoon "again and again."

It's when he holds me in our bedroom overlooking the neighbor's garage that I say, "I *had* to have Nana at our wedding. But I ruined everyone. Including you."

At first he listens, disagreeing heartily when I let him. One night, he snores. Another night, he says, "Please stop." The night after that, he slides a hand under my nightie and cups my breasts leisurely, sliding a thumb around each nipple. His patience eases me. He's back to being a panther with time, not a twitchy bat. He sits up, positions me so my back rests against his chest, lifts the thin satin higher, doesn't take it off. He slides a light hand over my stomach, over my underwear, doesn't take it off. Slides a finger into me, thickens behind me. He strips me drooling on my neck. Such pleasure, when others are in pain!

I push down. "I'm going to keep you in."

He lurches higher into me.

"Not yet. I'm going to keep you *in*."

He tries to slow down.

In the middle of the night, dreaming of Omarish sinuosities, I crawl on top again.

•

His salt and grease stay with me on my long drives into the salt-striped mountains. His family, and mine, complain that I go on digs "alone, with so many men."

Omar neither defends nor stops me. He's still looking for work outside his father's factory, and doesn't hear disapproval about anything else. When, after an evening with his parents, I point out that his mother kept hinting about so-and-so's *dutiful pregnant* daughter-in-law, he looks blank. It's not that he thinks I'm making it up. It's that at such times, he doesn't think. He can tune out, just like Mehwish, and I know he does it to protect himself from his father's snipes. His "emotional condom," as Zara calls it, has its advantages. If he listened to them, he might listen too much, and start interfering with me. Plus, his skin's also thick when it comes to greed and unkindness.

Still, frustrated that he can't feel a hurt not aimed at him, I consult Zara. "Right under his nose his mother looks at me and says it's shameful when girls are free with men. Omar says nothing. I would. I have, with my own mother."

"Mother is the Maker beside whom Man shrivels into infancy," she declares. "He becomes—primitive. But not in a hot way, huh?" She cackles, stretching on a rug.

"So, he's ignoring the chaos in the cave to focus on the chaos of the hunt?"

"Of course. But you're the hunter now, right? *You* can escape domestic pettiness. So escape. Go into the field with Abdul!" she cackles more. "Anyway, as long as Omar's lovely to behold and even lovelier to hold, so what?"

•

It's early November the following year and I'm on my way to a two-week dig in the eastern arm of the extinct Tethys. There are nine of us, including Henry (Brian works closer to home now). Henry has returned after a series of patchy visits, in which he carried back clumps of rock to the United States in his backpack. The rocks yielded turtle slivers and miniature elephants, plus another partial *Pakicetus* skull, and two of its teeth. This time he's hoping to at last complete the skeleton of the creature whose ear I once found.

We got the license after months of waiting for Ministries and Intelligences to flick their signatures on a dozen photocopies of documents unearthed from a time before the whales.

Their fists had barely unfurled from the Earth in their grip when there was a military coup.

Zara called the night it happened. "It's a *real* takeover!" (The last one was fake.) And Henry called to say it was his turn to plead with his country for permission. Finally, the coup being labeled "bloodless," both countries consented.

My joy's heightened for almost not having it, and not only because of bureaucratic pomp. My victory's personal. If peace and liberty were always mine, I wouldn't cherish them the way I do. I've never been included in a professional commitment of this scale. The day-long digs I've been on in the two years since my marriage (also after waiting so long) were stained by my wedding night and Junayd's death. Now, at last, I feel the thrill of my first ride into these hills, with Nana and Junayd, nearly twenty years ago.

Before I left Lahore this morning, Nana said, "Bring me back something I'll want to see." Receiving his hopes for me, I try to push away thoughts of Omar's mother, and mine, both of whom telephoned Omar before I left. "How can *you* let her go? What man would allow that? Catch her!" He offered his mother a pathetic apology, "Next time, we'll see what can be done…" and flirted with mine, "You know, I have no power!" He knows she adores him even more when she can pity him for being married to me.

All that fades now, as I roll down my window. I'm a creature of the open air, not of stale preservatives. Every movement and color is life reinforced: fingers of cool air sliding between the heat; sun-bleached river beds oozing crimson salt, sparkling like rubies in the sun; a porcupine holding up traffic with its spines. This is where I belong, this is where I'm balanced: at the edge of a remnant sea.

When the porcupine trudges off the road, the chatter in the car swerves between the coup; the twenty-first century, two months away; and Raja Mal, who once built a fort where the porcupine's quills, still erect, are pointing. Abdul also points to the ruins in the distance. He tells Kazuo Smith, one of Henry's team, "It was built eight hundred years after the Greeks left. It is fascinating, maybe, that Punjabi masons still remembered those fluted columns exactly the same way, with elaborate capitals and bases."

Kazuo Smith wears leather bracelets and loose cotton shirts. "Totally."

Feeling poetic, I add, "The design was imprinted on their fingertips."

Kazuo nods. "Yeah, inherited memory. Totally."

He's not like Brian, who used to get overwhelmed when conversation bounced from topic to topic.

Ibrar sits in front. Fawad's in the truck behind us. When Ibrar and Fawad are separated, they're slightly tolerable.

I say to Abdul, "I have to bring back the best ghee for Aba. Where do you get it?"

Ibrar tells Abdul to tell me, "Not for several kilometers."

I tell Abdul to tell him, "Thank you." The driver accelerates into fifth gear and races north, while my hair whips into my face and across my smile.

We pass brick kilns, marble and limestone quarries like Aba's—like the one that blinded Mehwish?—and fenced-off fields. We stop at last, just beyond a village on its way to becoming a town, north of the hill I climbed when I scratched my knee and came away with a piece of the first whale. The village has brick walls, not mud, stamped with drying dung. It wears a tin roof. Ibrar proudly tells Kazuo, "All the young men from here and lower in the plains enlist in the army."

Behind me, a broad-shouldered woman carries a basket into her house, while a cluster of men walks toward us. Behind them, the truck with our gear stops. The two drivers and the cook Ghafoor start unloading. One large tent; three smaller; one, even smaller, for me; sleeping bags; stove; tables; coolers (they'll drive into town every day for ice). Then the rock hammers and sledgehammers; brooms; plaster of Paris; ice picks; shovels; maps.

Short prickly grass sticks out in patches between crumbling stone. We walk around, stretching limbs and minds. It feels like cheating, being able to see in minutes what took millions of years to form. If after two weeks, we still don't find more of the puzzling *Pakicetus* (to Mehwish, still *Amalicetus*), what's two weeks? What's the twenty years since I first started looking?

I remember this paintbox-grid of color, how it traces the tides of the Tethys. These chocolate-sunset shades of mudstone and siltstone taught me that beauty in the abstract will never be enough for me. I have to taste.

After an hour or two of preliminary search, lunch is served.

•

The first night, Abdul asks if I have a lock for my tent.

"No."

"Your husband did not give you one?"

"No."

"Then take this." He fishes in his pocket, brings out a lock and key.

I laugh. "That's a bit—strange, Abdul!"

"Do not worry, it will fit, exactly." He crawls inside my tent, levels all three zippers—one vertical, two horizontal—and hooks the lock through them. "See?" He crawls out, points at the village behind us, then at Fawad—who *is* leering—and Kazuo, picking his nose. "I am surprised your husband did not give you one." He walks away.

I stare angrily at his broad backside. Now that he's put the fear in me—or encouraged me to dwell on a fear I was successfully holding back—it lingers oppressively. And I don't like his insinuations about Omar. Or me. But I tell myself he's just being a friend. After all, I'm married and have clearly rejected him. He could become hostile like Ibrar or hostile and sleazy like Fawad or simply aloof like some of the others. Instead, he really hasn't changed much. He's still Abdul, Wimpy Protector.

I slide into the sleeping bag. It smells of hair oil and old farts. It's too thin. The ground's bumpy. I've never slept outside before, except on our roof. Never in a tent. I'll be sore in the morning. I'm a creature of the outdoors who complains like a creature of the city. I fill the silence around me with the rustling of wild cats, the panting of wild dogs. My tent's pitched in the middle of the others—they're all my protectors!—and now I have to pee. Who will I pass? What if I squat in someone's view—or see someone else doing it? Doing *it*. An image from twenty years ago returns, unwelcome: a man behind a tent, shalwar down, penis erect. *Come here.* What if tonight it's Fawad? I peed carefully all day, afraid someone would sneak up behind me just as I dropped my shalwar.

I lie awake, worrying about nothing, my bladder so swollen I can barely breathe.

I know every night I'm away Omar will be at a party. I roll onto my side. Who's he with, right now? He won't be worrying about who I'm with or what I'm doing. He knows I work all day and think all night!

I decide to get out and finally do it. I sit up. Two legs, not four, outside my tent. *You're imagining it.*

To calm myself, I compliment myself. *You're the first woman in the country to do this, you know.* There's only one other woman paleontologist, and her family won't allow her on overnight digs. *You're the first.*

I feel better, but still can't sleep. *Thank God you don't have your period.* I roll onto my other side. Under my cheek, the ground speaks. Rock rumbles. Gas vibrates. Earth acoustics won't let me sleep!

Why do modern whales beach? I anthropomorphize freely. Because they miss the time before the sea seduced them. They miss the solid ground. A nub of rock on which to rest a chin. The sun on fur. So why did *Pakicetus* return to the sea, fifty million years ago? Why be sleek? Why swim, when you can flop?

It's with these thoughts that I hold my bladder all night. As soon as it's light, I fidget with the lock, run to the edge of our camp, squat, howl with relief.

•

We spend the next three days prospecting in twos and threes. Abdul's always with me (Kazuo asks if he's my husband). Sometimes I also walk with Mike Jha, the third member of Henry's team, whose father's Punjabi. Mike's paler than Henry, and even Kazuo, whose nose burned the moment he stepped out of the car. Ibrar and Fawad stick to Henry and the Department Head, Malik Sahib. Henry keeps trying to wander off alone.

By noon every day it's thirty-five degrees Celsius. The sparse ground reflects the sun like a sentence. We're a mix of turbans, dupattas, caps, sunscreen, water bottles (I don't pee more than four times a day, and it's orange), shovels and canvas bags. On my shorter digs, I did no "hard labor." My main task was preparing the cast, something I like doing. (I love the sound of shattering plaster when I break the cast later in the lab, and when the bone comes away clean, it's like finding it again.) But now, like the others, I hack off bits of rock with a sledgehammer. I find shark teeth, turtle bone, the fingers of a rodent. My back and shoulders are permanently sore. By the third night, I don't care who sees me walk to the place they all know by now is my toilet.

At lunchtime the fourth day, a group of men from the village brings us food. I'm the only one who can meet the women who prepared it, to thank them for their hospitality. I have a privilege I absolutely never expected to have: I can work beside men *and* enter the sacred *zananah*, the space consigned to women.

As Abdul walks me to the women's compound, I recall endless arguments I've had with Omar about The Village. He idealizes it the way expatriates like Munir Mamu (yes, I shouldn't speak ill of the dead) idealize the Motherland. It shouldn't change without his consent but he's delighted not to have to live in it.

"The village is the heartland," Omar will say, as if our home in Lahore has no heart.

"You know you can't do without your car and air conditioning," I'll answer. "You don't want to know the heartland. *Your* village is nothing but a pretty doll!"

"I do know it! It's where my family comes from, and I'm proud of it. You're not normal for feeling no pull to where *your* family first came from."

"How can you know where you've never lived? Your pride is only nostalgia for some imaginary tribe. But how far back can anyone trace his geneology? If we were Hindu warriors or weavers or Animists or descendants of the Prophet? And before *that?*"

He'll insist his tribe is *real* and that I substitute mine with pretend animal stories. I'll insist human geneology is also a story, mixed up with the real, to make a story to secure us, but all crocodiles are counterfeits because all history is selectively assembled by those in power, *it's the people who deny this who make trouble,* what else did Nana's bogus trial and poor Junayd's death prove?

Neither ever convinces the other.

Abdul leaves me outside the women's quarters. I pass two goats and a beaming boy who follows us everywhere while we dig, calling to his friends, "Nee-um." (I'm sure they watch me pee.)

"What's your name?"

"Mahmud." The face becomes serious, now that it carries a man's name.

I try to look equally serious. Immediately, he giggles.

Inside, late afternoon languor rolls over us like a raincloud.

"Which one is your husband?" a young woman asks. She's just washed her hair and combs it slowly, opening each long strand to the sun.

I don't admit he's not among the men here and only reply, "Omar."

All the women want to know his tribe. (*See?* He'd say. *It matters.*) Then my family's details. I say they were Partition refugees from Uttar Pradesh, and the women murmur sympathetically, their own wounds fresh after fifty-two years. They name the villages inhabited by *panahgirs*, refugees (after fifty-two years, they're still identified as refugees), and those that were here long before the land was divided.

An older woman, Neelum, asks how long Omar and I have been married, and how often he has sex with me. She cackles more lasciviously than Zara.

I smile. "Enough."

More cackles; many scowls. All intimacies are bared, from infertility to impotence. Jealousies surface. So does neighborhood news: an accident in a coal mine; a birth; a missing boy—abducted by the landlord's son? Somebody mentions a girl found in a well, but this is quickly hushed. Before I can ask about her, conversation turns quickly back to Omar. Are our children being looked after by my mother in Lahore? I don't deny it. But when I try to ask about the accident in the mine, if not the girl, again, more interest in my womb.

I fidget. The *zananah* is a shared sex organ. To desire privacy is to desire sex change. It's asking to be rejected, aggressively. Most don't ask. But, I look around, there must be a girl like me?

Wherever she is, she hides herself well. Perhaps in a well.

•

The fifth day we drive west, close to the North-West Frontier Province and the Suleiman Range. Abdul and I ride with Henry and Malik Sahib in the truck; Fawad grudgingly gets in the car.

Malik Sahib warns Henry that the villages are even more traditional here, "and if one of your boys so much as looks at their women, who are always beautiful, we can expect revenge. You have heard about Pukhtun honor."

Henry doesn't say *inner*esting. He nods gravely. His stomach's upset. He looks tired. So does Abdul, who seems to have the opposite ailment.

We go down a dirt road, but it's blocked off. At the next, a soldier asks for a permit. We show him what we have. He shakes his head, tells us to go back. The land lies mined, gray earth with silver glitter scattered in heaps. Looking for what? No one needs to ask. Before we left, I realized what the beaming boy who pointed me to the women's chambers meant by *nee-um*. Not his mischievous aunt Neelum, but uranium.

A convoy of three trucks with armed men passes us, *naswar* bulge in each cheek. Then we pass a semi-nomadic group of men and women on foot. No one looks at the women, not even me.

We finally stop and unpack. The next two days yield plenty of fish fossils, another fragment of *Pakicetus* skull, and more teeth. But we still don't find all of this elusive beast. After two more days, we circle east, back toward the Grand Trunk Road, pulling into a motel to replenish food stock, and, at last, to shower.

•

Day ten: a burst of energy runs through us like a current.

It's in the way our bodies lean toward each other. We ask more questions, and we listen. There's anticipation, excitement, and we can't be more thankful for it, because the fatigue of the last four days was becoming more oppressive than the heat. We smelled that on each other too. And we absorbed it even as it repelled us, because we're our own little tribe now, functioning as one organism, inescapably interdependent. If Fawad and Ibrar hoped I'd be holed up in a rusty resthouse by now—lulled by palms and cuckoos, cold towel on my head—till they finish out here, they can see they were wrong. This will make them worse back in our lab, but in the open, Fawad leers less and Ibrar stops telling Abdul to tell me to stop "going there" or "doing that."

Kazuo's flaky red nose smoothes to a light bronze. Henry ate a big breakfast and digested it. Ibrar and Fawad stop following him. Abdul stops following me (maybe he's trying to shit). It's Mike who walks with me, saying he's given up looking for his lost Punjabi tribe and is just happy to be going home in four days. "Meanwhile, it's a great day, blue sky, we're lucky there've been no storms, and bee-eaters everywhere."

The birds circle us in flocks of emerald green wings, each with a trim of salmon pink, before settling on matching pink-green rocks, long delicate beaks and tails beautifully aligned.

The steep shelf above is also pink and green, and as I break into it, instead of exhaustion, I feel exhilaration. My back is strong. My arm swings with ease. I don't have to use both arms. Beside me, Mike strikes a hammer with a violence almost loving. We tear into the rock a few inches above my head, then a foot above his, where I can't reach.

Abruptly, he stops. "Huh. Did you hear something?"

I look up at the crest of the hill. A sudden burst of recollection: *I should climb it.*

Mike swings his hammer again, even higher. This time I also hear it. We move quickly to a softer slope and pull ourselves up. The rocks are a darker pink, orange in patches, rough and bumpy ocean rocks, sculpted by layers of oyster beds. When Henry and Malik Sahib pass us below, Mike tells them, "There's something here!"

They bring shovels and join us. "These rocks are younger than the ones we've found *Pakicetus* in," says Henry.

"So maybe it *could* swim?" asks Mike.

Looking dubious, Malik Sahib cranes his neck to look over the edge of the hill. I also lean. Below me is a jutting nub of bone, lodged in the vertical cliff face. We start hacking off the edge, careful not to slip. We strike more bone.

•

We hit a tooth. An enormous spiral tooth, fused to an upper jaw. For the next three days, we keep finding more of this peculiar horn. Plant roots have snapped the lower jaw, but we find enough pieces to visually construct a broad snout, with the horn possibly four times its length. The animal lies buried diagonally on its right side, hind limbs sunk in the deepest layer.

Abdul scratches his beard. "That's a short reptilian arm, maybe."

I blurt, "What is it?"

"What the *hell* is it?" says Henry. "If it had flippers, I'd have guessed some kind of manatee. But, the horn! *Inner*esting."

"It looks like something from the future, not past!" says Mike.

Along with the huge twisting tooth, we find two small smooth teeth. Henry and Malik Sahib examine them, and get so excited they nearly fall off the cliff. "We've got to find an ear!"

On the last day, we do. It's the left ear, buried deep behind the jaw. And there it is, what we were all hoping for but dared not name out loud: the hidden *S*. The tympanic bone that houses the middle ear and curls in this shape for only one thing. We've dug up another kind of whale. A completely different kind. It walked like a crocodile and swam like a fish and charged like a rhinoceros and foraged like a manatee. It could have done little else with only two small canines. The only living horned whale we know is the narwhal—the creature with a tooth as long as Mehwish's imagination—which lives in the Arctic. What was this one doing, a long time ago, in the warm tropical Tethys?

•

It's our last night, and nobody wants to sleep. Pieces of *Cornucetus*, the horned whale, are carefully bound in wet plaster and foil. There's still a lot left to dig. We wonder when.

Nana said to bring him back something he'd want to see. For him, and for Mehwish, I sketch:

A whale with a horn is a vim zee dewil!

I can draw no better than when I was a child. I hide it from the others.

Kazuo and Abdul bring their sleeping bags out of the tent. Ghafoor and Dawood gather kindling for a fire. The stars are brilliant and more abdundant than the grains of dead sea around me. Mars blazes in the sky. I think I spot Jupiter too. We've been giddy with ideas all day. Now this shared silence is welcome. I look at us and wonder if we're all, like *Cornucetus*, only a stray association of Nature or God or something that keeps stretching, like a cinematic vocal chord? I have no answer, except to enjoy this last cold, clear night.

Ghafoor lights the fire. It quickly springs high and hot. For the moment, no need to dig up more silent letters. Enough that we're here, in this magical place, where pieces of the queer protowhale lying wrapped before us could be a constellation in the sky.

I have only ever wanted to be a humble voice in a mighty chorus. I have only ever wanted to be a small flame in a greater fire. Tonight, I am.

I wrap my sleeping bag around my shoulders. Jackals smell the burning wood and call closer. A star shoots across the glittering night.

•

They're washing his body when I get back.

Omar holds me in our gray shawl. "We called the university. They said you were on your way home."

"But we're not done."

"He died this morning."

"I'm going back! But first I have to show him what we found!" I look in my bag, for the drawing. He kisses me. A lot of people are kissing me. I pull away. "*Don't.*"

Omar steers me into the living room. "Mehwish is at our apartment. Ami's looking after her. Zara's promised to go there too."

"Zara and your mother together? Are you mad?"

He hushes me as if I'm the one who's mad.

Noman is here. He says something. Aba and Bilal Uncle and a few other men carry Nana's corpse out. Aba cries. He always hated how inferior Nana made him feel, but now he wails like a son. My mind burns as cold and clear as the air last night. When Junayd died, that's when I felt the grief. I look at the small body of the tall man with the long gait, lying in the middle of the room under a white cotton cloth, surrounded by roses and jasmine, and I know we're not done. I say it again, "I've brought back something to show you, as promised."

I hear a reply. "What does it matter if you come from water or soil when you don't decide which you become?"

It's Bilal Uncle. He puts a gentle hand on my cheek, smiling warmly.

I stare at him, this man I first saw in a photograph of the Samarkand Observatory, when Nana and Junayd were at their happiest.

He smiles again. "Though his professional hopes were thwarted, with the exception of losing Junayd, and of course his son, I think your grandfather died in peace."

Shocked, I snap, "I thought you knew him better than that!"

"I mean, he died the way he needed to, without saying who he was, because he is Zahoor. He is becoming. If you leave behind definable tracks, people first point to them, then own you, then put you in a box. That leaves your poor spirit with an impossible burden. But a soul not bent with the weight of mortals wanders freely. We will remember your grandfather in an infinite number of ways."

His voice carries no pity or tragedy. Only the frankness of love. Sometimes, it's the ones you never think about who say what you need to hear, or at least, the way you need to hear it. I doubt I'll see him again. Maybe he'll return to Samarkand. Maybe he'll fall asleep in a long dark stairwell deep underground and no one will want to disturb him.

Nana's hands are tucked in the cotton shroud. I loosen the sheet. A cold palm with lines like salt marks on a dry ocean bed. Inside, mine is still so small.

Noman

Carrying a bullet near my ribs was making me optimistic. I'm alive. What happened to poor Junayd didn't happen to me, for all those technical details Amal has to know. Hard bullets, soft bullets, ugly ballooning bullets and the mean ones that shatter like glass in your veins. I don't care about that. When you come this close to death, cause and effect don't matter. I'm alive. So's Mehwish. We survived the same bullet. It touched us both and we were saved. A miracle, there's a God.

The only stain on my newfound faith was Zahoor, who was and always will be my conscience. Since the shootings at Amal's wedding two years ago, every day I spent with him, I was reminded of my selfishness. When he lamented Junayd's death, and even his awful son's, I wished he would, just once, mention *my* injuries, the weeks *I* spent in hospital, *my* immobility and drips and wheezing and pain. He never did. I also wished he were back in his house in Islamabad. Again for selfish reasons. It was my only time with Mehwish.

I thought on Amal's wedding, in that second Mehwish leaned forward to touch me—just before the silent bullet shot through her and lodged in me—I thought she was going to stick her little finger between my teeth and say something, anything, just for me, the way she used to. It never happened. Zahoor's family sold his house and brought him to live with them here. Every day I spent with Zahoor I longed to spend with Mehwish.

But she and I were never alone. She wanted me alone with him, as if she knew he'd say things to me he couldn't say to her. She was right. Though he always sat up bravely in bed for his family, when I was alone with him, he let me see the rawness of his pain. Maybe he hoped I was finally man enough.

It wasn't just the surgeries and infections, the boils and fever and perpetual soreness that put the man who needed to walk—needed to drink the mountain air and feel the sunlight pitch and smell the graying shadows and trek all the way up to China just to see different sheep, for God's sake—on his back. Most of all: he'd lost his best friend, Junayd. He'd lost those conversations. It was the death of a way of looking at the world, that's what he told me. "*Holistically.* You know? A time when life had to be tasted, layer by layer." He couldn't lift his voice, but the whisper was still defiant. "But this"—cough, cough—"this is the age of categories. Space and time are tamed, like a lion in a pen. There are fewer sacred dimensions. Fewer places to worship the infinity inside a little tick. Why do we shrink ourselves?"

Another time, soon after the US bombing of Sudan and Afghanistan. "Listen to people everywhere. Categories. Buy their weapons you're developed. Make your own you're a savage. What about the guns that shot us? Wasn't there one of each?" The developed one didn't work, but I kept nodding and he kept talking—"At my age, you learn that people believe in God only if He created them first"—before Mehwish or her mother came into the room and he had to feel better.

He didn't know about the US missile that fell across the border into a Pakistani village. Soon afterwards, I saw some foreign reporters milling around Mall Road, wanting to know "how we're taking it." I tried to assure one of them that we take bombing very well. "Look around. There are hardly any protests."

She wasn't satisfied. "You're a Muslim?"

Wish she'd put the question to Zahoor. Never thought *I'd* have to confess my faith. *Say what you are! Say you're against us! Say it! Say it!* I smiled into the camera and asked if she works for the Party of Creation.

"I don't have much time. Are you a real Muslim?"

"No, imitation."

She walked away in a huff.

A few days before he died, while Amal was away on the dig, Zahoor couldn't have been talking to me but his accusers, when he murmured, "Have you ever turned over a rock or stroked the wing of a butterfly? I don't think so. What would you do with your hands if denied the power to sign your name across my life?"

Yes, those are the words that will haunt me most.

Now they're taking his body away. It isn't just a shell they remove but the vision that fueled it. I listen to Bilal console Amal: his soul will always be free; flesh is a transient illusion; the spirit still lives, uncategorized, unconquered. She looks... half-convinced. She's too tired from her trip and is going to have a nasty delayed reaction.

Me? It's as if the bullet waiting politely by my artery slips.

•

I celebrate the twenty-first century by becoming a monk. Not a holy one, a sulky one. I'm mean to my students. They grow fat on cable TV and silly portable gadgets that I immediately confiscate. My monk likes speed. I get a motorcycle to race other motorcycles with women seated side-saddle, slipper dangling on middle toe. How do they do it? They even balance children on their laps, still flaunting that five-inch heel. The secret of balancing a bike—fat man; fat woman; three to eight kids—is all in that middle toe. One day, a golden stilleto's knocked off a toe by an Elite Punjab Police van, and the bike skids. I'm not lying. And I don't race bikes that carry kids.

I find a spot between two peepul trees behind a lassi cart where I can sit in peace and not talk to anyone except the lassi wallah, Hamid. His oddball customers are almost as entertaining as my jaunts to Anarkali Bazar with Petrov, who seems to have evaporated with his jewels on a Baltistani glacier. Hamid's customers assemble at his stand to vent like chimneys, and we have names for them all: Khala Chimney, who always says the last time she had a glass of lassi, it was "do anna"; Chimney Chacha, who looks like he's from Waziristan and always gets a bit extra; Chimney Chapet, who slaps Hamid as if they're best buddies and tries not to pay. Sometimes there's talk of the New-President-General. Someone will mention Afghanistan. Are the Taliban doing what America promised but didn't, returning us to an Islam that was rich and pure, or is their jihad nothing but a bloody gang war? Both sides meet at the lassi cart, making almost enough smoke to asphyxiate my grief, my guilt, my unbearable self-pity.

What would you do with your hands…?

Zahoor never did see The Pen, my eloquent goodbye in *Akhlaq*. Aba saw it. He told me I'd never be welcome at home again. I never was.

I sit between the peepul trees and listen or read. I've read the eight-hundred-page *Moment of Mutazilites* three times, front to back, but I start a fourth time this year. Little details preoccupy me. What did Ibn Sina like most to eat, when he wasn't drinking himself silly? Was it sunny or raining, the day Al Kindi was accused of heresy, and his head was smashed with his own big book? What was the first flicker of recognition that drew Ibn Rushd to Aristotle? When Christians "reconquered" Spain, it was the Arabic translations of Aristotle they found. Now Aristotle is Arastoo and Plato, Aflatoon. If Arastoo went from Greek to Arabic to Castillian to Latin to English to Urdu—what's left of him?

Hamid has little time for my musings, though a lot for his own. "Aflatooni love is the only real kind of love," he states. "Especial, for a real Pakistan."

"Does this mean my love for Mehwish can only ever be Platonic?"

He nods. "It would be best, hunna?"

"*No*. It wouldn't."

He shrugs. "If she is as lovely as you say then you should not spoil her."

"But why does worldly passion spoil true love?"

"That is the question! It is as God wants. Maybe she belongs to Him, not you."

"*No*. She loves me, purely *and* passionately! And when her grandfather was alive, he would sort of... bring us together. Now he's gone, I don't know how to see her."

"You need an excuse?"

"Yes!"

He shakes his head. "You are not meant to find it."

I go back to the philosophers, who could teach this cynic something. "Plato loved this world but he loved the one that can only be imagined even better. Aristotle loved this world completely. He believed it possible to find happiness within its physical borders. I want his hope."

"Arastoo did not believe in heaven?"

"Only heaven on earth."

"I'm with Aflatoon."

"According to Mehwish's grandfather, so's she. He'd call her dreamy Plato and her sister earthy Aristotle. Isn't that the funniest thing you ever heard?" Instead of laughing, he puts extra salt in my drink because it's a very hot day.

•

I knock on Amal's door. She and Omar are never home. I leave messages. They're never returned. Should I bother her at the lab? Since Zahoor's death, she's probably buried even deeper in her work and won't want to be disturbed. Maybe our foursome, now that it can't be a foursome, can't even be a threesome. That's the message she seems to be giving me.

It's her hot friend Zara who helps me find her. Zara's opened a café in a strip where trendy new restaurants mushroom every day. It tries to be vegetarian but this is the Punjab. Vegetarian means lettuce—and chicken. It means spinach—and chicken. Cheese—and chicken. I go there with Faisal, and who's sitting at the table but Amal?

Faisal the Vulgarian, you should know, has joined Aba's party. He hasn't given up his habit, but he's given up talking about it. Now he only speaks of "alien ideologies that divide the Muslim against himself." He thinks this makes him "street." When we push open the café door, he's saying, "Your types will never have street power. Without religion, our people have nothing."

And I'm saying, "What's *my* type? And what's this 'our people' crap? Are you a Real Salman feudal-socialist now?"

We both stare at Zara behind the counter, making some frothy coffee drink in a tight T-shirt and bell-bottom jeans. I fear Faisal's going to reveal the full potential of his habit right here, right now. And I'm embarrassed that Amal's seen me ogling her friend.

She smiles. "Noman."

"Amal!"

"You look terrible."

"You don't."

"Sorry I didn't return your messages."

She doesn't look sorry and she does look terrible. Dark rings under her eyes. Thin. Doesn't suit her. Those bones need flesh. She's lost her glow. She looks at Faisal and decides quickly she doesn't like him. Deciding the same, he sits with his back to her but with a view to Zara.

I plead, "Can I call you?"

"I'll call you."

She doesn't.

•

Faisal and I often return to the café. Zara waves welcomingly, but whenever I ask after Amal, she finds an excuse to turn away. Her business rockets. The café-bakery attracts middle-aged sahibs, students, lovers and maulvis. It should be called New Mecca but goes by New Maza. Each time we take a seat near Zara, Faisal pronounces it too westryn. Then we wait for his new friends. Who are:

Surly Mullah. His frown suggests you can't even trust mullahs.

Jolly Mullah. Smile suggests you must.

Burly Mullah. God is muscle.

Sissy Mullah. Beard won't grow, sniff.

Playboy Mullah. Dumps Jewish Princess, returns to village for Muslim Virgin.

Hidden Mullah. Village virgins are uncouth; city virgins make cultured mothers.

Marxist Mullah. One God for One People.

Expat Mullah. I've never lived here but I know it's Paradise.

American Mullah. I've never lived here but I know it's Hell.

Which leads me to wonder, where are all the play*girl* mullahs?

I find her one day. I'm trying to swallow a soggy pastry when I sense it: fishnet hijab with stars. Skin so fragrant it salivates. Diamond missile in right nostril. Silk sleeves on stonewhite wrists. Fingernails like four-carat rubies. Trouser cuffs strictly at platinum anklets. Five-inch stilettos, silver. She swings the door, sashaying like Salma Hayek. Before I even look up, chromium lips have hard-boiled my quiche.

"*Yaar!*" Faisal and I gasp simultaneously.

Hidden Mullah: "She has the power by showing *nothing*."

Jolly Mullah: "She makes it dance like nothing!"

Burly Mullah: "She must have so many Mercedes."

Me: "Licensed at Emirates?"

Marxist Mullah: "Licensed at Army Rates."

Playboy Mullah: "Instead of stripping like Monisha Koirela, girls should groom like this one."

Expat Mullah: "All that western rubbish. She could lead a revolution."

Sissy Mullah: "I think she is."

Surly Mullah: "No she isn't."

In the following weeks, I know she is. I see more sexy saints than I know what to do with. Faisal dubs them Black Widows. "Just imagine what they *do* when they finally *give in*." But others aren't impressed.

Marxist Mullah: "Purity is not a commodity. It's a God-given gift."

Expat Mullah misses the innocence of the girl carrying water in a clay pot on her head. "That's the *real* woman."

Playboy Mullah: "I want a virgin, not a whore!" And Expat Mullah, Marxist Mullah, and Playboy Mullah are bonded for life and afterlife at Café New Taste.

•

Finally, Amal telephones. She doesn't have to ask how I'm keeping busy. Zara's told her. She doesn't want to talk about Zahoor. Or she does—but in her way. She tells me about her two weeks in the field last year, just before he died, and I can feel her excitement about the find, a sort of unicorn-whale with lizard feet. Maybe Aba's right. These scientists are all mad. But over the phone, I grunt happily.

She concludes, "There's still a lot left. I'm hoping we can return soon. Before it's buried again." She sounds doubtful. Either Omar doesn't want her sleeping in the mountains with a pack of lusty men, or her family doesn't, or the government doesn't. Or all of the above. "Maybe it's not meant to be completed? Maybe it doesn't want to be found? Do you believe in spirits? Even from so long ago?" I don't know what to say. She laughs. "I told Mehwish I saw you at the café. She misses you, you know."

"She does?"

"Of course."

She's teasing me. "You're teasing me."

"Of course."

"I want to see her."

"She wants to *see* you."

"Funny. Your parents won't like my Platonic visits to their daughter's room."

"*Platonic?* Well, if you keep it that way, you can meet her at our place."

"You're extracting this promise from *me?* After all I know about you and Omar?"

"I'm her big sister. And both of you have made my life difficult, in the past. Now I get to have some fun. A little power is just the thing!" She hangs up.

From then on, when Mehwish visits her sister and brother-in-law, I race over to their flat on my Vespa. ("That's Latin for wasp," says Amal. "No stinging.") After only a few minutes, Amal will tap her watch. *Time for you to go now.* When she sees my frustration, she'll yawn, gaze dreamily out a window, smile innocently. I'm in a tableau made of three giant sifrs floating around me: The devil Amal; frail and dazzling twenty-year-old Mehwish; and the ghost of the man that galvanized us, Zahoor, demanding: *You have spilled both blood and ink, what more will you do with your hands?*

Mehwish

I was saying.

When I poke the muscles on my back they are tight like a salty vocal chord. Amal says that is "normal." The bullet in Noman's back passed through me. The hole in my arm was not normal but a doctor stitched it with his finger like two letter dots. There is a scar it is uneven with edges thin and blurry.

When Noman visits us I stare at him it is my owlet look. "Does it hurt?"

"I have difficulty breathing sometimes but that is as much because of my injury as all the adult petrol fumes in the air. When you ride a scooter, you drown in them."

"Adulterated petrol."

"You're right."

I know he is smiling now. He is a little man who goes from serious to silly in the space of a smile.

I asked Amal not to leave us alone. I know what I feel for Noman now Amal says he feels it too I need to get used to it. The day Amal said this she also said, "The horned whale we found just before Nana died reminds me of you. It has one very long tooth, and that is your inner eye. The other two teeth are the outside eyes and they are weak." She made a drawing of it I have traced with my fingers it is uneven like my scar. The drawing does not talk. Clog talks less now also. After Nana died, he cried so much he got tired. That day Amal was telling me about the horned whale and about what Noman feels for me, I was going to tell her what happened in the bookshop but I did not. I think the one I want to tell is Noman. I said to Amal, "I will tell you when I want you to leave us alone."

"All right."

It is a few days later Noman is here at Amal's apartment she is here also Omar is at his father's factory. Noman says, "Sometimes I have trouble breathing because of nasty things like fumes, but sometimes for a good reason."

I stop staring at him and look down at my hands. He is saying I am the good reason. I think he is really going to say it but instead he leaves. First I am surprised then I am angry.

When I hear his scooter drive away, I ask Amal, "If you are right about Noman, why did he leave so soon?"

"I don't know, he must have had to go somewhere."

It happens again the next three times he visits. Just when I think he is going to talk about something other than the fumes or his students or Zara's café or Amal's horned whale, he leaves. The fourth time, he says quickly, "Mehwish, you are sweet to my lungs!" And then I think I hear him wrestle with Amal!

"What is going on?" I say to her afterwards. "I told you not to leave us alone but I did not tell you to push him out."

She starts to speak a lot of nonsense I do not want to repeat, about sperm ducks and kus and sex and money. "You have to know all this. You are a woman."

"Money?"

"Muny," she spells it, adding stupidly, "a homonym. You know, an overlapping sound—"

"I know what a homonym is."

"—with two meanings in Urdu. Sperm and egotism. Egotism is when you love your sperm ducks too much. Maybe because you don't have many!" She laughs at her almost homonym but does not say what sperm is. "Women have muny too, they just show it differently." I do not like this conversation it gives me two head aches.

"I am ready to see Noman alone next time."

She is quiet.

"You do not have to keep protecting me like a security issue."

"But you are the tail I need!"

"I am not a tail."

"I know, Mehwish. I was just joking."

She is not funny but I laugh anyway.

After a while, she says, "Your spellings are perfect now. You ask questions that are bigger than you."

"You are the one who told me you can never look far enough."

Noman is here and Amal leaves us. He sits next to me. I touch the gap between his teeth with my tongue. His mouth makes a lot of spit more than mine. "Do you have to open it so much?"

"You are supposed to open it so much. But we do not have to do this."

I am glad when he asks if I want to go for a ride on The Wasp. "All right."

He does not want me to sit properly which is when you keep both legs on the same side. He wants me to sit safely with one leg on each side.

"But nobody else sits like that."

"How do you know?"

"You just told me."

"Well, if they stare because you sit safely but differently, you won't know."

I like his frankness and I do not. "I can feel what people are doing if they are staring at me or Amal. I felt you, that first time."

He is quiet. The engine roars but we do not move. "I'm sorry. Sit as you want. But please be careful." I sit on one side only. "You can hold me for balance."

We take off, slowly. I stretch both legs and keep my hands on my lap it feels different as if I have no gravityG pull there is only the wind and the feeling that I am always on the up side of a swing.

Noman keeps talking. "There goes a woman on another motorcycle sticking out sandals so bright they're a traffic hazard! I'm always afraid of hitting a toe. Do you know, if the sandal falls, the bike will topple? How do they do it, without even touching their husbands, with children in their laps, and in the middle of all the may hum?"

Like Amal he tells me where we are if we are going around a park or between houses on backroads that are not too crowded. Now we are on a quiet street as quiet as a street can be in Lahore and I keep telling him to go faster and when he does I talk to him which is really the same as talking to the wind and when I am sure he cannot hear me I tell him all the things I have been wanting to say ever since the time at Nana's house when I knew I was not just saying hello when I touched him. And I start to miss Nana. Before he died I gave him some illegal ghazals Clog gave me I like that he never asked who Clog is he especially liked the one—

"Oh God! There goes another saint!" says Noman interrupting me. "You're lucky you didn't see her!" I always forget what I was thinking when I am interrupted. We pass under a tree his talk slips in the shade then comes out again. "That cat jumped down a high wall without even tripping! How does it do that?"

He keeps asking how this or how that I start to laugh. He goes in circles faster now I tell him please stop. "This is worse than a roundabout go straight!" We smell roasting corn it is a bhutta wallah he is fanning the coals I hear them spit Noman tells the man to put extra lime and chili. We are off again someone is watering a lawn or maybe a street I feel the sprinkles and the way the ground exhales as it cools. *Ah.*

I say, "Spin, spinning wheel spin!"

And Noman starts to go in circles again I hold him we have no gravityG pull.

At last we stop outside Amal's door. "Are you dizzy can you walk?" Noman asks. I show him I can. He takes my hand and kisses it. "I want to make sure you heard. You're sweet to my lungs, Mehwish. You're the opposite of the bullet inside me. You're the bloom." Then he does what I used to do to him. He puts his hands on my face and reads it. His fingers shake he is nervous. His thumb puts too much pressure on my eyelids. But now he is relaxing taking his time even poking between my teeth where I have no gap.

Amal opens the door I hear ice in a glass it is almond juice.

Noman tells her I never fell off. "I don't understand how that happens, do you?"

I walk inside brush the tangles from my hair comb the air from my face the shape is different. Behind me I hear Amal answer, "She has it in her."

Aba: father

Ahmadis: a denominational sect rejected as heretical by many orthodox Muslims

Ama/Ami: mother

arzoo: desire; wish

aur?: and?; what else? (Many conversations in Urdu begin with, and are punctuated with, "aur?")

baya: weaver bird

bhayia: older brother

bilkul: absolutely; completely

desis: South Asians; locals (Literally, "of the des," *des* meaning "soil.")

do anna: two annas; two pennies

Eid: the festival that marks the end of Ramzan, the month of fasting

gali: lane; alley

goras: white men; *gora*: white man; *goris*: white women

haram: a religious prohibition

haram zada: illegitimate child; bastard

la bes: Moroccan Arabic for "How are you?"

Mamu: mother's brother (Hence, also Nana's son.)

maulana: a religious leader (The title is loose; anyone can use it.)

maulvi: a religious preacher

m'hencha: Moroccan sweets

modryn: modern. ("Modryn" is how "modern" is typically spoken.)

Mooj: Mujahideen. Specifically, a member of the Islamic Jihad, armed and funded by the United States to fight the Soviet Union occupation of Afghanistan 1979–1989

Nana: maternal grandfather

Nani: maternal grandmother (Hence, also Nana's wife.)

naswar: tobacco, chewed like *paan.*

nawab: governor; ruler; prince

nichi zaat: lower caste

paan dans: a box for *paan*, which is a digestive of betel leaf and betel nuts

Ramzan: the ninth month of the Islamic calendar, and the month of fasting (The fast begins at sunrise and ends at sunset.)

Roos: Russian

sahib: sir. A term of deference originally used for the British

sehri: pre-dawn breakfast eaten during the month of Ramzan

shabash: well done

sher: lion; poem

acknowledgments

For generously sharing his work on the primitive whale fossils found in Pakistan, I am grateful to Dr. Hans Thewissen. All errors are entirely my own. Thanks also to the scientists at the Islamabad Natural History Museum, for striving in an environment where their work continues to be undervalued. Thanks to Rafay Alam for his legal expertise, and for sharing his work on the Blasphemy Law. It should be noted that the events and characters described in this book are fictional and are not meant to mirror or comment upon any actual case.

The following books proved indispensable: *At the Water's Edge* by Carl Zimmer (New York: Simon and Schuster, Inc., 1998); *Aquagenesis* by Ralph Ellis (New York: Penguin Books, 2001); *Islam and Science* by Pervez Hoodbhoy (London: Zed Books, 1991); *A History of Islamic Philosophy* by Majid Fakhry (New York: Columbia University Press, 2004).

Passages from the Quran are taken from *The Holy Qur'an*, translated by Abdullah Yousuf Ali (Lahore: Muhammad Ashraf, 1990), and *The Message of The Qur'an*, translated by Mohammad Asad (Gibralter: Dar al-Andalus Ltd., 1980), as well as from Abdul Wadud in *Phenomena of Nature and the Quran* (Lahore: Syed Khalid Wadud, 1971).